Finding Love in Eureka, California

Resort to Love Series

Finding Love in Eureka, California

Book four in the Resort to Love Series

By
Angela Ruth Strong

MBI

Finding Love in Eureka, California
Published by Mountain Brook Ink
White Salmon, WA U.S.A.

The website addresses shown in this book are not intended in any way to be or imply an endorsement on the part of Mountain Brook Ink, nor do we vouch for their content.

This story is a work of fiction. All characters and events are the product of the author's imagination. Any resemblance to any person, living or dead, is coincidental.

The author is represented by and this book is published in association with the literary agency of WordServe Literary Group, Ltd., www.wordserveliterary.com

Scripture quotations are taken from the King James Version of the Bible. Public domain.

ISBN 978-1-943959-42-6

The Team: Miralee Ferrell, Nikki Wright, Cindy Jackson
Cover Design: Indie Cover Design, Lynnette Bonner Designer

Mountain Brook Ink is an inspirational publisher offering fiction you can believe in.
Printed in the United States of America

DEDICATION

To God for adopting me into His family.

ACKNOWLEDGMENTS

My team at the Boise airport where I started working a year ago. You're my people.

Freedom Fitness where I teach fitness classes. You're my people too!

The woman who came to my yoga class and told me the story of why she has no toes. I hope she comes back someday so I can give her this book and let her know how much she inspired me.

Safe Place Ministries where I was inspired to write the best line in this book. (I'll let you guess which one that is.)

My mom and dad who love so well.

My kiddos who give me lots of practice with learning to love well.

My husband who challenged the love triangle in the book, making me go deeper. And for listening to me cry over my characters.

Kimberly Rose Johnson and Heather Woodhaven who suggested other very important tweaks to this story.

The rest of my writing group who helped me brainstorm and also listened to me cry over these characters.

Miralee Ferrell for working with me on this book like no other.

Dear Reader,

My editor and I debated whether or not to have yoga play a part in this story because the origin of yoga is Hindu, and we don't want to promote anything except Biblical truths. That being said, I could have taken the yoga out of this story, but it wouldn't change the fact that I'm a yoga instructor at a Christian fitness club. So rather than avoid this topic, I'd like to share my experience and encourage you to explore your views on a deeper level. I never want my writing to simply be safe and reaffirming of what you already believe but to promote questions for you to ask God because He is the only one with the answers.

I feel the danger in yoga is not the stretches and strengthening poses but the pagan goal of finding divinity within yourself and the encouragement to empty your mind. The Bible tells us to take every thought captive, so we are not to empty our minds. For that same reason, we shouldn't get drunk. We need to be in control of our thoughts, which includes the extreme focus of meditation. This is something more Christians should do and something I encourage my students to do at the end of a class. I give them a quiet time to lie on a mat and listen to whatever God is trying to say to them through things that have jumped out at them lately in scripture, songs, books, or through a friend. Sometimes my students will cry. Sometimes we sing along to the worship song playing. Sometimes I just enjoy resting in God's presence, while other times, I'm overwhelmed at the comforting words He gives me to speak.

Besides focusing our minds, the Bible also tells us to worship God with our strength. So often in America, we don't take care of ourselves physically, and this can affect everything—even our faith. I have been blessed when chiropractors or physical therapists tell their clients to attend yoga, they come to my class, and the pain or problem is relieved. I've even had one student who needed scoliosis surgery for his back, and after three months in my class, he only needed half as much surgery. What a gift.

Paul says in I Corinthians 10:23 that all things are permissible, yet all things are not beneficial. Yoga has been both for me. Besides God using it to heal bodies and souls, I've made some amazing connections in the class. I met a board member for Safe Place Ministries who invited me to a relationship class, which has made a huge impact on both my life and my writing. I've had students read my books and be inspired. I've had students ask for prayer. What an amazing opportunity.

Now I also need to add Paul's thoughts on eating meat sacrificed to idols. He said we are free to eat it because the idol means nothing to us, but if it trips others up, then we should refrain. I'm not here to trip anyone up. I'm here to point to Jesus and say Christianity isn't about rules or religion; it's about a relationship with Him and doing what He tells you to do. If God tells you not to do yoga, then don't do yoga. For me, God once told me to quit teaching a dance aerobics class I loved because the music lyrics weren't edifying. That doesn't mean I'm judging anyone else who teaches the class. God may very well want them there for a reason.

You'll see in *Finding Love in Eureka* that the yoga instructor Rosie (oh, how I love Rosie) teaches what's called Holy Yoga, and God does use it to meet my main character where she's at because God will meet us anywhere and use anything. I pray He uses this story in your life today.

In His Love,
Angela

CHAPTER ONE

GENEVIEVE WILSON HADN'T REALIZED SHE'D MISS seeing Matt so much. She had no idea why since he was simply a pilot she saw whenever he flew into the Eureka, California airport. He was way out of her league, so it wasn't like anything would ever happen between the two of them, but it was fun to pretend. And seeing him always made her day a little brighter.

Now that she was back from vacation, waiting in the airline office for a call from the incoming flight, it felt like she was checking the day's weather report. Would her day be sunny with a chance of Matt?

Static crackled. A cheerful male voice broke through the noise.

Gen sighed in contentment at the same time her muscles twitched with excitement. She picked up the radio that looked like a telephone receiver and pressed the button to respond. "This is the Eureka station."

"We are twenty minutes out. And we have one wheelchair on board." Matt sounded so professional, but she told herself he really wanted to say, "You are the wind beneath my wings." He just couldn't because, well, the co-pilot. And perhaps because they'd never actually spoken about anything other than departure times and passenger count.

She grabbed the clipboard to scribble down information. "Twenty minutes, one wheelchair," she repeated. The passenger in the wheelchair would probably be Olivia, which meant two of Gen's favorite people were flying into town on the same day. She'd count down the minutes until their arrival. "Gate three-bravo." Also known as 3B, but saying "bravo" made her sound as official as Matt.

"Gate three-bravo." He repeated. "See you at fourteen hundred hours."

Two o'clock. Gen looked at the watch she wore on her right wrist when at work to hide her tattoo. She had the normal amount of time to print out paperwork and get to the gate, though with the way her heart pounded, she might as well have been in a race. She rubbed her earlobes to help calm her the way her yoga-loving sister had taught her, then strode down the hall and out the door to the ticket counter.

Bianca printed boarding passes while Tyler struggled to check what looked like a surfboard in a case. If Genevieve wasn't in such a hurry to see Matt, she would have offered to help.

"The flight is twenty minutes out. I'm headed down to the gate. Please close the ticket counter at two-fifteen. Bianca, I'll have you help me board passengers. Tyler, you're free to go home after you make sure all the suitcases are picked up in baggage claim."

"S-L-A-P," Tyler called.

Gen squinted. He often spoke like he texted, but she couldn't always decipher the meaning to his acronyms.

"Sounds like a plan," he translated.

"Oh. Right."

The beads on the ends of Bianca's long black braids clacked against each other as her head spun to face Gen. Her teeth flashed bright against her dark skin when she smiled. "Matt's flying, isn't he?"

Really? How had the ticket agent read her so easily? Gen should have picked Tyler to help her board. He wouldn't tease her. But then *she* wouldn't get to talk about her infatuation at all. A giggle slipped out. So much for acting businesslike. "Yes, Matt's flying."

Her reaction drew the attention of a couple on the other side of the counter. "Matt's our pilot today?" asked the woman.

Genevieve considered getting jealous, but the passenger had to be in her forties. And she was with an attractive older man who appeared to be her husband. "Yes, Matt Lake is flying today. Do you know him?"

"He gave my grandchildren each an aviator pin when they came up for Memorial Day. He's a sweetheart."

Genevieve's heart warmed at the story. That was another good example of why she couldn't stop dreaming of him.

Bianca pulled the luggage to her side of the counter and motioned with her head to get Gen back on track. "See you down there, boss."

Gen nodded and turned to go. Her black ballet flats padded against the shiny tile floor as she flashed her badge at security and took long hallways to avoid having to go through the metal detectors. She dialed the phone number for the fuel truck to place an order then upon reaching the gate made announcements over the loudspeaker about arrival times and the boarding process. Finally she got to head down the jet bridge.

Warm sun shone through the windows, and for a moment, Genevieve wished she'd brought her steel toed shoes with her so she could join the crew below wing to drive the luggage carts and watch jets take off into the horizon. But once a dull roar announced Matt's arrival, there was nowhere else she'd rather be.

The plane slowed and turned toward her gate. Kevin led the way onto the ramp, waving orange wands. Gen snuck a peek at the cockpit. Matt sat straight in his pressed white shirt, all focus on stopping the moment Kevin crossed the wands overhead. The engines whirred into silence.

Her turn. She flicked the operation key and rang the bell three times before working the joystick that would move the jet bridge within inches of the aircraft. She lowered the canopy then knocked on the plane door to get the flight attendant's thumbs up through the small, round window before pulling the giant lever to release the lock. She used the weight of her hip to shove the door into its open position.

"Here you go." Michelle, the new flight attendant with shiny long dark hair, handed her the fuel slip.

Gen exchanged the slip for paperwork she'd brought down from operations. She should have pretended the paperwork wasn't printed out yet so she could have an excuse to track Matt down later. Next time. For now, she'd lead the passengers up the jet bridge and keep the door secure. Sometimes Matt got off the plane to buy coffee or lunch for his crew. She might see him then.

Bianca was already at the gate, logging in the flight arrival time on the airline computer. "Did you see him?"

If only the gate agent knew how to whisper. Gen would demonstrate. "Through the window."

"Bah." Even louder.

"Since you're here, I'll go back down and get the aisle chair ready."

"Olivia?"

"I think so. It's been a month since she visited her family." Not all passengers who needed wheelchairs from the gate needed the aisle chair to get them off the plane. Many could walk slowly with assistance. But Olivia was paraplegic.

Genevieve waited until the rest of the passengers were off before pushing the skinny version of a wheelchair down the aisle. She peeked through the cockpit door on her way past, but Matt was too busy scanning the paperwork she'd printed for him to notice her.

Olivia beamed from behind wire-rimmed glasses, her trendy blonde bob a little more silver than Gen remembered. "I was hoping you'd be here today. How was your Costa Rican monkey tour?"

Gen relaxed. Talking with the middle-aged woman was exactly what she needed to distract her nerves so she could act normal. "The monkeys were really cute at first, but then they got kind of annoying. They screeched all the time and stole my favorite pair of flip-flops."

Olivia laughed. "Flip-flops can be replaced, while I'm sure the photos you took are priceless."

Gen would like to think so. Owning priceless photos could really help her photography business. She lifted the armrest to slide Olivia from her seat onto the aisle chair. "If you want to wait for me to finish the flight paperwork, I can push you down to baggage claim and tell you all about my trip," she offered. Olivia had an electric wheelchair, so she didn't need pushing, but Gen hated leaving her alone. What if the chair tipped or the battery ran out?

"I'd love that, but I don't want to monopolize your time." Olivia leaned closer to whisper in her ear. "Matt's the pilot today."

Gen's pulse throbbed in her throat. At least Olivia knew how to whisper. "I know," she whispered back.

"Did you know he's right behind you?"

Matt strode down the aisle toward the redhead. She was back, which meant everything would go a little smoother this flight. Without her, the station agent had given him the wrong gate number and also let a TSA employee sneak on the plane so their passenger count was off. Not to mention the trouble they'd gone through when nobody else knew how to use the tiny chair on wheels that fit down the aisle of the plane.

Matt would check to see if the station manager had it under control, and then he'd make sure she knew she was missed. What was her name again? He'd have to get a peek at the badge on her lanyard because with all the times they'd conversed in passing, it would be embarrassing to admit he didn't remember.

"Need any help?" he offered.

She shot him a surprised glance over her shoulder, brown eyes wide. "Thank you, but Olivia and I have a system here."

The middle-aged passenger wrapped her arms around the redhead's neck as she scooped under the woman's legs. In one swift move, she scooted the passenger into the aisle chair.

The station manager turned to face him as the older woman strapped herself in. "Usually it takes two people to lift someone into an aisle chair, but Olivia weighs so little that I could give her a piggyback ride out of the airport without breaking a sweat."

The visual made him grin. He'd play along with the passenger. "You're pretty tiny, ma'am. I hope your weight isn't due to loss of appetite from our airline food."

The woman's dark eyes sparkled. "I *am* allergic to peanuts."

"And witty."

The station manager laughed. Unfortunately she was still looking at him, so he couldn't drop his gaze down to her nametag without being noticed. Goodness, she had intense eye contact, didn't she? One of her eyebrows arched as if she were waiting for something.

Matt cocked his head. What was he missing here?

She pointed past him toward the door. "We need to finish unloading the plane."

Oh, of course. He was blocking her path. He stepped backwards then pivoted to lead the way. He'd play it off because he hated admitting when he was wrong. Correction, he hated *being* wrong. He preferred people to think he could save the day. "It's good you're here to keep things running smoothly," he said. "The place fell apart without you last week."

She followed him onto the jet bridge, letting the new flight attendant push Olivia from behind. He stepped to the side, and the station manager maneuvered around him to enter the door code to the stairs so the baggage handler carrying Olivia's wheelchair could deliver it.

"Are you saying you missed me?" she asked.

The guy in the orange vest making the delivery slanted his eyes back and forth between Matt and the redhead before scampering down the steps.

Matt stuck his hands in his pockets to consider. She'd be fun to flirt with if he hadn't recently started dating Casey. "Actually I'm saying you need to stop being such a slacker."

Her mouth hung open, but her cheeks dimpled in delight. "What if I was sick? What if I had to have my appendix removed? Or I was diagnosed with a rare, incurable disease? Or perhaps..." She raised one finger. "Recovering from a gunshot wound obtained by rescuing a bank teller from a robbery?"

Either this woman was the kind of hero he'd always wanted to be or she had a wild imagination. Matt had to admire her passion one way or another.

Olivia rolled to a stop in front of them. "Or what if she went to Costa Rica to take pictures of monkeys?" she joined in.

Matt chuckled as the woman positioned Olivia's electric wheelchair next to her aisle chair and made the transfer. "You both have wild imaginations."

She then bent forward to flip down the footrests on the wheelchair and adjust Olivia's legs. She straightened to face him again, her dark eyes flickering gold with humor. "I *did* go to Costa Rica."

Matt scratched his head. "Really?" Apparently, there was a lot more than the woman's name that he didn't know. He peeked down at her nametag swinging on her lanyard, but she turned too quickly for him to read it. Undeterred, he fell in step beside her as she pushed Olivia up the jet bridge. He had to get coffee anyway.

She tossed her long red curls over one shoulder, but her arm still hid the name on her badge from sight. "I didn't go to take pictures of the monkeys though. I took pictures of people looking at monkeys. I like people."

She must like people to be in the airline industry. She must also be in the photography industry. "You're a photographer?"

She lifted her chin in what might be considered a nod. "Yes. I work here to get free flights so I can travel the world with my camera."

That made sense. But it also meant: "I should get used to this place falling apart from your slacking then."

"Or..." She pushed Olivia into the waiting area, scanning the passengers before making eye contact again. "You could learn to do your job without me."

"Touché." Coming from anyone else, such a statement would have rubbed him the wrong way. Made him work harder to prove his worth. But she was only teasing him the way he'd teased her. It made for a laid-back environment, which was one of the reasons he'd started flying this route in the first place. He smiled as the woman rolled Olivia to the side to start the boarding process. "I better go get a cup of coffee so I can keep up with you."

She snagged his gaze one more time as if giving him permission to walk away, her features soft but confident. That pretty much summed up her professional demeanor. She cared for people while getting stuff done. If only he could remember her name.

Matt ordered his coffee from Ramone's and watched Gate 3B from a distance. Everything was going a lot quicker with the station manager back. He might actually make it to that night's Giants game in San Francisco. Casey would be pleased. He owed her for the last couple of dates he'd missed. He should probably pick up a bouquet of flowers, too.

"Matt," the barista called his name.

He thanked the teenage girl, took the warm cup, and dropped two dollars in her tip jar. Wait. If the barista knew his name from his coffee order, maybe she'd know the station agent's too. "Hey." He pointed toward the gate. "Do you know the redhead's name?"

The barista wiped her hands on a towel. "Ginger?" She guessed.

"Thanks." Matt let the sarcasm drip from his voice.

She lifted a hand helplessly.

He made his way toward the jet bridge. Olivia remained patiently in her wheelchair on the sidelines. Perhaps she was waiting for an agent to push her once his flight took off. He should have offered to get her a coffee too.

He slowed. Smiled. Stopped. "Whatcha waiting for?" he asked.

Olivia pointed toward the station manager. "Gen wanted to accompany me to baggage claim."

Bingo. Jen. As in Jennifer. "Oh, that's nice of her."

"She's very nice."

He saluted with his coffee cup. "Have a great day, Olivia. It was good to see you again."

Now he could casually stride past the redhead and wish her a good day as if he'd never forgotten her name. He maneuvered around a family of four while she scanned their boarding passes. He caught her attention. "Glad to have you back, Jennifer."

She froze. The skin between her copper colored eyebrows dipped into a V.

Uh-oh.

"My name is Genevieve. Gen with a G."

CHAPTER TWO

MATT DIDN'T EVEN KNOW HER NAME? She'd been dreaming about him since the day they'd met while he had no idea who she was. How humiliating. Had Bianca overheard?

Genevieve glanced to the other side of the door to find Bianca shaking her head with her mouth pinched tight. At least she couldn't talk loudly with her lips clamped together like that.

Matt retraced his steps to stand next to Gen while she continued to scan boarding passes. She loved the idea of him wanting to stand next to her, but not out of pity. And not with everybody watching.

She chanced a peek at him. He'd struck a relaxed pose and one corner of his lips curved up. How did he do that? How did he come off as nonchalant and appealing after totally messing up? He should be the one saying sorry, but for some reason she was about ready to console him. Apologize for not being named Jennifer or something.

"Gen with a G?" he asked. "Is that like Anne with an E?"

Goodness gracious, he was quoting *Anne of Green Gables*. Was he going to call her Carrots next?

"Would you make that comparison if I didn't have red hair?" she challenged while continuing to smile at each passenger as they passed.

"Hmm. If you didn't have red hair, I probably would have compared you to Nellie Olsen in *Little House on the Prairie* because she is based off a real life historical person named Genevieve."

Gen knew of the real life character from looking up the history of her name, but hadn't expected anyone else to know. Most certainly not a man. Matt was more interesting than she'd realized.

She double checked her computer to make sure the chubby little baby in front of her showed up as a "lap child" on his mother's itinerary. Yep. She nodded them through. "You watch a lot of *Little House on the Prairie* and *Anne of Green Gables* when growing up?"

Matt shrugged. "My mom did. Those were pretty much the only

shows allowed on our television."

He was as innocently charming as the baby waving goodbye to Gen over his mother's shoulder. And though Matt wasn't tall, dark, or particularly handsome, he was cute. Likable. As in his smile could disarm TSA.

Gen wasn't the only one under his spell. There'd been the wife at the ticket counter. And Olivia who had to be twice his age.

"So that's your secret." She scanned the last ticket then clicked on the seating chart to see if any passengers were missing. "You learned how to charm women by watching Gilbert Blythe and Manly Wilder in action."

Bianca's deep chuckle drifted up the jet bridge as the other agent went in search of the baggage count form. Gen would be hearing about this from her later.

Was anybody else in hearing range? She checked on Olivia. Nope. Gen's favorite passenger appeared to be digging through her wallet. Probably looking for another dollar bill to give as a tip even though she had to know by now that Gen would refuse.

Matt cocked his head in that adorable way of his. "Are you telling me you think I'm charming?"

Oops. He was out of her league—obviously had more money, no doubt came from a better family, etc. If he found out about her crush, she'd be too embarrassed to have fun with him anymore. "No, I'm talking about the way you charm Olivia and other grandmothers. I'm not usually charmed when someone forgets my name."

There. She raised her chin triumphantly and reached by him for the intercom unit on the wall to page a late passenger.

"Ouch." Matt's voice echoed through the loudspeaker overhead as Gen pulled the receiver past him.

Olivia looked their way at the unexpected exclamation.

Gen's laughter filled the air in stereo now. She let go of the button on the receiver, but continued laughing. So much for paying attention to what she was doing.

Matt took a step backwards but held her gaze, the corners of his eyes crinkling in mirth. "I'll let you get back to work. But so you know, I'm really sorry about the name thing. Can I make it up to you somehow?"

A list of ways he could make it up to her scrolled through her mind. Dinner. Dancing. A private flight to Paris. He was a pilot after all. Oh, yeah... "We still need a pilot for our airport emergency exercise drill this weekend." Something inside her belly fluttered at the idea of working with him for more than forty-minute increments.

He stopped. Narrowed his eyes. Twisted his mouth to one side. "My boss already asked me about that, and I'm not sure I can make it with my schedule. My girlfriend's dad is the owner of the Giants, and I told her I'd go to the game with her."

Giants? They were probably a sports team. Gen didn't care about that. She cared that he had a girlfriend! Of course he had a girlfriend. It was a good thing Gen had kept her attraction a secret. Though the fact that it was hidden didn't keep her heart from feeling any less crushed. But what did it matter? He didn't even know her name.

She focused on her computer monitor so he wouldn't notice her blush. "Just call me Gen with a G next time, and I'll let you off the hook."

"Sure thing, Carrots."

Gen's pulse sent waves of disappointment through her veins as she peeked up to watch him walk away. It was stupid to be disappointed. Nothing had changed about their relationship. He was a pilot, and she was the station manager. Except now she knew he had a significant other in his life, while she was all alone.

"He called you Carrots?" Olivia rolled up. She must have tuned in after Gen accidentally announced the conversation over the loudspeaker. "That's what Gilbert Blythe called Anne Shirley."

"He called me Carrots because he can't remember my name." Gen grimaced. "*And* he has a girlfriend."

"Well, he's not married yet." Olivia patted her hand. The old matchmaker. "I've always said women should strive to marry a Gilbert Blythe."

Gen didn't want to talk about Matt anymore. Even if she couldn't keep from thinking of him. "Did you marry a Gilbert Blythe?"

"His name was Blaine." Olivia relaxed in her seat. "You would have loved Blaine."

Gen smiled sadly. She used to think Blaine had died, but after asking about his death once and having Olivia change the subject on her, Gen had started to suspect Olivia's husband hadn't died. He'd left her. Probably when she'd become paraplegic. So no, Gen wouldn't have loved him. He was no Matt.

Matt couldn't believe he'd called her Carrots—as if forgetting her name wasn't bad enough. All through flying home to San Francisco and taking a cab to the Giants stadium, he still wanted to kick himself for choosing the wrong response, but he didn't even know why he'd chosen it.

Because she'd said she didn't find him charming?

Because her eyes glowed gold when she challenged him?

Because he'd thrown her off her game with the loudspeaker incident, and he wanted to see if he could do it again?

He needed to let it go. He was dating someone new, and it was going pretty well. It also didn't hurt that his new girlfriend's dad owned the San Francisco Giants, though he wasn't like one of those other guys who only wanted to date Casey for the perks. Matt wanted to protect her from guys like that.

The elevator dinged, and he stepped into the lobby for the sky boxes at AT&T Park. With such a privilege, he should really attend more games. And he could, now that Gen had returned and would keep his flights on schedule.

Dang, he was thinking about the redhead again. Where was Casey? He only wanted to think about her.

He stood outside the owner's suite until he spotted her in a baseball cap chatting with a guy wearing a suit on the other side of the leather couch. Who wore a suit to a Giants game? Probably a business man. A "sponsor" who paid thousands of dollars to have his company logo displayed behind third base. That was Casey's job for the team—promotion. The two could very easily be talking shop, or the man could as easily be trying to steal Matt's girlfriend. Often there wasn't much distinction between those goals.

He'd interrupt. Rescue her.

"Matthew." Casey's Mom spotted him first and strode across the polished cement to give him a hug. She looked rich but casual in her team jersey, crisp jeans, orange Converse, and diamond earrings. She smelled like a flower Matt couldn't name, though he remembered it to be purple. "It's good to see you again," Valerie said.

Matt wrapped an arm around her shoulders in a hug. While Casey's dad was all business, her mom was all about relationships. He admired them both. "Good to see you too."

Valerie leaned away. "It looks like you brought Casey roses. Are you guys an official couple now?"

Matt gave a crooked grin. He'd kissed Casey for the first time at the game last week when their faces had been displayed on the Jumbotron as the PA system played the song *Kiss Me*. That couldn't have been a setup, could it? "I called her my girlfriend today."

Mrs. Holloway leaned in conspiratorially. "You did?"

"I did." For some reason he'd told Gen before anyone else. Was that weird?

"Matt." Casey's sweet voice interrupted his thoughts.

He met her bright blue eyes across the room and sighed in relief when she left the suite to bounce his direction. She threw her arms around him in a way that would announce to everyone else in the room that they were an official couple.

"You didn't tell me you were coming." She stayed in his arms but pulled back far enough for him to bask in the light of her radiant smile. Seriously, her teeth practically twinkled to the sound of a chime, her skin glowed from a summer tan, and her short, golden hair could certainly hide a halo.

Matt unwound one arm from behind her to hand her the roses. "I didn't want to disappoint you if I couldn't make it."

"I'm glad you're here." Her expression turned solemn as if letting him see the weight of her words. She gasped. "Oh, you brought me flowers."

"I did." He let go so she could lift the petals to her nose to inhale their fragrance. He didn't know her favorite flower yet, but roses seemed a safe choice.

"Thank you." She handed the flowers to her mother who was eagerly waiting to put them in water. Then she pulled Matt toward the seats lined up outside the room and overlooking the baseball diamond in the warmth of the autumn sun. He barely had time to make it to his seat before the national anthem played. That's when all light-hearted banter ceased as the family and their closest friends made serious work of cheering and talking stats and sharing personal information about the players. Matt could cheer, but that was about it. He really needed to start studying stats to fit in better if they were going to keep dating. Especially since the team would be the division champion if they won this game.

Casey leaned her head on his shoulder. "You're not going to miss any World Series games are you?"

Matt shifted to lift an arm behind her back. Boyfriends had that privilege, right? "I should be able to come more often. I missed the last few games because the station manager in Eureka was on vacation, and without their boss running things, they had a few delays."

"I couldn't—" Casey leaped out of her seat when Alan Anderson hit a pop fly toward left field. The outfielder caught it, and she sat back down with a groan. "I could never get used to the uncertainty you have to deal with every day at your job. I guess that's why I don't travel with the team."

He nodded as if he understood, but the idea of traveling with the team actually appealed to him. Visiting new cities. Seeing different stadiums, climates, cultures. That's why he'd become a pilot in the first place.

Casey shaded her eyes to better watch the next batter. "At least the Eureka manager is back now. Did you let him know how much of a difference he makes?"

"*She.*" Matt corrected, his guts flopping at the memory of how he'd handled his gratefulness. The guilt he felt over missing a couple of Giants games was nothing compared to calling a coworker by the wrong name. "I meant to tell her how much she's appreciated, but I kinda..."

Casey dropped her hand and turned to study him. "You kinda

what?"

He didn't mean to talk about his mistake, but he'd been thinking about it, which had caused the words to spill out. He shrugged and looked across the field. Maybe there would be another pop fly to distract Casey. Nope. Nothing but tinny organ music that sounded like it came from an arcade game. "I kinda forgot her name."

Casey tapped her fingers on the armrest in contemplation. Her family believed in empowering their employees, making each one feel special. That was one of the things he loved about them. Things he wanted to emulate. And exactly what he'd failed to do in this situation. "Well, that's not too bad unless you—"

"I did." He interrupted like he was ripping off a Band-Aid.

She sat up straighter. "You called her the wrong name?"

He definitely wouldn't mention the nickname thing. He pressed his lips together in contrition.

"Matthew Lake," Casey admonished. "Calling her the wrong name is the opposite of showing appreciation."

"Yeah, Gen made that clear." He pulled at the collar on his baseball t-shirt. Apparently having one woman upset with him was not enough.

"You have to make it up to her."

What? Did Casey want him to take Gen roses too? That might send the wrong message. "I did offer." He defended himself.

Casey relaxed in her seat. "I should have known you would. What did she say?"

Matt rubbed his jaw. At least Casey still had a little faith in him. "She said she needs a pilot for some kind of emergency drill they have coming up at their airport, but that's this weekend—the day of Oktoberfest here at the park. I already bought my lederhosen, and I don't want to miss doing *The Chicken Dance* with you, so I'll get her a vanilla latte next time I fly to Eureka instead."

Casey said nothing but crossed her arms.

He knew that look. "No vanilla latte?"

She shook her head.

"No Chicken Dance?"

Head shake.

"No lederhosen?"

Once more with the head shake.

That one was kind of a relief. "Are you sure you're okay with this? Because I told you I wouldn't miss any more games."

Her hand settled on his forearm. "The team is my job, and flying is yours. As much as I'd love to have you here, I'm dating you because I admire your responsibility…among other things."

He couldn't keep from smirking a little. "What are these other things you speak of?"

The crowd roared and leapt to their feet around him. Casey stood to join in and catch up on what she'd missed.

Matt stood by her side. Apparently she liked him, just not as much as baseball. So he'd go to Eureka that weekend for Gen's emergency drill, then once baseball season was over he'd be able to get to know Casey better.

CHAPTER THREE

THE HIGH SCHOOL DRAMA CLASS WHO'D volunteered to act like injured victims in a fake airplane crash had put on enough stage makeup to play extras in *The Walking Dead*. Gen didn't mind because it made for great photographs, but Bianca wasn't known for handling melodrama very well. Unless she was the one being melodramatic, of course.

"Listen, y'all." Bianca stood in front of the kids, one pointy French tip stabbing the air. "In real life, you would not have come into the airport as a group, wailing and pushing for attention. You're wounded and in shock, and you climbed off the plane one by one. So go back outside to take turns coming in. No more than three may enter at a time. And you must be respectful as we bring you inside the roped off area and pretend to treat you and contact your fake family. You can have fun with it, but we're not competing for Oscars here. I *will* remove you from this exercise if you overdo the theatrics."

The kids turned and trudged out quietly.

Bianca placed a hand on her hip. "You think I scared them?"

Genevieve lowered her camera and shifted her gaze from the solemn teenagers to the passionate black woman. "I think *I'm* a little scared."

Bianca smiled her first smile of the day. "Good."

"At least I know you can control a crowd."

Bianca arched a thin eyebrow. "Did you ever have any doubt?"

Gen thought back to the day they'd partnered up in one of her sister's exercise classes. She'd never had a tougher workout in her life. "No. In fact, if there's ever a zombie apocalypse, I'm headed straight to your place for protection."

A lone teenager wearing a ripped flannel shirt over a white t-shirt that had been squirted with bogus blood limped through the glass doors first. He paused, obviously awaiting a friend or two to join him so he didn't have to face Bianca alone.

"Are you sure those kids aren't zombies?" Bianca challenged.

Gen grinned as a couple of girls joined the first guy, all putting a lot of effort into sagging sideways as they walked. "They could break out into Michael Jackson's Thriller video routine anytime, couldn't they?"

"I'll be surprised if they don't." Bianca would handle them either way. "I'm also surprised you are in here rather than out at the plane with Matt."

Gen's pulse thundered in her ears. "I don't want him to think I invited him to this drill so I could hang out with him. He has a girlfriend."

Bianca readied her clipboard, preparing to admit zombie kids into her mock recovery center. "So you don't like him anymore?"

Gen bit her lip. She'd felt achy all morning—probably with the anxiety of knowing she'd see Matt again. "I'm going to try not to."

Bianca rolled her eyes. "You don't have to avoid him. You can still be friends."

Could she be friends with Matt? She was friends with Bianca, and they worked together. Gen looked down at her camera. "I need to go outside anyway. The airline asked me to take pictures for their training program, and I'll probably be able to sell a couple to the *Times-Standard* too."

Bianca swatted her shoulder with the clipboard. "Then go already."

Gen curled her toes inside the steel of her ugly, protective shoes. Supposedly Matt had joined the emergency drill to make up for forgetting her name. He was there because of her. But that didn't mean anything. The same way it didn't mean anything that he'd called her Carrots. She should go outside and treat him with professional courtesy.

She inched her way toward the glass door as a teenage couple entered, holding a plastic doll like they were the parents. That would actually make a good photo. Pausing to snap a picture, Gen focused her lens and adjusted the aperture.

"Want a coffee, Genevieve?" a warm male voice asked from behind.

Gen froze as if Matt were really asking her out. But he was not. He was only being his charming self. And probably also making the point that he remembered her name this time.

She lowered her camera and rubbed an earlobe. Today Matt had on a bomber jacket over his white button-up. He was practically Tom Cruise in *Top Gun*. "You look surprisingly uninjured for having crashed a plane."

"I know." One corner of his lips curved up as he watched the fake parents hobble through the lobby. "*They* look awful. You should simply be glad I'm alive."

He had no idea. "Yeah, well if you need to get imaginary medical care, check in with Bianca." Gen pointed to where Bianca had snatched the plastic doll and was waving it around while lecturing the teens on respecting their elders once again.

Matt clicked his tongue. "I'm pretty sure all I need is a coffee. Did you want a cup? I still feel like I owe you."

She would have loved it if he'd invited her for coffee before. Would have considered it a date. But he wasn't asking her out now. He was only guilty about forgetting her name. "I'm headed out to take pictures of the accident response teams, so I won't have an extra hand to hold coffee, but thank you for offering." She was moving one way while the person she wanted to be with was heading the opposite way. Story of her life. "Hey, don't you need to be out there, too?"

He lifted a shoulder. "Yeah, but it would help if I stayed awake. Do you know how early I had to get up to fly here?"

Her heart throbbed, and her skin burned. He'd gotten up early for her. He may not be asking her out, but he did make a sacrifice to improve their relationship. Having a good working relationship...worked.

Matt didn't mind flying on a Saturday, but really, his job was pretty much over. He'd simply had to get the plane to where the airport needed it for the emergency response drill. Now he could sip coffee and watch the action until it was time to take the Airbus back home to San Francisco.

There was a lot of action too. Ambulances, firemen, police, crew, and a bunch of teenagers walking around, pretending to be the undead. Genevieve ran around, recording it all on her fancy camera. Curious to see her pictures, he ambled her direction, sipping his earthy brew to stay warm in the dewy morning air.

Gen knelt at the bottom of the emergency slide that had been inflated for the crew to practice assisting "passengers" out of the plane. She angled her camera toward Michelle and clicked away as the new flight attendant zipped down to the ground.

The wind lifted Michelle's long black hair, and she landed with a giggle. She smiled up at Matt then turned serious when she noticed Gen. "You didn't take a picture of me, did you?"

Gen stood, but kept her gaze focused on her camera screen. "I did. I'm photographing the event for corporate."

"Can I see?" Michelle moved to look over Gen's shoulder. "Oh, wow. That's not bad. Can you send me a copy for Facebook?"

"I guess." Gen bit her lip, her gaze meeting Matt's.

Obviously, Michelle didn't realize Gen's photo was not a standard selfie snapped on a cell phone. What the flight attendant requested was similar to his buddies trying to bum free flights—only Gen was too giving to say no.

Matt stepped forward. "Let me see." He'd casually ask how much Gen usually charged for her work then hopefully Michelle would get the point.

Gen tilted her camera his way.

The vivid color struck him first. Though the slide was gray and the plane behind it white, it was so bright that it made Michelle's navy blue uniform boldly stand out. "Oh, man."

He leaned in to get a better view of the photo but also picked up the scent of baby powder. Did Gen have a baby, or was that her perfume? He flicked her a quick glance and decided the soft smell matched her personality. Now to check out her art.

Even on the small screen, the photo radiated brilliant clarity. Every strand of Michelle's hair stood out against the background, and with the way her skin glowed, he would have assumed the photo had been touched up. He looked first to the sky to pinpoint the sun still low over the trees behind them then toward the slide as more people slid past. The "passengers" didn't look nearly as good in real life as Michelle looked in the photo. Had Gen lucked out with the perfect lighting and timing, or was she that skilled at her craft?

He glanced at the photo once more before meeting Gen's watching eyes. "That is an impressive shot."

Her cheeks rounded in a smile. "Thanks."

"Thanks." Michelle's hair toss drew his attention back her way.

Wait. Did the flight attendant think he was complimenting her? Before he could say anything else, she'd turned her back and sauntered away with enough swing in her hips to hold up a hula hoop.

No time for subtlety. "That's really nice of Genevieve to give you a copy of this picture," he called after her. "Usually you have to pay big money for professional photographs."

No response. Not from Michelle anyway.

"It's okay." Gen scrolled through her photos. "If she'd rather I give her the photo than sell it to the local news, I don't mind."

Matt suppressed a smile. They both took Michelle to be the kind of person who would have preferred media attention. He crossed one ankle over the other and leaned against the side of the inflatable slide. "If you're still looking for a model, I'd be happy to pose," he offered in his deepest voice.

Her smile grew to laughing size, and her brown eyes sparkled when they met his. "Talk about big money."

All right, he deserved her sarcasm. In fact, if it kept her teasing, he'd set himself up again. "What? You don't want to photograph this?" He motioned from his head down to his feet with the coffee cup in hand.

"Hmm." She surveyed him, and he wondered what she saw. He should have pulled a ball cap on that morning as he was due for a haircut. "Thanks, but I'm pretty sure I already have a photo that would work." She stepped forward and lowered her camera so he could see the shot to which she was referring.

Had she snapped a picture of him when he wasn't looking? He

tilted his head. It took a moment for the image to register. He squinted to focus. Instead of a plane, he saw vibrant green leaves of the jungle, and instead of his own image, there was a furry little monkey sticking his face in a red coffee mug on a patio table.

"I think I'll title it 'Pilot Monkeys Around During Airport Emergency Drill.'"

His mouth fell open. The pleasure of laughter vibrated inside and released through a guffaw. "*Real*-ly?"

He studied her with this new perception of her sass. Her cheeks burned pink against pale skin, her grin revealed teeth so straight they must have once been adorned with braces, and her dancing brown eyes invited him to tango.

"You don't like it?" she asked, her tone full of artificial sweetener.

He lifted his free hand from the side of the slide to point at the screen. "I can see how you mistook me for your subject since we both seem to have a thing for coffee." He wouldn't mention their similar out-of-control hairstyles. "But I'm pretty sure that photo was taken in Costa Rica. Since, you know, it's a photo of a *monkey*."

Her giggle poured over him, refreshing like the rain. "Oops."

He crossed his arms, tucking his coffee cup under one elbow. This changed everything. "Well, I'm not going to worry anymore about calling you the wrong name."

She lifted her camera to take pictures again. "You never had to worry about that in the first place."

"*Now* you tell me." Though he was kind of glad she hadn't mentioned it before. Because being compared to a monkey wasn't nearly as bad as having to wear lederhosen.

Pure unrepentance lighted her face in a grin.

He couldn't let her think she'd gotten the best of him. He wouldn't wave the white flag. Even if his goal in coming had been to improve their relationship, it was more fun like this. "Well if that's the case, I'm going to go back to calling you 'Carrots.'"

Her lips pursed, and her eyes flashed a warning. But the dimple in her cheek betrayed her delight.

"Hey, Genevieve," a fireman called. "We're going to put out the fake fire now. Do you want a photo of us with the hoses?"

Her enthusiasm faded into a professional demeanor with a couple of blinks of her rust-colored eyelashes. "Excuse me," she said in perfect civility, but her gaze slid his way one last time to let him know they weren't through.

Matt watched her move to different angles around the firetruck to get a variety of photographs. Each time, it looked like there was a person in the foreground with the water spraying behind them. She really was all about making people her subjects. Even people like Michelle.

The flight attendant wasn't assisting fake passengers anymore. She was hanging out with Matt's co-pilot, Ethan, on the other side of the plane. Matt eyed the firehose one more time to make sure he could join his crew without getting wet. He circled the low engine on the side of the Airbus then strode underneath.

Ethan casually rocked back and forth in his shiny shoes, hands in his pockets. He was a little older than Matt with a wife and teenagers at home, but he stayed in good shape and kept the buzz cut from his time in the military. "Hey, Matt," the co-pilot greeted over the white noise of rushing water. "I was telling Michelle how you offered to get my family a rafting trip with your brother in Idaho in exchange for me flying here with you today."

No other pilots had wanted to give up their Saturday to hang out at the airport either. Genevieve's emergency drill would have had to be rescheduled, and Matt would have had to find another way to get in her good graces—back when he thought this would get him in her good graces. He chuckled at the idea now.

"You're lucky. Not only will you love Idaho, but if I hadn't had the means to resort to bribery, I would have twisted your arm until you agreed to come. I may not have combat training, but I'm younger, and I could still take you."

Ethan crossed his beefy forearms. "I'd like to see you try."

That would never happen. Because Matt knew he would get his butt kicked. "Anytime, old man. Anytime."

Michelle studied their size and stature, resting a little longer on Ethan's broad shoulders. "I don't know, Matt. I think my money's on Ethan."

"Thanks, sweetheart." Ethan only needed a fedora and cigar, and he'd be Humphrey Bogart.

Matt grinned, but the other two didn't even notice. They were looking at each other. Matt's smile slipped. Was he missing something here?

Nah. It had to be friendship. Or his imagination. Ethan's family went to the same church as Matt. He was a good man. A good husband. Plus, he had a lot to lose if anything happened with a flight attendant. Not that it ever would. Besides it being completely wrong, it was cliché.

Maybe the moment was only awkward because Matt was staring awkwardly.

The click of a camera drew his attention to Genevieve. She'd joined them, though her camera hid her face. If Matt's staring had been awkward, this wasn't going to help.

Gen lowered the camera then frowned at her screen. Her eyes rose to meet Matt's then shifted toward Ethan and Michelle. She'd seen it too.

"Are you taking pictures of me again?" Michelle fluffed her hair.

Ethan's gaze remained focused on the flight attendant. He could be attracted without ever doing anything about it, right? That was human. Matt shouldn't judge.

"Of course she's taking your picture, you're gorgeous," Ethan answered for Gen. "Wanna go get coffee?"

No, Ethan, no.

"Yes," Michelle said, turning her back on both Matt and Gen.

Matt should invite himself to go along, but he already had coffee in his hand. He looked down at his cup then up at Genevieve who bit her lip as she watched the pair head toward the airport. Could she get Ethan fired if she reported the start of an illicit relationship? Matt would talk to Ethan later. For now, he'd distract Gen.

"Get good shots of the firemen?" he asked.

She released her lip. "What? Oh, yes. I hope." She glanced at her camera, at Matt, then at the other pilot again.

Matt had to do better. "So why people?"

"Why people?" Her eyes turned toward him then narrowed in

contemplation.

"Why do you take pictures of people rather than airplanes landing at sunrise and fire engines shooting water and even monkeys in the jungles?" It seemed the most well-known photographers took pictures of landscapes and scenery. Well, the only one Matt knew of was Ansel Adams, but anytime he turned on his computer he was always greeted with a magnificent scene of a waterfall or ocean or forest. That's what people wanted to look at unless they knew the person...or knew *of* the person. Maybe Genevieve was part of the paparazzi and traveled to stalk famous people.

Understanding eased the lines around her eyes. "Oh... Why do I take pictures of people?"

He nodded.

She studied him for a moment before looking at her camera as if shy. "My dad bought me my first disposable camera when I was eight for our trip to Yellowstone. My brothers and sisters all took pictures of Old Faithful and the Paint Pots, and I did too, until I saw a woman with long, red hair."

Matt's gaze shifted to Gen's long, red hair. Where was she going with this?

Her eyes lifted to meet his once again. "I'm adopted, and when I saw the woman, I thought she could possibly be my biological mother."

His lips parted. His heart clenched. He never would have imagined this. "Wow," was all he could say.

"Yeah," she agreed. Maybe wow was enough. "The woman had kids with her, and I thought they might be my brothers and sisters, so I took their pictures too. They weren't, of course. They had a funny way of speaking, and when I asked my adopted mom about it, she said they were British."

He couldn't keep from giving her a small smile—an encouraging smile. Because...wow. "You don't think you were born in England?"

She scrunched up her nose, and he noted she didn't have freckles usually associated with redheads. Her fair skin was like the plane in the background of her pictures—it made her other features stand out more prominently. Could she be Irish?

"Nope." She answered with certainty.

"Did you ever find your real parents?" Or maybe she'd had her blood tested for heritage. Was that an insensitive question? He didn't know, and he hated not knowing. It meant he could mess up.

"Nope." She repeated but looked away this time. "I was born in Oregon, and when they passed the law that I could order my original birth certificate, I did. I never picked it up though. I already have wonderful parents."

Well, that was good. But as she gazed off down the runway, it looked like her eyes were glassy with unshed tears. Why would she want to cry if her family was wonderful?

"But...you still take pictures of people you think might be your relatives?"

Her mouth fell open in laughter and her shiny eyes were dry when she swiveled to face him. "I do. I also make up stories for them. It's fun."

Oh, that was too good for Matt to leave alone. He hooked a thumb over his shoulder. "So, Michelle? Is she your long lost sister?"

One hand left her camera to shove his shoulder.

He stepped wide to catch his weight. "She's pushy too. You have a lot in common."

Gen shook her head, eyes toward heaven. Then her gaze dropped back to his. Her eyebrows lifted, and her head tilted. "Maybe you're my brother."

Something uncomfortable twitched in his ribs. But he wouldn't think about it. He'd play it off. "You compared me to a monkey earlier, and now you think I'm your brother. What does that say about you?"

Her free hand covered her mouth though it didn't hide the sparkle in her eyes. "I didn't think that one through."

He waved his hand as if to erase her embarrassment, even though it had blossomed into a pretty pink stain on her cheeks. "Don't worry. I know you're not my sister. My mom wanted a girl and got five boys instead. If she'd have put anyone up for adoption, it would have been one of us."

Her hand slipped down revealing her dimples once again. "How very kind of you to say."

Yeah. He was being kind. That's all. The jolt in his chest meant nothing. It probably wouldn't be a bad idea to think of her as a sister.

CHAPTER FOUR

GEN COULDN'T CHANGE INTO HER SILK pajamas fast enough. She swung her living room door closed behind her in the old, pink, Victorian house that her sister Rosie had converted into a Holy Yoga studio with apartments above. She unhooked her purse from the way she wore it bandolier style then kicked off her stupid steel toed shoes. They always made her back ache, but her whole body was starting to ache now for some reason. Could be stress from the chaos of an emergency drill or maybe the result of nervous tension from all the interaction with Matt.

Though really, Matt was fun and charming, and she was getting more comfortable in his presence—not counting that last part of the drill where she'd used the other pilot and Michelle as a cover for taking a picture of Matt. She couldn't shake the feeling the co-pilot and flight attendant might need a cover of their own.

Groaning, she set her camera bag on the antique secretary desk by her computer and continued down the tiny hallway decorated with enough picture frames to tell the story of her life. She'd return and upload the new photos to her hard drive after she changed.

Gen pulled open the top middle drawer on her teal shabby chic dresser where she kept her piles of PJs. The royal blue ones with the white piping sat on top. Perfect. The silk cooled her skin. Maybe a little too cool. Goosebumps popped up on her arms and legs. It might be time to start turning the thermostat back on, though the sun was still warm during the day.

She looked longingly at the pastel patchwork quilt on her bed. She usually didn't take naps, but it had been a long morning. At least she didn't have anything else planned for the day except to start editing photographs to be sent out for submission. She could always stay up and do that all night long if she wanted to. It wouldn't hurt to catch up on a little sleep now. After she downloaded the photos and saved them to a thumb drive first, of course.

She trudged back up the hallway. Her feet felt as heavy as if she were still wearing her work shoes. Was she that out of shape?

Gen stared at her camera bag next to her laptop. She usually loved diving right into the images she'd captured, but for some reason, her usual enthusiasm wasn't there.

Could it be because looking at a photograph of Matt didn't compare to spending time with Matt in person? And the photo of him now felt tainted by Ethan and Michelle while her memories of laughing with him were not. She'd much rather close her burning eyes and relive the moments they'd shared together.

She sank onto her puke green couch brightened up with an abundance of throw pillows and reached for her purple chenille blanket with the tassels. Usually the ugly couch was comfortable, but not today. Everything felt stiff and lumpy. And she didn't want to move to readjust because it hurt too much.

So she stayed there and thought about Matt. Things like how much warmer she would be if he'd let her wear his jacket. Or maybe if she'd taken his offer of coffee. Her favorite thought was the one about the heat of his arms were he to ever wrap them around her. After he broke up with his girlfriend of course.

A loud pounding on the door made her heart jump, and it took her a few moments to reorient herself in the dark living room. She must have fallen asleep. She shifted to push herself up, and the thin pajama material clung to her damp skin. She wiped her sweaty brow. At least she wasn't cold anymore.

The hot room suffocated her though she hadn't turned on the heater. And her head throbbed from her temples to the base of her skull.

"Gen?" The quick, enthusiastic voice belonged to Rosie.

What time was it? Did they have plans together? Had she slept all night, and Rosie was there to pick her up for church and the weekly visit to see their brother?

"I'm coming." Gen rocked to her feet with a grunt then stabilized herself with a palm to the wall. She finally made it to the door and swung it open. She'd tell her sister she wasn't up for going out today.

Rosie stood a good six inches shorter. She was dressed in a tank top and yoga pants stretched tight over thick thighs. Specially-made running shoes covered her stubby feet. Not church clothes.

Rosie peered past Gen into the dark room. "Are you in bed already? It's not even nine o'clock on a Saturday night."

So it was still Saturday.

Rosie's palm cooled her forehead. "Are you sick?"

Gen shivered in the rush of evening air. Lovesick? she wondered. If spending the morning with Matt had this kind of effect on her, she would be better off giving up her crush. "Matt has a girlfriend."

Rosie stepped past her, flicked on a stained glass lamp, and led her to the couch. "Did he still come to your rescue today?"

"He did." Gen returned to the couch and let Rosie cover her up with the blanket.

Rosie sat on the oversized ottoman and smiled down at her. She was one of the most beautiful people Gen knew—not in a way that could get her into *People Magazine*. No, she had missing toes and some missing fingers, so the world would consider her deformed. But in spite of her deformities, or perhaps because of them, Rosie could love like no one else.

"And?" Rosie asked.

And what? Gen's brain grew foggy, and her scalp ached as she tried to think of what to say. What had she and Matt talked about? "I told him I'm adopted."

She never knew what to expect from people when sharing that part of her story. Would they look for flaws in her to discover why her parents might have given her up? Would they be extra nice out of pity? Or would they be able to relate somehow? That was her favorite response. Besides Matt's joking, of course.

"How did he react?" Rosie knew the importance of the reaction too. Even more so than Gen.

Gen smiled at the memory. "He said he's not my brother because if his mom had given up anyone for adoption, it would have been one of her five boys."

Rosie rubbed Gen's leg. The light touch meant to comfort felt more like bruising on Gen's unusually tender skin. "That's a good thing to know. Remember when I found out my first kiss had actually been my bio cousin?"

"Eww." Gen lifted a hand to plug her ears but lost the energy halfway there and dropped her arm back to the couch. "Don't remind me."

"Does he have red hair?"

Gen let her eyes drift closed. What were they talking about again? "Who? Your cousin?"

"No. Matt. Why would he even consider the possibility of being your brother?"

Gen processed the information slowly. They were talking about what Matt looked like. She sighed in contentment. She couldn't describe Matt in words. Rosie needed to see for herself. Gen peeked one eye open to make sure she'd set her camera on the desk. She pointed. "I took a picture of him if you want to see."

"Oh, awesome." The sound of Rosie's sneakers squeaking across the wood floors was followed by the whirring of a computer coming to life and then the click of cords being plugged in. "I actually came over to talk to you about your photography. I decided to start a goat yoga class, and I'd love for you to take some pictures for my website."

Maybe Gen really was sick. Hallucinating. Because it sounded like Rosie had said "goat yoga."

"It's the new thing. I bought a bunch of kids—you know, baby goats—so they can come in my studio to play around and jump on participants while they're stretching. I've already got a waiting list."

Gen's head throbbed. Her sister used to live with Gen when she'd first moved to Eureka, then her career as a motivational speaker had taken off, and she'd ended up buying this place and renting half of it to Gen. Rosie's life had gotten better, but that also meant Gen's life got wilder. How responsible was Gen going to have to be for raising goats in their backyard for this new craze?

She didn't have the energy to consider all the ramifications. She'd agree to the photo shoot so she could go back to sleep. "Okay."

"I knew you wouldn't mind."

Quiet. At last. Gen's thoughts drifted as the soft rhythm of a clicking mouse lulled her to sleep.

"You got some good shots. Is Matt the guy in the bomber jacket?"

Gen jolted. Rosie was still there? She forced her eyes open despite the bright light of the computer screen. If Rosie was looking at pictures of Matt, she wanted to see him too. "Yeah."

She'd actually gotten a good shot of him. At least the other two people in the pic were out of focus. Or maybe her brain was just fuzzy. She let her eyelids block out her surroundings once again.

"He's kind of got a baby face. Like Tom Cruise in *Top Gun*."

Gen hugged a pillow to smother the fluttering in her belly. She still didn't know if the reaction was physical or emotional. "I thought so too."

"Makes me want to invite him to play in a beach volleyball game."

The buzzing in Gen's temple overrode her sister's humor. That reaction had to be physical, because normally she would want to laugh and joke some more. "Can you get me a pain killer instead?"

"Of course." The chair scraped floorboards. "Are you feeling that bad?"

Gen sighed and sank deeper into the pillows. "Only when I'm awake." This was more than exhaustion, wasn't it?

Footsteps. Cupboards thudding shut. Running water. More footsteps.

The ottoman puffed with Rosie's weight. "Can you sit up?"

Ugh. Gen hadn't thought her request all the way through. Taking a pain pill would require more movement than she had the energy for. But if Rosie had gone through all that trouble...

She pried her eyes open, lifted her head, and pushed to a semi-seated position.

Rosie opened her palm to reveal a little white tablet. "You think you're getting the flu?"

"I hope not." Gen couldn't miss any more work. She pinched the pill and placed it on her dry tongue. Water might actually help. She reached for the cool glass and tilted her head back to guzzle.

Rosie gasped. "Gen, your neck."

Rosie gasped all the time. Usually over silly things like when she remembered she had hot fudge in her fridge and usually at inopportune times like when Gen was driving. So Gen should be used to this. But still, she set her glass down and reached for her neck in concern. "What?"

"You have a rash."

Really? Could it be heat rash from a fever? An allergic reaction? A never-ending blush from the way Matt made her feel that morning? It didn't itch. Only felt puffy and warm.

Gen stood. "I'm taking you to Urgent Care. You've already had chicken pox, haven't you?"

Gen wanted to argue. Not only were the couch cushions calling her name, but she didn't have time for an illness. She preferred to save her time off to use for travel. Especially since she had that Rome trip coming up, but if her rash didn't go away, then she wouldn't want to travel anyway. And she couldn't miss her first trip to Europe.

"You don't ever want to go to Europe?" Matt repeated in disbelief, on the drive to Grace Cathedral the next morning.

"I don't want to *fly* to Europe." Casey shrugged as if it were no big deal. "I would do a cruise. Though it would have to be in the winter when baseball season is over, and that might not make the best cruising weather."

He should have known. They'd met when he'd been flying Casey's dad's charter plane to New Jersey for the MLB draft, and she'd been scared to go with him. Matt had encouraged her, comforted her, and ultimately distracted her enough to get her on the plane.

"What if *I* were flying the plane?" he countered, pulling into the parking lot across from the cathedral where Casey's family attended church.

"I'd take a cruise and meet you there."

For some reason he'd thought dating him might make her more open to airline travel. "So if I invite you to Idaho to meet my family, you'll want to drive?" It would be a fifteen-hour drive compared to a two-hour flight. He'd never driven it.

Casey pursed her lips for a moment. "Why don't you invite them here? I mean, Dave came for a Giants game. Wouldn't your other brothers want to come too?"

They probably would. Matt could get them free flights, and Casey could get them free tickets. He'd call Tracen when he got home. His middle brother had been mourning his broken heart for a little too long now. He needed to get out and try new things. But that didn't mean Casey couldn't go visit them, as well.

Matt parked between a Mini Cooper and an old-fashioned woody wagon. "Your family would love Sun Valley. Everyone from Arabian princes to Oprah vacation there. And my brother recently mentioned there are also plans to film a movie."

Casey climbed out, and he stood to face her over the roof of his silver Audi. "I'm sure Idaho is great, but we get all those celebrities here too, you know. Did you see who was at the game yesterday?"

"No." He hadn't been at the game; he'd been getting to know Gen with a G. But that wasn't the point.

She leaned forward and patted the top of the car with each word as she spoke it. "Jack. Jamison."

Matt couldn't place the name. Actor? Singer? Politician? Casey was clearly a fan of the mysterious VIP, so he'd play along. "No way. Did he wear lederhosen?"

Casey's head dropped back in laughter. "I wish."

She did? What did that mean? He shook his head to clear out the confusion.

She circled around the trunk of his silver coupe, her eyes sparkling. "Of course, not as much as I wish you'd been there in your lederhosen."

"That's better." He joined her and reached for her hand. "I think I still have my green felt hat with the feather in the backseat if you want me to wear it to lunch."

"Oh, I do."

Matt shot her a grin before tugging her toward the cathedral. This was the Casey he liked to hang out with. The one who wasn't obsessing about baseball.

His gaze rested on a family already crossing the street. Ethan's family. His co-pilot was still bringing his family to church, so there probably wasn't anything going on with the flight attendant. Ethan's son bounded up the wide stairway while Ethan, his wife, and daughter followed more slowly. From a distance, their lives appeared perfect. And Matt hoped they were.

"How well do you know Ethan's wife, Stephanie?" he asked casually.

Casey followed his line of sight toward the middle-aged woman who looked like an athlete with her trim physique and dark hair cropped short. "Stephanie White? I've had coffee with her a couple of times. She's always asking me to donate baseball tickets to raise money for the PTO. I'm also sponsoring her in the Run for Education coming up. She invited me to run too, but I'd rather do the fun runs where you dress up like a superhero or something."

That sounded like Casey. She wanted her events to have themes — hence the lederhosen.

"Raising money for education really would make you a superhero. You could still dress up." He wanted Casey to connect with Stephanie in case Ethan's wife needed a friend...or some advice.

"Ooh, I think I have a red cape in my closet somewhere."

"I'm sure you do."

She squeezed his hand. "You are *so* wearing your felt hat at lunch today."

He chuckled despite the heaviness in his gut. Was he overreacting to worry about Ethan's marriage? He might get a better feel for what was going on if he hung out with them together. "Wanna invite the Whites to lunch?"

Casey lifted her face toward his, mouth open in awe as if he'd come up with the best idea since the Wright brothers invented the glider. "I would love to go on a double date now that we are an official couple."

They could do that too, but... "I was thinking their whole family would come."

"Oh sure." She picked up her pace, pulling him along. "I would love to have a family like theirs someday. Wouldn't you?"

Yeah, he wanted a family someday, though it seemed like they were skipping a few steps if they talked about it now.

Casey leaned forward to step into the street, her focus on the

Whites.

Matt planted himself in place and tugged her back to keep her out of oncoming traffic. "Hang on, Case."

She swung around until she faced him, her nose at his chin level. He studied her beauty, knowing it went a lot deeper than her skin. She was precious. In every way. So why did the thought of following in the Whites' footsteps bother him? Was it only because Ethan's attention could be wandering from his wife? That had to be it. Matt would never do to Casey what he suspected Ethan was doing to Stephanie.

CHAPTER FIVE

MATT CHECKED THE CONTROLS BEFORE REACHING for his radio. Now that he knew more about the woman on the other end of the in-range calls, radioing in seemed more personal. "This is Flight 348, calling the Eureka station."

He grinned in anticipation of Genevieve's response. He was looking forward to talking to her today because a huge redheaded man in a kilt had boarded the plane, and he wanted to see her reaction when he suggested the man might be her father.

Static crackled. "Uh…Eureka station." The response came in a deeper voice than expected. It wasn't Gen. It wasn't even female.

"Oh, man." Ethan grunted. "She's gone again. Hopefully they send us to the right gate this time."

Why was Gen gone? She'd just returned. Even Ethan was bummed.

Matt would worry about it later. He pressed the button on the radio to respond. "We are twenty minutes out. No wheelchairs today."

"Great. We'll see you in twenty minutes at Gate 3B, I mean…uh…three-bravo."

Ethan shook his head and sighed.

Maybe Matt's co-pilot wasn't having an affair with Michelle after all. Ethan didn't seem excited that Gen's absence could create extra time at the airport with the flight attendants. Plus he'd been pretty attentive to his wife at lunch on Sunday. The extra attention from a flight attendant could be nothing more than a little ego boost. Or perhaps Ethan wasn't even aware of it on his end, and he was simply being a nice guy.

Matt went through the motions to land the plane then filled out the fuel slip for Michelle to hand to whoever opened the plane door. It looked like the same agent who'd been lecturing high school students on Saturday. Bianca. He'd ask her about Gen.

Michelle stuck her head in the cockpit as passengers filed past. "You guys hungry at all?"

A burger did sound good. If Matt offered to run into the airport and get burgers for everyone, he'd have an excuse to talk to Bianca. "I'll buy."

Michelle smiled past him at Ethan. Red flag.

Matt should have thought this through better because now he was leaving Michelle alone with Ethan in the cockpit. If these warning alarms in his head kept going off, he'd have to have a talk with his co-pilot.

"Thanks, Matt." Ethan hung up his headset like he didn't have a care in the world. "No onions on mine."

Michelle stepped out of the way so he could pass. "And I'll take sweet potato fries."

Matt nodded without looking her in the eye. After collecting orders from the rest of the crew, he headed up the bridge.

"Hey there." Bianca greeted him at the gate. She ignored her computer and all the passengers to grin at him.

"Hey." He stopped. "Gen off today?"

Her grin grew wider. She leaned forward and held a hand to the side of her mouth as if she was going to whisper, but her voice remained loud enough for the rest of his crew on the Airbus to hear. "She got Zika down in Costa Rica. It's a virus."

He rocked forward and jutted out his chin. "Zika?" That sounded bad. Like something that would require quarantine and Hazmat suits and a pandemic alert. "Is she going to be okay?"

Bianca waved a hand. "It's basically a really bad mosquito bite that causes flu like symptoms. She'll be back within the week."

Matt blew out his breath. Crisis averted. "That's...crazy."

"That's Gen. Risking her life for a little adventure." Bianca busied herself with plugging a scanner into the computer for boarding. "I'll tell her you asked about her."

"Thanks." At least she was okay. Matt turned to head toward the lone airport restaurant.

There, in his path, the big Scotsman knelt to strap a small child into a stroller. How did he do that modestly in a kilt? Looked dangerous. Though it also looked pretty cute the way the child beamed up at the gruff giant as if he were a teddy bear. Gen would want to take a picture and make up a story.

If Gen were related to the man, she could be long lost Scottish royalty. Ha. Matt was making up a story for her. Might as well take a picture to go with it. He moved backward to appear inconspicuous when pulling out his phone.

The Scotsman stood and stepped behind the stroller. Matt needed to act faster. He tapped on his camera app, centered the image, and tapped again. Not bad. Definitely not the same quality of the photos Gen took, but it still told a story. Too bad he'd have to wait to show her. Unless…

Matt glanced over his shoulder to see if Bianca had begun boarding passengers yet. Nope. She was pulling out a portable Bluetooth speaker to play "boarding music." Something she didn't do when Gen was there.

The strum of a guitar introduced the lyrics to the song *Leaving on a Jet Plane*. A few people chuckled around him.

He strode to the podium.

Bianca swayed side to side as she sang along. Matt never would have taken her for a John Denver fan.

"Can I interrupt real quickly, Bianca? I'd like to get Gen's phone number to let her know the flight crew wishes her well."

The gate agent didn't stop her performance, simply pulled out her cell phone as if it were part of a choreographed routine. Her voice was actually pretty good. She stayed on tune though she changed the lyrics. "Call her or text instead. Tell her to get her rest in bed. Wish her well so she'll come back to work…"

If the two of them hadn't already had the attention of all the passengers around, they did now.

Bianca held the phone up for him to see Gen's number. "Sing with me," she cried.

She couldn't be serious.

The crowd joined in, the chorus surrounding him. He smiled at the magic of the moment, but he couldn't stay for an encore. He had to get those burgers. And text Gen.

"I'm leaving…" the crowd sang.

He punched in the number and held up his phone in thanks. *"I'm leaving."*

Bianca waved before looping her arms around the gate agents on either side of her. Matt left them to their show, wound around the line of waiting passengers, and pulled up his messaging app.

Gen lay on her side in bed, her laptop open in front of her where she could follow the flight information. The plane had landed and everyone was off, but boarding for the next flight still hadn't begun. Bianca probably had them all singing along with John Denver again.

She closed her burning eyes. If she hadn't taken one of those extra strength pain killers the doctor prescribed her, she could have gone in. Except then Matt would have seen her gross, icky rash.

Her phone buzzed. Her eyes flew open. Bianca? Were they missing bags? Was there an inebriated passenger they had to deny boarding? Had they crashed the luggage cart into the jet bridge again? There went her annual bonus.

Gen dug around in the quilt until she found the cool, smooth cellular device. An unknown number flashed, signaling a message received. It wasn't her team. Her stomach unclenched.

She slid her thumb over the screen.

Hey, slacker. –Matt

Her stomach knotted tighter this time. Matt? Matt the pilot? How did he get her number? More importantly, why did he want her number? Was he joking, or were things really falling apart at the airport? The drugs made her brain too fuzzy to think straight.

She had to respond. But what did she say? *Forget my name again?*

She covered her mouth as if she'd said something wrong. Maybe she had, maybe she hadn't. She wouldn't know until he responded. If only she could see his face. Hear his tone.

Sorry. Hey, Carrots.

She squealed aloud to make sure she hadn't died and gone to

heaven. Forget *Top Gun*. This guy was straight out of *Anne of Green Gables*. Teasing her and calling her nicknames. Sure, he probably did that with everyone, but for the moment it made her feel special.

Rolling onto her back, she let herself float as if on a cloud before gripping her phone again. The nice thing about texting was that she could make all kind of giddy noises and throw her arms wide in ecstasy without Matt knowing.

Was this a thing now? Could she text him whenever she wanted? Surely not that much. As far as she knew, he still had a girlfriend.

She had to act like it was no big deal. *Airport falling apart without me?*

I wouldn't say that, though Bianca started up her karaoke again.

Gen knew it. Though that didn't explain why he'd texted. Hmm... *Things could be worse.*

Yeah. We're fine here. I'm texting to find out how you're doing. I've never heard of the Zika Virus before.

Bianca must have told him before she started the sing-along. Had she said anything else embarrassing? Like, "Gen wants to marry you someday"? He really could be messaging to let her down gently. He'd called her Carrots instead of Gen to keep his distance.

Cringing, she tapped her fingers across the keyboard. *It's not too bad. The drugs help. The worst part was giving blood so the doctor could run the test.*

There. She sounded positive. And friendly without being needy. Right?

Well, take it easy and come back soon, okay? I was hoping you'd be here because I think I saw your dad on the plane.

So much packed into that one message. First, he wanted her to come back soon, so he couldn't have found out about her crush because that would have totally creeped him out. Second, he hadn't only wanted her there for business reasons but to goof off.

He had to be goofing about the dad thing. She'd started it by telling Matt about her photography. What kind of man would he suggest to be her father? Probably a redhead.

Papa Carrots?
In a kilt.

Her phone buzzed a second time in a row, revealing a photo of a large man with a bright red beard and even brighter white stumps of legs underneath what looked like a plaid skirt. He was pushing a toddler in a stroller.

And that's my nephew?

Your brother. Your father has been looking for you for a couple decades and was finally forced to give up and create another heir to take ownership of the castle that has been in your clan since the 17th century, but by some quirk of fate, they were able to track you down here, and he's probably about to knock on your door.

Matt was good at this game. He not only gave her a loving family, he practically made her royalty. Gen curled her knees in to snuggle on her side. She'd linger in the fantasy a bit longer. It beat a headache and sore joints.

Is it one of those castles where they play elephant polo or one that had its walls painted by Brazilian graffiti artists?

She hoped he'd say the one with Brazilian graffiti artists. She'd always wanted to visit that one.

I'm pretty sure it's one filmed in the Christmas episode of Downton Abbey.

Now that was too much. No man was that perfect. *You blamed your mom for making you watch Anne of Green Gables and Little House, but I don't think you can blame her for Downton Abbey.*

I'll blame that one on my girlfriend.

Game over. Since Matt was perfect, he deserved a perfect girlfriend like Giants' heir, Casey Holloway. She'd googled.

Sure. Gen attempted to keep the tone light with sarcasm.

I'd plead the Fifth if I had time, but I gotta go fly an airplane now. Get better.

Gen smiled sadly at her phone. Even if she wasn't sick and was goofing off with Matt in person, he'd still be getting back on an airplane to fly away. He was the highlight of her day, while she'd only ever be a blip on his radar.

She'd take what she could get. *I'll try. In the meantime, keep me posted if I miss out on any more relatives.*

Oh, I'm sure I'll find more.

CHAPTER SIX

IN THE NEXT WEEK, MATT FOUND more relatives than Genevieve could possibly have been related to. And they weren't all Scottish either. The pictures kept getting more and more bizarre. It started off pretty benign with a guy sleeping on an air mattress in the SFO airport. Followed by the girl with the peeling sunburn, who easily could have been related to Gen. But then came the punk rocker with the pink hair and gage holes in her ears. Then the Indians and the older African woman wearing a beautiful orange scarf on her head. It made Gen's boring week go by a lot faster. But it also made her miss Matt even more.

She told Rosie about it on the way up the 101 to visit their brother Damon that Sunday. "Last night he sent me a picture of Emily Van Arsdale. Do you know who that is?"

Rosie glanced at her in surprise from where she was perched on a pillow to see out the windshield of her new Jeep Cherokee. "The actress?"

Gen smiled. "Yeah. Matt spotted her in the airport."

"I hope you *are* related. Then you can introduce me. I'd love to get an endorsement from her for my website."

Gen chuckled. "You think she'd like goat yoga?"

"Oh, I know she would, but I'm talking about my speaking website."

Gen considered writing Matt back with Rosie's request, but she wasn't ready to talk about her real life family yet. It was more fun to imagine she might be inheriting a castle one day. "If Emily and I are ever reunited, I'll definitely mention it."

Battery Point Lighthouse, with its dome sticking out the center of a white stone building, signaled their arrival in Crescent City. During low tide, a land bridge connected the tiny wildflower covered islet to the mainland. Just one of the many views that made the 80 miles of rugged coastline and majestic forests fly by.

Though she loved the area, the prison was actually what had brought Gen to Eureka after Damon was convicted for rape. She'd wanted to be there for her big brother when nobody else could or would. His crime was heinous, and he'd be forever considered a monster no matter how sorry he was. This was a just punishment for his sin. And the reason he needed more love now than ever.

Their parents had tried to move down, but Dad's engineering job in Seattle as well as the resources Mom needed to take care of their youngest brother's disabilities prohibited them from following. It had been easier for Gen to relocate. Damon was sentenced the same year she'd graduated from Seattle Art Institute, and Dad's contacts at Boeing had helped her get the airline job. She hadn't wanted to move to California at first because she'd thought of it as plastic and stuck up, but Eureka wasn't like that at all. It embraced the arts, which made it a good fit for her. It was just too bad her discovery of the area had required such devastating circumstances.

"You know Damon's parole hearing is coming up, right?" Rosie asked.

Gen had been counting down the days until he was set free. "I'm sure he'll be released. Though the prison will miss him running the library and leading Bible studies."

He'd been sentenced for eight years and could get out at five. Only Gen didn't know what he was going to do once he was a free man again. He'd become a doctor so he could go on mission trips to his home country of Haiti and treat the sick, but after his conviction, the state of California had revoked his license to practice medicine.

Gen wanted more than this for him. A product of rape himself, he'd somehow justified the crime in his mind. Probably because his dad had gotten out of punishment in Haiti simply by marrying his mother—not that the arrangement had worked out for anyone. But when Damon had fallen for an associate and didn't know how to pursue a relationship, he'd sadly resorted to force.

Gen hurt for both his victim and for him, and she wondered where the pain would end. According to her understanding of the Bible, he would be punished for the sins of his father. It didn't seem fair as none of her siblings even knew their birth parents, so she'd quit reading the Bible when she'd gotten to generational curses in the Ten Commandments and preferred to pretend everything was all right.

She was there to help him make everything all right again. "You think he'd want to become a yoga instructor?" she asked as Rosie turned onto a side road.

Rosie grimaced. "I'm not sure how comfortable my female students would be with that."

Gen clicked her tongue because Rosie was right. If his own sister wouldn't hire Damon, who would? "I'm going to hate watching him flip burgers."

"Me too."

Damon was their big brother. Gen had looked up to him. He'd taught her to tie her shoe by folding the laces into two rabbit ears when she couldn't get the whole loop thing. And he'd given her piggy back rides when her feet were tired from Christmas shopping at the Alderwood Mall.

"It'll get better," she told herself as much as Rosie. But would any woman ever want to date him? Would he ever have children of his own to give piggy back rides?

A chain link metal fence topped with barbed wire flashed its ugly silver fangs through openings in the trees on their left, and Rosie flipped on her blinker to turn toward the visitor's gate. A blue steel watchtower stood over them, resembling the lighthouses they'd seen along the way, but here workers were more prepared to take a life than save one.

Rosie pulled the Jeep next to the guard's booth and rolled down her window to hand over her ID. Gen retrieved her wallet with the gold bow to do the same. She knew the process well enough to set herself on cruise control until they reached the ammonia scented visiting center in the Security Housing Unit and took a seat at a cold, metal table. Once again, it was easier to simply block out the sadness that surrounded her.

A few conversations buzzed at the other tables in the visiting center. Then the clanging of an outer gate announced Damon's arrival. A tattooed guard led him in, looking more like a criminal than Damon.

Her brother was tall and lean like a basketball player, though his glasses made him appear more studious than athletic. The deep creases in his brow were newer and ran parallel with the straight hairline across the top of his forehead. He smiled his bashful smile.

The guard remained at the door, one hand on his Taser. At least Gen hoped it was a Taser.

She waited her turn for a hug from Damon. Rosie currently had her arms wrapped around him. He patted her awkwardly.

"Hello, Genevieve," he greeted over the top of Rosie's head. Always so formal. Not the stereotype of the kind of person who needed to be tasered.

"Hello, Damon."

He was the oldest Wilson kid, and as far as Gen could remember, he'd always had a bit of an old soul. Her parents had fallen in love with him at the age of three on a mission trip. His adoption was followed by Trina's adoption from China. After that, Mom and Dad started fostering kids in the States and ended up with three more.

As for Gen, someone had specifically requested the Wilsons adopt her the week she'd been born. Who knew where she would be if they hadn't? Though all her siblings had been well loved and cared for, unfortunately it hadn't been enough to keep Damon out of jail or reverse the effects of any of her other siblings' cursed family trees.

That had been the real reason Gen didn't pick up her original birth certificate. She didn't want to know her curse.

Rosie let Damon go so Gen could step in. He held her at arm's length to look her in the eye. "I researched the Zika Virus, and I was happy to find it's not airborne. Were your symptoms pretty mild?"

Her lips curved up. That was his way of telling her he missed her visit the week before. She leaned in to complete the hug. It didn't last long. It never did. And Gen always wondered if it was because he was scared of his own strength.

"I was achy like with the flu. The worst part was the rash, but it's finally gone away. See?" She pointed to the neckline of the hooded sweatshirt she'd put on over her church clothes to hide her body from leers and cat calls of inmates.

"Good. Good." He pulled out chairs for the sisters to sit then circled the table to join them. Folding his hands, he focused on Gen. "Was Costa Rica worth your illness?"

She hadn't thought of it that way. Though the two were related, they didn't even compare. "Definitely. It was incredible. I hiked volcanoes and waterfalls and kayaked and visited an alligator farm, not to mention the monkey tour. I'd probably just take more insect repellent next time."

Damon nodded in concern. "And you'll want to make sure your immunizations are up to date before you travel to Rome. Italy is having a measles outbreak."

Measles. She'd definitely prepare for that so she didn't miss any more work than she had to. "Good to know." Hey, he'd be out of prison by then... "Do you want to go with us?"

Rosie widened her eyes and shook her head as if sending a warning. What?

Damon blinked and pressed his lips together. "I will consider your suggestion, but my first priority is to find a job and an apartment."

Oh. That.

Well... "I know an apartment owner." Gen tilted her head toward her sister. "I bet she'd give you a good deal—as long as you don't mind having goats running around your backyard."

"Goats?" Damon lowered his glasses to peer at Rosie. "Because having a pink house isn't strange enough?"

Rosie laughed her contagious laugh. "What do you expect from a girl with no toes?"

A few heads turned their way at her remark.

Damon smiled, his teeth flashing bright against dark skin. This was the Damon Gen missed. He came out to play every now and then. Usually when Rosie laughed.

"I should have expected goats," he said.

An inmate headed toward the guard at the door stopped and squinted at their table. He would have been handsome if not for the scary looking scar down his cheek. "Whoa, lady. You're missing fingers, too. That is so gross. Did you get in a fight with a lawnmower or somethin'?"

Damon's chair scraped back. He shot to his feet, towering over the shorter man, the smile in his eyes now replaced with a warning gleam. His hands fisted and a vein bulged in his neck. "Do you assume she was cut by a lawnmower because that's what happened to your face?"

The guard stepped forward and pulled out his Taser.

Gen's pulse pounded in her ears. She forgot to breathe. Damon was overreacting and it could lose him his chance at parole.

"Damon." Rosie held up a mutilated hand in a stop signal then quickly lowered it as if to prevent any more insults that might further enrage their brother. "It's okay. I'm okay. This isn't anything I haven't heard before."

"Dude." The inmate lifted both of his palms to show he meant no harm.

The guard leveled the Taser on Damon. "Sit down," he barked. "Sit down now."

Gen covered her mouth. She'd never seen her brother treated like a dog before. She'd also never seen him snarl like a pit bull. He could be scary.

Damon kept his eyes on the other inmate while slowly lowering to his seat.

Laughter echoed around them. Only it wasn't the contagious kind.

The guard shoved the other inmate toward the door. "Get."

Metal doors clanked. Followed by an eerie silence.

Damon cleared his throat and pushed his glasses higher on his nose. "I apologize," he said as if he'd simply forgotten to pick up the dry cleaning or something.

Rosie curled her hands on her lap. "Damon, you don't have to defend me from him. I'm used to those kinds of jokes. I make them myself. You were just laughing at one."

Damon sat up straighter, on edge. "That thug wasn't laughing with you. He was laughing *at* you."

"So?" She shrugged. "He's going back to a jail cell. I'm returning to my pink house and my goats in my brand new Jeep, and soon I'll be headed to Rome. I don't care what he thinks. My life is good."

Gen took a deep breath. "Rub your earlobes, Damon. It will help you relax." Even if he got parole, behavior like that could land him back in prison. She wanted more than that for him.

He obediently pinched his earlobes between thumb and forefinger.

"You can't fight." Rosie nodded and started to reach for his arm but stopped herself. Either she was avoiding the possibility of triggering another confrontation with the people around, or the first man's insults had gotten to her after all. She looked at her lap. "You're going to be out soon and leaving this all behind. If our coming here is going to jeopardize your release, then we're not going to visit."

Gen held her breath. How could Rosie make a threat like that? How would Damon respond?

He watched Rosie pull away. His eyes didn't hold anger anymore. They were empty. Resigned. "Okay," he said. "I want you to keep coming. You're the best part of my week."

Gen sniffed to keep the tickle in her nose from betraying her emotions. She also had to avert her gaze so Damon didn't notice the unshed tears before they had a chance to dry.

It was really hard to ignore the sad things when they were right in front of her. When they were a part of her family.

So she'd think about Matt instead. About his claim that she would inherit a castle. Yes, that was better. She'd simply keep pretending life was a fairytale, and someday her favorite pilot would rescue her, and they'd fly off into the sunset.

Matt slid into a rocking, orange kayak. He'd offered to take Tracen to a Giants game, but he'd mistakenly assumed they'd be attending the game, not cheering from the bay. He should have known better. Tracen was a rafting guide.

"I hope there are some splash hits tonight. Can you imagine if I caught one?" Tracen dropped into his own kayak and waved the net he'd rented in hopes of fishing baseballs out of the water in McCovey Cove. "I'm so jealous of myself right now."

Energy hummed through the air in the form of chattering from other enthusiastic kayak renters at South Beach Harbor. Casey wasn't one of them. She stood on the dock, one hand shielding her eyes from the sun overhead. "Tracen, are you sure you don't want to *watch* the game? This is the World Series."

Matt lowered the volume on the waterproof radio so he could hear their conversation above the announcer's pre-game show.

Tracen lifted his chin to be able to see Casey from under the brim of his baseball cap. As much as he loved the sunshine, he had to protect his eyes or he'd sneeze like crazy. "Are *you* sure you don't want to paddle out with us? Get a different experience of the game? I mean, where else in the world is there a stadium on the water's edge?"

Casey lifted her free hand in a shrug. "Where else can your brother get you into the owner's suite?"

Tracen shot a pointed look Matt's direction from behind his dark lenses as if waiting for his brother to step in and explain the differences between growing up an heiress versus growing up with five brothers in Idaho.

Matt shook his head. If he was going to have to choose a side, it would be Casey's. He was her boyfriend now. "She's got you there, bro."

Tracen sliced his paddle through the water, sending a shower of icy droplets Matt's direction.

Matt rubbed a hand down his face to dry it. He'd splash back if there was any possible chance that Tracen wouldn't retaliate hard enough to drench Casey. There wasn't, so Matt would wait until later to return the shower. For now he'd resort to sarcasm. "Now *that's* going to change her mind and make her want to join us."

Tracen's smug smile gave the impression he knew exactly what he was doing, but he acted all innocent when facing Casey again. "I'll have to return on a foggy weekend to watch from the suite. Today is too nice to not be on the water."

She tilted her head to soften her stance. "You're always welcome."

"Thanks." Tracen pushed off from the dock and spun his kayak around.

Matt shook his head to smooth things over with Casey before trying to catch up. "You'd have to have a little brother to understand."

She attempted a smile. "I doubt I would ever understand, but I hope you have fun out there anyway."

"Oh, I will." He let go of the dock to allow his own kayak to drift away. "You'll probably hear us cheering from your seat."

She nodded. "I'll say hi to Mom and Dad for you."

"Thanks, Case." He tilted a paddle to push against the water and propel himself after Tracen.

If not for Tracen's height, Matt wouldn't have been able to find him in the masses. A group of college guys on inner tubes bounced a beach ball designed to resemble a baseball back and forth overhead. An earthy looking couple wearing orange and black cowboy hats slipped by on paddleboards. Two older men floated past in a raft, pulling a giant inflatable baseball glove holding a cooler behind them. Every kind of water craft from ski boat to cabin cruiser floated outside the no motor zone, and, in the distance, ferries and water taxis shuttled people to the game.

Tracen twisted to face Matt once he'd caught up. "Sorry your girlfriend didn't want to come."

Matt shot him a sour expression. He didn't mind having guy time; but he wasn't going to tolerate any lies about it. "No you're not."

Tracen broke into a grin. "You're right. Nothing against her, she just reminds me of my ex. All blonde and celebrity-ish."

Matt grunted. Would Tracen ever get over his former fiancé leaving him to pursue a career in Hollywood? "You don't have to make excuses."

Tracen held up a hand as if to smooth things over. "She seems perfect for you. You know, if you are into perfection."

What did that even mean? Tracen made Casey's perfection sound like a flaw when really it was why so many other men wanted to date her. Matt was honored she'd chosen him. He wanted to live up to that choice. He wanted to believe she needed him.

Tracen surveyed their surroundings and pointed toward an open spot in the water on the other side of the stadium wall. Matt angled his kayak to follow.

He'd felt responsible for protecting his brothers ever since Tracen had tried to raft a Class-VI rapids at the age of fifteen. Like a selfish idiot, Matt had let him go by himself, and their family had spent the night in the hospital praying Tracen would survive the slashing of his intestines. Since then, Matt had started taking a little more obligation for everyone around him.

Cheering erupted from the stands and echoed across the water. A fraction of a second later the radio announcer detailed a pop fly caught by one of the Giants.

The boaters shouted and laughed and splashed in response.

Tracen groaned. "Too bad it didn't pop a little farther."

Matt didn't mind. He stilled his kayak, lifted his paddle into his lap, and laid back to rock in the sunshine. He'd never tell Casey, but this beat the suite life.

"So?"

Matt cracked an eye open to find Tracen studying him. "So what?"

"You don't mind having a perfect girlfriend?"

They were still talking about Casey. Or was this really about Tracen? Matt propped himself up on his elbows. "Why would I mind it?"

Tracen removed his hat, scooped it in the bay, and replaced it on his head. If he liked the feeling of all that water running down his face, there was no way Matt would be able to ever win a paddle battle. He wouldn't even try to get Tracen back for splashing him earlier because Tracen was immune to water as a weapon. "I mean, isn't it exhausting to be around perfect people all the time? Do you ever get to do what you want to do, or do you always have to hang out with her family?"

Matt frowned. The expression both blocked the sun from his eyes and conveyed his confusion. "Her family is great."

Why wouldn't he want to hang out with them? Simply because he got tired of baseball games? He still got to do what he wanted to do during the off season. He had his bicycle polo team during the summer. And he could fly year round. Though not with Casey.

"Are you ever going to bring her to Idaho?"

"Of course. We were talking about it last week." Matt left out the part about how they were going to have to drive.

"Okay." Tracen shifted his attention to their surroundings. The lapping water. The distant roar of boat engines. The seagulls. The crazed fans.

None of it slowed the thoughts Tracen had swirled up. "Mom isn't her biggest fan, but Mom is super protective after the way Serena treated you."

Tracen grimaced and turned to accept a couple of sodas from the guys in the raft. He passed one to Matt then popped the top on his own. "Don't remind me."

"Sorry." Matt held the cool can, too busy contemplating other arguments to take a drink. "Everywhere I go, people rave about Casey. They all tell me how lucky I am. She's sweet and beautiful and smart and fun and hard-working."

Tracen nodded slowly. "Perfect?"

Why did he have to say it like that? "Yeah, and I'm her hero."

"Matt," Tracen interrupted. "You don't have to make excuses."

The exact words Matt had used on Tracen. Only Matt hadn't realized he was making excuses. He didn't need to make excuses. He was dating the world's most perfect woman. "I'm not—"

The crowd cheered. A small dot flew from beyond the stadium wall right over their heads. Matt grabbed the mitt he'd brought just in case.

The dot grew larger as it dropped towards the water. It was going to be out of reach though. Closer to those guys in orange wigs and fake beards.

Tracen splashed overboard, losing his hat as he swam in a race against gravity. Hey, maybe he could beat it. Or maybe he could if there weren't so many rafts and kayaks blocking his route.

The ball splashed down next to the guys with the wigs and inches out of Tracen's reach. The fake redhead in the raft scooped it up and held it overhead, shouting as if he were a caveman.

A smile crept across Matt's face. The guy who'd beat Tracen to the ball could be related to Gen. He had the right colored hair.

Matt put down the glove to unzip the waterproof pouch attached to the inside of the kayak and retrieve his phone as celebration erupted around them. He clicked to open the camera app and focus on the guy with the orange hair. He snapped a shot, scrolling through a mental list of ideas about how the guy with the ball could be related to Gen.

Could he have been a former baseball player? Maybe Gen's dad was a married athlete who got another woman pregnant. He'd offered the woman to support her financially if she would give the baby up for adoption and keep quiet about their affair.

Matt scrunched up his face. That wasn't a good story. That would mean Gen's mom had practically sold her.

Hmm…

Tracen's head popped up next to Matt's kayak. "So close." He grabbed onto the front of the craft, making it tip sideways.

Matt's phone tilted forward over the edge of his fingers. He tightened his grasp. The action squeezed his phone upward and out of his grip. It tumbled toward the water.

Matt stretched to catch it. Only he fumbled it against the side of the kayak before it plunked into the bay and disappeared.

Tracen reached inside his own kayak, retrieved his net, and scooped the phone out of the water in one smooth motion.

Matt's heart sank as he stared at his dripping phone. Would it ever dry out, or had he lost everything saved on it?

Tracen shot him an understanding look. "Had to take a picture for Casey?"

Casey? She probably would have liked that pic, but he hadn't even considered it. "Actually…" He blew out his cheeks in frustration. "It was for my friend Gen."

Tracen's forehead wrinkled above the top of his sunglasses. "Uh, who's Gen?"

CHAPTER SEVEN

MATT DROPPED TRACEN OFF AT THE gate for his flight back to Idaho before heading to get his own plane ready. Tracen's last words had been, "Say hi to Gen for me." Matt rolled his eyes at the memory. He should have known better than to mention any other woman's name besides Casey's. Tracen had issues.

As for Gen, Matt hoped she'd recovered from her Zena Warrior Princess disease and was back at work. He'd ask how she was doing except his phone never dried out from its swim in the harbor, and he'd lost his contact information. For all he knew, Gen could have tracked down her birth parents over the weekend and be moving to live with them in Scotland.

Ethan joined him in the cockpit for a pre-flight check. "Fog's rolling in."

Matt had noticed but hadn't worried about it. "We have time to get off the ground."

"Can we get back?" Ethan's gaze flicked toward the cabin. "We should probably check the Portland weather too." That's where they headed after the stop in Eureka.

Matt pressed his lips together. Was Ethan thinking about Michelle? About spending the night with her if they got stuck in Eureka? Was it time for Matt to say something? Or should he simply continue watching them for now?

"There's always the chance we get stuck somewhere," Matt said evenly. Then he kept his eye on the weather radar through their flight with a sinking feeling.

The alert came right before his in-range call. They could load passengers, but they wouldn't be taking off until they got the okay from PDX, and even then they might have to divert to Eugene or Seattle.

Matt shot Ethan a wary look as he picked up the radio. "Flight 348 calling the Eureka station."

Static crackled. "This is the Eureka station." Gen's voice came across as both soft and authoritative.

Matt wanted to shout Eureka. Because now he wasn't going to be alone in his concern. Gen had seen what was going on with the other pilot, and though Matt hadn't wanted her to know about it at first because she could get Ethan in trouble, he now doubted she would. She cared too much for family and what might be the breakup of a family. "We are twenty minutes out with a weather advisory on our continuing flight."

"The ticket counter is informing passengers of the advisory. We will see you in twenty minutes at gate three-bravo." Gen sounded so distant. Or perhaps simply professional.

"Gate three-bravo." He'd fight the urge to call her Carrots. For twenty minutes anyway.

How was Gen going to be ready in twenty minutes? She hadn't even had time to daydream during Matt's inbound call. If she'd had time, she would have imagined that he apologized for not texting her yesterday because he'd...hmm...maybe he was saving a beached whale, or he'd volunteered with a mission in the Tenderloin District.

"Gen." Bianca stuck her head in the office door.

Oops. She'd accidentally started daydreaming anyway.

"There's an angry aunt out here who wants to talk to you about why her niece, a Sylvie Emerson, can't fly by herself when there's a weather advisory."

Gen hated this part of the job. Not to mention that if the flight was delayed, passengers weren't the only ones stuck at the airport. They never seemed to realize how it also affected her plans.

She jabbed at the print button on her computer once more before standing. "Will you see if you can get paperwork printed while I talk to her?" If they'd had more warning on the weather, she would have looked up the manifest to see if there had been any kids scheduled to fly alone and then called them ahead of time before they arrived at the airport.

Bianca frowned at the computer. "I'd probably make it worse. You know I'm not good with technology."

True. "Okay, will you trade places with Tyler so he can print paperwork?"

"Sure thing."

Tyler would rather play on the computer than deal with upset passengers any day. Both women headed through the door to the ticket counter.

The angry aunt stood with her arms crossed, squinty brown eyes looking for someone to accuse. They focused on Gen.

Gen glanced at the teenage girl next to her. With her slouched posture and timid peek from underneath a curtain of dark hair, she appeared to be more scared of her aunt than worried about missing her flight.

Gen gave her best apologetic smile. "You must be Sylvie."

The girl glanced up again and nodded.

The aunt practically stepped in front of Sylvie to get Gen's attention. "Yes, and she has a ticket on this flight. Why would everyone else who paid for a ticket get to go while she can't?"

Gen swiped a flier from the counter. If the aunt read their policy on how to deal with a weather advisory, then she might turn her wrath away from the ticket agents who had nothing to do with making the rules. "I'd love to put Sylvie on the plane, but if the low cloud ceiling in Portland doesn't permit our pilots to land, they will have to fly to another airport. As your niece is under eighteen, she doesn't have the ability to rent a car or a hotel room, and we don't want to put any children in that position."

The aunt snatched the paper from Gen's grip. "Her mom can drive two hours to Eugene and pick her up."

Gen understood. She really did. She just hoped the aunt would try to understand her side as well. "While that would be a possibility, the flight could easily be diverted to another city. I'm sure you wouldn't want your niece stuck in Seattle overnight."

The aunt waved the flier helplessly. "What am I supposed to do?"

Gen tilted her head in compassion. "You can call the number on the bottom of that sheet to reschedule a flight for tomorrow."

The paper crinkled in the woman's fist. "I have to work tomorrow."

The whir of a wheelchair battery buzzed louder. Olivia. "There's a weather advisory?" she asked from her seat. She wore her usual sweet smile, but light brown eyes held a fire that told Gen she knew exactly what was going on.

Gen wasn't sure whether to be thankful for backup in the confrontation or worried that if the older woman took sides she might create even more drama. "Yes." She explained the advisory once again, and for the first time realized how such a situation might affect Olivia. Would she be okay on her own in an unknown city? She did pretty well traveling alone, but she needed Gen to move her in and out of her wheelchair. How did she get into bed at night? How did she bathe? "We are hoping there won't be any issues, but if either of you want to reschedule for tomorrow or get a refund, you can call our customer service line."

The aunt eyed Olivia for a second, her face softening as if comprehending for the first time that her situation could be worse. "I guess I'll have to figure something out. Come on, Sylvie."

Whew. Gen wanted to wipe her brow in relief. "Please let me know if there's anything else I can do to help you," she said instead.

The aunt didn't respond, but she turned and walked away, which gave Gen a chance to breathe. She reached for Olivia's fragile hand and squeezed gently. "Thank you," she mouthed.

Olivia squeezed back.

The door to the hallway swung open, and Tyler emerged with a stack of paperwork held triumphantly overhead. Maybe Gen should delegate her weaknesses to those who were strong in them more often. Then they could all enjoy their jobs more. For example, she would really enjoy pushing Olivia through security. She had to catch the other woman up on all Matt's text messages.

"Tyler, why don't you head down to gate 3B, make announcements, and check the jet bridge operations? I'll push Olivia and meet you there."

His face lit up. "I love working the jet bridge. It's like playing a video game. Y-M-M-D."

You made my day? She'd go with that. "Thanks. Bianca, you good to close the ticket counter?"

Bianca made her crazy eyes and motioned toward Sylvie's aunt headed out the door. "I am *now*."

With a sigh of relief, Genevieve wrapped her fingers around the wheelchair handles. "Thanks, guys. See you down there, Tyler."

"H-F."

Have fun? "You too." If she'd typed her message to him, she would have spelled it with the letter U and the number two. He'd probably appreciate it more.

Olivia chuckled as they started off. "Matt must not be flying today."

Gen angled the wheelchair around the corner toward security. "Why do you say that?"

"Because you're staying with me instead of rushing to the gate."

Gen smiled. She usually did feel more rushed when she knew she was going to see Matt, but being with Olivia put life into perspective. In the same way Sylvie's aunt had seemed to discover, Gen was also reminded that though life didn't always work out the way you wanted it to—hey—it could be worse.

"Maybe I'd rather talk to you," she suggested, taking the shortcut around the line of people waiting to walk through the metal detectors.

"You mean you want to talk about Matt?" Olivia's insight colored her words with warmth. She held up her boarding pass and ID for the TSA agent to scan.

Gen shrugged even though Olivia couldn't see her. Hopefully the motion helped lighten her tone. "We could talk about Matt if you want." She lifted her badge for security then entered her clearance code into the touchpad.

Olivia chuckled. "What is there to talk about?"

Gen pushed the wheelchair forward so the TSA agent with the metal detecting wand could scan Olivia and pat down the chair. "Matt's been texting me."

Olivia held her arms above her head for inspection, but twisted to beam over her shoulder at Gen. "So you two are friends now?"

Gen smiled and nodded.

The female agent looked up from where she'd crouched in front of the wheelchair. "Matt the pilot? Isn't he dating Casey Holloway?"

Gen refused to let her smile slip. "Yes."

The agent smiled knowingly. "You're not the only employee here with a crush on him."

Gen blushed and looked away. "We're friends, like Olivia said." Though if other people had a crush on Matt, was it really that bad if she did too? She turned her back on the woman to step through a metal detector, and she kept her back turned until the agent pushed Olivia around the side.

Olivia reached for her hand before Gen had a chance to resume her position behind the wheelchair. Once the TSA agent returned to her post, she whispered. "Don't you worry about her. She's probably jealous."

One corner of Gen's lips curved up. No reason for anybody to be jealous of her, though she appreciated the fact that Olivia let her live in her delusional bubble without attempting to pop it. She squeezed a thank you then resumed pushing the wheelchair toward the gate. "He only texted because he heard I had the Zika Virus."

Olivia turned sideways again, her eyes wide with alarm. "You had a virus? When?"

Gen nodded at the agents working for the other airline at the gate next to 3B. She'd have to quiz them about how her team did while she was gone. Find out if Bianca's antics affected passengers other than their own. "Don't worry. It's not contagious."

The older woman shook her head. "That's not what I'm worried about. Are you okay?"

"Better than okay." She parked Olivia next to a pillar and scanned the area to make sure everyone was taken care of. Passengers sat around looking bored while Tyler made intercom announcements without using his usual acronyms instead of words, so she was able to return to her conversation. "You know I'm adopted, right?"

Olivia looked up. "I think so."

"Well, Matt also discovered that I take pictures of people and make up stories to myself of how I might be biologically related to them."

Olivia squinted. "I didn't know *that*."

It probably sounded silly, but Gen had started when she was young, back when silly things were taken very, very seriously. She waved her hand as if to brush it off as no big deal. "Yeah, so while I was gone, Matt saw a big guy with red hair, and he took a picture for me, joking that the guy could be my dad. That's how the texting started." She gazed out the window to see if he'd landed yet or not. Nope. Her stomach knotted. "He hasn't texted me for a couple of days though."

Olivia twisted an earring. "Maybe he hasn't seen any more redheads."

Gen's gut churned to a stop. The older woman always knew how to make her feel better, even if her sweet suggestions were way off base. "Maybe."

"Or maybe he's been flying a lot. You know how cell phones have to be turned to airplane mode when in flight."

Gen pulled out her cell to check anyway. No more messages. She clicked on the photo attached to Matt's phone number in her contacts list and twisted her wrist to show Olivia. "I also got a photo of him at the emergency drill."

Olivia's lips parted, and her gaze shifted from the phone to Gen's face. "He came after all?"

"Yep." Gen's stomach tightened at the idea his appearance had been anything more than an apology. It was a delicious thought, and like most delicious things, it might require her to pick up some Tums from the gift shop. Did the antacid company make a product that could bring relief to the pain caused by a one-sided crush? She flicked a gaze in the direction of the shop in curiosity, and the newspaper on display caught her eye. "Oh, hey. That looks like my photo."

From a distance, the top half of the weekly newspaper above the fold resembled the red blob of a firetruck and the white blob of a plane with a few darker blobs in front that could be people. Now she needed an antacid for overexcitement.

Olivia followed her line of sight. "Did you sell them one of your pictures?"

Gen nodded, afraid that if she moved closer to the shop, the blobs of color would focus into someone else's photo entirely. If she stayed in place, she could continue pretending she'd made the front page.

Olivia lifted a five dollar bill in front of Gen's face. "Go get us both a copy."

Gen's feet magnetized themselves to the floor. "No, it can't be. It's probably something else. Like a red rose. Or an apple. Or Jessica Rabbit."

"I like Jessica Rabbit too. It's a win-win either way. Go get us copies."

Gen went numb. She couldn't let herself feel because if the photo really was of Mrs. Rabbit, she wouldn't only feel disappointed; she'd feel like a failure. And that was a feeling she preferred to avoid.

Why had she even let herself hope in the first place? Yeah, her photos were good, but nobody would choose them over bigger news for the front page. And now Olivia would know it.

On autopilot, she plucked the money from Olivia's hand. Her feet moved across the floor as if she really were controlled by magnets. Her eyes remained glued to the newspaper. With each robotic step, the shapes on the page formed an image she'd seen before. Her heart hammered harder against her tin chest. And as the fire engine came into focus, the metal shell fell away like the braces that had kept Forest Gump from running.

She'd made the front page.

She picked up her pace for the last few steps into the store and gripped the crinkly paper to her stomach. She turned to beam at Olivia.

Her favorite passenger beamed back, two thumbs stuck in the air like she was a reviewer. Or Fonzie.

Gen pulled the paper away to double check her dream come true. Because what if someone else had taken a photo at the emergency drill? Nope. Underneath the picture on the right side in italic print, it read *Genevieve Wilson.*

She grabbed another issue and rushed to the counter then rushed back for a third issue. Rosie would also want a copy. And what about Mom and Dad? She turned to stare at the stack of papers. She needed to buy them all.

Another customer blocked her way, and she glanced up to see a stream of passengers filing off the jet bridge. Oops. She'd have to clear out the store's newspaper inventory later. For now, she'd take the three copies and return to assist her team. She handed the cashier the bill and dashed back to work.

Olivia held up eager hands. "Let me see."

Gen dropped one issue of the paper on the woman's lap and continued past to help Tyler. She'd let him keep an eye on the door while she ran down to the plane and made sure everyone was off so they could board for the next flight. Plus, she had to show Matt her photo on the front page. She hoped talking about photography would make him want to text her pictures again.

A slow-moving couple stepped to the side so she could board the plane. She checked the seats out of reflex, barely registering the fact they were all empty, before turning toward the cockpit. She ducked through the door and nearly ran into Ethan and Michelle standing face to face, only inches apart.

"Oh." She stopped and averted her eyes so they couldn't read her discomfort. Doing so also prevented her from seeing past them to find Matt, but surely if they were getting this intimate, then Matt wasn't in the vicinity.

Michelle's giggle sounded forced and a little guilty. "Did you need something?"

Gen shook off the stickiness of the situation. "I was wondering if you had any more information on the weather advisory," she said, though her gaze betrayed her by flicking past them into Matt's empty seat.

Ethan placed one hand against the doorjamb and leaned onto it. "You can go ahead and load the plane, but we won't be taking off until we get the go-ahead from PDX."

"Thanks." She forced herself to look him in the eye as she spoke, but his were hard and challenging as if telling her she had no room to judge his behavior. As if her own crush wasn't as innocent as she wanted it to be.

"Matt went to get coffee," he said. He knew why she was really there.

CHAPTER EIGHT

MATT CROSSED HIS ARMS AND SURVEYED Gate 3B as he waited for his beverage. Gen had answered his in-range call, so why wasn't she here? Did she get sick again? Was there some emergency at the ticket counter?

His gaze landed on the paraplegic woman sitting across the walkway by a pillar and reading a newspaper. Olivia. Maybe she'd know where Gen was.

"Matt." He barely registered a voice calling his name.

As soon as his coffee was ready, he'd go talk to Olivia. He could play it off like he was concerned about getting her into her seat without Gen there to assist. Which, he truly was.

"Matt the pilot." The voice registered this time.

He jerked toward the coffee stand to accept his drink from an irritated barista. Hopefully the caffeine would help him pay attention to what was going on around him. He dropped a dollar in the tip jar before striding across the tile.

"Good morning, Olivia."

She glanced up and blinked a couple of times before grinning. "Good morning, Matt. Look what I'm reading." She shook the newspaper to straighten it before angling it his way.

He respectfully glanced at the headline then did a double take. The photo was from the day of the emergency drill. He tilted his head. "Is that Gen's work?"

"It sure is." She folded the paper and placed it in her lap. "The girl is talented, isn't she?"

"Very." He'd already come to such a conclusion but hadn't assumed media professionals would agree. Art was subjective and competitive. "Speaking of Gen, have you seen her?"

Olivia's smile softened. "I have. And you'll probably see her when you take off since she's walking on clouds after getting her photograph published on the front page."

Matt visualized such a scenario. It wasn't hard to imagine, and he was happy for Gen if not proud. "Say I wanted to talk to her *before* takeoff, where could I find her?"

Olivia scanned the waiting area from the counter to the door that led to the jet bridge. "She's here. Maybe she went down to the plane looking for you."

Matt scratched his head. Their paths must have crossed somewhere, though he was surprised he hadn't noticed her. She was hard to miss with all that red hair. "Thanks. I'll go check."

The trickle of passengers arriving from San Fran had run dry, so she should be at the gate, getting ready to board for the next flight. He'd meet her in the jet bridge on his way back to the plane. He checked his watch. They had another half hour before the scheduled departure. That should leave a little time for catching up.

He rounded the corner inside the tunnel and smacked into someone jogging the opposite direction. The smell of baby powder and flash of red hair told him who it was before he had time to stabilize Gen with his free hand. A drip of warm coffee splashed onto his wrist. "Hey, where's the fire?"

A newspaper fluttered to the floor, and she rocked backwards before gripping his biceps to help find her balance. She froze, and her eyes widened into that deer-in-headlights look he hadn't seen since moving away from Idaho. "Very funny," she said.

What was funny? All he'd said was...oh. *Where's the fire?* Since he was always teasing her about her hair, she probably assumed he was referencing its color again. He grinned, because it actually was kind of funny. "I didn't mean your hair." A chuckle slipped out.

She let go of him like she'd been burned, but the smirk on her face told him to prepare for her to fight fire with fire. "Then how did you mean it?" She squatted to retrieve the pages of newsprint.

He stooped to assist her since there were a lot of pages. More pages than were normally in the small newspaper. Two of the pages looked the same. She must have bought two copies. He grinned and pointed at the photo Olivia had shown him earlier. The one with the fire truck. "I meant it like, 'Hey, where's the photo of the fire truck?'"

Her cheeks dimpled, her dark eyes danced, and she paused in her cleanup. "Nice save. Did Olivia show you the picture?"

He grinned back before focusing on folding the newspaper in half and studying the cover photo again. "She did. That's pretty cool they put your picture on the front page."

She stayed in her squatted position as she studied the image for herself. Her shoulders relaxed, and her cheeks tinged pink. Matt knew that feeling. It was the one where you worked so hard and cared so much and all your efforts were finally appreciated.

Footsteps shook the jet bridge. "Gen? Do you want me to—" The young guy who sometimes worked as a gate agent rounded the corner and stopped. He glanced down at them in surprise. "Uh…Are you going to help me load the passengers?"

She stood and brushed her hair out of her face. "Of course. Sorry. I'll load Olivia then scan tickets while you announce the boarding zones." She tossed Matt a wave before hurrying up the jet bridge.

Matt stood too as Gen disappeared around the corner toward the terminal. He hadn't gotten a chance to ask her about her sickness or tell her the story of losing his phone in the bay or even say hi for his younger brother. Maybe he'd leave out Tracen since Tracen had the wrong idea about them. He looked down to find her newspaper still in his hands. He stepped around the corner so he could see her again. "Gen."

She slowed and glanced back.

He held up the paper. "Do you need this?" She *did* have an extra. And it *was* an article about an event he'd attended. "Or can I take it home to show Casey?"

Her mouth opened. She glanced down at his hands. "Yes. You keep it."

He waved it in appreciation for the paper as well as her artwork. She really did have a lot to offer. "Thanks."

Genevieve rubbed an earlobe with one hand while plugging the scanner into the computer with the other. She knew her infatuation was all one-sided, but that didn't make it any easier when Matt went from holding her in his arms to talking about his girlfriend within moments. He teased her, he texted her, but he didn't feel that zap of electricity that caused her pulse to fibrillate.

Come on, Gen, she chided herself. *This is how you wanted it. This is why you picked someone so completely out of your league to fall for. Relationships are much safer this way.*

Plus, she would never really try to steal someone's boyfriend. She wasn't like Michelle. No matter what Ethan assumed.

Pasting on a smile, she motioned Olivia forward. The wheelchair buzzed closer.

"Did Matt find you?" the older woman asked.

Gen's heart squeezed in her chest. Why did Matt have to look for her? Her crush had been simpler when he didn't even know her name. Though at the same time, she would never want to give up their newfound laidback banter.

"Yes," she answered.

The older woman had probably waved Matt over and displayed the newspaper like a game show model. Gen gave a small smile so as not to stifle the older woman's enthusiasm before pushing her wheelchair down the jet bridge.

"What did he want?" Olivia asked.

Gen frowned as she placed the aisle chair next to Olivia's wheelchair. She'd simply figured Matt had been looking for her because Olivia had shown him the picture. "I don't think he wanted anything."

Olivia nodded thoughtfully. "He must have just wanted to talk."

That sounded sweeter than it really was. Matt hadn't even mentioned their texts, so it wasn't like chatting meant much to him. He'd probably only needed to discuss the weather advisory. She'd call operations as soon as she got a chance. "Probably about work stuff," she said.

Gen bent toward Olivia and scooped under the woman's legs. Olivia wrapped her arms around her neck. She smelled like roses and tea.

"I don't know," Olivia pondered. "I might have to come visit my family again sooner than usual to stay updated on these talks with you."

Gen gave a genuine smile this time as she lifted Olivia to the other seat. Olivia not only let her dream, but Olivia dreamed even bigger than Gen did. Had anybody ever believed in her that much?

Gen's smile slipped because she was sure to let Olivia down, and not only into an aisle chair.

"There are other things we can talk about too," she said. "My brother is getting out of prison soon, and my sister is starting a goat yoga class. I'm supposed to go take photos for her website after work today."

Olivia's grip tightened on her shoulders. Had she never mentioned Damon's imprisonment before? It was sure to make some people uncomfortable.

"Goat yoga?" Olivia repeated as if that was the real shocker. "With live goats?"

Gen handed Olivia the straps to buckle herself in. "Baby goats."

Olivia patted her hand. "Never a dull moment with you, dear."

Gen smiled. It was nice to have a relationship where the delight in the other person's existence went both ways. She rolled the aisle chair to Olivia's seat and removed the armrest to scoot the woman over. With a quick hug, she was back at the gate, scanning tickets and directing traffic.

The light outside grew darker before the last passenger boarded, then the sky opened up and sheets of rain poured down to the sound of a drumroll. This was the kind of weather that made Gen want to crawl under her covers with a bowl of hot cereal but also the kind of weather that would keep her at the airport. It was even worse for the guys working the ramp below. Hopefully they brought ponchos.

She scribbled down the passenger count for Tyler to verify with the flight attendants before pulling out her phone and looking up the number for Operations. She hit send.

"Operations," a woman's voice answered the phone.

Gen released the lip she hadn't realized she'd been biting. "Hi, this is Genevieve Wilson at the Eureka Station. Do we have a landing time at PDX?"

"Checking the flight status for flight 349."

Gen shut down her computer and let herself into the jet bridge as she waited. Her job was essentially done, but she couldn't leave unless the plane took off. She switched the phone to her other ear so she could look at the watch on her right arm while holding the phone with her left. She'd told Rosie she'd be home in time to photograph the noon yoga class, but if they had a delay, she wouldn't make it. She liked her job, but she hated when it interfered with her passion.

"Ma'am, it looks like you are now on an edict. Don't push the plane out until we have a landing time for you."

Edict? That was worse than a weather advisory. Rather than the forces of nature the crew could work around, she was dealing with positions of power. They were all stuck until the other airport gave them a landing time.

She scrunched her eyes and wrinkled her nose. "How long do you think that will be?"

"I'll get back to you within the hour."

An hour? They were going to leave passengers on the plane for an hour? She was going to have to stand around and do nothing for an hour? And she'd have to call Rosie to say she couldn't make it to yoga because she was too busy standing around doing nothing?

"Thank you." She tapped her phone with her thumb to hang up then raised her fists to heaven and shook her arms silently so her team around the corner couldn't hear, but that wasn't enough to get rid of all her frustration. She hopped up and down a couple of times then stomped her feet quicker and quicker until she easily could have been auditioning for a role in *Riverdance*. Of all the days for an edict…

"I take it you heard about the edict?"

Gen's energy drained out her fingertips and toes. She shifted herself into a normal stance and readjusted her button down to hide the strip of skin at her waist that would have been revealed during her little jig. Matt stood there casually, hands in pockets, smirk on face.

She shrugged her shoulders as if he hadn't caught her acting like a wild woman for a second time that day. "What makes you think that?" she asked all casual like.

"I don't know." A corner of his lips curved up, and he motioned toward the plane with his head. "Come on. I'll have the flight attendants get you some cookies to make you feel better."

Cookies were good. Not quite baklava at Top of the Mark, but still a sweet offer.

She couldn't help laughing at herself. Silly to imagine a guy was going to invite her to the fanciest restaurant in what residents of the San Francisco Bay Area referred to as "The City" after witnessing her little fit. "Thank you."

He chuckled as he strolled beside her back down the jet bridge. "Did you have somewhere else you have to be?"

Dare she tell him about goat yoga? He'd probably seen enough of her crazy for one day. "Photo shoot, but I can reschedule."

"Oh, that's a bummer." He ducked into the plane.

She found herself surrounded by Tyler and the three guys in orange vests from the ramp who'd climbed the stairs to hide out from the rain on the jet bridge. They reclined on the floor around her. Might as well make herself comfortable too. She leaned against a wall and slid down to sit next to Tyler.

"Hi, boss," he said.

"Hi," she said, glad he hadn't seen her fit. Hardly mature behavior for a boss. Not that sitting on the floor was the pinnacle of good leadership either.

Matt returned and everyone seemed to sit up taller. He'd brought enough Lady Fingers to offer them each a snack package.

Tyler jumped to his feet. "I'll go get sodas and water. B-R-B." He'd apparently be right back since they kept a stash of beverages underneath the gate desk to offer the guests on delayed flights.

Matt watched him go. "I should have thought of that."

Gen waved a hand at his regret then busied herself ripping open the crinkly wrapper. She hadn't had a Lady Finger since Mom's lemon dessert at Easter. "This was very kind of you." Would he return to the cockpit now? "Wanna join us?" The words slipped out before she could stop them. She shoved a cookie in her mouth to keep it from saying anything else without her permission. Mm...sweet vanilla.

Matt looked back inside the plane. Gen chewed as she followed his gaze to see Michelle joking with the other flight attendants. He seemed to also be suspicious of her and Ethan. If so, he had nothing to worry about at the moment.

He turned and leaned against the wall in Tyler's spot, though he didn't slide down the way she had. Of course, he hadn't been running around for the past two hours. He'd probably enjoy some time on his feet after being stuck in an Airbus all morning. Then again, maybe he was more of a professional than her.

"How are you feeling?" he asked.

Gen wiggled her toes in her ballet flats. Should she stand up so he wasn't looking down at her? She swallowed to answer. "My feet hurt."

He glanced at her shoes then shook his head, lips pressed together like he was trying to conceal a smile. He failed. "What about your virus? You all better?"

"Oh." Her lips pursed with the word. She should have known he was referencing her time off of work. If she had to choose, she'd prefer to talk about her feet than the rash. "I'm fine now. Thanks."

"I would have texted to ask, but I dropped my phone in the bay and lost your number."

He'd lost her number? At least he hadn't chosen to stop texting her, but was this it for them? The end of their communication outside of work? He'd asked Bianca for her number when Gen was gone, but he didn't have an excuse now. Her heart sank. She'd really enjoyed the silly pictures he'd sent. They made life lighter. More whimsical. As if each of those people in the photos were really related to her, and even if they weren't, she wanted to hug them all just in case.

"I guess I'll never find my family now," she quipped.

Matt snapped his fingers and pointed at her. "I think I found them actually. Two guys with orange beards. There's a possibility the beards were fake and part of their Giants costumes, but they also could have been your brothers."

There he went, making her want to hug everybody in the world again. "I've always hoped for two brothers with fake orange beards."

Matt nodded in mock solemnity. "I knew it. I was trying to take their photo when I dropped my phone."

Gen's employees across from them looked at one another. She

ignored them and smiled wider at Matt. Because now she knew why he hadn't texted that weekend. Her fingers itched to type her number into his new phone, so she scratched them and shoved another cookie in her mouth to keep from suggesting it.

He reached inside his pocket and pulled out the device. "You better give me your number in case I see them again."

Her mouth went dry, and not only because of the cookie bits caking her teeth. She ran her tongue along her gums and spoke around the chunk of food in her cheek. "Okay." She reached for the phone.

Kevin elbowed Shane.

She considered glaring, but she could always do that later when Matt wouldn't be around to see. He was a nice guy. Nothing more. Or so her head said. Meanwhile her heart had started a tap dance of its own. She pictured it wearing a top hat and holding a cane.

Tyler reappeared, a pile of beverages in his arms. He looked at Gen with the phone in her hand. "Did you hear anything new from Ops?"

He thought she was holding her own phone. Now she had to explain out loud that Matt had asked for her number, and she had to do it without grinning like a jack-o'-lantern.

"She's adding herself to Matt's contact list," Kevin explained for her.

Tyler's lips parted, and his eyes darted to Matt and back.

Gen had to say something before Tyler did, even though he'd probably say something like *worried eyebrow emoji*. But bits of cookie still clogged her throat. Maybe she could simply create a distraction. "Water?" she reached for the bottles in Tyler's arms like a dying man crawling through the desert.

He handed her the bottle then passed out the remaining drinks. Had Matt noticed the kid's curious look?

Gen watched from the corner of her eye as Matt popped the tab on a Coke Zero and guzzled freely. His nonchalance over the incident could only mean one thing: he didn't even consider the implications of asking for her number because he was so completely smitten with Casey Holloway that the idea he could ever be attracted to Gen hadn't entered his head. Maybe if their friendship continued, she'd eventually get to the place where she didn't daydream about kissing him and planning a honeymoon together, but she wasn't there yet, and his indifference stung. Especially since her team could see it too.

She lifted Matt's phone to hand it back to him and unscrewed the lid to her water. Hopefully it would cool down both her parched throat and burning face.

Tyler snatched the phone before Matt was done drinking. "You need to add a photo, Gen."

Say what? With the rain outside, her hair was sure to be particularly frizzy, and even if she wasn't blushing anymore, taking a picture of her sitting on the ground would not be the most flattering angle.

"Oh, I can send him a pic," she offered. Preferably one where she was hiking in the forest and far enough away that she looked tiny next to the redwood trees. That would also give her time to edit out hair frizz and blotchy skin.

"That's no fun," said Tyler.

Her eyes scanned the row of men across from her. They were all watching. All witnessing her crush at its most humiliating moment.

Kevin rolled over to his hands and knees and crawled her way. "I'll join you," he said.

He didn't want her to feel alone, which was sweet. Even sweeter, the shine from his bald head and the reflection off his glasses in the photo could actually make her look better.

"Me too." Shane stood and crossed the narrow bridge to squat between her and Matt. She'd forgive him since his intentions were in the right place.

Lance rolled in front of them and held up a peace sign.

Gen laughed. How petty of her to worry about looking good for Matt. He was never going to be in love with her, but her team made her feel loved.

Tyler held up the camera. "Say 'edict'."

"Edict," they chorused.

A phone rang. Not the one in Tyler's hands, but the one in her pocket. She fumbled to pull it out as the guys peeled themselves away.

Her screen read: Operations.

She slid her thumb across the tab and lifted the device to her ear. "This is Genevieve."

"Hi, Gen. I've got good news and bad news. Portland has a time slot for you to land, but you have to be off within ten minutes."

She shot to her feet. "We'll do it," she said. Then there was no more time to chat. She pocketed her phone and sent the ramp crew scurrying into the rain.

Ethan stuck his head out the door of the plane. "If we're not off in ten minutes, Matt, we could be stuck here overnight."

Matt nodded but stayed in place when Ethan disappeared. Gen's pulse hammered in her ears. She pinched her lobes in hopes of quieting the sound. Why wasn't he in a hurry to go? Did he have something to say to her now that almost everyone else was gone?

He held out his hand toward Tyler. Oh. He was waiting for his phone.

Tyler jerked like he'd been asleep. At least now that the plane was leaving, Gen didn't need the agent's help for anything else. She could close the plane door herself and back the jet bridge away.

Matt took the phone and grinned at the screen before holding it up for her to see. She didn't look beautiful, but she looked happy.

"It's like you have a fan club." He retreated through the door.

She followed to close the door, scrunching her nose at the idea anybody thought of her the way she thought of him. "Hardly."

Matt pocketed the phone. "Seriously. Even my brother Tracen is a fan. He wanted me to say hi for him."

Matt's brother? Was Matt trying to set her up? Because why else would he be talking about her to his family? How did she respond to such a statement? She reached inside the plane to push the button down that would allow her to shut the door.

"Tell him 'hi' for me." That's all she could think of in the moment. She'd probably come up with something better later.

But it wasn't like Matt was waiting around for her response. He'd headed into the cockpit to don his headphones that would allow him to talk to the ground crew until they unhooked the cart from the plane on the tarmac.

She gripped the handle sticking up from the door and slid the door shut before forcing it all the way down into a locked position. Back at the control panel, she lifted the canopy and rang the warning bell three times, though it couldn't be heard over the sound of wind and rain. With mixed emotions, she pulled the joystick to send the bridge in reverse.

Matt made eye contact through the storm between their windows and saluted. That's what he would do to any agent before he flew away, though, as far as she knew, he didn't have any other agent's phone number. How long would it be until he texted?

CHAPTER NINE

GEN SMILED AT THE LATEST PIC from Matt. This one featured a man who'd spent a little too much time in a tanning bed. Matt's text suggested that maybe she wasn't only related to guys with orange hair but possibly orange skin, as well.

"Gen." Rosie snapped in front of Gen's face. "Are you paying attention?"

Gen looked up to focus on her job photographing goat yoga. She hadn't made it to that last class after the flight edict, so they'd rescheduled for the next day.

Rosie had been teaching her own version of yoga for years. The kind that incorporated stretches, strengthening exercises, and balance poses, but also made God the focus through worship music and meditation on scripture. She'd also done a really nice job decorating the yoga studio with bamboo flooring, the silhouette of a tree painted on the wall, and a fountain in the corner. She'd picked up all the candles off the floor and tied the gauzy curtains up in preparation for the baby goats.

"I'm ready," Gen said. There wasn't much else she could do until participants arrived and the baby goats were let in. "You simply want me *not* to take pictures of goats peeing on yoga mats and trying to give people wedgies by nipping at underwear, right?"

Rosie swatted at her. "That's only happened a few times."

Gen grinned. This was one of Rosie's classes she hadn't attended yet. The waiting list was too long already, and professional photographs hadn't even been posted on Rosie's website. "What's next?" she asked. "Cobra pose with real life cobras?"

Rosie narrowed her eyes in mock indignation. "Only if Indiana Jones joins us."

Exactly the segue Gen needed. "Speaking of cute men, want to see my latest text from Matt?"

Rather than look at Gen's phone, Rosie moved across the room to peek out the front window. "Why's he texting you so much?"

Gen's skin prickled. Rosie knew about her crush. She knew the joy these texts brought. Her sister should be giggling with her. "Because it's fun."

Rosie didn't even look at her. "But he has a girlfriend to have fun with."

Gen's spine straightened. She wasn't doing anything wrong. It was one thing for Ethan the cheater to assume the worst of her, but not her sister. "We're friends," she argued. "I know nothing is ever going to happen between us."

Rosie faced her again with a sigh. "Your head knows nothing will happen, but that doesn't stop your heart from hoping."

Was Rosie right? No. Gen wasn't hoping. She was pretending. Like when they used to play that what-would-you-do-if-you-won-the-lottery game. She was never hurt by not winning the lottery. In fact, winning the lottery would have probably caused more trouble than it was worth. Most of those winners went bankrupt eventually.

"I don't think so," she said. But should she stop texting Matt to be on the safe side? Could she? She didn't want to.

Rosie strode back across the room and took her hand. Holding Rosie's hand wasn't the same as holding anyone else's hand because there were empty spaces where fingers should be, but that made holding her sister's hand unique and special. Rosie was there for her like only Rosie could be. "I want you to find love, Gen. Real love. The kind that lasts. And how can you find that with anyone else when your heart is too busy having fun with someone who is already taken?"

Real love. Like the way their father had loved their mother. It was a rare find. None of her adopted siblings had found it. And most likely none of their bio parents had found it. Why did she think she would be any different? God was punishing them all for the sins of their fathers.

She didn't want to voice her fears to Rosie because either Rosie would wave them off as ridiculous or point out that Gen probably had a better chance at love than she did with her deformities. And then Gen would feel like a guilty pansy. So she'd say something else. But what? And even if she thought of something, could she get it past the ball of emotion in her throat?

Stupid emotion. Why couldn't she keep pretending everything was all right? She had a good life with photography and travel and goat yoga. It was enough.

The ball in her throat throbbed like a heart aching for love. There was no way she could answer now. Not without letting loose a trickle of tears.

The doorknob twisted, and the front door scraped lightly over bamboo, letting in a chilly breeze. To distract herself from their serious conversation, Gen let herself wonder what Rosie was going to do when the rain started up for the fall. The baby goats would track mud all over the place.

Rosie met her gaze with concern and gave a final finger squeeze. Gen wasn't ready to interact with anyone yet, so she focused on Rosie's one hand with the three cranberry colored acrylic nails and gold rings. She was the brave sister. She flaunted her flaws. Like, *Take me or leave me, suckers.* While Gen didn't want anyone to leave her. Ever. She needed therapy, but goat yoga would have to do.

Twenty participants including Bianca arrived, giddy to workout with farm animals. They set up their mats before Rosie opened the back door and called the kids.

Gen had helped Rosie name the goats. They'd gone in alphabetical order as if the animals were hurricanes, which really wasn't too far from the truth. Alfred and Bridgette ran around from person to person while Cynthia looked for something to nibble and Dale practiced his jumping skills. Eugene made a beeline for Gen's legs. She reached down to rub his fuzzy head for a moment before gently shoving him towards the participants who'd paid to hang out with him.

Once the chuckling and baby talk died down, Rosie instructed participants to sit cross-legged and breathe. Gen squatted to get a better angle for photos of goats climbing in and out of laps, and she did the breathing exercises too. Usually the room smelled like clean linen mixed with honeydew, but the goats had brought in an earthy animal scent. It created a farm-fresh vibe that reminded Gen of home.

Though Mom and Dad had plenty of money from Dad's engineering job, they'd never displayed it. Instead, Mom had homeschooled them on the small farm where they'd learned the meaning of hard work. It wasn't likely any of the adopted siblings could have been raised better by their birth parents, but the fact that they weren't raised by their birth parents made them all feel like something was missing. Like Rosie's toes.

Rosie instructed everyone to climb onto their hands and knees to set up for down dog pose. Gen moved to the other side of the room to better use the natural light filtering through the curtains.

She sighed. Every now and then she got this sense that what had been missing from her childhood was gratefulness for what she'd been given. In those instances, she'd experience a desire to return home to see the old farm with fresh eyes. Or maybe it was only a desire to run and hide in the one place she hadn't felt like an outsider. Even now, she was the outsider.

Was that really why she'd chosen photography? For a chance to peek into the lives of others and try to figure out what she needed to do to fit in? That could be why Matt's texts were so great. He took photos of such strange people that it made her seem like the normal one. It also made her feel like he saw her as normal.

She smirked at the reality of what he would think if he could see her in the yoga studio, surrounded by people with their butts sticking into the air and goats either climbing on their backs or tunneling underneath them. Yeah, she and Matt were better off as texting friends. Problem solved. Rosie could think what she wanted, but Gen was nothing more than Matt's digital pen pal.

The goat on Rosie's back attempted to step across to another yogi's back. Gen dropped to her belly to catch the maneuver while the animal stood on two different people like a cheerleader in a pyramid. She pressed the shutter. Perfect.

Her heart did a cheer. *Alfred, Alfred, he's our man. If he can't do it, no goat can!*

Maybe Gen didn't want to be normal after all. Because then she'd miss out on stuff like this. Smiling, she twisted to take a photo of Bianca on the other side of the room. Bianca bent her knees and lunged one foot forward as directed. Gen focused her lens.

Bridgette stepped into the frame the very moment Gen snapped the shutter. Had she gotten the shot or not? Pulling the camera away from her face, Gen scrolled back to see the photo she'd taken. If she'd thought the photo of Alfred had been perfect, this one was even better.

With Bridgette so much closer to the camera than Bianca in the background, the shot looked like the African-American gate agent was doing yoga on a large goat's back. Gen never would have thought to plan it that way, but it would probably be her favorite photograph.

She'd have to show Matt even though it meant revealing one of her eccentricities. She bit her lip. How would he react?

Matt felt like a pack mule with all the bags Casey wanted him to carry, but at least he was needed, and he got to spend time with her doing something other than watching a baseball game. He gazed down the quaint main street of Sausalito, past the reflection of the sun off the harbor to the Golden Gate Bridge they'd crossed.

These were the kind of days he enjoyed spending on the ground. When it was gray like yesterday, he preferred to get up above the clouds in a plane.

He inhaled the warm, greasy scent coming from a nearby restaurant. It reminded him of the stovetop popcorn his dad used to make, and his stomach growled. "How about a basket of fish and chips?"

"That sounds good." Casey stopped in front of yet another store window. "Ooh, look at those little glass frogs. They're like cartoon characters but fancier." She pointed. "I love the one playing baseball."

Matt eyed the rest of the art displayed in the window. That glass frog wasn't going to be cheap. "I'll buy it for you," he offered. It would be a reminder of their first baseball season together, which is something that meant a lot to her. Yeah, she had more money to spend than he did, but he still wanted to be her hero.

She shook her head. "Oh no, I'm going to buy it for my mom."

"Okay." He'd have to think of something else to get her. He looked off toward the bay on the other side of the street. What could he possibly give her that she couldn't get for herself?

A man with the appearance of a Hawaiian Santa Claus held a parakeet on his arm in front of a fountain. It had been a while since Matt had seen the bird man. He grinned. Maybe he could get Casey a real-life pet once they grew to know each other better. For now, he wanted a pic of him with the birdman to send to Gen.

"Hey, Case, I'm going to go have my picture taken with the bird while you buy the frog."

She paused in the doorway but continued peering through the shop windows rather than look at him. "Okay. I'll meet you down there then we'll eat. I promise."

Matt hoped so. He didn't want to look weak, but his shoulder was really starting to throb from hauling around the bag of pottery. "Sounds good," he said, though she'd already gone inside and probably couldn't hear him.

He strolled past the Spanish fountain and set the shopping bags under a bench to wait his turn with the bird man. A couple with small children had beaten him to the street performer. Matt watched as the bird man motioned for a little girl to hold her arms out wide. He set the bird on one of her hands then used a seed to lead his winged friend up the girl's arm, behind her neck, and down the other arm.

The girl giggled. She wasn't a redhead, but her joy reminded him of Gen. Of the way people were drawn to her.

He reached inside his pocket to pull out his phone. If Gen's mother had been a teen mom, then this could be Gen's little sister.

The bird man didn't speak, but he motioned for the girl to bend her elbow to bring the bird closer to her face. Then he stuck the seed between her lips. Her parents also snapped photos when the bird leaned in for a "kiss."

Matt smiled down at the photo he'd taken. Yeah, he had to send it to Gen. He clicked on the share button. His list of most-used contacts popped up. Gen was on the top. Above Casey. But that would only be because he didn't have to text Casey since they were always together. Though it might seem a little odd to someone else. He shrugged as if shaking off his actions then clicked on Gen's name and hit send.

"Matt!"

Matt jumped. He hadn't meant to upset Casey. She'd understand his explanation. She wasn't the jealous type, and even if she was, she didn't have any reason to be jealous.

Casey charged toward him from the direction of the fountain. She couldn't have seen his phone from over there.

"What's wrong?"

She marched until they were almost nose to nose. Her arms lifted and dropped to her sides repeatedly. She shook her head like a horse whinnying in protest.

Did he do something wrong? "What?" he asked with a little more caution than before.

"Our team photographer is stuck in Leavenworth."

His shoulders sagged in relief. This wasn't his fault. And it wasn't even something to get upset about. Unless the photographer was in prison. "Did he get arrested for something?"

"No." She shook her head as if he'd made the situation worse. "You're thinking of the prison in Leavenworth, Kansas. The Leavenworth in Washington is a Bavarian village. He went there to shoot their Octoberfest, but they cancelled all the flights out of the nearest airport due to fog. Can you fly up there and get him?"

Matt blinked. How did she think he was going to do that? He didn't have his own aircraft.

"Dad can charter you a plane."

Of course he could. "Even if you get me a plane, I'm going to have to follow the same protocol as other pilots. If they can't land in Leavenworth, neither can I."

Casey's hand covered her mouth like she was watching a horror movie. "Our World Series campaign kicks off next week. I have to have those photos."

Matt lifted a palm helplessly. "Can't the guy drive down?"

"Oh." Casey pulled her phone out of her purse. Presumably to check the distance and drive time from Washington and either coordinate a train ticket or rent a car.

Matt stuck his hands in his pockets and rocked back and forth from his heels to toes. It was likely with the marketing emergency that he'd end up taking Casey to work even though she was scheduled to have the day off to spend with him. What would he do for the rest of the afternoon? He could go for a bike ride. Or paint his guest room. Or get that haircut he really needed.

His phone vibrated in his pocket. Gen? He pulled it out and smiled at her name on his screen. He tapped to open her response. Only she'd sent a photo in return. A photo of a giant goat. Strange but creative. How would he ever top that?

Casey's groan pulled his gaze her direction. "He doesn't drive. We booked the one photographer in the world who doesn't have his license. There's always the train or bus, but that would take him two days. And we have the players all planning to shoot tomorrow."

Matt glanced at his phone again, the seed of a plan starting to sprout in his imagination. "You'll have to hire another photographer."

Casey ran a hand over her head. "All the good photographers are going to be booked. And I even got a deal to have a huge poster displayed on the side of a building downtown."

Matt's pulse picked up speed. This could be even better than he'd thought. "Remember the newspaper photo I showed you that my friend took?" He held his breath.

She tilted her head in consideration. "Yeah, it was good, but we aren't taking candids here. This guy said he had a great twist to make the photos unique. Your photographer friend isn't going to come up with some brilliant idea in a day."

Matt couldn't believe the timing. He held up his phone. "I think she already did."

Casey peered closer. "How is that an idea? It's trick photography that makes it look like a lady is doing yoga on the back of a giant goat."

Matt pressed his lips together and nodded. She still didn't get it. "*What* kind of goat?" he prompted.

Her perfect forehead produced a tiny wrinkle. "Giant?" Her mouth fell open. Her eyes rolled from side to side in contemplation. "We're the Giants."

There it was. "What if Gen photographed the players next to San Francisco landmarks in a way that made them appear giant? They could hold the Golden Gate Bridge in their hand or look down on Alcatraz."

"Oh…" Her voice got all breathy. "That's gooood. You think she would do it?"

"I'm sure she would." It's what she lived for. He couldn't wait to tell her. If only he could see her face in person when he did.

Hey, maybe he could. Maybe he could work it out with Bianca so that if he flew into Eureka as a passenger, he could take Gen back to San Francisco with him on the return flight. He'd need to make sure she could get the time off. And that she had her camera equipment. She'd never suspect.

"Matt, you're the best." Casey pressed his cheeks between her palms and lifted onto her toes to plant a kiss on his lips. "What would I do without you?" she asked.

It was nice to feel needed. Though Tracen's words from the weekend whispered in his memory. *Do you ever get to do what you want to do?* Here he was, supporting the things she wanted to do again.

Casey looked at her watch. "I hate to ask, but would you mind dropping me off at the stadium offices? I have to get everyone updated on this new campaign idea."

It actually didn't bother him. He'd known she was going to ask. Plus, he had stuff to do now too. He had to plan Gen's surprise.

CHAPTER TEN

GENEVIEVE SLAMMED HER VAN DOOR IN the employee parking lot and jogged toward the airport. Oops. Her camera. She retraced her steps and manually unlocked the old Caravan. Usually she didn't bring her photography equipment to work, but Bianca said she had someone special coming in on the flight, and she wanted Gen to be able to take photos. And not photos on her cell phone.

Friends often took advantage of Gen's experience with a camera, but she enjoyed it. Especially with Bianca. And especially since taking the photos wouldn't be taking any time away from Matt because she knew he wasn't flying today. Pilots only flew about fifteen days a month, which meant he had the rest of the week off.

Maybe she could send one of Bianca's photos to Matt too. He'd really seemed to get a kick out of the giant goat picture, which was a nice surprise. She'd been worried he might think her too strange to keep texting. Nope. Just the opposite. He'd even asked that morning if she had any photo shoots scheduled for today. Nothing on the calendar, but after goat yoga the day before, she'd felt inspired to take more pictures of people with animals. She'd probably head to the Sequoia Park Zoo after work. If she got some good shots, the zoo might even buy them from her.

She unlocked her office and filed paperwork from the last flight then filled out the whiteboard with information on how many passengers and bags they should be expecting today. It looked like two lap children, one service animal, and no wheelchairs. There was also someone scheduled to arrive in the jump seat. Perhaps an auditor? She'd have to warn her team that they might be under inspection so definitely no singing John Denver songs as they loaded the plane. While fun, Bianca's boarding music always distracted her enough to lose focus.

"Hey, girl." Bianca appeared in the door, her white teeth flashing.

"You remember your camera equipment?"

"I did." Gen scrolled through her computer to open the stats on their flight and make sure it would be arriving as scheduled. "So who is this mystery person you're so excited about seeing? Is it a guy?"

Bianca laughed her belly laugh. "Oh yeah. He's definitely a guy."

Gen swiveled in her chair to face her friend. She'd never heard Bianca get this excited over a man before. Bianca went on lots of dates, but she always outlined her expectations up front, which seemed to scare most men away. With the way Bianca was literally dancing in the doorway, this new guy must have agreed to her list of requirements. "Where'd you meet him?" Gen asked.

Bianca threw her head back in laughter this time. She was still laughing as she opened the mini fridge to grab a water bottle. "You know what?" She pointed a manicured finger Gen's direction. "I'm going to let him answer all your questions. I don't want to give you any preconceived notions."

Gen shook her head but couldn't keep from smiling. After Bianca left to help check bags, she pulled up the manifest once more to look through the names of passengers. There were only a handful of men flying by themselves, and all but three of them were too old or too young for Bianca. She was either waiting for a Calvin Gray, Jason Hutchins, or Brett McDonald. Gen couldn't take the suspense. She stood and strode out to the ticket counter.

Tyler and Bianca looked up from their computers when she walked out.

"Hi, guys," she greeted.

Tyler grinned. No passengers waited in line so she could quiz him about what he knew.

"You know about Bianca's guy?"

Tyler frowned. Bianca howled. She had it bad.

Gen faced Bianca. She tried to keep a straight face like a detective, but giggles even punctuated her own words. Darn Bianca's contagious laugh. "Who is it? Calvin, Jason, or Brett?"

"You..." Bianca actually slapped her thigh as she fought for breath. "You searched the manifest?"

Gen leaned against the counter and crossed her arms. "Of course I did."

Tyler joined into Bianca's hysterics. Did he already know? Maybe Gen was way off. Maybe Bianca's grandfather was flying in.

Gen clicked her tongue. "You guys."

They kept laughing. Bianca wiped tears from her eyes to prepare to help the family weaving through the roped off maze that led people to their counter. Gen would apparently have to let the subject drop if they were ever going to get anything done.

"All right. I'll go wait for the in-bound call. You two try to get it together in case an auditor surprises us. There's someone in the jump seat, and that very well could be corporate coming to check us out."

Another round of laughter. They were losing it. She escaped through the door but waited for them to calm down before abandoning passengers to their insanity. She'd find out who Bianca's guy was soon enough, and she had plenty of work to do until then.

After the in-bound call from a female pilot with an Aussie accent, Gen let herself daydream about Matt on the way to Gate 3B. What did he do on his days off? She knew he'd been in Sausalito the day before because he'd sent her the picture of the girl with the bird man. Had he ridden a bike over the bridge, driven, or taken a sailboat across the bay? As the sailboat and car would likely include the incredible Casey Holloway, Gen preferred the bike scenario. She'd once rented a bike to ride over the Golden Gate Bridge but hadn't been expecting the hills to be so steep. She'd gone so slowly that joggers had actually passed her. But Matt wouldn't have that problem. He probably rode miles every morning before his flights to stay so athletic looking. Or maybe he did yoga. Just not with goats.

She stashed her camera equipment under the podium and made announcements to prepare passengers for the upcoming flight. She was watching for the plane to land through the window when both Bianca and Tyler showed up. Usually she'd only need one of them to help board passengers, but since she'd be taking pictures today, she'd asked both of them to come.

"I'll run the jet bridge so you can stay out here and photograph," Tyler offered. Did he really enjoy working the jet bridge that much or was Bianca's guy a pro athlete, and Tyler wanted to see him first? The name Jason Hutchins did sound vaguely familiar.

"Get your camera ready," Bianca ordered.

A few passengers glanced up with curiosity. Gen gave them a professional smile. *Nothing to see here, folks.* Not yet anyway.

She let Bianca take over so she could adjust her shutter speeds and snap a few practice shots to check the lighting. An elderly black man nodded at her, but he walked right by Bianca without a glance. Not Grandpa.

The captain and co-captain even emerged and lined up alongside Bianca. That was odd. Where was their passenger from the jump seat? Perhaps it was a ramp inspector, and he'd gone down the jet bridge stairs to check on the ground crew. She exhaled in relief. Now she wouldn't have to worry about an auditor watching her shoot Bianca's happy reunion.

"Here he comes," Bianca shouted.

Gen lifted her camera and focused on the tunnel. A family emerged. Then a familiar face. Matt. Out of uniform. But he looked every bit as good in jeans and a black polo as he did in his pressed pants and white shirt.

Her pulse took off like a jet. What was he doing here? He hadn't been on the manifest, so he must have been the one in the jump seat. She was tempted to lower her camera to talk to him, but she couldn't miss Bianca's reunion.

Matt's face grew larger. He stopped right in front of her so that all she could see were his smiling lips through her viewfinder. She lowered the camera and squinted in confusion.

"Don't waste your time taking pictures of me," he said. "Not when you could be taking pictures of the San Francisco Giants."

She blinked. Nothing he'd said made sense. She wasn't there to take pictures of either him or a sports team. She was there to take pictures of...

Wait.

She shifted her weight to peek around Matt. Bianca pointed at Matt repeatedly. Did that mean Matt was her guy? That made sense of half his statement. But as for the other half? He wanted her to photograph the baseball team owned by his girlfriend's father?

Her heart hammered even louder. That would be incredible. Too incredible to assume. Though it would explain the earlier hysterics at the ticket counter.

She shifted back to face Matt once again. If the Giants wanted to hire her, he would have been the one to arrange it. But then why didn't he just call. Why did he fly up here to tell her? How did everyone else already know?

His teal eyes shimmered like the bay on a sunny day, and all that light was focused directly on her. Of all her daydreams, she'd never even come close to imagining such a scenario. Matt *and* the photography opportunity of a lifetime. How was this even possible?

Matt watched Gen open and close her mouth a couple of times before words finally came out.

"I don't understand."

Seeing her reaction in person had been worth the effort. It was like he'd been given the power of a genie. He had the ability to make her dream come true.

He nodded to her camera. "The Giants need a photographer today, and I suggested you. Are you interested in the job?"

Her knuckles turned white as she clutched the camera tighter. "I...I..." Her eyes widened then her gaze darted around the terminal. "I can't. I'm working already."

He turned and placed a hand on her shoulder to guide her toward the jet bridge. "I hope you don't mind that I took the liberty to make sure your employees could cover for you."

Bianca held up a ticket for flight 350 with Gen's name on it and Gen's purse.

Tyler held up a baseball card. "Will you have Alan Anderson sign this for me if you get a chance?" The rascal.

Gen clutched her camera to her chest, obviously still in a state of shock. "I don't know who that is."

Seriously? The homerun hitter known as A-Plus for his excellent batting average? Matt was taking her to meet some of the biggest athletes in America, and she didn't know who they were. He'd have to go through the roster with her on the flight so she didn't offend anyone. Namely Casey's father.

Matt took the plastic covered card from Tyler and stuffed it in the back pocket of his jeans. "I'll take care of this for you."

Tyler pumped a fist in the air. "T-Y."

Thank you?

Gen remained frozen in place. "I can't believe this is happening."

Bianca laughed and hooked the frilly girly purse over Gen's shoulder. "We put you guys in first class. Row four, seats A and B. Perks of working for an airline."

Matt had to push Gen forward toward the plane. A strand of her long hair came loose from her braid and tickled his fingers. An unexpected shiver ran through his body, adding to the magic of the moment.

The melody from Bianca's favorite John Denver song floated down the tunnel after them.

"I can't believe this is happening," Gen said again.

He smiled so hard his face hurt. "You can't believe Bianca's playing that song again or that you're the one leaving on a jet plane?"

Her shoulders relaxed. Her cheeks dimpled. She broke out of her trance to grin up at him. "Oh, I'm used to Bianca playing the song."

She was going to be okay. He dropped his hand to his side and let her step in front of him to board the plane.

Gen stopped in front of Michelle. "I'm going to San Francisco to photograph a baseball team."

Michelle arched an eyebrow and glanced over Gen's head at Matt in challenge. What was that all about? "I know," she said.

Gen moved on to the next two flight attendants. "Did you know?" she asked.

They both nodded.

She looked over her shoulder at Matt, and he ducked his head to hide his laughter. The line of passengers behind him weren't finding the hold up so amusing.

"Let's take our seats so we can get out of the way." He motioned toward their row.

Gen continued to their seats then sank into one with a sigh of contentment. "Am I on a flight back tonight, or did you somehow get Bianca to pack a suitcase for me too?"

Matt took his spot next to her and strapped the seatbelt across his waist. He hadn't thought to ask Bianca to bring a change of clothes, but Gen looked too happy to care. It would be a long day for her. Well, for them both. "There aren't any flights scheduled from San Francisco tonight, so Casey's dad chartered me a plane to fly you home."

Gen stilled as much as she could with the passengers behind them jostling their seats. "No, he doesn't have to charter a plane for me. And you don't have to go through the trouble. That would be ridiculous. I'll wait until tomorrow."

Of course she would see it as excess. She didn't see how Casey's family lived. As for him, he didn't get to fly small planes very often anymore. He shrugged. "It'll be fun."

She shook her head and held a hand to her heart. "No, really. I can't let them—"

"Don't worry about it, Gen. It's pocket change for the Holloways. And if they like your photographs today, this could very well become a regular thing."

She searched his eyes, giving him a glimpse into the warmth of her heart. She was more concerned about the Holloways' efforts than the expectations they'd placed on her. As the enormity of her position sank in, her brown eyes glowed gold, and she leaned in to whisper. "How much are they paying me?"

This was the question Casey had prepared him for with a check that she'd thought might need to be used as a bribe. Matt had known better. But he hadn't known Gen would go all secret agent on him, like they were performing some illegal back alley transaction.

He played along by peering furtively over his outside shoulder then palming the check and grasping her hand to pass it to her without letting the other passengers see. Her fingers were soft as they curled around his. A small V appeared between her rust colored eyebrows. She glanced down at their clasped hands then blushed when she felt the piece of paper and realized his intent.

"Ahem." Michelle cleared her throat on his other side.

He slid his hand away from Gen's, leaving her the check, when turning to face the flight attendant.

Michelle ignored him and focused on Gen. "Bianca wants to know if you have any extra earplugs she can use when taking some gate checked items down to the ramp."

Matt twisted again to look at Gen. She stared blankly at the unfolded check in her hand, her expression not registering that she'd even heard Michelle's question.

Matt grinned. He'd prefer to talk about that check, but first he'd have to get Michelle to leave. He leaned toward Gen and placed his fingers on her forearm to attract her attention. "Bianca wants to know if you have any earplugs."

Her gaze lifted to his, but her expression didn't change. She was in shock.

"Earplugs?" Michelle enunciated as if Gen was wearing them in her own ears.

"Oh." Gen blinked. "I don't think...no...no, they are in the pocket of my high visibility vest underneath the podium."

Michelle gave a tight smile. "Thanks."

Matt shook off her attitude and faced Gen, waiting.

Now that she'd come out of her shock, she appeared uncertain. She gingerly folded the check then unzipped her purse, but paused as if contemplating whether her frou-frou handbag was safe enough to protect such a large sum of money. Where else would she put it? Her shoe?

She bit her lip and peeked up at him. "Does this amount include the payment for the plane charter?"

Matt couldn't help grinning at the question. She was too sweet. Or humble. Or both. A nice change from dealing with Michelle. Or anyone for that matter. "No, that's what the Giants' pay a photographer when they are planning to use her images for banners and billboards and to cover the whole side of a skyscraper downtown."

Her trembling fingers curled tighter around the check. Her blush paled. Her chest rose and fell hard. "I think I might need one of those vomit bags to help me breathe."

Matt scrambled to grab the bag in front of him. Hopefully she wouldn't actually vomit. He punched it open and handed it to her.

Gen tipped forward and cupped the bag to her face. It crinkled with each inhale.

Michelle's voice came over the intercom, starting her spiel on how to buckle and unbuckle a seatbelt. Like anybody didn't know.

Was there something else Matt could do to help Gen? At least he'd been here with her in person when she got the check. He patted her awkwardly on her back. That probably wasn't very soothing. He switched to a rub, running his hand up and down the soft knit material covering her spine.

Michelle's voice echoed around them with advice on oxygen masks. Too bad he couldn't pull one down for Gen.

What else would make her feel better? It had to be embarrassing to have a panic attack in front of a coworker. Especially since she had nothing to worry about. This was only the beginning for her. He grinned. "Someday I'll say I knew you when."

Her laugh came out like a snort. She stayed bent over but left the bag between her knees when turning her face to address him. "I want to tell my parents what I'm doing, but if I can't believe it myself, how am I ever going to explain it to anybody else?"

She'd get used to it in the same way he was getting used to dating Casey. "You can bring them to San Francisco to show them."

Michelle's speech moved on to directions for what to do in the event of a water landing because *that* was sure to keep everyone calm and collected if the plane crashed into the sea.

Gen sat upright, her long braid flipping down her back. "I will," she said, awe making her voice breathy. "My parents are coming down soon, so I'll take them to The City for a day." She paused. "Dad's a big fan of his team in Seattle, so he might think I'm a traitor though. Wait, did Seattle's baseball team move away?"

It was kind of refreshing to be around someone who knew less about baseball than Matt did. Even if it meant he'd be tutoring her for the duration of their flight. "Seattle's basketball team moved away, not their baseball team, so your dad *could* consider you a traitor, but really, you're only cheering for your home team now."

"True." She rubbed her earlobes. "It would be silly not to cheer for my home team. What are they called again?"

He tilted his head. Why did she keep rubbing at her ears? Would it help her remember things? Hopefully. He'd explain the campaign idea so she'd be able to associate Giants with the giant photos she would take of the players. He really wanted her to do well today. Not just for the team but for herself. "The Giants."

She scrunched her nose in embarrassment. "Oh yeah, the Giants."

Static crackled over the intercom. Michelle's voice rang out one last time. "We'll be landing in approximately one hour and ten minutes. That's all for now, and if you weren't listening...good luck."

Passengers chuckled around them.

He smiled. Gen didn't need luck. Once she got over her fear of being pushed out of the nest, she was going to find out she could fly on her own.

CHAPTER ELEVEN

GEN WANTED TO REMEMBER EVERYTHING MATT tried to teach her on the flight, but it sounded like gibberish. Especially since her brain was exploding with ideas for poses and lighting. Who cared about names and stats if she made the players look good?

That was the important thing here. Not how she didn't know to let the chauffeur open the door for her when they were picked up at the airport by a limo, or how she'd almost had an anxiety attack on the plane when she realized how much she'd be getting paid for this job, or even how she'd thought Matt had been holding her hand when he'd given her the check.

She'd daydream about that last one later. Or she would have if Casey Holloway hadn't glided out of her office at the ballpark like she was doing a little turn on the catwalk.

"Genevieve?" The beautiful woman held out both hands to reach for Gen's.

Casey's touch was smooth and firm, though it pricked Gen with guilt all the way to her lungs so that it hurt to take a breath. This was Matt's girlfriend. Gen was holding the very hand on which Matt would most likely one day slide a wedding ring.

"I'm so thankful Matt was able to talk you into coming today." Casey made life look effortless. She was dressed in a black suit that was both businesslike yet feminine with its form fit and well-placed ruffles. She had corn silk for hair, styled in a bold, fun, short style. And her eyes had an exotic tilt despite their sky blue color. Gen imagined Matt could stare into them and feel like he was flying.

Gen opened her mouth like a character having a conversation in a comic book strip, but her talk bubble remained empty. What could she say to the woman who'd offered her the chance of a lifetime while she was still daydreaming about the other woman's boyfriend?

Matt winked from behind Casey. He thought she was being

modest or speechless with awe. It was more like being guilty and speechless with shame. Her heart's fluttery reaction to his wink didn't help.

She needed to be professional here. Matt was a friend who got her this job. She couldn't let him down.

Gen smiled at Casey, and her genuine happiness surprised her. Not only because she really was grateful for the woman giving her this opportunity, but because Matt deserved her. Matt deserved this angel of a woman. "It's an honor," she said.

She wouldn't think about Matt anymore. She'd embarrassed herself enough. Instead, she'd focus on her craft. On Casey's goals. On making the players look like titans.

A whirlwind of creativity transported her through the city much like Dorothy in *The Wizard of Oz*. She had the first baseman pretend to skateboard on a trolley for his photo. The catcher posed like he was resting an elbow on top of The Palace of Fine Arts. An outfielder with a beard like a caveman "pinched" Coit Tower between his fingers. And a shortstop squatted like he was sitting on top of the Dragon Gate at the entrance to China Town.

Up last was the guy known for getting straight As. He wasn't much of a giant. More of a little guy, but Casey was determined he was the one to act like he was as tall as the Golden Gate Bridge. At least the timing was perfect. The six o'clock setting sun created a golden glow, and the silhouette of the city behind the bridge would soon start to flicker with lights.

Gen opened the door to climb out of the limo at a place called Battery Spencer. Then she saw the chauffeur walking her way and quickly pulled her foot back in to shut the door so he could open it for them. Her faux pas didn't even faze Casey or the baseball player as they were used to it by now, but Matt watched her with a bemused smile. She sent him a mock glare in an attempt to hide her embarrassment, but her face still heated up. Finally the limo driver released her into the cooler air.

She focused on the cement fort that had once held cannons to protect the bay. Now it was just the spot where everyone went to photograph the bridge. She'd come here a couple of times before with

Rosie, though those trips didn't compare to this moment. Not at all.

Casey climbed out of the limo and stuck her hands casually in her pockets. The wind ruffled her hair as she followed after Gen. She made being a professional business woman seem simple. "How do you want to do this?" she asked, probably ready to finish up their shoot so Matt could fly Gen home then return to spend the rest of his evening with her.

Gen ignored her twinge of jealousy. Infatuation had been fun, and out of it had come the realization of what she truly wanted someday. If she ever overcame her fear of falling in love, she'd look for someone like Matt. She glanced at him one more time over the top of the limo to store his image in her memory. His gaze caught hers, but the only reaction she could afford was to curl her toes inside her ballet flats.

He tilted his head as if to ask her thoughts.

He was too far away to talk, but even if they were back in the limo alone, she could never tell him what was on her mind. The questions in her head weren't something either he or anyone else could answer. It was a question for God alone. Much like the ones she asked about her birth parents. *Why couldn't I have met Matt before he met Casey?*

God had never answered any of her other questions, so she didn't expect an answer for this one either. The only answer she could ever figure out was reminding herself that her life could have been worse, and that was certainly true here too. Life could have been worse than riding around San Francisco in a limo with a huge paycheck in her purse. She needed to focus on her job. She needed to focus on Alan.

The guy wasn't much taller than her, but he had a presence that could be felt like static during a lightning storm. He climbed out of the limo and never stopped moving. He shifted from foot to foot, straightened his collar, smiled at people, and hopped on rocks for a better view of the bay. He actually had an A+ shaved into the back of his head, and she couldn't help thinking that the strips of hair removed from his skull could have been the same ones that circled over his top lip and then down underneath his jaw in a finely trimmed goatee.

"Think you can stand still long enough to cross one ankle over the other and pretend you're leaning against the bridge?" she asked.

His mischievous smile flashed her way. "Is that a challenge?"

She twisted her lips together. "If it helps."

He punched a fist into his opposite palm. "I hate standing still, but I love a challenge."

She might have to move quickly to make this happen. Kind of like when photographing Rosie's goats. Lifting her camera to her eye, she found an angle that worked then shifted to bring Alan into position. "Cross your arms."

Alan folded one arm over the other then twisted back and forth making pouty faces or lifting his chin, probably like he assumed models did. Gen snapped away, but even if she caught him when he was in the perfect position, he'd still most likely be a blur. She lowered her camera to view the images on screen.

Matt chuckled from behind Gen where he and Casey watched. "You're scaring me, bro," he said to the ball player.

Alan unfolded his arms to strike the Thinker Pose. "Why? Because I'm so GQ?"

"Yeah, that's it." Matt's voice dripped with both sarcasm and humor.

Alan propped one hand behind his head and stuck his hips out. "This is my good side. You should photograph me from this angle."

Casey stepped closer to look over Gen's shoulder at the images as the guys continued to banter.

Gen stopped at the first photo she'd taken of Alan. If it was the best she could get out of him, it would be okay, but not something she'd want plastered to the side of a skyscraper.

Casey shook her head. "He needs to have the most dynamic photo out of all the players."

That's what Gen had been afraid of. She scrolled through photos to compare Alan to the other guys on the team. The others were fun yet intense, while Alan looked like a goof.

Alan appeared over her other shoulder. He pointed to the pic of the trolley/skateboard. "That's cool. Why don't I get to do something like that?"

Casey took a deep breath and rolled her shoulders as if to ease frustration. "We wanted you to have the most well-known landmark since you're the most well-known player." Smooth. That's why she got paid the big bucks.

"Ah, yeah." Alan plucked at the front of his shirt. "Maybe I can look like I'm hanging off it like Godzilla or something. How's this, Genevieve?" He turned sideways and assumed a rock climbing position. Then roared.

"Now I'm really scared." Matt grinned.

Gen took advantage of the opportunity by backing up to make it look as if Alan really was climbing up the side of the bridge. She almost backed into Matt. His breath on her neck gave her chills. "Sorry." She pulled away from the warmth of his body.

"Wait."

She fought off a shiver. *I want someone like Matt*, she reminded herself. *Not Matt.*

He stepped beside her, and the breeze wafted his woodsy scent her way.

Matt's taken.

His eyes glanced up to meet hers, and she realized she was staring. "Can I see the photos?"

She jumped. "Oh, yes." She tilted the camera his way.

Matt grinned. "I love them, but they are more like blackmail material than an advertisement."

"Hey." Alan sent them a mock glare. "That's not nice." Just as quickly, the glare disappeared and he danced in place. "I want you to make me look good, Genevieve. How you gonna make me look gooood?"

It was really hard to capture his energy in a still image. "What's he known for?" she whispered to Matt.

Matt slanted his eyes her way. He'd probably told her this already on their flight down, but she didn't remember. "He's a great hitter, but he's also an amazing runner. He's got a record for the most in-the-field homers, and it's because he can't be stopped."

"Makes sense."

"That's right." Alan pretended to swing a bat. "Back at the University of Washington I played ball, but in high school I was able to play ball *and* run track."

U-Dub? That's where Damon went. She'd tell Alan later. For now, she'd focus on the track part of his statement. "Did you run hurdles?" she guessed.

Alan stood up straight. "Oh, yeah. And those skills came in handy that one time the Dodgers got me in a pickle. I leaped right over the third baseman. Did you see that?"

One corner of Matt's lips curved up. "Yeah, did you see that?" he repeated, probably knowing full well Gen had never watched a baseball game in her life.

"No." She narrowed her eyes at Matt before turning to usher Alan back to his spot in front of the bridge. "But the world is going to see you hurdling this bridge."

"Say what?" His tone got all squeaky. "Ain't nobody that can hurdle a bridge."

She smiled as she marked a line in the sand with her toe. "You can with my help. Take off here and try to get..." she surveyed the bridge for an idea of where he would need to be. She lifted her palm to about chest height. "...this high."

Alan rubbed his hands together. "Oh, I see what you're doin'. You're gonna make me look gooood."

Hopefully. "Can you smile at the camera as you jump?" she asked. His smile was likely even more well-known than his batting average.

"Girl, I can smile at the camera in my sleep."

Like when letting Tyler run the jet bridge at work, this pose was going to cater to Alan's strengths. She wasn't going to make him look good as much as he was going to make her look good. "Somehow I knew that."

It took a few test runs and changes to the lighting and aperture before she got the stop action she wanted. She clicked back through a couple of frames, and her heart shimmied. Whether anyone knew a thing about Alan's career or not, they were going to know he was a superstar simply by looking at this pic.

Casey gasped over her shoulder. "Oh my," she said on her exhale.

Matt just stared at the tiny screen from Gen's other side. He lifted an arm and held it there.

Gen loved talking to Matt, but making him speechless gave her an even better feeling. Like she'd exceeded his expectations. And if she were being compared to Casey, this was probably the only time she'd ever be able to do that.

Matt couldn't take his eyes off the camera screen. It was as if time had frozen with Alan Anderson in the air, and the whole sky and city lit up perfectly around him like a frame at the Museum of Modern Art. When the image was blown up to building size, it was going to look like A-Plus was leaping right into the city.

Gen could quit her job at the airport if she wanted to. Everyone from the Golden State Warriors to The North Face was going to try to hire her now.

"What?" Alan did his little parrot head bob thing. "Do I look like a champion? Because we are winning the pennant, and I don't want no lame photo going on World Series baseball cards."

Casey crossed her arms and strode toward him. "Your photos are taken care of, mister. Now you can focus on winning."

Matt could tell Casey was pleased too. These images were going to get them all kinds of recognition whether Alan lived up to his claim or not.

Gen gazed at Matt as if waiting for something. "Baseball card?"

He stared into her searching brown eyes, and it took a moment for her words to sink in. She was talking about the flimsy little baseball card in his pocket. While she'd taken what would most likely be the photo that would be associated with A-Plus for the rest of his career, she was concerned about getting Tyler his autograph. For the first time, Matt realized he was in the presence of greatness, and it wasn't because he was riding around in a limo with Alan Anderson.

"Oh...ye-yeah." He pulled the card out of his pocket. What could he say to convey his amazement of her skill?

She bit her lip and peered at him out of the corner of her eyes. Probably a little weirded out by his stuttering. Letting her camera hang freely from her neck, she plucked the baseball card from his fingers. "I'll do it."

He grinned. He had the rest of the night to think about what to say to her. For now he'd settle on watching her play the fan to a superstar she knew nothing about. It would be fun to see her poke a hole in Alan's inflated ego. Especially with the irony of how her talent was going to make him an even bigger star. "Okay."

She gave him another measuring look. "What?" she challenged like she knew there was something he wasn't saying.

How did he explain? Did he have to explain? He had to say something or they might keep staring at each other like this while Casey and Alan climbed into the back of the limo and drove away.

"You." He answered her simply.

Her eyes widened, and her eyebrows lowered at the same time. If he hadn't freaked her out before, he certainly had now. It was kind of fun.

"Let's go," Casey called from the door of the limo. She wasn't used to being kept waiting.

Had Matt really been staring that long? He must have been because he was still staring as Gen turned her back on him, shot him one more confused glance over her shoulder, and ducked inside the car to take a seat next to Alan.

Matt followed. He should feel accomplished after the day they'd had. Not only had he gotten Casey the best photographer in all of California, but he'd gotten Gen a job that would most certainly blow the door open for more opportunities. He lived for days where he got to be the hero like this. Yet there was something unsettled inside him. Something not quite satisfied with the results.

He climbed in the limo to take the side seat next to Casey and wrapped an arm around her shoulders so he was better positioned to look past her to where Gen and Alan sat in front of the partition window. Since the sky was dimming outside, the driver had switched on the interior lights for them to better see each other. He'd watch and listen and try to figure out what was bothering him. Even if he couldn't put his finger on it, the card-signing was sure to make good entertainment.

"Oh my word, Matt." Casey patted his leg. "I am going to get a promotion after this campaign. Thank you so much for recommending

Genevieve."

Matt nodded, forcing himself to make eye contact. The truth was that Casey could get a promotion anytime she asked her dad for one, but he was glad he could make her happy.

Casey sighed in contentment and rested her head on his shoulder, giving him a chance to look over her to Gen and Alan as the limo began its trip to drop Alan off on the way to the airport.

Alan whipped a Sharpie out of his sock to sign the baseball card Gen presented him. Matt wouldn't even feign surprise.

"I'll sign it: To Gen, my favorite fan." Alan removed the lid to the Sharpie with a flourish.

Matt opened his mouth and held up a hand to stop him, but Gen beat him to it.

Her hand flew between the pen and the card. "Oh no. You have to sign it to Tyler."

The Sharpie marked her hand then paused in midair. Alan's face pinched as if in pain. "Who? I don't know no Tyler."

Gen grinned, obviously enjoying the entertainment as well, despite being written on. "Tyler. He's a friend I work with."

"Oh." Alan leaned toward her and wiggled his eyebrows. "A close friend?"

"Not that close." Gen's eyes slid Matt's direction. Perhaps a cry for help.

"He's a little too young for Gen," Matt explained.

Tyler probably wasn't that much younger than Gen, but she seemed more mature. More driven and passionate and…classy. She deserved a man's man. Or at least someone who didn't play videogames in all his free time. But Matt couldn't quite think of anyone good enough for her.

Alan flashed him a delighted smile. It held some kind of dare. The baseball player turned toward Gen and scooted closer to her in a very obvious and playful way. "Are there *any* close males in your life?"

Matt stiffened. He wanted to tell Alan to back off, but he knew that would only encourage the man's advances. If Gen was asking Matt for help earlier, she'd be ready to send out an SOS in Morse Code. He watched for her distress signal, contemplating the best excuse for switching seats.

Gen threw back her head and laughed. Huh. Clearly she wasn't threatened at all. Was it because she could see right through Alan? Or was she so not interested that the pickup line sounded like a joke to her? It couldn't be because she was enjoying the attention.

She lifted her head up enough for Matt to see her eyes flash. "Actually…" she said.

Actually? Actually there was a close male in her life? How did Matt not know this?

But why did he think he would know? He'd probably know if it was another crew member of the Eureka station. All the guys had been sitting in the jet bridge when he'd asked for Gen's number. None of them had said anything. Bianca hadn't said anything when he'd gotten her number the first time either. But they probably all knew Matt had a girlfriend, so they wouldn't think anything of it. Which they shouldn't. His texts had been nothing more than friendly. But still. If he and Gen were friends, she could have said something. He'd told her about Casey.

"You might know him." Gen answered Alan's question though her eyes caught Matt's. Her lips curved up.

Matt's breath hitched. How would Alan know her close male friend? Unless she was talking about Matt? Yes, the two of them were becoming close friends, but not the way Alan meant.

She faced Alan as if forgetting Matt completely. "He probably went to the University of Washington at the same time you did. What year did you graduate?"

Matt rubbed his chin. He didn't like the fact, he had no idea who she was talking about. Especially not after he'd thought she'd been talking about him.

Alan stretched out his arms along the back of the seat. Not quite touching Gen, but close. "It's been eight years since I graduated. Can you believe that? So who's this guy?"

Matt braced for impact.

Casey's head rolled along his arm, bringing her lips toward Matt's ear. She whispered something. Matt strained to hear both her words and Gen's but ended up comprehending neither.

He raised a finger as if he were going to hold it to his lips and hush Casey, but he stopped himself in time. That wouldn't go over very well. His skin prickled in frustration.

"Damon?" Alan's mouth fell open as he responded to whatever it was Gen had told him. "Damon was my tutor. Smart guy. Did he ever become a doctor?"

"He did." Gen wasn't as animated. In fact, when she shot Matt a sideways look, her eyes seemed a little sad.

But why? Didn't all women want to date doctors who were smart guys? If Matt was going to pick out a boyfriend for her, this man probably would have been his choice. Though he hadn't been consulted in her choice at all. And for some reason he felt he should have been. It made him a little sad too.

"Matt." Casey's voice called to him. Again.

He blinked and looked down at her, lifting a hand to rub over her satin hair to make up for his moment of inattentiveness. "What, Case?" he asked. He hoped she answered quickly. Because there was more he needed to know about the smart doctor.

"I asked if you're okay."

He stared at her. Why wouldn't he be okay? They'd had a wonderful day. He let his subconscious search for the right words to say as he consciously strained to hear the other conversation in the car.

"He's your brother?" Alan's voice was loud enough the driver probably heard through the partition.

Her brother?

Matt sighed. His shoulders sagged.

Gen had been teasing Alan. The athlete only asked if there was a close male in her life, and she'd used that as an opening to both turn the player down and create a common bond through a mutual acquaintance. Matt should have known she could hold her own.

He smiled at Casey. "I feel fabulous." Because not only had he had a wonderful day, but it wasn't over yet.

CHAPTER TWELVE

THIS VERY WELL COULD HAVE BEEN the best and the worst day of Gen's life. Best because she loved every minute with Matt and the opportunity he'd given her. It had been better than she'd ever imagined, and she could imagine a lot. But it was the worst day because now that she'd met Casey, she had to quit imagining.

Casey was too real. Plus Casey was perfect for Matt. They were super cute together. And they seemed really happy. Daydreaming about him would now be like daydreaming over a friend's fiancé. It made Gen feel selfish as well as insignificant.

She crawled after Casey to climb out of the limo. The driver hadn't taken them to the curb in front of the airport. He'd driven them to a private hangar with a little Cessna. The plane was so little the cockpit looked about the size of the front seat in a car. And she'd be riding in it for an hour in the dark with Matt. That was the worst possible situation for not imagining.

"Are you coming with us, Casey?" she asked. Then she could sit in the backseat. Be the third wheel. Nothing romantic about that.

Casey shook her head emphatically. "I hate even flying in an Airbus. There's no way I'm going to get into one of those death traps."

Really? Gen eyed the plane again. Was she crazy to be excited for the adventure? To get away from reality and find peace among the clouds. Flying was actually a little like daydreaming, wasn't it?

Back to her problem. She eyed Matt hesitantly.

"Don't listen to Casey," he said. He must have thought her hesitation involved the flying part of their trip. "Cessnas are safe. I know what I'm doing, and I'm going to take good care of you."

How was she going to keep from daydreaming with him saying things like that? "Okay." The sooner she agreed, the sooner they could take off, and the sooner she could get home to bed and escape from her daydreams into sleep.

Casey reached to hug her. She smelled delicious like peaches. Why couldn't she smell like rotten eggs or garlic? If she had at least one flaw, then normal people might feel less insecure around her. Not that Gen was normal.

"I'm sure you'll be fine" Casey patted Gen's back. "I simply prefer to fly as little as possible."

Gen got out of the way for Casey to hug Matt goodbye.

He dropped a kiss on Casey's forehead then stepped away with a small smile and an eye roll. "Of course we'll be fine."

Maybe this was Casey's flaw. Matt would probably see it as a flaw anyway.

Casey nudged him with her shoulder. "He puts up with my fear because without it, we never would have gotten together."

Oh. Gen quirked her lips to one side.

Matt shrugged before turning to do some kind of pre-flight inspection on the plane. "Her dad hired me to fly their family to New Jersey, and she tried to chicken out, but I wouldn't let her."

Okay, so it wasn't a flaw after all. It was one of the many ways in which they balanced each other out.

"Well, I'm glad I got to meet you, Casey." Gen really was. Because of the day's photo shoot, she had new opportunities for her career as well as the desire to let go of her crush so she could look for someone like Matt who was available. She knew what she wanted now. And she wanted it to be real. Like Rosie said.

"Same here." Casey's shoulders dropped as she sighed. "I can't tell you how stressed I was, but you exceeded all expectations on the photos. You've got my email address so you know where to send the files?"

Gen checked her pocket for the business card. Edges of cardstock poked her fingers. "Yep."

"And she's got my number if she loses it." Matt spoke up from behind.

"Yep," Gen said again. This time with a little less enthusiasm. Because that might be the only reason she used Matt's number now—for contacting Casey.

"All right." Casey side-stepped gracefully toward the limo door the chauffeur was still holding open and gave a princess wave. "I'm headed out. Fly safe, honey." She threw a kiss to Matt.

Gen stood there between Matt's plane inspection and Casey gliding away in the limousine. As far as real life went, the moment was completely surreal. "Just yesterday I was photographing goats," she said.

Matt laughed. He lowered his clipboard to his hip with one hand and opened the passenger side door for her with the other. "They were easier to deal with than Alan, huh?"

Alan certainly had the energy of a kid. She chuckled at the comparison. "Perhaps." Then she held her breath to keep from inhaling Matt's scent when stepping past him to climb into the plane.

Her heart trilled anyway as she took her seat in front of a dark dashboard of dials and gauges and two steering wheel thingies. She buckled up to help calm down. Was she more nervous about the fact that above the dashboard there was nothing but glass that would give her a toe-tingling view of their distance off the ground or about the fact that Matt's seat was only inches away from hers? A couple weeks ago, she'd wished he'd fly her to Paris for dinner. And now she really was his only passenger.

If only he wasn't doing it all for Casey. But he was.

The flimsy little door shook as he shut it beside her. He walked around to the pilot's seat, flashing an excited grin before focusing on dials and gauges.

"Did you always want to be a pilot?"

He twisted his steering wheel shaped like the letter W and squinted past her through the window to make sure whatever made the plane turn would do its job. "I actually wanted to be a pirate." He spoke as if it were the most normal thing in the world.

"Oh." She smiled. "Like Captain Hook?"

He ran his hands over a number of buttons, presumably checking to see if they were pushed in or not. He met her eye contact in the intimacy of darkness. "More like Dread Pirate Roberts from *The Princess Bride*. He was such a great hero."

Matt certainly was going to get his princess bride. "Wise choice."

Matt worked a knob out and in; similar to how she did when

priming her lawnmower at home. "I thought so too. Then my family went on our first vacation on a 737 where I found out the pilot of a plane is also called a captain. Plus he could explore over both water *and* land."

Gen pictured Matt as a child, staring in awe out the window of a plane kind of like she was doing now. He turned a key, and the propeller in front of them whirred to life, the engine vibrating their seats and echoing around them.

"So you basically wanted to be an explorer?" she surmised.

"Basically." He pressed a couple of buttons and a screen flashed on with a GPS program. "An explorer with a really cool hat. And possibly an eye patch." He grabbed a headset to cover his ears. "These are as close as I got."

He didn't seem to mind much. Though as cute as he looked in his headset, he'd probably look even cuter in a Jack Sparrow hat. "There's always Halloween." She closed her eyes and shook her head to get rid of the image.

"I should dress up this year. That would be fun."

The image returned. But what did it matter? Matt would be spending his holidays with Casey. Not Gen.

He gripped the steering wheel thingy, and the plane rolled forward, headlights leading the way toward a runway no wider than her driveway. "If you want to wear your headset, we can talk a little bit easier." He gestured toward the set.

Gen smiled sadly as she raised the headset and placed it over her ears. She did want to talk to him. And she didn't want their conversations to end when she took the earphones off. So she would be his friend. She'd consider him like one of her brothers.

Matt taxied around a corner before speeding up. The engine roared louder. Lights of buildings lined the ground in the distance. He got permission from the tower and before she knew it, the rumbling of tires faded away. They'd lifted off.

Her body wavered between pressure of velocity and the weightlessness of flying, creating a dizzy sensation at first. Once she found balance, sitting in the cockpit became as ordinary as a pew on Sunday morning. Except the space between her feet and the earth was growing. And she could see more lights than the standard skyline on either side. It was as if both the ground and the heavens shone with stars.

She exhaled. "It's beautiful."

The horizon tilted, and Gen shifted right. She grabbed onto the handle for stability then quickly let go to prevent from accidentally opening the door. Her eyes flew to Matt to register his expression and confirm this was supposed to happen.

She could only make out his profile in the red glow of the instrument panel, but a flash of teeth revealed his delight. "I'm banking north. Scare you?"

She released the bite of her fingernails against her palms. Her pulse slowed to dam the flood of blood through her veins. She sank deeper into her seat. "You're enjoying this, aren't you?"

He adjusted a variety of instruments and scanned the horizon. "Every second."

She watched him with the freedom darkness afforded her. His passion was like fine wine—rare and intoxicating.

He glanced past his shoulder to see her and came back for a double take when he found her staring. She blinked and shifted her gaze out the windshield.

"I feel alive in these little planes, you know?" It was as if he thought he needed to explain himself to her. He didn't.

"I know."

He studied her for a moment. She allowed herself to peek at him a couple of times but only quickly like when swiping her finger through the flame of a candle. If she stayed still, she'd get burned.

Could he feel the heat? Was he thinking the same thing?

"I can do things in a Cessna that I can't do in an Airbus."

He was most definitely thinking of different things than she was. "Um…" Her cheeks flushed, and she told herself it was too dark for him to tell. "What kind of things?"

He let go of the steering wheel. "I could let you fly."

Her hands splayed wide. Tingles exploded down her legs and arms. She didn't want the plane uncontrolled, but she didn't want to be the one in charge either. "What?"

"You fly." He nodded toward the steering wheel in front of her.

"What? What if I crash?" Even as she blurted out her greatest fear, she knew she didn't have that power. She could angle the nose of the plane directly toward the ground, and he'd pull them out of it. She just didn't want to mess up. She didn't want to do anything wrong.

He tilted his head, the red glow picking up the smug tilt at the corner of his mouth. "Oh, Gen. What if you soar?"

Dare she? She hadn't prepared for this. Yet something inside wanted to flip the plane upside down in an inverted dive as if she were Maverick.

"Here." Matt reached for her.

She stiffened. But he was only taking the camera from around her neck.

Why? Less distraction? She ducked her head so he could unhook the strap.

"We'll both learn. You don't know anything about planes, and I don't know anything about cameras. You fly, and I'll take pictures."

That seemed so backwards. Maybe he saw in her the passion for photography that he felt with flying, and he wanted to share it. But if he wanted to take pictures in this light... "I need to change the f-stop for you." She reached for her Canon.

Matt let her work in silence, and it wasn't until she looked up that she caught his watching smile and realized he'd intentionally calmed her fears by letting her return to her comfort zone.

She narrowed her eyes. "You know you're getting off easy here, right? Snapping photos isn't nearly as dangerous as taking over the controls of a plane."

"I told you I'll take good care of you, and I will." His fingers brushed hers, and it took a moment to realize he was reaching for the camera. If she wasn't scared before... "Now grab hold of the yoke."

The yoke. AKA the steering wheel thingy.

Gen took a deep breath and wrapped her fingers around each side. They were still alive. "Hey, I'm pretty good at this."

Matt lifted the camera to his face and peered through the viewfinder. He was looking at her. What did he see? She wasn't used to being on this end of the lens. And she certainly wasn't used to having

Matt's concentrated attention. Had she put on any makeup that morning? She couldn't remember. It seemed so long ago.

Matt clicked and kept the camera to his face. "Now try to steer."

Steer? Weren't they on a straight course to Eureka? She didn't want to mess that up. "Where?"

"You pull out or push in to go up or down. And you'll turn right or left to bank."

She didn't want to bank. So maybe she'd go down a little. She tightened her grip and pushed the yoke in.

The plane dropped. Her hips pressed against the seatbelt. Her heart enlarged like a parachute within her chest. A scream ripped from her lungs.

The plane steadied. Her breath raced to catch up. Her fingers continued to squeeze the yoke, but she tore her gaze away to see how Matt handled her kamikaze stunt.

He only had one hand on the wheel. The other hand held her camera, still pointed at her. He arched an eyebrow. "You okay?"

How did he remain so calm? She'd almost killed them. Her throat had gone dry. She didn't even think she had the spit to answer, so she nodded solemnly.

"You sure?" He cranked his wrist around to turn the screen on her camera her direction. "Because right here you look like you're on that freefall ride at Great America."

He'd caught her mid panic, eyes wide, lips parted, hair flying. And it was actually a pretty cool shot since not only was her hair red, but her whole profile glowed eerily. It was the kind of photo one would have paid big bucks for at an amusement park. If only Matt could have snapped a picture of both of them. Though he probably would have appeared as one of those calm rollercoaster riders who wore shades and crossed his arms at the exact spot where he knew the automated camera would click.

She swallowed. "I didn't scare you at all?"

He shrugged a shoulder. "Remember when I said I can do things in a Cessna that I can't do on an Airbus. That's one of them."

Her mouth dropped open. He hadn't only set her up; he'd been the one to dive the plane? She didn't think she'd pushed the yoke in that far. She pointed. "You?"

He pressed his lips together and nodded like a mischievous ten-year-old, caught in the act. "Sorry. I couldn't help it."

She released the yoke and pressed both hands to her heart. Her body puddled in her seat. And then the laughter rose up, shaking her from the inside out. He got her good.

Knowing about Matt's prank made the picture he took even funnier. She laughed louder and had to wipe at her eyes. After thinking she was going to die, she was now more alive than ever. Her leftover adrenaline gave her the feeling she could conquer the world.

"So you're not mad?" he asked. Was this why Casey wouldn't ride with him? Or had he known from the beginning that he couldn't pull such a prank on his girlfriend?

Either way, Gen wasn't mad. She was thrilled. "Can you do it again?"

Matt couldn't remember when he'd had that much fun flying. He'd taken a risk by playing the prank on Gen, but somehow he'd known she would enjoy the rush and be able to laugh at herself. What was even funnier was that she couldn't keep from screaming, even when she knew he was going to drop the plane. Every time he'd lower their elevation suddenly, her mouth would involuntarily open and the noise burst out. She'd tried a few times to keep quiet and failed. Her exuberance was going to make the trip home seem even quieter. He felt lonely already.

After landing, he'd tried to walk around to Gen's side to open her door for her, but exactly like in the limo with the chauffeur, she'd popped out before he'd had a chance. She looped her purse and camera bag over her chest bandolier style, a silly grin on her face from the fun they'd had. Was there anything better in the world than a silly grin?

Her shoulders relaxed, and her smile faded into solemnity. "Thanks for making this day happen," she said. "It's almost ending, and it still doesn't feel real."

Matt stuffed his hands in his pockets. It was going to be a late night for him, but he had the next few days off, so he could sleep in. "It's not over yet." He motioned with his head in the direction of the employee parking lot. "Come on, I'll walk you to your car."

Gen waved a hand. "You don't have to."

He leveled his gaze on hers. "I know." She was too modest. Too humble. Too giving. She may not let him open a door for her, but he wasn't going to let her walk through a deserted parking lot alone at night.

She gave him one of her shy little peeks before turning to stroll side by side with him. Funny that she could act so shy with Matt when he did nothing but offer to walk her to her car, but she brashly laughed when Alan put his arm around her. Maybe it was because she knew Matt had a girlfriend, and she was being sensitive. Or maybe she really was interested in Alan. Hmm.

She did her earlobe rub thing as he entered the security code to open a gate in the chain link fence. "Are all your brothers as chivalrous as you?" she asked.

She thought him chivalrous? Even after the whole plane prank? He'd let her keep thinking that. As for his brothers... "My oldest brother is engaged, so he must be doing something right. My youngest brother is too busy snowboarding to even know women exist. Josh is the charmer, so I guess you could call that chivalrous. Then there's Tracen." He shook his head and held the gate open for her to pass through. "Tracen couldn't even be chivalrous to Casey."

Gen shivered in the cool night, and he wished he had his jacket to offer. So much for all this talk of chivalry. Her eyes caught his as she passed through. They were still like deep water, and he wondered what lay underneath.

"Tracen doesn't like Casey?" she asked, revealing that she was still thinking of his brothers. Kind of disappointing for some reason.

He stuffed his hands back in his pockets as he followed her through the fence, letting the gate clang shut. "He thinks she's too perfect."

Gen nodded and looked off in the distance. Was she still thinking about Tracen? "Casey is pretty perfect."

She'd moved on to thinking about his girlfriend. And she didn't sound judgmental like Tracen had been. Her tone held a breathy amount of awe mixed with a touch of heaviness that could be mistaken for jealousy. His pulse gave an extra pump at the idea Gen might be jealous of his girlfriend. Though most people were jealous of Casey. Which had nothing to do with him. So he shouldn't even consider jealousy a factor.

He and Gen were friends. Even if he wasn't dating anyone, Gen lived a different lifestyle in a different city. A relationship with her would take work. It would include travel. And adventure. And the craziness of their families. Wait, wasn't he supposed to be convincing himself they weren't compatible?

Matt rolled his eyes. He must be really tired to even consider dating anyone other than Casey.

He needed to focus. He studied the deserted parking lot, completely empty except for some old, dented minivan that probably belonged to a janitor. He stopped. Scanned the area. Stiffened, as if expecting joyriding kids to do a Dukes of Hazzard out of the parking lot in Gen's vehicle. "Where's your car?"

Gen pulled her keys from her purse and pushed a button. The van beeped.

Matt relaxed the same way Gen probably had after her scare in the airplane. This situation struck him as funny as Gen found his prank. "You drive a minivan? Do you have four kids that I don't know about?"

Gen walked past him and swung the driver's side door open, depositing her belongings next to the seat. "Not yet," she said.

Did she want four kids? She'd be a good mom. But she wasn't one yet, was she? "Why do you drive a minivan?"

She faced him again, revealing the return of her carefree smile. "So I can go on photography road trips and save money by sleeping in the back of the van rather than getting a hotel."

She did what? His spine straightened. "That's not safe."

"Neither is flying airplanes."

"Touché." She had him there. Hopefully after that job with the Giants, she could afford to sleep in hotels. Though with the kind of person she was, she probably didn't care. He lifted a hand to rest it on the top of her roof, slick from recent rain. He was tired, but he didn't want to go yet. He wanted to relive the day with her one more time. "You had a good day?" he asked to hear her rave.

Her cheeks softened. She leaned against the van by his hand. "I did. I'll probably have to pinch myself when I wake up tomorrow."

Without thinking, he reached for the soft skin on her forearm underneath her short sleeves and pinched.

"Ouch." She pulled the arm to her chest and rubbed it with her other hand.

"That hurt?" He hadn't meant to hurt her, just to make a point.

"Yes." She over pronounced the word with mock disdain.

"Then you're not dreaming."

She looked down at her arm and sighed. "Not anymore."

What did that mean? Maybe that he'd made her dreams come true.

He'd let her go. Let her head home to bed where she could dream up more ideas. As a friendly gesture, he reached the hand from the van around her shoulders to pull her in for a hug.

Her palms caught on his chest, holding them apart. He looked down to find her eyes boring into his, both demanding and skittish at the same time. "What are you doing?"

What did she think he was doing? He eased his arm from behind her and held them out innocently. "I was hugging you goodbye?" He turned the statement into a question so she had a chance to give him permission if that made her feel more comfortable.

She looked down at her hands on his chest and stepped away. If she was going to react so strongly to a hug, then she definitely wasn't jealous of Casey earlier. She wanted Matt firmly in the friend zone. Which shouldn't bother him. They were friends. But didn't friends hug?

"I don't know if we should hug since we're coworkers."

Really? Did she have some bad experience in the past? He wouldn't make it worse. Though it rubbed him the wrong way. She felt safe enough to let him dive their plane toward the earth, but not safe enough to give him a hug?

He retreated to give her space. "It's not like I'm your boss or anything."

The farther away he moved, the more a twinkle returned to her eyes. "If anybody was boss, I think I'd be your boss."

Back on even footing, despite her claim. He relaxed. "Why do you think *you'd* be boss?"

She tilted her head in challenge. "Because you can't fly anywhere unless I put the passengers on the plane and pull the jet bridge away."

He returned to his spot and dropped the same hand onto her van roof. He wasn't going to back away from a challenge. "Then with your reasoning, Kevin is also my boss because he pushes my plane from the terminal for every flight."

Gen lifted her chin. "That's true. I think I'll trade him places next time you fly. I'll put the headset on and climb in the pushback cart, and I'll make you call me boss before I drive you out to the tarmac."

She did silly so well. She did cute and sweet and silly. And it was a miracle she wasn't married with four children yet. Or maybe it was these grand ambitions of hers that kept her from settling down.

"I'd have to call you boss then," he conceded, one corner of his lips curving up. "But there's still a problem."

She turned to get in her car and looked over her shoulder, an eyebrow arched high. It was like she was poised to make her escape after getting the last word in. "What's that?" she asked.

He wouldn't let her escape so easily. He stepped closer until he stood above her.

Her gaze lifted to remain on his, though her haughty act faltered like a mask slipping off. He couldn't wait for it to slip all the way off and reveal her smile.

"With as much money as I make, I'm pretty sure my boss wouldn't drive a dented minivan."

Her elbow struck his gut with enough force that he sidestepped the remaining impact. He hooked the crook of her arm in the crook of his so she couldn't fight anymore. But she wasn't fighting, she was laughing—leaning back into him, head resting on his shoulder, smiling at the stars and laughing.

"I love my dented minivan," she wailed, making herself laugh harder.

He laughed along. Though there was something in his heart that hitched. Something that longed to be loved like a dented minivan. Wasn't that what everyone wanted—to be seen as their imperfect selves and loved anyway. To not have to be the hero all the time?

Did he have that with Casey? Or was he trying to appear perfect for her because he didn't think she'd love him otherwise? He'd ponder the thought on the way home. Which is where he should have been headed. It was late, and he was getting loopy.

He released Gen's arm, freeing her to go home too. Only she turned with that silly smile on her face and stepped into his embrace.

The hug. The one he'd asked for. Soft and warm and comforting. Exactly what a hug should be. And he didn't want to let go.

CHAPTER THIRTEEN

"I LET HIM GO." GEN SHIVERED outside Rosie's front door at one a.m. in her pink and white striped silk pajamas. It was too hard to sleep when she couldn't stop reliving her day over and over in her head. Especially the part where she hugged Matt goodbye. She needed to tell Rosie so her sister could keep her accountable.

Rosie stood in the doorway wearing an oversized t-shirt and basketball shorts, rubbing her eyes. "What?" she mumbled.

Gen expected a little more drama from her. This was a big deal. "I let Matt go."

Rosie blinked then craned her neck to see around Gen as if she thought Matt had been here. "When?"

"When he flew me home from San Francisco."

Rosie yawned. "Are you going to start making sense, or do I need to go brew a pot of coffee?"

Gen had thought the only part that would matter to Rosie was the letting go part since she'd been the one to encourage it. But Gen might as well start from the beginning. "Matt got me a photography job for the Giants where I met Casey, and she's incredible. I probably love her as much as he does."

"Coffee it is."

If Rosie drank coffee, she'd be up all night. That hadn't been Gen's goal. She turned to leave. "You can go back to bed. I just wanted to tell someone what happened so I could sleep."

"Wait, Gen." Rosie's hand caught hers. "I know what you need. Let's go downstairs."

The yoga studio. Was she going to make Gen lay on a mat and do relaxation exercises, or worse, cuddle with a goat? "It's okay. I'll head to bed now. Sorry I woke you."

Keys rattled as Rosie grabbed them off a hook and followed her onto the balcony. How did Gen get out of goat cuddling now?

"You'll like it. I promise."

Gen sighed. She should have written in her dusty prayer journal and called it a night. Would God still want to hear what she had to say if she didn't want to hear what He had to say?

Yoga it was. Then maybe she could drift off to sleep like that one time in Rosie's class when she thought she was on a boat then woke up to find everyone staring at her because class was over.

Rosie's Wonder Woman slippers scuffed the steps as she trudged down to the first floor. She unlocked the entry then flicked a light switch to reveal silky looking scarfs hanging from the exposed ceiling beams. "Aerial yoga," she said. "I'm adding it to my class schedule."

Gen scratched her head. Maybe she *had* gone to sleep, and she was dreaming. If only Matt were there to pinch her again. She scrunched her eyes shut. No, she wasn't supposed to be thinking of Matt that way anymore. If nothing else, Rosie's crazy idea would be a distraction.

She walked over to one of the scarves and fingered it's strong, cool fibers. "So, what do I do? Hang upside down?"

"You could if you want to." Rosie clicked on her stereo to start worship music then lit candles and dimmed the old wall sconces. "Or you could do this." She turned her back to one of the scarf loops and reached up as if hoisting herself into a swing. Once sitting on the scarf, she spread the edges of the material to expand from head to toe like a hammock.

Okay, this was exactly what Gen needed. She followed suit and found herself surrounded by what felt like a cloud. She arched her back to get all the kinks out of her spine before sinking deeper into the swinging hammock.

"Did you say you got a photo job with the Giants?" Rosie's voice asked from beyond the purple cocoon.

Gen closed her eyes, letting the scarf rock her like a baby. "Yes. Did you know Damon tutored one of the players in college?"

"A-Plus. Their heavy hitter. How did you not know that?"

Gen shook her head at her own ignorance and at the irony of the heavy hitter getting nowhere when hitting on her. "Well, I took his picture today. It's going to be on the side of one of the buildings downtown. We should take Mom and Dad to see it when they come for

Damon's release."

"Wow, yeah." They rocked to the music for a moment. "How did you say you got this job again?"

Gen smiled as she shared the story of the way her station teamed up with Matt to surprise her. To think that had been less than twenty-four hours ago.

"And he brought you home, too?"

Gen played the scene like a movie trailer in her mind. "Yes. I hugged him goodbye." She'd fit into his arms so well. Unfortunately, she'd never be there again.

Her stomach churned in regret, so she laid a hand over it in hopes the pressure might be calming. Matt was only a man. He'd been fun to have a crush on. He'd been fun to daydream about. But there would be other men, and now she knew what to look for.

"Who initiated the hug?" Rosie sounded like she might as well have been shining a spotlight in Gen's face for interrogation. Did she think Gen had thrown herself at the man?

"He tried to hug me, and I wasn't going to let him, but then I realized it would be my only chance. So I hugged him goodbye."

Rosie didn't say anything. Gen opened her eyes to wait. The candlelight flickered, sending shadows dancing against the silk. The rafters creaked. The music soothed.

"What if he's falling for you?"

Gen's lungs filled like a balloon. This was the story she used to make up. This was the figment of her imagination she was letting go like a bubble bound to pop. She blew out her cheeks. "No, he did it all for Casey. Casey needed a photographer. He's in love with her. She's perfect."

They rocked a little longer. "What do you mean perfect?"

Gen wiggled her toes out in front of her. The glittery turquoise nail polish had already chipped halfway off. Casey would never have chipped nail polish. "She's sweet and intelligent and hard-working and beautiful and she makes life look easy."

"I'm sure being rich helps."

Gen dropped her head back farther. "We did ride around in a limo today."

"Oh, I'm wide awake now. You rode around San Francisco in a limo with A-Plus? I can't believe you didn't text me pictures."

Gen extended her arms overhead to stretch out even more. "I didn't quite believe it myself," she said. It still felt surreal. Like she needed to go download all the photos to her computer to actually convince herself it happened.

"Gen, giving up Matt should be about doing the right thing, not about waving a white flag in surrender because you don't think you can compete."

Gen's heart squeezed tight. She pulled her arms down to press hands against her belly again. "I'm not going to compete because I was never going to compete, but especially not now that I've met Casey. I wouldn't want to steal a boyfriend." Not that she could.

She waited for Rosie's response. Waited to find out if she'd given the right answer. With the way her silk had spun, Rosie was now behind her, and even though they couldn't see each other in the swings, she didn't want to have this conversation facing opposite directions. Gen tilted her head and shifted her weight to get the hammock to continue its rotation.

"I respect your decision since Matt is already in a relationship. But I don't want you to think Matt would choose her over you. You're beautiful too, Gen."

Tears blurred Gen's vision. She wiped them away and swallowed the lump in her throat to hold back any more. Rosie wouldn't be able to see them, but she would be able to hear them when Gen spoke.

Gen might be the same kind of beautiful as Rosie. But Matt would never see that. Most people didn't. She wiped at the tickle in her nose and forced her voice not to quiver. "I think I could be beautiful if I tried more. You know, wrinkle creams, hair defrizzer, a boob job."

"I didn't know you want a boob job."

"I don't." Gen's face heated. If she ever had a breast augmentation, she'd be so embarrassed that she'd never stop blushing. "I don't even want to use the hair defrizzer that's sitting in my bathroom because it takes too long in the mornings. There's so many other things I'd rather do with my life than defrizz my hair."

"Like eat cereal on the balcony and watch the sunrise?"

"Yes."

"That's what makes you beautiful."

Gen's chin wrinkled, but she kept from crying this time. "I do make the time to put on mascara though. Otherwise my eyes completely disappear since my eyelashes are red."

"Beautiful and *wise*," Rosie joked then sighed. "Just be like the mustard seed Jesus talks about in the Bible. Though it's tiny, it's not insignificant. It grows into a huge tree."

No wonder Rosie did so well as a motivational speaker. She could make an ugly duckling feel like a swan. Though Gen was more comfortable with the jokes about wisdom than parables from scripture. "You're the wise one. I've decided you're right about dating available men. I want what Matt and Casey have."

They rocked to the worship music long enough for Gen to wonder if her sister had fallen asleep. Then she heard a soft "in Jesus's name" and realized Rosie had been praying. Either that or she was ending their yoga session the way she ended all yoga sessions.

"I'm proud of you, Gen," Rosie said, still inside her hammock, so she must have been praying. "Simply because love hasn't worked out for any of us yet, doesn't mean you won't be the first."

Gen hadn't voiced her fear to Rosie. Were her thoughts that transparent? "How did you know I thought that?"

"Because of the way you always talk about generational curses."

"Not *always*." Gen may have mentioned it once or twice after they'd both planned to read their Bible from cover to cover. The curses theory made sense with the lives her siblings led despite being raised in a good home. Why did they struggle so much when others seemed to have it all? "Sometimes I talk about blessings. Do you think Casey's life is so easy because she's blessed?"

Rosie's voice grew clearer as the hammock spun in Gen's direction. "I think we're all blessed in different ways, but we often take our blessings for granted."

Gen pressed her lips together. Was this a direct message to her? She was blessed to have all ten fingers and toes. She was blessed to be born in America. She was blessed not to have a drug addiction like their other brother Craig. Yet here she was, comparing herself negatively to someone who had more than she did. She was focusing on what her curse might be rather than how she was blessed. Maybe that was the real curse.

"Also, I think people who seem to have it all on the outside also have what you would consider a curse." Rosie continued. "I mean, Casey Holloway's in the spotlight all the time. She may not feel like she has the choice not to use a defrizzer in the morning."

Gen rolled her eyes. "What a curse."

Rosie laughed.

Gen had to smile. And add on. "She's also cursed not to experience the joy of sleeping in the back of a minivan or doing goat yoga."

"Poor girl."

Rosie may be half-joking about Casey's curse, but she was right about Gen's blessings. Focusing on her blessings would keep her mind off the remorse over giving up Matt. She'd consider herself blessed simply to have him as a friend.

"Look what your friend sent me." Casey dropped next to Matt in the row of seats overlooking the Giants' baseball diamond and held up her smartphone to reveal the email app with attachments.

"Gen?" he prompted. His friend had a name. And she should be Casey's friend too. If the two of them were both friends with Gen, and they were both in contact with her, then he wouldn't feel that uncomfortable prick of guilt when texting photos of possible relatives—like the one guy downstairs who'd been wearing a NY Giants football jersey instead of one for the SF Giants.

That discomfort had been getting stronger since their hug, which was really ridiculous. It was a hug. Exactly like Casey had hugged Gen. Right?

"Yes, Gen. Don't you love her?" Casey's voice snapped him back to attention.

"Wh—what?"

Casey waved her phone in front of his face, displaying Gen's touched up photograph of Alan. "She's by far the best photographer we've ever hired. I'm so glad you told me about her."

"Oh." Matt huffed. "Yeah." Of course that's what Casey meant. What else could she possibly mean?

"I have to show Mom and Dad." Casey jumped up and trotted into the owner's suite behind them.

Matt turned his head to watch her go. She was still as gorgeous as ever. And he couldn't deny that dating her put him in an enviable position. But there were so many other things he'd rather be doing in that moment. Like laundry. If he got a couple of loads done, he could take off for the weekend to Maui. Except the Giants were in the World Series. And there was no way Casey would let him miss that.

Maybe that's what he and Casey needed. To get away from baseball and reconnect. Was he a bad boyfriend if he secretly hoped the Giants lost their game?

His phone vibrated in his pocket. Gen?

He refused the instinct to glance over his shoulder to see if Casey was watching when he pulled out the device. He had nothing to hide. He'd even share the text with her when she joined him again.

Sliding his thumb across the screen, Matt opened his messaging app. Gen and half the Eureka station smiled at him from her profile picture. He smiled back.

You think the guy is related to me because he's wearing a blue shirt instead of an orange shirt like everybody else?

Not only did the woman know nothing about baseball, but she knew nothing of sports in general. He smiled and shook his head, trying to formulate a way to explain.

I think the guy might be related to you because he knows as little about baseball as you do. He's wearing a football jersey.

I get it. Yes, that's something I would do. Are you at a game?

Of course she didn't know about the game. The game his girlfriend lived for.

Yes.

Say hi to Alan for me.

Matt looked out to the field where the team warmed up. Did Gen think he was down there in the dugout with them? Did she think A-Plus climbed into the stands to sit next to Matt between his turns at bat? She was kinda like the youngest Lake brother, Sam, who'd run out to first base to hug Matt when he'd got his first hit in the Babe Ruth baseball league. Except Gen hugged better. He should invite her to come join them in the suite sometime.

That discomfort Matt got from texting Gen made him shift in his seat in an attempt to shake it loose. Why was he uncomfortable about inviting her to a game? It would be the same as when he invited Sam. He'd invite Sam too.

There. Take that, overactive conscience syndrome.

Wait. He could do even better. He tapped the messaging icon that would let him respond.

Matt: Alan isn't with me, but Casey is. I'll say hi to her for you.

Almost instantly, the phone buzzed and a hand waving emoji popped up.

Gen: Hi, Casey!

See? There was no jealousy on Gen's end. Nothing between the two of them to worry about. So why was he worrying? And why did that itch underneath his ribs grow from her response? Was it because Casey wasn't really with him? He'd let her run off to do her own thing while he texted Gen.

Casey brushed his leg as she dropped back into her seat. "I guess Mom's not coming today. She's not feeling well, but Dad thinks the photos are gorgeous. I'm sure we'll be hiring Gen again in the future. And we'll probably need to get something scheduled with her right away, because after these photos go on display, she's going to be in high demand."

If they were going to hire Gen again in the future, would Matt get to be part of the shoot again? Would he fly her home? Would they hug?

There went his imagination. He needed to control it. He needed to show it who was boss.

He held up his phone. "You want me to tell Gen right now? I told her we're at the game, and she said to say hi."

Casey squealed. "Here." She reached for his phone. "I'll tell her how much everyone loves her work."

Okay... She had his phone...

"Cute profile pic," she said.

The one with all the men? Would that make Casey suspicious of Gen's character? Was she going to scroll back through their conversation? Was she going to see how much they'd been talking? Would she want him to delete Gen's number from his phone? Would he?

Yes. He would. Once the baseball season was over and he got his girlfriend back then he wouldn't have time to be attracted to another woman. Not that he was.

Gen's long red hair flashed through his mind. She was pretty. But if he was attracted to her, it wouldn't be because of model good looks or a voluptuous body. It would be her laugh. Her spunk. Her heart. She was so ludicrously likeable.

Which is why they made good friends. And that was all.

It wouldn't be that big a deal if he deleted her phone number.

Casey tapped her thumbs on the screen. She gasped. Here it came...

Matt cringed.

"Hank's here. I heard his voice." She handed Matt his phone as she twisted to look behind them.

Matt took the phone. He watched her jump from her seat for a second time. He listened for the deep male voice belonging to the former Giant and Hall of Famer. It rumbled from the suite, confirming Casey's reason for abandoning their conversation.

Good timing. Now Casey wouldn't be hurt, and Gen wouldn't have to be deleted. Yet for some reason, Matt was disappointed.

Yes, that was the unsettled feeling that had been eating at him since the photo shoot. Disappointment. But if he was disappointed with anyone, it should be himself. He had everything a guy could ask for, and he wasn't satisfied.

Matt sighed. Maybe he needed to quit texting Gen. Sure, it was just texting, but he really enjoyed their texting. More so than dating Casey at the moment. And Casey deserved better than that.

He rubbed his face and looked down at the screen. What would he say?

The response Casey had written displayed next to an icon of his picture, and he realized on Gen's end it would read as if he'd written the text. Maybe Casey's words had come across as formal enough to start to put professional distance between them.

We want to hire you again for photography. You're so brilliant, I could kiss you.

Matt's eyes bugged. His skin grew numb. His breathing stopped.

Did Casey understand how her words would be taken? How *would* they be taken? All Matt knew was that the message was labeled "read," and Gen had yet to respond.

CHAPTER FOURTEEN

MATT KEPT HIS EYES ON THE ramp agent holding the orange light wands overhead as he taxied toward the gate. He wanted to check and see if Gen was watching through the windows on the jet bridge, but he needed to be ready to brake the moment the orange wands crossed.

He usually didn't land in Eureka late enough for the wands to be lit up, but the flight had taken a four-hour delay for mechanical work in Portland when Ethan's headset quit transmitting. That meant Gen would be dealing with upset passengers, and Matt would need to make their turn as quick as possible to keep from timing out. Of course, if he reached the daily time limit, he'd take an extension to keep Ethan and Michelle from having the opportunity to hook up in Eureka.

"Tyler's running the jet bridge." Ethan must have checked for him.

Matt grunted in response and pulled to a stop. He had told Ethan about the crazy text Casey sent and how this was the first time he was going to see Gen since that day. At the time of the text, Matt had immediately explained the misunderstanding. Gen had responded, "LOL." And then they'd never mentioned it again. But the ideas she must have imagined when first reading Casey's text hovered in the back of Matt's mind like an invisible fence, waiting to zap him if he got too close to crossing boundaries.

"Probably good we're in a rush, huh?" Ethan asked. "Then there won't be time for any awkward interaction with Gen."

"Yep," Matt said. Listening to Ethan talk about Gen was awkward enough. He'd meant to make the story sound offhand, as if it didn't affect him at all. But here he was, tensely awaiting his chance to head up the jet bridge and offer her a coffee to make up for this misunderstanding the same way he had the time he'd forgotten her name.

Matt slid his eyes sideways to watch the jet bridge roll toward them and confirm Ethan had been telling the truth. Sure enough, Tyler worked the joystick like he was in a live version of Pac Man. Did Gen send him to open the door so she could avoid Matt? She'd been her distant, efficient self over the in-range call, which also meant she knew he was the captain.

Michelle opened the cabin door and peeked in, or more accurately, peeked at Ethan. "Long day, huh guys?"

"I'm going to go get a coffee." Matt stood. "You two want anything?"

Ethan removed his headset then lifted his eyes in that direct way of his. "I'll get the coffee if you want to avoid a certain redhead."

The offer came out more sardonic than authentic. Especially since Ethan always stayed in the cockpit with Michelle.

Matt flicked his gaze toward the flight attendant. She didn't know what was going on, and he would have preferred to keep it that way. Though with as much as Ethan and Michelle talked, she probably would find out anyway.

"That's okay. I need to stretch my legs."

Michelle backed out of his way, and he nodded a thank you.

Passengers moved to the side for him as well, since Matt could walk faster without luggage. Usually they thanked him for flying when he passed, but today they were too frazzled from the delay and not thankful at all.

Gen's eyes caught his the moment he strode out of the jet bridge. With a giant sigh, her shoulders released, and her head sagged to one side. "I can't tell you how happy I am that you're our pilot today. If it was Ray again, I know he would have chosen to time out, and I'd be stuck here until midnight waiting for San Francisco to gather a new crew and fly up a rescue plane."

Matt couldn't help grinning down at her. She looked as frazzled as the passengers with strands of her long hair sticking haphazardly out of her braid, but despite her weariness, she focused on the positive side and made him feel like a hero in that dramatic way of hers.

Bianca snapped her fingers. Matt peeked at her out of the corner of his eye. If Gen had told the gate agent about his text, Bianca might give him a piece of her mind. She was actually the dramatic one. Gen was more the joyful one.

"Nuh-uh." Bianca shook her head. "I would have made Ray take the extension. I've got a salon appointment scheduled for tomorrow morning, and I am not going to miss it so he could get his beauty sleep. I'm already missing my Grandma's birthday party tonight."

Gen dropped her hands to the podium and leaned forward. "You're missing Nana's party? Why didn't you say so? We could have gotten someone else to fill in for you."

Bianca narrowed one eye until she looked a little crazy. "Are you kidding? I ain't no wussy pilot. I finish all the jobs I start."

Matt had to hold up a palm to that one. "Whoa there."

Bianca planted one hand on her hip and looked off into the distance. "No offense, Matt."

Matt eyed Gen to see how he should respond to that. Gen pressed her lips together in warning, even as her eyes shined with laughter. Apparently, the two women handled stress very differently. He'd err on the side of laughing at their problems along with Gen.

"Well, this wussy pilot was going to offer you girls some coffee since you've had a long day, but Bianca, I'm not sure I want you getting any more amped up."

Bianca's head swiveled back his way. "Venti Cocomo Breve please. Double shot if you're thinking of timing out."

Matt splayed his hands wide, though Bianca was already strutting down the jet bridge. He called after her. "Get the plane loaded so we're ready to go in half an hour, and I won't time out."

Bianca completely ignored him, and Gen gazed at her computer screen, but he knew her smile was for him.

"I'm guessing you'll want a triple shot to deal with her."

"Always think you have to buy me coffee to make up for your mistakes, huh?" She did her little trademark peek move, and the jitters hit Matt like he'd already consumed a triple shot.

He rubbed a hand over his jaw to stall. Because if she was referring to Casey's text then they were going to discuss kissing. And he hadn't prepared himself for that. "Are you talking about the flight delay?"

She clicked the mouse on her screen a couple of times then

smirked. "Nope."

Was it getting hot in there? Hot like the fire he'd jokingly accused her of running from when she'd crashed into him in the jet bridge. The first time he'd held her. How had he forgotten about that? He might have to get himself an iced coffee.

"Oh." He frowned then feigned enlightenment. "You mean Casey's text on my phone."

She tapped a couple of keys before looking up triumphantly. "Yep."

What had he been thinking when he'd assumed his attraction to her had to do with her personality alone? Not only was she the sweetest woman he'd ever met, but her sweetness made her skin glow, her eyes shine, and her lips curve. She was beautiful.

Like Casey.

Wow. Casey. His girlfriend. The woman who'd caused this problem in the first place. He had to be the one to fix it. Which meant pacifying Gen then taking off like a jet from an aircraft carrier.

"Just like this flight delay, Casey's text was not my fault either," he pointed out. "I've got nothing to make up for. I'm simply a nice guy."

Was he? Because her gaze was pulling him in like a tractor beam. He hadn't wanted this moment to be awkward between them, but he hadn't wanted it to be the opposite of awkward either. He hadn't wanted their connection to be so natural that it made what he had with Casey feel fake and lifeless. Because it wasn't. It was him.

Gen's smile flashed. All innocence. Like she had no clue how true Casey's text had become. "Well, Mr. Nice Guy, I appreciate the offer, but I'm going to pass. If I drink coffee, I'll be up all night."

He was going to be up all night anyway. Even more so than after the night she'd hugged him. "All right."

Bianca emerged from the tunnel. "Offloading complete." She scowled at Matt. "You better hurry up if you're going to keep from timing out."

Right. He glanced at Gen who'd turned to read her boarding announcements over the intercom like it was a normal day. He'd play along by leaving to order coffee, but while waiting for said order, he couldn't resist watching her scan tickets. Did she feel anything for him or not? Was he imagining things? Or was this real?

He needed more time to figure it out. Figure out what he wanted.

Ethan's crewcut blocked his view. "We've got a problem, Captain."

Another one? Matt narrowed his eyes to focus on his co-pilot. "What's that?"

Ethan crossed his arms like he was hiding something. "My headset quit working again."

Matt's suspicions grew. Could the guy be disabling his own equipment to keep them grounded. He'd play it off. "Get a mechanic."

Yeah, they'd take another delay, but he wouldn't time out. He'd wait it out. Maybe this was the time he needed with Gen to figure out what was going on in his heart.

His eyes wandered to watch her work again. Should he stop the boarding process or let the passengers get on the plane so he and Gen could hang out in the jet bridge again, eating cookies? At least if the passengers boarded, then they'd be venting their frustrations to the flight attendants and not the station manager. She wouldn't have anything distracting her from him while they waited for a mechanic to do his job.

"I think we should time out," Ethan advised.

"Of course you do." The words slipped out before Matt could stop them.

Ethan tilted his head, eyes dark with warning. "What does that mean?"

Could Matt backtrack? Sidetrack? Make a run for it? He accepted his steaming paper cup from the barista and sipped in hopes it would give Ethan time to cool off. Instead, he burnt his tongue. Hey, if that would keep him from running his mouth...

Ethan glowered in the way only a guilty man could. "Why do you think I want to time out, Matt?"

Matt lowered his cup and looked up. He'd confront the issue if it was going to get them home that night and keep Gen from needless hassle. "So you can spend the night with Michelle."

Ethan shrugged as if adultery was something you could shrug off.

"It's not like you're any better, Matt."

Ethan's words punched him in the gut. Matt's stomach cramped. His world spun. He wanted to argue that he would never have an affair, but he certainly had feelings for a woman who was not his girlfriend. Sure, they'd snuck up on him, but they were there. Not that he was going to act on them. "I wouldn't—"

"You want to." Ethan stared him down.

Ethan went to his church. He could easily pull out scriptures about committing adultery in his heart. Though Ethan had no room to talk, Jesus did. As did Matt's father. Matt had been there when Dad gave Dave marital advice at their family reunion. *Don't say you won't ever have an affair. Say you won't even have coffee alone with a woman. If you don't ever cross that line, then you won't ever have an affair.*

Matt looked down at the paper cup. He wanted more than coffee.

"My marriage died a long time ago." Ethan relaxed his posture and rubbed the back of his neck. "Stephanie spends all her time with the kids and doesn't even care when I'm gone. I've tried, and I've been rejected."

Matt had no idea it was that bad. Though how hard had the man really tried? And was this reality or an excuse?

Ethan shook his head and focused on Matt. "How are *you* ever going to stay true to an imperfect spouse when you've got this perfect girlfriend, and you can't even stay true to her?"

"That's not fair." Ethan was comparing his own infidelity to Matt's uncertainty. Matt didn't know what he was going to do, while Ethan blatantly planned to sin. But the facts didn't block Ethan's accusation from hitting his target. The fact was that Matt was dating one woman while he couldn't stop thinking about another.

"Really?" Ethan mocked. "What's fair? Watching you take the extension so you can flirt and laugh with the station manager while your girlfriend sits at home alone?"

Casey wouldn't be home. She'd be in her happy place, preparing for the next game in the World Series.

Ethan shook his head. "It's not fair to Casey, and it's not fair to Gen."

Gen. Matt checked on her again. She had one arm around Bianca, as both women swayed and sang the jet plane song. Gen rarely allowed Bianca to play it, but they thought they had reason to celebrate the end of their shift. They didn't know about the headset. If Matt refused to take an extension, she'd be stuck here for hours. That wouldn't be fair to her either.

Ethan was only manipulating the situation to get his way.

"No, Ethan. I'm not timing out." He left Bianca's coffee behind and slammed his own in the trash with a thunk. He was hot enough without the beverage.

Gen grinned when she spotted him. She lifted an arm for him to link onto her and join their kick line. He wouldn't. He couldn't.

He'd tell her about the delay then hide out until they got clearance to fly. Because if he spent the evening with her, not only would Ethan be watching, but it would give Matt the opportunity to cross a boundary that shouldn't be crossed. And more than anything, more than he wanted to pull Gen into the privacy of the jet bridge and nuzzle his nose in her soft hair and run his hands up and down her spine, he wanted to do the right thing.

Gen giggled along with Bianca. She didn't normally allow the gate agent to play boarding music, but after dealing with angry passengers for four hours, she was ready to kick up her heels. And Matt had just enough time to finish the song with them before he took off. Except he looked more ready to shoot someone than dance. Hopefully TSA hadn't spotted him because they might very well tackle him to the ground, and then he couldn't finish flying his route.

"What's wrong?" she teased. "Is Ramone's out of coffee? I wouldn't be surprised with as much as the passengers have been drinking all day."

Matt didn't crack a smile. Not even one corner of his lips.

She stopped swaying and untangled her arm from Bianca. This was serious. "What?" She held her breath. Hadn't they had enough bad news for one day?

Matt shook his head, and his gaze bounced around before meeting hers again. Still no trademark twinkle. He'd been laughing when he'd left her, and she'd been feeling pretty good for how nonchalantly she'd handled the whole kiss misunderstanding.

She hadn't been so nonchalant at the time of the text. She'd panicked, not knowing whether Matt really wanted to kiss her or if it was a figure of speech. She'd nearly hyperventilated in her attempt to tell Rosie what was going on. Rosie, being Rosie, had offered to cool her down by driving them to Mt. Shasta for some "snoga," which was basically yoga in the snow. Thankfully Matt had explained before they'd gotten that far.

It was good to find out Casey wrote the text. Good because if Matt's girlfriend had any questions about his relationship with Gen, she never would have written such a thing. Which meant the message showed there was absolutely nothing romantic on Matt's end at all. And Gen could go back to telling herself she'd given up on her daydreams of him.

Matt looked past her. "The headset isn't working again."

Oh. She exhaled. With the way he was acting, she'd thought someone had died. A broken headset might mean another delay, but Matt could take an extension, and the plane would get off the ground eventually. The passengers were boarded, so they were out of her hair for the moment.

"Did you let Operations know? Have they called a mechanic?"

He ran fingers through his clean-cut hairstyle, giving it an adorable lopsided messy look. "Ethan took care of calling Ops. He thinks we should time out."

Gen rolled her eyes. Ethan was as bad as Ray, though she was pretty sure his desire to time out had something to do with a certain flight attendant.

Bianca leaned between them. "Did you say time out?"

Oh boy. Gen needed to give Bianca something to do before she worked herself into a tizzy. The gate agent had nothing to worry about, and her theatrics would only upset Matt further.

"Hey." Gen moved around Bianca to stand next to Matt. "I'll get this figured out. You go see if the flight attendants need anything from us."

Bianca threw her arms in the air but dutifully headed off down the jet bridge. "And he didn't even bring my coffee."

Gen pinched her earlobe before turning to face Matt again. If she was getting a tension headache from dealing with upset people, he was likely feeling the same. His eyes met hers, but they smoldered with more frustration than she would have expected. Was there something else going on? His jaw remained rigid, so it wasn't like he was going to open up about anything without her asking.

"What is it?" she asked.

He simply looked at her, eyes narrow either to study her deeper or to shield his own expression from being read. Her heart grew heavy like a stone dropped in a pond. Something else had happened.

Movement behind him caught her eye. Ethan leaving the coffee shop. Had Ethan said something? Done something? This could have to do with Ethan's desire to spend the night in Eureka. Maybe Matt also had suspicions of infidelity with his co-pilot. Maybe they'd been confirmed.

She leaned in closer and lowered her voice so the other man couldn't overhear. "Is it Ethan?"

Matt's jaw shifted though he didn't open his mouth to respond. He must not want to say anything. If she was right, his words had the potential to end a marriage, and the weight of being in such a position had to be burning him up inside. She could even feel the heat of it radiating from his skin. His chest rose and lowered. His head tilted, and his eyes pleaded as if begging her to understand why he couldn't talk.

She understood. She gave a small nod and laid a hand on his forearms crossed between them. "I'm here for you."

He groaned and dropped his arms to his sides. Poor guy.

Ethan's heels clicked past them. He lifted his coffee in a kind of salute. "Looks like you two have the airport to yourselves. I'll be awaiting your orders on the plane, Cap."

Gen watched Ethan go. How could the man be so glib on the verge of a situation that would likely lead to divorce? Her stomach churned. She closed her eyes in a desperate prayer, though she had trouble believing God would answer desperate prayers if He was willing to punish people for mistakes their parents had made. She peered back at Matt.

He stood rigid, his gaze as penetrating as a laser. Was he looking to her for answers? It would help if she knew the question.

"What do you need?" she asked.

He blew out a breath and lifted his eyes toward the heavens. God was probably more likely to answer his prayers anyway.

His gaze returned, and its warmth seeped into her. She'd give him anything he asked for.

"I'm overwhelmed. I need to go." His voice had turned gravelly.

Go? As in timeout? She'd give him anything except that. Naturally, he'd be tempted to call it a night and head for a hotel, but he wouldn't really do that to her. He wasn't Ray. "I know it's been a long day. I'm sure the mechanic will get this taken care of shortly then you can fly home. I'll hang out with you until then."

He lifted both hands to run them down his face. "I can't do this."

Warning bells rang in her head. His decision wasn't about her, but it would feel really personal if he took off to go to bed while leaving her here to offload 150 irate passengers and wait with them for another plane. She wouldn't go that route. She'd appeal to his sense of right and wrong—the battle he was obviously fighting within himself at that very moment.

"If you don't want to fly home with Ethan, I understand." She'd probably feel the same way in his shoes. "But if you time out, you'll be giving Ethan exactly what *he* wants."

Matt grimaced. Shook his head. "I know."

Gah. Okay. It was true. She wouldn't put that burden on his shoulders. Ethan was responsible for his own actions. But as captain, Matt was responsible for every passenger currently sitting on his plane.

Ray had been a selfish jerk who'd walked away whistling when he stranded passengers in the airport, but Matt wasn't like that. He had heart.

"You know what? Forget Ethan. Think about everybody else. Think about the frantic mom running out of formula for her baby. The hurting family trying to attend a funeral in the morning. The hopeful college grad trying to make it to a job interview with Google. He's a bright kid, by the way." The kid had fixed her computer settings when he'd seen her struggling with the print button. "I bet if you got him in the cockpit, he could fix your stupid headset."

Matt gave her a sad smile. Why sad? That had been a funny suggestion. Maybe even brilliant.

He held out a hand then let it drop to his side. "How can I fly them safely anywhere, if I'm too distracted?"

Was he seriously that distracted? He had a job to do, and he got paid pretty well to do it. She wanted to grip his shoulders and shake the nonsense out of him. But then TSA might tackle *her*.

She needed another way to get through to him. Yes, finding out your coworker was about to throw his life away was unnerving, but Matt could rise above that. Unclenching her fists she lifted her hands to his shoulders and leaned in, giving him no choice but to look directly at her. She widened her eyes to let him see how much this meant to her. How much she believed in him.

"Focus," she whispered.

His eyes darkened from the color of calm waters to the shade of a stormy sea. "Gen," he warned. Like he was a lifeguard.

But she was the one trying to save him here. All of them. There was no need for anyone to abandon ship. Couldn't he see that?

As for being able to see, she'd never looked at him so up close before. She noticed the creases in the skin at the corner of his eyes. The stubble on his jaw. The champagne pink color of his lips. If she weren't so serious about doing her job, she might wonder if tasting them would be as intoxicating as sipping champagne.

His hands flicked her wrists away like she'd learned to do to an attacker in self-defense. That couldn't be good. "I have to go. I'm timing out."

CHAPTER FIFTEEN

MATT SAT IN HIS RENTAL CAR the next morning, staring at Gen's house. She'd said she lived in a pink Victorian house, and this was the only one the locals knew of. The place was charming, quirky, and endearing, which fit her well enough to make his stomach warm just looking at it. But he'd only come to apologize.

She probably hated him now. She'd think of him like Ray. Which would be a good thing. Then he could go to work with her and not worry that she might grip his arms again and stare at him and whisper like he was the only person in her world who mattered.

His heart skipped a beat at the memory. Though she probably had no idea what kind of effect she'd had on him. Again, a good thing. Because he was committed to Casey. Which was why he'd had to leave the night before.

He couldn't have spent the delay with Gen without thinking things he shouldn't have been thinking. And he couldn't explain to her what he was struggling with because then she might start thinking those things too. And even if he could have found a way to both keep quiet and keep his distance, Ethan still would have known. And been watching. If Matt was going to be any kind of witness to Ethan, he had to start by being an example.

Though Matt wasn't sure he'd done the right thing. He'd cost his company some big bucks for having to make the extra flight. Not to mention all the passengers who would badmouth their airline on social media and refuse to fly with them again. His boss had already scheduled a meeting to debrief. And Casey was horrified he wouldn't be at what could be the final World Series game with her that day. Though if she knew why he was still in Eureka, then she'd be even more horrified.

The right thing would have been for Matt to be a better man. For him to have never gotten into such a position in the first place. But looking back, his motives had been pure. Yeah, he'd texted Gen, but he'd never thought it would lead here. He'd been thrilled to get her the photography job with the Giants, but that had been a way to help both her and Casey. And though he'd initially tried to initiate a platonic hug, he'd backed off at her hesitation. She'd been the one to throw herself into his arms.

After a night of prayer and wrestling with God, Matt finally came to the conclusion that were he not in a relationship, he'd pursue a deeper friendship with Gen. But as he was, he needed to focus on Casey, and what he wanted with her or didn't want with her. Until he decided where they were headed, he'd put some space between him and Gen.

But he still needed to apologize.

Gen stared at her ceiling. She didn't have the energy to get out of bed yet. She'd simply soak in the peacefulness of the golden sunshine reflecting off her hardwood floors and the gentle coo of doves outside her bedroom window. She rolled over to feel the cool caress of silk pajamas against her skin. After the night she'd had, she deserved this.

Deep down she knew her lack of energy didn't come from not getting enough sleep. It came from Matt's abandonment. Thoughts about the way he'd left the night before echoed against the walls of her internal emptiness.

She'd been a fool to believe he might care. And she'd been even more foolish to think she'd released him from her heart. She might have given up romantic daydreams, but she'd hoped to keep him as a friend. Apparently, he didn't feel even that for her.

She wanted to be angry. She wanted to compare him to Ray. To ignore him the next time she saw him as if they'd never texted or flown together or hugged. But that wasn't the truth. The truth was that they'd done all those things, and it had meant a lot more to her than to him. The truth was she'd been abandoned. Again. Only this time, there was nobody to adopt her and try to convince her she was still lovable.

A knock pounded on the door.

Gen sighed. She'd agreed to go hiking in Fern Canyon with Rosie. The good thing about Rosie was that she let Gen vent. The bad thing about Rosie was that she gave unwanted advice. And she was usually right.

Flipping the old quilt off her legs, Gen rolled up to a sitting position. There were no flights to San Francisco that day, so she didn't have an excuse to get out of hiking. She'd probably feel better from a little physical activity anyway. After pushing her achy limbs to stand, she reached overhead to stretch them out.

The knock pounded again.

"Coming," she called with a groan. Why was Rosie being so impatient? Usually if Gen didn't answer immediately, her sister would go back to her own apartment and make herself comfortable until Gen was ready to join her.

She braced her lower back with her hands like a pregnant woman and trudged forward. Her feet still hurt from last night. She was not cut out for fourteen-hour shifts.

Her stomach rumbled. Maybe Rosie would be up for stopping at Los Bagels. She needed a Chorizo and Guac Scrambagel to get her going. She needed to pamper herself.

Gen reached for the brass doorknob while rolling her head back to get the kinks out of her neck. The door squeaked on its hinges. Let the venting begin. "You do not even know what I went through last night."

"I'm sorry." The male voice shook her like an earthquake. It couldn't be.

Gen snapped her head up. She gripped the doorknob tighter. Matt stood in front of her, looking manly in jeans and a plaid flannel.

Had he really come over to her house to apologize? Did that mean he cared?

He glanced down at her outfit, and his eyes widened. "I didn't mean to wake you."

She looked down. Of all the days to wear the kissy lip pajama set Rosie had given her on Valentine's Day. Should Gen slam the door in his face or invite him in while she disappeared into her room to change? She needed to hear what he had to say first in order to make an informed decision.

She blew out her breath before raising her chin to confront him directly. "I was up pretty late last night."

He pressed his lips together as if he had no excuse, though the shadows in his eyes spoke of humility. "Do you hate me?"

How could she hate him? She couldn't even be angry at him. She was simply hurt. Though to tell him the depth of injury would reveal the strength of her attachment. She needed to get back to their easy banter. "Yes," she stated firmly.

His head twitched to one side like she'd slapped him in the face. He blinked. Nodded as if he deserved such a blow. "All right." He looked away. Ran a hand over his head. "I don't want to bother you anymore. I just wanted to apologize because —"

"No, I don't hate you. Come in." She pulled the door wide and stepped to the side.

He may not care about her the way she cared about him, but he was a good man. She'd salvage what she could of their friendship even if that only meant they were coworkers who didn't hate each other. He probably didn't have that kind of relationship with Ethan anymore.

His eyes zeroed back in on hers, reflecting both gratefulness and hesitation. "I wouldn't blame you for hating me."

He was beating himself up so much that she almost felt sorry for him. She gave a playful smirk in hopes of taking them back to the day he'd first called her Carrots. "You know, red hair doesn't mean a person has to have a temper."

The corner of his lips did not curve up, though a small glimmer lit his eyes with humor. "If it did, then Bianca would be a redhead."

Yeah, he was going to get it from Bianca. Gen would give him a little more grace. "I hate what you did, Matt, but I'm sure you had your reasons."

His glimmer dimmed. "I did." He looked over his shoulder. "I should go and let you get back to your day."

"Right. What are you going to do? You're stuck in Eureka." She narrowed her eyes, knowingly. "Come in. I'll go get dressed."

Matt dropped his gaze to her hardwood floors before entering obediently. Gradually his scrutiny rose to her ugly couch, antique desk, and framed photos decorating the walls.

Goodness. She hadn't thought about how he would see her home. What story would it tell? Frantically she searched the room to see if there was anything she needed to hide before he saw it.

The living room was bright with color. And it was relatively tidy except for a couple of cereal bowls sitting out from both yesterday's breakfast and dinner. Everything was old except her computer and her photos. Would he look at her photos? Her breath caught at what they might reveal.

A door creaked. Footsteps slapped against wooden planks.

"Hey, Gen. What time did you get home last night? It was pretty late when I went to bed, and..." Rosie's voice faded off as she appeared in the doorway. Her lips parted. She scratched her cheek and stared.

If Gen was worried about what Matt might be thinking of her, it couldn't even compare to what Rosie was probably thinking. Gen had come home late, Matt was in her living room, and she was in her pajamas. They'd laugh about it later. For now, she had to iron out the awkwardness.

"Matt!" Okay, yelling his name probably wasn't the best way to ease tension here. "Meet my sister Rosie."

Matt pivoted. His gaze flicked to Rosie then back. His eyes took in Gen's pajamas once again and enlarged with new awareness.

"Matt?" Rosie pointed at Matt, though her question and her regard remained focused on Gen.

Gen's mouth opened to explain. It froze in that position when no words formed in her brain. Because how did she stop Rosie from saying anything revealing without revealing something herself?

Matt stepped forward. Reached to shake Rosie's outstretched hand. "Nice to meet you, Rosie."

He did a double take at Rosie's missing fingers, but that was the least embarrassing part of the whole thing. Rosie knew how to handle such reactions. Maybe it could put them in familiar territory again.

Rosie accepted the handshake. "I'm really not trying to flip you off," she said. "Not yet anyway."

Oh boy. Gen stepped forward before Matt had time to process her sister's words and take offense. She inhaled to pour the story out in one breath. "I got home late last night because Matt's flight was delayed, and he timed out, so we had to have a whole new crew called into SFO to fly a different plane up here and rescue the passengers. We had to use another gate which required stairs rather than a jet bridge. The stairs weren't high enough for the Airbus, and they were broken so they wouldn't adjust. We had to call out another mechanic…" That got Matt's attention though Rosie's eyes glazed over. Back to the part her sister cared about. "Matt was stranded at a Eureka hotel last night, and he just came over to apologize for his part in the delay."

Rosie thawed. "You *just* came over?" she repeated to confirm Gen's story with a second source.

"Uh…yeah." Matt waved off Rosie's concerns, his concentration directed toward Gen. "You had to call out the mechanic again? How long did that take?"

Gen shifted under the weight of Matt's gaze. She'd been trying to defuse the situation, but here he was, more intense than ever. She fiddled with the hem of her nightshirt. "Half an hour for him to get to the airport. Another hour or so for him to fix the stairs."

"Oh, man." Matt stepped backwards to drop onto her couch. Surrounded by frilly cushions and a tasseled throw, his masculinity stood out more than ever. Gen wished she could grab her camera and snap photos without him noticing. "If I'd known it was going to cause this much trouble, I would have taken the extension."

"Oh…" Rosie crossed her arms. "So why didn't you take the extension?"

Gen shrugged. She could explain the whole Ethan thing to Rosie later. As for Matt, there was no sense in him making a big deal out of it now. "You couldn't possibly know that was going to happen, Matt."

Matt groaned and leaned his head back. "I'm so stupid."

Rosie glanced Gen's way, her face softening in compassion. Here came her motivational speaker persona. She strode to the sofa and took a seat next to him. "Matt, you made a mistake. Admitting that doesn't make you stupid. It makes you smarter than you once were."

Gen edged toward the hallway. Rosie's spiel would give her enough time to change into something decent. "I'm gonna go get dressed, guys."

Neither seemed to hear her. She stared for a moment at the scene in front of her—another scenario she never would have imagined. This one bittersweet. Sweet because her sister was sharing her heart with the man of Gen's dreams in her living room. Bitter because if she'd imagined this situation ever happening, it would be with the expectation that she could also share her heart with him. But she couldn't.

Matt stayed on the couch when Rosie went to pack a picnic lunch for them. Yes, them. She'd convinced him to go on a hike in the Redwood Forest. She claimed with all the times he'd flown to Eureka, he should have visited the Redwoods by now. She argued that if he was stressed, which she could somehow tell, he needed to get away from the noise and be closer to God. Then she clinched it by reminding him how George Lucas filmed the speeder bike scene from *Return of the Jedi* in the Redwoods. As a kid, he'd dreamed of flying on a speeder bike.

If Gen had been the one to invite him, he would have said no, but with Rosie there, it seemed safe. Like pushing a reset button on their friendship.

How would Gen feel about it? She didn't hate him, but that didn't mean she wanted him tagging along. He hadn't exactly started their day off smoothly by showing up when she was in her pajamas.

He caught himself smiling and forced the corners of his mouth into a frown. He was supposed to be creating distance between them yet here he was sitting on her ugly old couch. It was probably even older than her minivan. She was a unique one. He shouldn't even try to figure her out.

His eyes scanned the room of their own accord. There wasn't much to look at apart from the walls covered with photographs of people from all different cultures. Chinese. Alaskan Eskimos. An African safari.

One photo in particular caught his eye. He stood and crossed to the frame sitting on her desk. Gen smiling next to a black man with his arm wrapped around her.

Is this why her sister freaked out when she found Matt in her apartment? Was this why Gen felt so comfortable with Alan? Could it be why she didn't seem fazed at all last night when standing so close and whispering to him? She was taken?

Disappointment warred with relief. Part of him wanted it to be true so he could let his guard down. The other part of him wanted Gen available in case he decided to break up with Casey. It was a selfish desire. One he had to get rid of. Because it made his guts churn.

"Is this your boyfriend?" he called.

Bare feet padded against the floor. Gen's head popped around the corner. She had half her hair in a braid. The other half hung loosely with a few strands trying to veil her confused expression. "Who?"

He held up the frame. If she was confused, then who was this guy?

Her lips spread in a grin. "Remember when Alan asked me if I had a man in my life?"

How could he forget? He narrowed his eyes. "You told him you had a brother."

"Yeah." She nodded.

He stared, still not comprehending. This guy was a different race. How could he be her brother? Unless she was… Oh yeah. She was adopted. "Ahh. The doctor."

She disappeared again.

He set the photo down but continued to ponder. He was close with his siblings, but he didn't live in the same apartment complex as any of them. He didn't have their photos on his desk. "Are you this close with your whole family?"

If so, it made sense why she wouldn't need to track her birth parents down. She had something even better.

She rounded the corner, both braids complete and carrying hiking shoes. "No. I don't see my other three siblings nearly as much as Rosie and Damon." Either she purposely avoided eye contact as she spoke or she was extraordinarily intent on sitting down and lacing her boots.

Should it be the former, he'd respect her sensitivities and talk about Rosie instead. "Can I ask what happened to Rosie's hands?"

"Sure." She grinned then sat up fast enough to flip her braids behind her back. "But you'll have to ask Rosie since it's her story to tell."

He'd never do that. He wasn't that insensitive.

"It won't bother her. She makes a living off telling that story."

Yeah, no.

Rosie knocked this time. Not only was she carrying a backpack full of food, but she'd also donned a Giants' baseball cap over her ponytail. Did she know about his connection to Casey, and this was in his honor, or had she recognized his attraction to Gen the way Ethan had, and she wore the hat as a reminder of who he should be thinking about while on their hike?

"Nice hat."

She winked underneath the brim. He didn't know what that meant, but she'd been the one to invite him to join them, so he'd take it as a good sign.

He offered to drive, but Rosie felt her Jeep could handle the winding forest roads better than his rented Hyundai. He also offered to sit in the back, but Gen wouldn't allow it, saying he needed more leg room. He felt like a schmuck at first, but the seat actually allowed for great views of their surroundings and the perfect position for hearing all the stories both women told.

If he'd thought their pink Victorian to be quaint, it was nothing compared to the Old Town area they drove through with its colorful rows of storefronts across from the bay. There was even a gazebo surrounded by a bubbling fountain and brick walkway, not to mention the horse-drawn buggy. It was like a step back in time.

Once they drove up the unpaved park road into the forest, he felt like he'd taken a giant *leap* back in time. With the massive trees overhead and the way moss and ferns grew up canyon walls, the place was positively prehistoric. He certainly wasn't in The City anymore.

On their hike to Fern Canyon, they had to take off their shoes to wade through a few creeks and use fallen logs as balance beams. The air was a lot chillier where hidden from the sun, but the peaceful ambiance of trickling water and sweet smell of greenery made it one of the most gorgeous places on earth.

"I can't believe I've never been here before." He'd certainly have to bring his brothers next time they visited. And Casey might like it. He wasn't sure. She was kind of a city girl. So he'd stop thinking about bringing other people up and simply enjoy it with Rosie and Gen.

They'd reached the end of the trail, but Gen circled them from a distance, her camera aimed their way. Matt didn't know whether to smile or give Rosie bunny ears. She certainly couldn't give him bunny ears with her missing fingers.

Gen lowered her camera and waved away their attention. "Pretend I'm not here."

Right. If it was that easy, he wouldn't have had to flee the airport the night before.

Rosie explored beside him like she was used to living under a spotlight. She ran her hand along a wall of ferns then leaned back to look up at the tops of the giant trees. "This place gives me hope," she said.

Hope? Matt could use a dose of hope. Hope that he didn't make any decisions that would veer him off the course he'd set for himself. He peeked at Gen who was so busy scrolling through the photos she'd taken that she didn't even seem aware of his existence, and he found himself hoping something else. "How so?"

Rosie lowered herself to a damp log and patted the spot next to her. If he took it, he'd have a front row seat to watch Gen work. It would likely be the only time he ever got this chance. He sighed and took a seat.

"Gen invited me to move down here when I was in a very dark place," Rosie began. "I'd just found my birth family, and long story short, they didn't want anything to do with me."

Matt's attention shifted from Gen to the woman beside him. He couldn't imagine being in her shoes. Yeah, his brothers gave him a bad time about everything, but it was always out of affection. His Mom was a little bossy, but that was out of her desire to protect him. As for Dad, he didn't always talk a lot, but when he did, Matt knew to listen. What would life have been like if he hadn't had that? If he'd wanted it, and they'd refused him.

Did Rosie's rejection have to do with her missing fingers? Such a rejection said more about them than it did about Rosie, though it would still be sure to hurt. Worse than losing a finger.

"I'm sorry."

Rosie shrugged off his apology. "I was too, but then I got down here. I fell in love with this place and with these trees. Do you know how old some of these trees are?"

Matt scanned the forest as if it would give him a clue, but his gaze didn't make it past Gen climbing a fallen log. He shook his head to both answer Rosie's question and bring himself back to reality.

"Two thousand years."

Matt looked past Gen this time into the whispering leaves and dancing branches. No wonder this place felt so ageless. Some of these trees had been here when Jesus walked the earth. "Oh, man. I grew up on a Christmas tree farm, but we cut down our trees when they were six to ten years old."

"These trees are survivors." Rosie tilted her head toward the treetops. "They survived earthquakes and mudslides and typhoons. They survive by sticking together."

A peace settled over Matt. The kind of peace that came from knowing he wasn't alone. That Gen wasn't alone. Even if he couldn't be by her side, she had her adopted family.

Rosie waved an arm overhead. "Though some of these trees are more than three hundred feet tall, their roots don't go much deeper than twelve feet. Rather than deep, they spread their roots wide and intertwine with the roots of the trees around them." Rosie laced her few fingers together over her heart. "In the same way, the roots of my family tree don't go very deep, but we will survive because we can help hold each other up. Gen held me up, and now I'm here for her."

Anybody with Rosie on their side was sure to go far. "I'm glad." His gaze wandered back to find Gen making her way down the tree trunk. Had they met in another time, he would have offered her a hand. Maybe even wrapped his hands around her waist to lower her to the ground. Held on when she tried to step away.

"I don't want to see her get hurt."

Matt jolted upright, his eyes locking on Rosie's. Though hers were hidden by the shade from the brim of her hat, he could still read a warning in them. She knew.

His heart plummeted. He couldn't stop his feelings; he couldn't even hide them. It was like everyone knew except Gen. He had to keep it that way. That would cause the least amount of damage for everyone.

"What are you guys talking about?" Gen leaped across a small stream to join them. She lifted her chin, a curious smile making her eyes dance. "I took pictures of you in a very intense conversation."

Matt shot to his feet. He needed to be able to step away if she came any closer. "Trees," he blurted. "Rosie was telling me about trees."

"Yeah?" She planted her hands on her hips while she caught her breath and grinned at Rosie. "Why don't you show him your tattoo?"

Rosie stood, as well. She shot him a measuring glance.

Matt didn't want to see Rosie's tattoo. He wanted to put distance between them so she would know that he would never do anything to hurt Gen. He was only here because she'd invited him.

Rosie didn't seem so inviting now. She reached for her right wrist and rolled up her sleeve. The tattoo inside her wrist was small and round with the branches and roots of a tree forming the edges of a circle despite the way her deformity seemed to create scars that distorted it. The image was simple, yet he knew the meaning was profound. She may have been rejected from one family, but that wasn't going to keep her from growing.

His heart softened. Because this wasn't about him. This wasn't an attack. This was Rosie loving a sister the way she should have been loved.

"It's beautiful."

Gen stepped forward and tugged up her own sweatshirt sleeve then held out her arm next to Rosie's. She had a matching tattoo on her wrist.

She met his gaze sheepishly. Probably because they weren't supposed to have visible tattoos at the airport. How had he never noticed it before?

"I hide it under my watch."

She wouldn't get in trouble if she kept it hidden, but he was still surprised. Surprised she would take such a risk. Surprised she prioritized a person above a rule. But that was only because he wouldn't take such a risk. He was too worried about not messing up. As for Gen? People would always come first with her, wouldn't they? He shouldn't be surprised at all.

Gen smiled at Rosie. "We may not look like sisters, but we have the same family tree."

"It's beautiful." He said it again. He'd never meant anything more.

Looking at Gen made his heart ache. No, he wouldn't ever hurt her. He'd keep the pain inside himself. Because that was the right thing to do. Rosie had pretty much made that clear.

CHAPTER SIXTEEN

GEN FOLLOWED ROSIE TO THE BACKYARD to feed the goats. Matt had left over ten minutes ago, and Rosie still hadn't said anything about him. Gen would have expected they'd be giggling together by now like they used to in college when she'd had a crush on Eric Shultz. Granted, she didn't have a crush anymore, but Matt was still a super sweet guy. And Rosie had talked with him for quite a while.

"Well?" Gen leaned against the edge of the pen as Rosie climbed over into the hay.

The kids bleated and split their time between bouncing after Rosie and climbing up the wall by Gen. Gen reached down to scratch Alfred's fuzzy head.

"Well, I'm going to need your help feeding these guys when I have my speaking engagement in The City next week."

That was next week? Gen eyed the goats warily. She hadn't fed any animals since leaving the farm nine years ago. And she rarely ever prepared herself anything to eat more than cereal. But she would do it. Especially if it meant moving on in their conversation to talk about Matt. "Sure. But that's not what I was talking about."

Rosie poured a milk substitute into the bucket encircled with what looked like bottle nipples at the base. Alfred bounded away from Gen to suck on the rubbery contraption. "I know what you're talking about."

"And?" Gen prompted. Why was Rosie being so secretive? Had she developed a crush of her own?

"And…" Rosie leaned against the railing, so she was close enough to talk, but she still had her back to Gen. "I can see why Casey Holloway fell for him."

Gen climbed one of the split rails and leaned forward to look Rosie in the face. "I know, right?" Now they could laugh together.

Hair tugged against Gen's scalp. She looked down in surprise to find Alfred chewing at the end of her braid.

Rosie laughed and knelt to release the goat's hold on Gen's hair. Not the laughter Gen had been hoping for. She'd have to remember to put her hair up when she fed the goats next weekend.

She dropped from the pen and wiped her hair dry. Maybe Rosie would go back with her into her apartment and look at the photographs Gen had taken at Fern Canyon. That might spark more conversation. "I'm going to go download pictures. Want to come over, and we'll order a stuffed mushroom pizza?"

Rosie pulled her hat off and wiped her forehead. Her hair frizzed from her ponytail like the fur on a baby goat. "A bribe?" she asked. "I think you've still got it pretty bad, Gen."

Gen widened her eyes and gave her sweetest smile. "What have I got bad?"

Okay, she really wasn't that innocent. She knew Rosie thought she was still daydreaming about Matt romantically. But she wasn't. She simply liked him as a person. He made her smile. And it had meant a lot that he came over to personally apologize for his decision the night before. Rosie was probably still being cautious after finding them together in her living room that morning.

Rosie climbed after her out of the pen and wiped her hands on her pants. "I will come over and talk about Matt if you will promise to go on a date with someone else this month."

Gen scrunched her nose. A date? Where was she supposed to find a guy to date that quickly?

Rosie shrugged. "Looks like you're having cereal for dinner again."

"Gah." Gen dropped her head back and flopped her arms to her sides. What did Rosie want her to do? Join some crazy online dating site? Was there a Goat Owners Only dot com? That would at least prove Rosie had the wrong idea. "Fine."

She'd go on a spite date. Maybe with that guy at the library who ran the children's program. He talked to everyone like he was putting on a puppet show. That would at least be entertaining. And then Rosie would apologize for pushing her before she was ready.

"Really?"

Gen looked up to find Rosie studying her in disbelief. Her sister shouldn't be so surprised to get her way. She usually got her way. "If you want me to go on a date, I'll go on a date."

Rosie bit her lip, her eyes darting toward the goats. "Gen, the reason I want you to go on a date is because—"

The thud of a door slamming sounded from overhead in the general direction of Gen's apartment. Her heart tripped. Maybe Matt had forgotten something. She wracked her brain to think what it might be. Nothing came to mind. Could he be bringing them a pizza to thank them for the hike? He seemed to like to do things like that. He was always getting coffee for his flight crew. She bounced toward the back steps.

Rosie grabbed her arm. "Wait. We should call the police."

Gen tugged her arm away. "Don't be silly." She didn't want Rosie to think she was giddy over the thought of seeing Matt again. "Maybe it's some guy who wants to ask me on a date."

Rosie pulled her phone out anyway and pointed toward the giant spatula hanging from the barbecue grill. "Take a weapon."

Gen laughed at what Matt's response might be to find her brandishing a spatula. *I'd flip for you.* Oops. She wasn't supposed to be having those kinds of daydreams anymore. She'd blame Rosie's concern.

Brandishing the metal spatula, she charged up the stairs and peeked in the back window from the deck into her room. One of the most attractive men she'd ever seen stood in her bedroom doorway, hands in the pockets of his denim jacket. It had been years, but she'd recognize that thick dark hair and stubble covered jaw anywhere.

"It's Craig." She whirled around and called down to Rosie, drawing her brother's baby blues her direction.

Today was certainly a day of surprises. Good surprises. Craig's appearance wasn't equivalent with her daydream of having Matt bring her a pizza; it was better since Craig could take her mind off Matt. Hanging out with her brother would be even better for her than a date with the librarian. She knew that's what Rosie was going for with the whole date thing—get her mind off the guy she'd claimed to not be thinking about.

Craig held his hands wide and walked toward the back door in his casual confident way, and Gen had the crazy thought that if he wasn't a high school dropout and recovering drug addict and selfish player, she would have loved to introduce him to Casey. Were they to get together, the two of them would look like they'd just stepped out of a perfume ad in a magazine. But though Casey was gorgeous, she was too smart for him. She went for good guys like Matt.

"What is Craig doing in your apartment?" Rosie responded in her typical concerned older sibling tone right as Gen opened the door.

"Genevieve." Craig wrapped her in a hug. His musky scent would have confirmed her idea that he belonged in a cologne commercial if not for the way it mingled with the smoky odor of cigarettes. In his case, she'd forgive the fact that he'd been smoking, for that was the lesser evil. "I was looking for you girls, of course." He leaned over the balcony to see Rosie. "You didn't hear me knock, so I hunted down the key above the door post."

"Trespassing." Rosie gave him her best deadpan. He'd have to prove he was clean and sober in order for Rosie to let him in her side of the house.

Gen pulled away so she could look him in the eye and gauge their clarity for herself. All she knew about drugs she'd learned from visiting Craig in rehab. They considered it a disease there. They'd said that some people didn't think it was a disease because if you held a gun to an alcoholic's head and told them not to drink, they could choose not to drink. The rehab center argued that though they could choose not to drink, they couldn't control the shaking or the way their mouth watered. In their minds, getting drunk or high equated itself with breathing. That's why an addict would lie, cheat, steal, and hurt others to get drugs or alcohol. They felt they were doing it to survive.

Gen didn't know what she could do to help Craig with that, but like she'd been there for Rosie, she wanted to be there for him too. Whether addiction was a disease or not, it had been passed down by his parents. It was his curse.

Craig smiled the kind of smile that melted women's hearts. Her heart didn't melt, but her lungs sighed in relief at the way his eyes appeared cognizant.

"Want some pizza?" she asked. She would need even more of a bribe to get Rosie over now.

"I'd love pizza."

Rosie stayed below and crossed her arms. "How long are you here for, Craig?"

Craig ran a hand through his thick hair. "I'm here for Damon's release. Thought I'd come down early to hang out with my family."

Gen wanted to believe him, though she didn't like the way he said family. As if it was a wild card in the game of Uno. As a family, they shouldn't be playing against each other. They were a team.

"Do you think it's wise for you to be here?" Rosie asked.

Gen knew what she was really asking. Would Craig have come at all if they didn't live in the Emerald Triangle—the area where the most marijuana was grown in the United States. It was legal for him to smoke it now, but if he got started, he wouldn't stop there.

"I missed you too, sis." Craig's deep voice dropped even lower with sarcasm.

Gen reached for his arm to pull him inside. "We're glad you're here." Even if he'd come for drugs, he was there. She couldn't do anything for him if he hadn't come. But now she had a chance to make a difference in his life. To support and encourage him the way she had for Rosie. Had Rosie forgotten the way *she'd* once hurt everybody?

"We'll order the pizza and give you time to get cleaned up, Rosie," she called down. Hopefully by then her brother and sister could be civil to each other. Because whether they liked each other or not, they were really all she had, and she couldn't lose them.

"I still can't believe we lost." Casey stared blankly at Matt.

Even though Matt knew the Giants had lost all four games in a row, it took him a moment to connect Casey's stoic demeanor with the baseball team. She looked like she'd lost a puppy or her job or something. And this was what he'd been secretly hoping for. He was a terrible boyfriend. Now that he had all her attention, she might start to notice too.

"I'm sorry, Case." He placed a hand at the small of her back to usher her across the street from the Aquatic Park with its bleacher-like steps in front of the cove toward the entrance into Ghirardelli Square…and to avoid eye contact. "I know we were going to walk along the Presidio after church, but I think you deserve a hot fudge sundae." It could help him drown his sorrows, as well. Thankfully he hadn't been in trouble with his boss because pilots were allowed to time out, but he'd been viewed as less than a team player. He hated being viewed as less than.

She let him guide her while she walked in a daze, not seeming to register the afternoon mist that chilled their skin or even the street musician who sounded like he was making up a song just for Casey. Oh no. Those rhymes came from the poem Casey at the Bat. He'd put it to a melody in her honor. "Mighty Casey has struck out." He sang the words over and over. Matt ignored him.

She climbed the steps, her feet dragging. "It's over. Though Alan's face is still smiling down on Union Square." She stopped and stared up at the giant letters spelling out Ghirardelli above their heads as if seeing Alan grinning in its place. "I'd been hoping those gorgeous pictures Gen took would be the start of something great."

Matt's mind rewound to the day Gen came to San Francisco. The day they'd laughed for the whole flight back to Eureka, then she'd hugged him. It could have been the start of something great. But Casey was right. "It's over."

Solemnly they walked across the brick courtyard then into a glass storefront claiming to be the original chocolate shop. The sweet scent of candy permeated the air and invited them to weave through barrels of treats, past a random carousel horse, and to the counter covered by a striped awning. During the summer and on weekends the place had a line out the door, but today the quietness matched Matt's mood.

He sent a cursory glance to the menu. "What do you want?"

Casey gazed past him toward a chandelier. "I want to throw an end of season party. Because though we didn't win the pennant, we still made it to the World Series. And that's worth celebrating."

So much for getting her attention back. He rubbed his jaw. "Uh, yeah. Did you want to order their world famous sundae or something else?"

She blinked and fluttered her hand. "That's fine."

Matt placed their orders with the woman in the light blue polo, making his a rocky road sundae. Seemed appropriate.

Casey led the way to a round table in the corner to wait for what would be their lunch. "I need to throw the party soon before the players head out of town for vacation. The Gotham Club behind the scoreboard is available this weekend." She reached across the table to grab Matt's hand. "You don't have any flights over the weekend, do you?"

Matt squeezed her hand. Of course she would want him at the party with her. They'd been going their separate ways so much lately that he hadn't even thought to check his calendar. This was why he'd wanted the Giants to lose, wasn't it? So he could have time with her again. But he couldn't help wishing for the weekend to himself to escape and clear his mind. "Let me check." He pulled his hand away to retrieve his phone and open the calendar app.

Two little green bars underneath the date on Saturday told him he had something planned. He clicked to find out what he had going on.

The first bar held one word: Sam.

"Oh, my baby brother is visiting this weekend."

Casey lifted an irked eyebrow. "Tracen again?"

Clearly Tracen's distaste had been mutual. Though he'd been intrigued with the idea of Gen.

Matt shook his head. "No. Sammy is my baby brother. He'd been planning to come watch a home game." Sore subject. He'd steer the conversation to a happy place. "You'll like him."

Casey sat back, her gaze lifting above Matt's head again. "Then bring him along."

Matt shrugged and looked at his phone to message the kid. Probably make his day. Except the second bar under the date caught his attention. He didn't remember any other plans. He clicked.

Halloween.

"Were you thinking of throwing the party on Saturday, Case? Because that's Halloween."

Both her palms smacked the table. "That's perfect. We'll make it a costume party."

She did love her themes. She'd probably pull out her Bat Girl cape, though he wasn't wearing the green felt Oktoberfest hat again. Ethan had teased him mercilessly when they'd gone out to lunch. Not that Ethan's opinion mattered.

Matt sank deeper in his seat as Casey's spirits lifted with her party planning. Matt watched from a distance, his thoughts returning to Ethan's accusations. The truth was that despite his choice to stay in a relationship with Casey, he was attracted to Gen. How long until that attraction went away? It *would* go away, wouldn't it?

He hadn't felt the attraction at first. He'd simply appreciated Gen's hard work and cheerful attitude even in the face of adversity— like how she dealt with being adopted. Then he'd been proud of her creativity and entertained by her playful banter with Alan. After that, he'd enjoyed pulling the prank on her in the plane and the way it made her laugh. Then, she'd intrigued him with her love of a dented minivan. Probably because it was different from the life he'd been pursuing. The perfection. The prestige.

But was her minivan really that different from the life he'd wanted as a kid? He'd told Gen he'd wanted to be a pirate. He'd wanted to explore the world. Which was exactly what she was doing with her minivan. With her life.

Maybe it wasn't even Gen he was so drawn to. Maybe it was her freedom. Was there a way he could have both Casey and the freedom Gen represented?

Glass bowls of overflowing ice cream and toppings clinked to the table in front of him. He shivered. He should have ordered a hot chocolate instead. Ice cream in cold weather was Sam's thing.

"Thank you, Matt."

Matt focused on his girlfriend. She smiled at him so sweetly. She was everything he'd thought he'd wanted. Just like his ice cream had been. He picked up his spoon and dug in. "You're welcome."

"For the party, we should dress up as a couple." Back to the party. "What kind of costume would you want to wear?"

At least there was one decision he didn't have to second guess. "I want to be a pirate."

Craig set his feet on Gen's ottoman and crossed his legs. Besides drugs, alcohol, and women, movies were her brother's vice. While she didn't have a television to entertain him, she did get Netflix on her computer. He hadn't even gone to visit Damon with them on his first full day in town—claimed he was too exhausted from traveling to even get out of bed. And ever since then, he'd been doing nothing but watching movies. At least if he was in her home, she knew he wasn't doing drugs. Though looking at her computer screen made Gen itch to edit photographs...or actually go outside to take more photos.

"Wanna go paddleboarding in the bay?" she suggested.

Craig glanced up with a grin to laugh at what he thought was a joke. "It's cold outside."

True, but if they kept moving, they would warm up. "You can paddleboard without getting wet. Unless you're taking one of Rosie's paddleboard yoga classes, that is. Then you'd probably fall in."

Craig's forehead wrinkled in the kind of look he often gave Rosie—the kind that said he thought she was insane. "There's no way I'm taking paddleboard yoga. I can't even touch my toes."

"That's exactly why you need Holy Yoga. It will help you with flexibility as well as stress relief."

Craig turned back to the computer. "I think Rosie is the only one of us who needs stress relief. She's so not calm."

Gen rolled her eyes. Craig couldn't ever see situations from other people's perspectives. Especially if it meant he had to prove he'd changed in order for someone to trust him again. Gen had wanted to have something to offer him, but he was sucking her dry. Hopefully Damon's parole hearing wouldn't have any hiccups that could prolong Craig's stay on her couch. "Just because she's not calm with you, doesn't mean she's not calm."

Craig tossed a piece of popcorn in the air and caught it in his mouth. "I don't really care about calm; I just wish she was more like you. You're the best. I don't know where I'd be without you."

Gen relaxed against her throw pillows. Every time she started to get upset with Craig, he'd go and say something so completely flattering that she'd adore him all over again. It made her feel like everything could be okay.

Her phone buzzed on the end table on Craig's side. She jolted upright. She'd told herself it was good that Matt hadn't texted or been flying into Eureka, but that didn't keep her heart from jumping at the chance to talk to him again.

He might be done playing the family photo game now that he'd met her sister, saw their tree tattoo, and realized she had all the family she needed. Hey, she could send him a selfie with her and Craig so he could see her brother too.

Craig handed her the phone, a glimmer in his baby blues. "Who is he?"

"No one." She answered before checking the caller ID to find an unrecognizable number flashing. It really was no one. She sighed and slid her thumb over the glass.

Hi, Gen. This is Alan. Casey gave me your number.

She frowned. Alan, the Giants player? Why would Casey give him her number? Had he asked for it? Yeah, he'd been hitting on her in the limo, but she'd figured he would have hit on any woman sitting next to him.

Oh no. She'd told Matt to tell Alan hi for her. Maybe the baseball player thought she was interested.

Craig twisted sideways, now watching her with an expectant smile. "What does 'no one' want?"

She didn't even look up. "I don't know." She was a little afraid to ask. So she settled for: *Hi.*

Are you busy this Saturday?

Gen tucked her feet underneath her and sat up straighter. Was Alan going to ask her out? Was this going to be the date Rosie suggested she go on?

"He wants to know if I'm busy this weekend." If she was going to go on a real date, she needed the support of both her siblings.

Her stomach cramped. Going on a real date with a jock might be a little different than with a librarian. He would probably be more...experienced with dating.

Craig plucked at his t-shirt. "It's a good thing I'm here. I can play Dad. Make the guy come to the front door when he picks you up. I'll shake his hand and tell him my expectations for how you should be treated."

Gen grimaced. As much as she appreciated Craig's offer, dating Alan would be a little more complicated than that. For starters, she'd probably have to go to San Francisco. And this time, the flight wouldn't include hanging out with Matt. She bit her lip. She wasn't ready to commit to anything yet.

Why do you ask?

Her phone buzzed the quick response. *I need a date for an end of season costume party at AT&T Park Saturday night.*

Gen sank into the throw pillows. He didn't really want to be with her. He only needed a date. Or maybe a photographer. If she got in over her head, Matt would be there to bail her out. It was a safe first step into the dating world. She smiled as she typed.

I wouldn't be bringing my camera, but I can take photos with my phone.

That's cool.

She knew it. Nothing to worry about with Alan. She'd hop the last flight down on Saturday then sleep in the airport to save money before flying back the next day. Airports were some of the safest places on earth with all the security. *Sounds fun.*

"You're smiling."

She beamed up at her brother.

"That really isn't 'no one' you're talking to, is it?"

Gen laughed. How would her brother react? Maybe with even more disbelief than she felt. "Have you ever heard of a baseball player named A-Plus?"

Craig froze except for his jaw, which dropped like the Cessna with Matt behind the yoke.

She laughed. "He asked me out."

CHAPTER SEVENTEEN

MATT ADMIRED CASEY'S WORK. THE BLACK and orange team colors blended seamlessly into the harvest party theme with jack-o'-lanterns spelling out GIANTS at the entrance. Orange twinkle lights flickered around the room, and a band warmed up in the corner.

Sam snapped his fireman's suspenders. "I am so jealous of myself right now."

Weren't those Tracen's same words when visiting San Francisco last month? They both seemed to love Matt's life more than he did.

"Glad you could come, Sammy." He hoped the kid would enjoy his visit as he'd just announced he'd enlisted in the Army. Matt didn't want to be there when their mom found out about that.

Sam grinned down at him. When had the baby of the family gotten so huge? "You're going to introduce me to the players, right? I can't wait to meet A-Plus."

Matt rubbed his temple. He couldn't tell if the pounding in his head was coming from the repetitive drumbeat from the live band or the start of a migraine. "You can't miss A-Plus."

Sam studied the growing crowd around them. "He might be hard to spot in a costume."

"I doubt it." Matt lazily surveyed the few costumes around him — a clown, a rabbit, and an angel. Not fancy enough for Alan.

Sam spun slowly, stopping when he faced the entrance. "There he is. Though I'm not sure who he's supposed to be."

Matt wasn't sure he wanted to know, but he pivoted dutifully to see if he could figure it out. Alan had dressed in a newsboy cap, collared shirt, vest, neck scarf, and, to top it off, a gold chain attached to a watch in his pocket. His swagger did not go with the time period, and Matt would have had no idea who he was supposed to be if Gen wasn't walking next to him in a dress with puffy sleeves.

They were Anne Shirley and Gilbert Blythe. But Matt was the one who wanted to crack a slate over Gilbert's head.

While Alan looked around to see who was watching him, Gen looked around in delight, and Matt couldn't keep his eyes off her. If he'd thought her quaint little town was a glimpse back in time, the way she wore that dress made it look like she'd stepped right out of the history book. She even had on long white gloves and high-heeled boots. He noticed these things when her heel tripped and she reached for Alan's arm with a gloved hand.

At the same time, fingers slipped between Matt's side and bicep. Casey.

"You invited Gen?" he asked. But it made sense. Gen's photos were displayed all through the stadium. She was part of the franchise success.

"No. Alan must have invited her. He asked me for her phone number."

And Gen had said yes. But that could be a good thing, couldn't it? She wasn't available anymore. So even if Matt were to consider breaking up with Casey, Gen would already be taken.

Though Gen with Alan? That was wrong on so many levels.

She spotted him. He knew because her face lit up, even more than with the golden glow of candlelight. She waved and headed his way, looking him up and down.

"You're a pirate." Her voice rose over the sound of the band's first song. "I was hoping you'd dress like a pirate."

She'd been thinking of him?

"Look." She brushed her fingers over his arm, though with the jolt he felt, she might have shot him with a cannon. "We're both wearing puffy sleeves."

"So am I." Casey pointed to her own, as she'd been the one to pick out their couple's costume. Her sleeves were a little different from theirs with the way they came off her shoulders.

"You look gorgeous." Gen smiled at Casey to include the other woman in their conversation. "Do you know who I am?" she asked.

Matt had known the moment he'd laid eyes on her red braids, made more fiery with the orange light from overhead. But he'd let the others guess first.

Casey shook her head.

Sam tilted his fireman's hat. "You're Gen. I heard about you from my brother."

Matt's eyes slid Sam's way in confusion. He hadn't said a word about Gen.

Sam tilted his head and spoke so only Matt could here. "Tracen told me about her."

Matt narrowed his eyes. What could Tracen have possibly told Sam? He'd never met Gen.

Gen beamed and extended an arm toward Sam to shake hands. "And you are?"

Sam clasped her hand in his. "I'm Matt's youngest brother, Sam. I thought I'd be coming to a World Series game this weekend, but meeting you is even better."

Casey leaned forward to look around Matt at Sam. "What did he say?" she asked. "I don't think I heard him right."

Gen released Sam's hand and held hers to her belly while throwing her head back in laughter. When she looked up, she was smiling at Matt again. "And you said he wasn't chivalrous."

Sam frowned in mock offense. "He told you that?" Maybe the kid had become chivalrous after Matt moved out. Or maybe he thought it was fun to put Matt in the hot spot.

Casey's gaze landed on him, as well. It was the most attention she'd given him in a while. Was she curious as to why he'd been talking to Gen about chivalry?

He'd get out of answering the question by giving a demonstration. Turning his smile on Casey, he rubbed a hand down her back. "I still have a few things left to teach him."

"Woo-hoo." Alan did a side step to slide into their circle and wrap one arm behind Gen. "Matt's got the moves." He hooted the words, obviously unaware Matt would rather be in his shoes.

Gen playfully shoved Alan away with a shoulder, though Matt still couldn't tell if she was enjoying the man's company or simply excited about attending a pro-ball party.

"I don't know, man." Matt eyed Alan's costume. "You're like Gilbert Blythe meets Michael Jackson. That's a pretty tough combination to beat."

Alan bobbed his head. "I like it, I like it." He twirled in a full circle to face Gen. "You ready to mingle?"

Gen shrugged like she was up for anything. "Let's mingle."

Alan did a two-step before sauntering off toward the nearest group.

Gen watched for a second then leaned forward and cupped one hand around her mouth as if she didn't want her date to hear what she had to say. Not that he was listening. "Alan pretended he was asking me out, but it turns out he was just hoping I'd bring my camera and take more pictures of him."

Casey stepped closer too. "That sounds like Alan."

Gen's eyes twinkled. Clearly she wasn't slighted by the backhanded invitation.

Matt rocked onto his heels. He could relax now. Gen wasn't going to get played by the baseball player.

"See ya later." She waved and trotted off.

Sam watched her go after her date, a stricken look on his face. "Nobody introduced me to A-Plus."

"Oh my goodness, Sam." Casey turned to face them both so they were now their own group. "Why didn't you introduce yourself?"

The kid motioned after Alan, opening and closing his mouth a couple of times before getting any words out. "Because he's A-Plus."

Matt slapped his little brother on the shoulder. "He's only Alan to us, but I'll try to remember to tell him who you are next time."

Casey linked her fingers with Matt's. "Let's go show Sam around the park so he doesn't miss anything else."

Matt gripped her hand firmly, reminding himself they were a team. This was what he'd chosen for himself. So he'd do his best to be there for her. "Good idea."

They made it through the locker room and dugout up to the trolley at the top of the stairs with a view of the brightly lit bay on one side and the dark field on the other. Then Casey got called away.

She clicked on her phone screen to end the call. "I'm going to run and talk to my dad real quick. Do you want to wait here or meet me back at the party?"

Sam sank into the trolley seat overlooking the field. "It's a gorgeous night. I'll chill right here for a while."

Matt would enjoy the break too. He dropped down next to his brother before Casey had time to rise on her tiptoes to kiss him. "Sounds good to me."

Casey studied him for a second before turning to go. "Hopefully I'm not long."

Matt smiled and nodded. He was putting on a pretty good show, wasn't he?

Sam stretched his arms along the back of the bench and crossed one ankle over a knee as they watched her go. "I really like her."

Matt kept smiling and nodding. Everybody liked Casey. Including him. "Me too."

"As much as you like Gen?"

Sam might as well have kneed Matt in the gut. He groaned and leaned forward to cover his face with his hands, resting elbows on knees. Why did he have to like Gen so much? And why did everyone have to see it?

Of all the times for Sam to visit. Though maybe with Sam's outside perspective, he could help. "What am I going to do?"

Sam scratched the back of his head. "That depends."

"On what?" Matt sat up. His brother made it sound like the answer could be simple.

"On why you haven't done anything yet."

The answer wasn't simple. What was Matt supposed to have done? He waved a hand after Casey. "Because I don't want to hurt anyone."

Sam nodded thoughtfully. "That's a good answer. I thought maybe it was because you didn't want to give up all this." He tilted his head toward the field.

Matt huffed. He'd thought dating the daughter of the team owner had been pretty cool at first, but he didn't share her passion for the team. It seemed to be pulling them apart. Whereas with Gen, they had more similar interests—apart from her choice of driving a minivan. Though that moment where she'd leaned into him, laughing and declaring her love for her beat up vehicle haunted his dreams. She didn't need things to be perfect in order to be happy. She was simply happy.

Ethan had made it sound like Casey wasn't enough for him, but maybe he wasn't enough for Casey. Which he hated admitting to himself. And he needed to admit to himself.

"I have to break up with her tonight."

Sam gave a knowing nod. Maybe it really was that simple. Once he was single, he'd be free to pursue his attraction toward Gen and see if perhaps she felt the same way.

As if conjuring her from his thoughts, a shadow with puffy sleeves moved silently from the darkness of the bleachers toward the light of the bay. The figure swung the silhouettes of boots in her hands, which explained the lack of echoing footsteps.

"Hey, Carrots."

She spun, braids flying. Then her shoulders relaxed, and she moved his way. His pulse quickened its pace with each of her steps. He couldn't pretend he didn't feel something anymore. Even if Gen didn't feel the same for him, it was unfair of him to stay with Casey.

"Hey." She stopped in front of the trolley, peering to see them better in the darkness. "You guys are facing the wrong way. The view's behind you."

The lights from the bay kissed her pale skin, turning it a peaceful shade of blue. He wasn't missing anything. But he stood to walk with her toward the spot that overlooked the harbor entrance to the park. Sam followed, and Matt shot him a warning look because little brothers were kind of known for making things awkward for their older brothers. Matt had enough little brothers to know.

Sam pressed his lips together to signify his lips were sealed. Good.

"Did you come up here for the view?" Matt asked Gen. How was it that he was always running into her? She seemed too innocent to have planned this.

She set her shoes on the ledge and stared out at the sailboats rocking in their docks. "I was actually trying to get away from all the people who wanted to interview Alan and get his autograph. Did you know he's famous? Like really famous?"

Matt looked to Sam. "I had my suspicions."

Sam smirked. "Did the Nike posters give it away?"

Matt chuckled. "I think it was the Gatorade commercials."

Gen shook off their humor. "You guys." Her eyes met Matt's and held. And there was absolutely nothing in the world he wouldn't do for her—including giving up the life he'd planned for himself—the chance to be a hero to the most sought-after woman in the Bay Area.

Movement below caught his eye. Casey and her father. He had to talk to her now, before he made the mistake of talking to Gen first. "Excuse me."

Gen massaged her earlobes as she watched Matt go. He'd given her a look that caused her heart to quiver and her palms to itch, then he disappeared. Which was a good thing. Because she was on a date. Even if she wasn't, he was. And even if Casey wasn't absolutely perfect, it was wrong for Gen to think of Matt as anything but a friend. Though that look he'd given her could fuel her daydreams for years to come...

Oh, crud. Sam was watching her daydream right there.

She straightened. Dropped a shoe. Swiped it off the ground and straightened again. It could be worse, right? She could have knocked the shoe the other direction off the ledge of the building.

"How long have you had a thing for my brother?" Sam tweaked a brow.

Gen jumped. Clutched the shoes to her chest like a shield though she obviously couldn't hide anymore. "You can tell?"

"Oh, I can tell."

She'd told friends about her crush at first. Friends like Bianca and Olivia and Rosie. Then others started noticing like Ethan and Michelle. She thought she'd gotten her crush under control since then. But now Matt's brother knew. And his brother would likely say something to him. Which would make her professional relationship with Matt difficult. It could also ruin her photography job with the Giants. All for nothing—because she'd known from the beginning that nothing would come from her attraction.

She took a step toward Sam. He was a sweet kid. He might understand. "I'm so embarrassed. Please don't tell Matt. I don't want to lose his friendship."

Sam tilted his head as he studied her. One cheek dimpled, and his eyes sparkled. "Don't worry. Your feelings aren't one-sided."

The world faded around her. The lights dimmed, the sounds hushed, and the cool breeze had no effect on the warmth crawling up her skin. She had to be dreaming. This wasn't real. But then the memory of Matt pinching her arm returned in full force bringing with it memories of his texts, their laughter, and the hug they'd shared. Could he have been falling for her the way she didn't want to believe she'd been falling for him?

Her heart fluttered, but she couldn't believe it. Not Matt. He was on a pedestal. Unreachable. As far out of her ballpark as the splash balls that got knocked over the fence. And even if she was more beautiful or more rich or more anything than Casey, Matt was too good a person to have feelings for someone other than his girlfriend. If he'd ever felt any kind of attraction for Gen, he would have immediately stepped back.

Like when he'd timed out at work.

She gasped. What if he'd timed out to get away from her?

He'd stopped texting her.

He disappeared after that look he gave her a moment ago.

It was a boundary.

Oh no. Her pulse hammered, throbbing behind her elbows and her knees. She alternated between the sensations of falling and being frozen. According to Sam, Matt felt for her what she'd dreamed he'd feel for her, which meant now she was going to lose him completely because of it.

"I have to go." She'd get a taxi to the airport. She'd fly home to Rosie. Maybe she could stay numb enough to keep from crying until then.

Sam shook his head. "Gen, you don't have to do anything. Matt's already doing it. Come here." He motioned her toward the ledge.

She took a hesitant step. As light-headed and weak-kneed as she was feeling, she could easily topple over the edge. Plus, she was afraid to see what Sam was pointing at—afraid to see something that might confirm his words.

There. Below. Matt the pirate jogged toward Casey. But that didn't mean anything. They were a couple. He probably jogged toward her all the time. Gen wouldn't assume.

"He's breaking up with her." Sam crossed his arms on the ledge to watch the show for himself.

Gen couldn't breathe. Her hands trembled. Matt was giving up his perfect girlfriend for her? How could she ever live up to that?

How long would he wait before asking Gen out? Surely he wouldn't do it here. Maybe at the airport. Maybe he'd text. What if she was a disappointment to him? And Matt wanted all this back, but it was too late?

Reality was so different from a daydream. In reality, she could get rejected again. Was that kind of pain worth the risk? Matt's words from the plane rang in her ears. *What if you soar?*

What if? What if this was what she'd been waiting for her whole life?

Both shoes fell to her feet as she covered her mouth to watch.

CHAPTER EIGHTEEN

MATT WAS REALLY DOING THIS. HE was going to break off his relationship with Casey. He didn't even know if he had a chance with Gen. For all he knew, she was in love with Alan.

The truth was that Casey deserved better than this. Yeah, she'd be hurt at first, but honestly, there were plenty of men who would eagerly step into his shoes. It may be hard for her to figure out which of them was the one, but he knew it wasn't him.

"Hey, Case?" He couldn't look her in the eye as he jogged toward her. Because then he'd have to see her adoration. Her trust. Her hopes for their future together.

He might never have a future with anyone. This could be it for him. Maybe it was all a case of cold feet because he was a commitment-phobe, and he'd never say 'I do.' But he hadn't felt this way before Gen.

Casey had a lot to offer him, but he wanted to offer what he had to Gen. And that should be what a relationship was about.

Casey's pirate boots came into view. If he couldn't look her in the eye before, how could he now? She was going to see the heartache all over him.

"Matt." Her voice cracked. Could she already tell?

He looked up to find the blue pools of her eyes spilling over. Had he done this to her? Had she known what was coming before he did? His throat constricted. How could he possibly say anything to make it better?

"My mom." She whispered the words, stepping into his arms and burying her face in his shoulder.

Her mom? Mrs. Holloway? What did she have to do with any of this? She hadn't even come to the party.

Matt lifted his hands in reflex, but where did he place them? Her waist? Her back? Her head? He'd only been through a few breakups in his life, but none of them had gone like this. He settled for patting her on the back. He'd do that to a buddy. Though it felt very similar to how he'd held Casey in the past. This wasn't how he imagined things going. But it could be worse. She could have yelled or slapped him.

"My mom has breast cancer."

The words circled around him as if looking for a place to land. What did they mean for Valerie? Chemo? Radiation? Death? That word landed with enough impact to cause his soul to shudder.

"Oh, Casey." Whether her mom lived or not, Casey had to be dealing with the thought of losing her. He wrapped his arms tighter in support. He'd never lost anyone close to him. Tracen had been in that bad rafting accident, and it had changed Matt forever. Life would have been even harder if they'd lost him. What would Casey's life be like if she lost her mom?

"She didn't want to tell me, but Dad had to take her to the hospital tonight."

Casey just found out? That's why her dad had called? "How serious is it?"

She clutched the back of his shirt as if it would help her mom hang on. "Dad said we're going to fight it. Dad thinks he can win any battle, but he's never fought this one before." She looked up, revealing lines of heavy pirate makeup smeared across her face. She didn't look like the perfect Casey he knew. "Will you take me to see her?"

He let out a deep exhale. Of course he would take her. He couldn't break up with her now. He couldn't send her to see her sick mother alone. He couldn't say, *I'm sorry your mom might be dying, but I realized tonight I want to be with someone else.* Who would do that? He'd thought letting Casey go was the best thing for her, but at the moment it certainly was not.

Casey needed him. He'd be there for her at the hospital because he cared for her. But what would happen if her mom passed? She'd need him even more then.

Oh, man. Was he only going to pretend to love Casey, waiting to see if Valerie survived? That was heartless. Plus, if Sam could see through him, then Valerie would, as well. She knew people. And she'd likely be in a mindset of making sure her daughter would be taken care of without her around.

"Thank you." Casey wiped at her eyes. "I don't know what I'd do without you."

Matt pulled her head back down to his chest to comfort her. And to avoid talking.

Why? Why was this happening?

Matt wanted to be with Gen, but he couldn't let Casey down. Did he have to make a choice right then, or could he figure it out later?

He thought of Ethan's choice. The way his co-pilot picked one woman, but then when that didn't work out the way he wanted, he chose another. Ethan had accused him of doing the same. Is that what he was doing here? Being wishy-washy about love when really the act of love was a choice.

He couldn't be with Gen without hurting Casey, but should he decide to stay with Casey, Gen would never know any different. He closed his eyes.

It would be wrong to leave Casey alone with her pain.

It would be wrong to stay with Casey with intentions to break up later.

The only right thing to do was to commit. His heart would follow later.

Life with Gen would have been brilliant and adventurous and fun. The image of her in puffy sleeves smiling out at the harbor played like a DVD he had to shut off. He'd choose to let her go. To do the right thing. Even if it hurt as much as finding out a parent had cancer. He'd take that pain on himself so he never had to hurt anyone else.

Lifting his hands to cup Casey's face, he lowered his lips to her forehead. He was going to be the man she deserved.

Gen couldn't look away. She remained frozen in place as Matt kissed Casey on the forehead. Had she really thought Matt was going to give up all of this for her? Even if he was somehow attracted to her frizzy hair and vampire pallor, he probably took one look at Casey in the moonlight and fell in love with her all over again.

Nothing had changed. Nothing except the realization of how much Gen had wanted it to change. She'd dared to let her heart step out of the nest only for it to fall. It wheezed within her chest like it had actually splattered against the ground.

"Gen." Sam reached a hand toward her as if that would help.

It would have been better if he hadn't been there at all. If he'd never made her think Matt could possibly love her. Because he couldn't.

Now Sam had witnessed her rejection. He knew. He knew everything. Matt would not only hear about her crush but that he'd crushed her. There was no way she could hide it.

She couldn't face him tonight. She had to get away before he showed up in front of her with his arm around Casey and a big smile on his face.

She'd once read that couples often broke up right before an engagement. They tried life without each other and realized how much they missed being together. Matt hadn't even gotten that far. Either Sam had been wrong about Matt's feelings for Gen, or she'd been the catalyst needed to bring him and Casey closer together. She'd be remembered for the rest of Matt's life as a mistake. Probably how her bio mom had thought of her when she was born.

"Goodbye, Sam." She swooped down to grab her boots before she forgot and left them behind. She was no Cinderella.

"Gen, wait."

For what? The tears to fall? It wouldn't be long. They were already burning the back of her throat with her efforts to swallow them.

She twirled and padded barefoot across the ground, feeling its chill for the first time. She'd focus on the icy sting of her toes rather than the iceberg in her chest, threatening to send an avalanche of emotion through her veins.

"There has to be some explanation!"

The explanation was that Sam was young. Naïve. Not to mention incredibly sweet for thinking his brother might actually choose her over an heiress. He'd had her thinking it too.

How could she be that stupid? She knew how love worked. Or

didn't work, in her case.

Rosie knew too. Rosie had warned her about this, but Rosie would comfort her anyway. Maybe offer Gen a personal "tantrum yoga" session where she could lay on a mat and scream until she got out all her pain and frustration and was left with inner peace. Though it might take a while.

She dashed down the stairs, her heart pounding in her chest. Was that from the physical exertion or the fear of running into Matt before she could make her escape?

One thing at a time. She had to find Alan. Or did she? It would be easier to leave him behind so as not to have to explain, but she had to get her purse that she'd left at his table.

She pulled open the door to the clubhouse and was hit by warmth and the vanilla perfume of candles. Her stomach churned from the new sensations or perhaps in spite of them. Music and conversation swirled around her, carrying her forward through the dark room in anonymity. She kept her eyes down when weaving between bodies.

There. Her purse. She looped it across her body to keep from having to juggle it with her shoes. She'd stop to put the shoes on once she got outside. Once she got far enough away to breathe.

"Gen. There you are." Alan blocked her path, his head bobbing and fingers snapping. "Do you want to dance?"

He was too much. Alan on top of everything else. She'd laugh about it later with Rosie. Though the turbulence inside her at the moment could just as easily pour out in the form of hysterical laughter as it could in uncontrollable sobbing. She had to keep going before she exploded in front of everyone.

She placed a hand on his arm so she could swing him to the side like pushing through a door. "I'm not feeling good," she yelled over the music. "I'm going to go home. You stay here and enjoy yourself."

He tailed after her, almost tripping her up. "Do you need a doctor?"

If Alan followed, eyes were sure to follow too, which was the last thing she needed. Why was he not striking poses for his adoring public or dancing on stage or something? "No."

He caught her arm. "Are you sure? Because Matt and Casey are headed to the hospital, and I'm sure they can give you a ride if you need."

She stilled, though her mind reeled. Why were Matt and Casey going to the hospital? She would have guessed Vegas for a quick wedding, but the hospital? Were they okay? And more importantly, how did Alan know where they were going? Had they come inside and told him?

She scanned past unfamiliar faces to find Matt by the entrance, helping Casey into a caramel suede jacket. Gen needed to retreat. Disappear backward into the crowd.

Alan cupped his hands and yelled across the room. "Matt."

Matt's eyes lifted and locked with hers. His jaw shifted.

Her pulse skittered to a stop.

Alan dragged her forward. "Gen's not feeling good."

Matt rested his hands on Casey's shoulders and said something to her before stepping their way.

Gen dug in her heels—tried to pull out of Alan's grasp. He held on like she was a baton in a track relay, and he was about to pass her off.

Matt stopped in front of them, but the force of his gaze continued forward and hit her like a tsunami. If only it could have swept her away. "What's wrong?"

He'd know what was going on with her as soon as he spoke with Sam, but it wasn't anything they could talk about here. Not that she ever wanted to talk about it with him. She'd have to go with the sick excuse she'd given Alan. It wasn't a lie. She looked past him, seeing nothing. "I don't feel well."

Matt didn't move. She chanced another glance to read him. She shouldn't have. For the concerned wrinkle above his eyebrow drew her in like fingers slid behind her neck and into her hair. Though how would she know what that felt like? He'd never touched her like that, and he never would.

He lifted his hand. She jolted as if trying to wake herself from a dream, but he only rested a palm on her forehead to test her temperature. It rose. Her cheeks burned. She opened her mouth to suck in oxygen. Her chest heaved.

His head tilted to study her deeper. What did he see? Probably more than she wanted him to. "The Zika Virus?" he asked.

"Worse." The word had slipped out before she could stop it.

He reeled back slightly, his hand dropping from her head. His lips parted, but he didn't ask any more questions. He wouldn't want to hear the answer, but a spark of panic in the depths of his aqua colored eyes said he already knew—and he wasn't going to do anything about it.

So why was she still standing there?

Matt longed to follow Gen into the elevator. He needed privacy to discuss what he thought she was talking about. Though could he even say anything at all?

No, he couldn't. If he'd read Gen right, he'd already hurt her, and telling her why would hurt Casey. Though how had he hurt Gen? How had she known he'd chosen Casey over her? He'd made that choice with the belief she would never know. The belief that she might not even care. She'd been her happy self up by the trolley with Sam.

Sam.

Matt whirled to find his little brother standing in the entrance to the club, fire hat in hand. Had he followed Gen down? Had he seen what happened? Had he *caused* what happened?

Matt strode past Casey, holding up one finger so she'd continue to wait for him, though her eyes were dazed enough to not comprehend the drama around her.

Alan comprehended. "Where's everybody goin', man? Do I need to take Gen to the hospital?"

Matt didn't respond. By the time Alan got downstairs, Gen would likely be gone anyway. So Matt focused on Sam. Narrowed his eyes. Ignored the cramping of his stomach. "What did you do?"

Sam stared right back. "What did *you* do?"

Matt did what he had to do. He'd made a sacrifice to save the day. Sam better not turn this on him. He spoke slowly to relay the gravity and a warning. "I told Casey I'd take her to see her mom at the hospital because Casey just found out her mom has cancer."

Sam's eyes bulged. "You're kidding."

"I've never been more serious."

Sam's head fell backwards. He turned to pace away, muttering to himself.

"Sam?" This was not good.

The kid returned. Flinched. Shook his head. "I was only trying to find out if she was attracted to you."

Matt's chest ached to know the answer to the question, but he would not ask. Her answer had been clear in the way she'd described her own pain as worse than the illness she'd contracted in Central America. His heart throbbed for what could have been.

Their friendship must have turned into something more for her, as well. And when she'd admitted as much to Sam, he would have told her how Matt felt. "What did you tell her?"

Sam's dark, sad eyes spoke their apology before he even opened his mouth. "I told her you were breaking up with Casey to be with her. I said if she didn't believe me, she could see for herself."

The fight drained down to Matt's toes. This wasn't about what Sam had said. It was about what Gen had watched. He'd struggled seeing her on Alan's arm, yet she'd seen him wrap his arms around Casey and kiss her. It wouldn't have meant anything a few days ago, but tonight, with the realization that he was falling for her, what she'd seen was him choosing Casey over her. And she wouldn't know why.

CHAPTER NINETEEN

GEN SKIPPED CHURCH WITH CRAIG, BUT she wouldn't skip a visit to Damon. Talking to him could be a good distraction. Or even a reminder that life could be worse, though it felt pretty bad. It felt like the sunshine of her heart had gone behind a cloud. Even outside gray rain ran in rivulets down the windows and distorted the beauty of the forest and ocean beyond.

"He's just a guy." She whispered the words.

"A-Plus?" Craig asked from where he sat next to Rosie in the front seat. "I'm pretty sure he's more than 'just a guy.' You went out with a superhero last night."

Gen allowed a small smile for Craig's benefit. Rosie knew who she was talking about. After catching a late flight home, Gen had spent the night at Rosie's. Rosie even let her sleep in her bed and rubbed her back as she'd cried herself to sleep.

"She's not talking about A-Plus." Rosie turned the windshield wipers higher. "She's talking about Matt Lake."

"Who?"

"The guy dating the team owner's daughter."

"Then he's not 'just a guy' either. He's a *lucky* guy."

Gen dropped her head back against the seat, her empty stomach churning bile. Maybe she shouldn't have come after all. "No. She's a lucky girl."

"Oh." Craig twisted to look at her. Perhaps realizing for the first time that her red eyes were not a result of partying all night long the way he'd likely assumed. "You have a thing for the Matt guy."

"Yes." Ugh. Why did she have to have a thing for the Matt guy? It had been fun at first when she hadn't really known him and simply thought he was adorable, but now she knew him. She loved spending time with him, and for just a moment, she believed he might feel the same way.

"I told him not to hurt you." Rosie growled.

Gen lifted her head. When had Rosie told him that? *Why* had Rosie told him that? "What?"

"I told him not to hurt you," Rosie repeated. "I could tell he was attracted to you on our hike. He couldn't take his eyes off you."

Her heart clenched. Was Rosie right? Matt had honestly been attracted to her? Well, not enough.

He'd been smart to douse that small spark with water before it started a fire. Though the resulting smoke threatened to smother her. She dropped sideways into the seat the way firemen always recommended when dealing with smoke.

"I should hurt *him.*" Craig punched a fist into his other palm.

Gen groaned. "It's not his fault." The upholstery muffled her voice, so she turned her head sideways and rested her cheek on the cushion. "If Sam hadn't gotten my hopes up, they wouldn't have come crashing down. Matt was a perfect gentleman."

"Okay, I'll hurt Sam then." Pause. "Who's Sam?"

Rosie snorted. "You can't fix this, Craig."

Gen sighed. Nobody could fix it, but it was nice to know Craig wanted to fix things for her as much as she wanted to fix things for him. That could create a bonding moment between him and Rosie, which was something Gen had been hoping for. He'd actually seemed to stay out of trouble over the past week by simply chilling in her apartment with her. She should quit focusing on what she didn't have, and be thankful for this gift.

Her pain wasn't unique. People lost loved ones all the time. To death or divorce or prison. At least she wasn't left alone. She had her crazy family to support her.

She allowed a sad smile and forced herself to look at the humor in her situation. "Sam is bigger than you, Craig."

Craig shrugged. "Damon will be released soon. The two of us can take him."

Gen rolled her eyes. Men. But they were the only men in her life now. Besides Dad who would be down next weekend for Damon's release. He'd help put everything into perspective with his logical, engineer's mind.

"Hmm." Rosie flicked on a blinker to turn into the prison. "It sounds like Sam had his hopes up too. Maybe Sam thought you were a better fit for Matt."

Craig twisted to take a closer look at Gen as if confused by all the attraction. She'd like to think he'd never considered her to be pretty before because he only saw her as a sister, but she'd always known Craig was drop-dead gorgeous, so that excuse didn't fly. "You've got all kinds of men interested in you," he said, his voice filled with wonder. "What's your secret?"

She flopped her arms wide to reveal how pathetic her situation really was, laying in the backseat with a sob-fest hangover and wearing day-old braids. As for the three men she'd hung out with the night before? Alan appreciated her photography skills. Sam had been completely mistaken about the possibility of her being a good fit for his brother. And Matt was probably, at that moment, wondering how he could avoid Gen—and the awkwardness she'd created—for the rest of his life. She'd be surprised if he ever flew to Eureka again. "Do I appear to have any secret?"

"No." Craig gave a sympathetic twist of his lips. "Not really."

The Jeep slowed and pulled to a stop at the guard station, the swish of the windshield wipers sounding loud in the sudden stillness. Gen continued to lie on the seat, but dragged her purse across the floor so she could reach inside and retrieve her ID. She passed it up to Craig who gave both their driver's licenses to Rosie when she rolled down the window to pass them over for inspection. It was long enough for a few drops of rain to splash in Gen's face.

She wiped at her cheek while staring at the tan ceiling and contemplated the next step for her life. With Damon getting out of jail the following week, she didn't have to stay in Eureka anymore. It would be hard to leave Rosie, but Rosie didn't need her the way she used to. Her sister was also starting to travel more for speaking, so she'd be gone a lot anyway.

Gen lay there, thoughts spinning. Where would she want to go? With her photography and flight benefits, she could really go anywhere. And actually, with the kind of money the Giants had paid her for her last photography job, she could afford to go into photography full time and wouldn't need to work at an airline. She'd probably be doing Matt a favor if she quit.

"What's taking so long?" Rosie whispered. "Craig, do you have a warrant for your arrest?"

Craig looked up as if he were actually trying to remember. "Not in California, I don't think."

Crud. Gen hadn't thought her day could get any worse.

"Gen, sit up. You might be making us look suspicious."

She hadn't considered laying on the backseat much of a threat. She'd assumed anyone who looked at her could tell she was suffering from a broken heart. She blinked and rolled up in slow motion to keep her depression from affecting others.

Putting on her bravest smile, she turned toward the guard so he could see she bore no malicious intent, but the man in the booth wasn't even looking at her. He was talking on a phone.

"It doesn't normally take this long?" Craig asked, shifting toward the door like he was about to make a break for it.

"Touch that handle, and I will punch you." Rosie continued to smile at the guard though the threat came through in her tone.

Craig held his hands up. "Why do you automatically assume I'm the one who messed up?"

"Gen, have you ever puked in my dryer, thinking you were puking in a toilet? Have you ever taken my car without permission and crashed it in a ditch because you were too high to see straight? Have you ever found a dead body in the marijuana field you were stealing from then lied about it so the police had to track you down at my place?" Rosie directed a scowl toward their brother though her rhetorical questions were for Gen. "No? I didn't think so."

So much for Rosie and Craig's bonding moment. So much for Gen counting her blessings. Her life was cursed. No wonder she preferred to daydream.

"I apologized for every one of those things." Craig narrowed his eyes.

"Yeah, and then each time you charmed your way back into our hearts, you took advantage and did something worse."

"I checked myself into rehab."

"And we're supposed to believe you're clean now?"

Craig's voice rose. "What else do you want me to do, Rosie?" It never worked to get mad at him because he could always get madder.

Gen slid her gaze sideways to see how the prison guard was reacting to their family feud. She wanted this to be her last visit to the place. She didn't need another brother in jail.

The man knocked on their window. She jumped then leaned forward to get a glimpse of the expression on his face as Rosie rolled down the glass again. He didn't look happy, but he wasn't looking at Craig either.

He bent forward, giving them an even better view of his ruddy complexion. "I'm sorry to tell you folks this, but Damon Wilson can't have any visitors today."

Gen shook her head. That wasn't right. In five years, that had never happened before. But he'd never been released on parole before either. Hope expanded in her chest like a balloon. If she didn't have hope, she wouldn't have anything. "Is it because he's getting ready for release? Does he have to pack?"

The man's beady eyes turned her way. "Packing a prison cell doesn't take that long."

Something was off. "Is he hurt? Is he sick?" Maybe her virus had been airborne after all. The state had better have given him the care he needed.

The guard handed Rosie their IDs. "I can't tell you anything more, but you should be getting a call from his attorney."

Gen slammed back into her seat. Damon's attorney? Why would he need an attorney unless he'd done something wrong again? But he wouldn't have done anything wrong. He was the Bible study leader.

Rosie rolled up her window and circled her car the direction the guard pointed to turn around. Gen caught sight of Rosie's fingers on the steering wheel. Damon had almost gotten into a fight over her fingers on one of their last visits. Could that be what all this was about? Gen's hope deflated, dropping the load it had been lifting like an anvil in her gut.

Craig looked back and forth between his sisters. "I don't understand."

"Gen, call Mom." Rosie jerked her head toward the backseat. "Damon's attorney would have contacted her. She'll know what's going on."

Oh, Damon.

Gen only dialed because Rosie was driving and because Craig would create even more drama. She didn't want to be the one to have her suspicions confirmed over the phone. She didn't want another reason to be sad.

Matt could hear the sadness in Gen's voice. Even though she was trying to sound strong. Even though all she said was, "Gate three-bravo."

Or maybe he didn't really hear it. Maybe he only thought he did because he felt it. Like a weighted blanket designed to help insomniacs sleep. Which was something he might have to invest in if he ever wanted to sleep again.

It had been three days. Three days of not talking to Gen or texting her. That wasn't only because he'd been at the hospital comforting Casey, it was because he needed to talk to her in person. If she was ever going to understand his position, she needed to see the sincerity in his eyes.

He also needed to see the strength in hers. He needed to be reassured that she was a fighter. That she was surrounded by people who would support her and her dreams.

Between Gen and Casey, Casey was the one who'd looked like she had it all. But that's because she was the beautiful orchid protected by perfect conditions in order to bloom. Those conditions resulted in her being admired by everyone. Once those conditions were tampered with, she could wilt. He didn't want her wilting to be his fault. So he'd stay there for her to protect her from the elements.

Gen, on the other hand, was the one who could forge her way through stone. She was like a wildflower on the top of Half Dome in Yosemite National Park, finding a way to bloom despite life's obstacles, but only the bravest explorers would ever fully experience her beauty. He hoped one day there would be a man courageous enough to find her and treasure her. He couldn't.

He finished up his announcement of their descent over the intercom and powered off the speaker and reduced elevation.

"What's with you?"

Matt ignored his co-pilot. He didn't need any more advice from an adulterer.

"If you're not going to talk, I will. Tonight I'm going to tell Stephanie that I'm leaving her for Michelle."

"You're an idiot." Any other day Matt would have taken a little more time to consider his words, but he'd spent his whole weekend pretending, and he couldn't do it any longer. He thought Ethan was an idiot, so out it came.

Ethan laughed. "Tell me how you really feel, man."

Normally Matt would have shared his feelings with his co-pilot in an attempt to reach him. Not today. Not when he already had enough hopeless things to focus on. He set the flaps. "I don't think it matters what I say because you won't listen."

Ethan lowered the landing gear. "The feeling is mutual."

Like Ethan had any good advice to offer. The guy didn't know the difference between lust and love. Matt thrust on idle and lined up with the runway. The ground seemed to move quicker, the lower they got. "Then there's really no reason for us to talk."

Ethan blew out his cheeks, shook his head, and raised the nose of the plane to slow them down. Buildings zipped by in the distance. "I'm going to lose a lot more than my family, aren't I?"

Was that self-pity? An attempt at giving Matt a guilt trip? If anybody should feel guilt, it was Ethan. Matt absorbed the jolt from the rear wheels landing and used the speed brakes to gently set the nose down. "Is there anything worse than losing your family?"

"Losing yourself," Ethan said, effectively ending the argument.

The silence after Ethan's answer roared louder than the jet engines as they worked in tandem to slow the plane and steer it toward the gate. Matt was better off not having to converse. He didn't like Ethan's insinuation. He wasn't losing himself. He was laying himself down.

If Ethan couldn't understand, would Gen? He finished up his flight and made his way up the jet bridge to face her and find out.

Gen was glad she wouldn't have to face Matt alone. Rosie was flying to San Francisco for a church conference where she'd be keynoting, so Gen made sure she was sitting next to the podium at the door to the jet bridge. Matt might not even talk to her at all, in which case, she'd need Rosie's support even more.

Rosie seemed to be struggling as much as Gen. Only her struggle was over the fact that Damon had gotten into a fight with the inmate who'd been making fun of Rosie's fingers. She blamed herself for Damon being denied parole.

The gate door swung open. Gen jumped. It was only Bianca, holding the fuel slip Matt must have filled out. Had he expected to be handing it to Gen? Would he care that she wasn't the one who'd opened the plane door?

Passengers filed through the door behind Bianca, but as the agent didn't get out of their way, they had to part to go around her. Bianca didn't even pass Gen the fuel slip. She held onto it as she crossed her arms. "What's going on?"

Was Gen that transparent, or had Matt said something? No, Matt wouldn't do that. They'd both be better off if Bianca didn't get involved.

"Bianca, why don't you set up your speaker for your boarding music? I'm having a bad day, and a little John Denver might lift my spirits."

Bianca gave her the fuel slip grudgingly. "I know you're avoiding my question, but I agree that you could use some John Denver right now."

Gen watched the other woman turn and head toward the desk before sending Rosie a smile over the small triumph.

Rosie flashed the A-Okay hand gesture before looking down at her mutilated hand and burying it in her lap once again.

"Gen."

She jumped for good reason this time. Matt stood behind her. Chills popped up on the back of her neck. How had she not sensed his presence the moment he'd gotten off the plane?

"Can I talk to you about Saturday?"

She made the mistake of meeting his gaze before busying herself at the computer. He had kinda squinty eyes, but that didn't diminish the power in their aqua depths.

Was Bianca playing the soundtrack to Jaws over the loudspeaker or was that all in her imagination? She certainly wanted to scream like she'd seen a shark. She needed to get on solid ground.

"It's fine," she said, though the way she rubbed her earlobe raw was sure to give her real feelings away.

She dropped her hands and focused on the screen then moved her finger along the mousepad like she knew what she was clicking on. A random screen popped up. Gen stared at it intently.

"It's not fine."

Why was he arguing? She'd taken him off the hook and thrown him back into the water. He was free.

Meanwhile, her fingers trembled. Where was Rosie when she needed her? She sent a furtive glance toward her sister who was not being furtive at all in the way she watched Matt. So much for having a wingman.

That's probably how Matt had felt about Sam. She'd let the kid brother off the hook too. He must not have known what he was talking about when he'd told her Matt was going to break up with Casey for her. "Sam was mistaken."

"No, he wasn't."

Her breath spasmed. Her stomach clenched. Her eyes found his.

Their intensity sent tingles down her spine. Their sadness made tears pool in her heart. He was saying that he really had been about to break up with Casey for her. But then he hadn't. And here they were. She was still single, while he was not.

"It's fine," she said again. It had to be. Eventually.

"No, it's not."

Anger rose up like the armor she'd need to drive Matt away

before he hurt her even more. What did he want? A girlfriend at every gate? She'd thought he was better than that.

"Then what are you going to do about it?" she demanded, her voice barely above a whisper. She didn't want to attract attention, and she didn't want Rosie to step in now. Not when she'd taken a stand for herself. Not when Matt was about to admit which side he was on.

He didn't draw his sword. Rather, he gave her a pleading look, like he was waving the white flag. "I want to explain."

Explain? As in tell her exactly why he'd picked Casey over her? List everything she lacked like she didn't already know?

She'd applauded his choice. She'd expected him to choose Casey from the very beginning. Everybody had. She'd thought his unavailability had made him safe for her silly attraction. Then he had to go and ruin it by making her feel like she had a chance.

She would not take her armor off now—not when that would give him the power to gut her.

She studied his face one last time. His average looks turned into classic good looks when he smiled, but even when he wasn't smiling, his eyes still smoldered in such a way that they had the power to heat her up inside.

He couldn't fix what he'd broken. He needed to leave. "Explaining will make this harder."

His eyelids lowered in a flinch. If it hurt him too, why was he prolonging their pain? Couldn't he rip the Band-Aid off already?

"Matt." Rosie stepped in. "I have something for you."

Gen would have thought such an interruption would have helped her relax, but, knowing Rosie, that "something" for him might very well have been a wave goodbye with the middle and only finger on her left hand. Gen tensed in trepidation. She also wondered how she could explain such a conflict to her boss should any passengers report it.

Her sister did indeed extend her left hand, but pinched between thumb and middle finger were two cardstock tickets. "I'm speaking at Grace Cathedral tomorrow night. If you're not busy, I'd really love for you to hear what I have to say."

Gen's shoulders relaxed at the sight of such a gesture, but then they rocketed back up toward her ears at Rosie's words. What was her sister going to speak about that she thought Matt needed to hear? Usually her talks were on the history behind her deformity and how God had helped her overcome, but why would she want Matt to hear that? Was she going to add to the message? Was she going to say something about Gen? That was the downfall of having a sister who sparkled on stage. It put their whole dysfunctional family in the spotlight.

Matt looked down at the tickets slowly as if not sure the invite was genuine or a diversion technique. Gen hoped it to be a diversion. She'd use it as one anyway.

Grabbing the speaker for the intercom, she swallowed down her nerves to steady her voice and announce pre-boarding for anyone with a disability or who might need assistance getting on the plane. Then she scanned the crowd in hopes Olivia would be waiting so Gen could excuse herself and use the paraplegic woman as a shield, but as Olivia hadn't flown into Eureka lately, it would have been a little difficult for her to be there to fly out.

"I have a disability," Rosie stepped to the front of the line with a giant wink towards Gen. Neither the wink nor the need to pre-board were necessary and surely wouldn't be lost on Matt. "Are you headed back to the plane, Matt? I'll walk with you."

Matt shot Gen one more look that could either be described as longing or long-suffering. She'd consider it to be long-suffering. Because as much as she used to pretend he longed for her, she now had to pretend the longing didn't exist.

CHAPTER TWENTY

IN TWENTY-FOUR HOURS, MATT HAD not only painted the spare room, but he'd fixed the neighbor's doorbell, balanced his checkbook, cooked fettuccini Alfredo for lunch, then biked to Sausalito and back in a dense, cool fog. All this was done before he had to pick Casey up for an evening trip to the hospital. He'd hoped that expending so much energy would help him sit still and feel less anxious while Casey cried on his shoulder.

He wanted to be there for her and her mom. That's what a good boyfriend would do. That's what they deserved.

It just killed him knowing that Gen deserved more than he could give her too.

He pulled in front of Casey's new high rise condo and let the valet take his car. He rode the glass elevator up the side of the building until he reached the perfect view of the bay from Casey's floor. All the glass made her place feel like she had a house in the sky and should have freaked her out with her fear of flying. He didn't have that fear, but it *was* a little too modern for his taste. Perfect but cold. Which strangely had never bothered him before.

Casey met him at her door. She was still dressed professionally for work, and her expression seemed every bit as detached. She held up her phone. "Dad texted. Said Mom could use rest tonight after all the testing they've been doing, and he thinks we should go out and do something fun instead of spending the evening crying over her."

Matt didn't have the appetite for fun, but this wasn't about him. "How do you feel about that?"

Casey didn't move. She didn't look like she had the appetite for fun either. "There's nothing I want to do."

Did that mean she wanted to spend the evening crying here if she couldn't cry at the hospital over what the test results might be? He'd be there for her either way.

He shoved his hands in his jacket pockets. The corner of a paper poked at his fingers. Tickets. For Gen's sister's speaking event. He hadn't planned to attend, but it would get Casey out of her house. It would distract her from her own pain—if she was up to it. He didn't know what Rosie had to say, but it was sure to be entertaining.

He pulled the squares out to check the date. Yep, it was tonight. "I have these tickets to hear a motivational speaker if you're interested. Might help."

Casey stared at him for a moment before reaching out her hand. He passed her the tickets. Her eyes scanned the information. "It's at our church. Who's Rosie Wilson?"

Matt looked toward the gray tiles to avoid letting her read his emotion when he spoke of Gen. She didn't need any more pain in her life. "Gen's sister. She's missing some fingers, so I think that's probably part of her story."

Casey's lifeless gaze sparked with curiosity. "Do you know if she lost fingers because of cancer or tumors?"

He shook his head. He had no idea. This had never been a topic that would have appealed to Casey, but she was looking for encouragement now. It might be exactly what she needed. "You want to go?"

Casey glanced at her watch—a diamond encrusted timepiece given to her from her father after five years of working for the Giants. She'd once been so proud of it but would surely trade it now in exchange for her mother's health. All those beautiful belongings Casey used to prize didn't mean anything anymore. Except maybe for the glass frog she'd bought Valerie on their shopping trip to Sausalito. That could very well have been an unintended parting gift. And it might become a memento from better days. Guilt pricked at Matt's conscience for his previous ambiguousness over Casey's purchase. He had a lot to make up for.

She bit her lip. "Can we go but leave early if it doesn't help?"

"Yes. Of course." He was there to help.

Once at the church, Rosie's words gripped him from her very first line. He had trouble seeing her from the spot they'd staked out in the last pew, and she was dwarfed by the stone columns, soaring ceiling, and arched stained glass, but that didn't matter. It was as if she were speaking to him.

"I'm really hurting tonight." Her voice resonated with both the room's powerful acoustics and her own transparency.

Was she hurting because of Gen? Had his desire to avoid hurting anyone caused even more pain? Was she going to announce his unspoken feelings in front of Casey? His gut twisted. How had he messed things up so badly?

"Usually..." she held up both hands to display their odd array of fingers. "I tell my sad story and how I survived it, and that's the end. You all go home all happy and inspired and maybe tell someone else about my story so they can be inspired too."

That was exactly what Matt had been hoping for. He shifted on the hard wooden seat and glanced at Casey to see how she felt about the change of direction. She watched with rapt attention, so Matt focused back on the stage, as well.

"The thing is that my life isn't over. There are going to be more challenges."

Yeah, that was the opposite of encouraging. Especially if *he* was part of her challenge.

"So tonight I'm going to be real about what I'm struggling with. Then I'm going to tell you why I keep on going."

Matt rubbed a hand over his face. Did he want to stick around for this?

"I was adopted into a family of six kids. We all had a great childhood. It was fabulous. But because I didn't know my birth parents, I felt like something was missing."

Matt dropped his hand to his lap and cocked his head. That was the opposite of what Gen had said. She'd claimed that because of her fabulous family, she didn't want to meet her birth parents. Were the sisters that different or were their stories somehow connected?

"With as much as my adopted parents loved and cherished me, I figured my biological parents would feel the same. I thought there must have been some horrible accident where I lost my fingers and toes, and they were injured too. Or even killed. But I was wrong."

Rosie shook her head. "I tracked them down and discovered that they didn't need me because they had two daughters just like me already. And when I say 'just like me,' I mean *just* like me. I'm a triplet."

Matt pressed back into his seat in shock. Had Rosie's parents kept the other daughters and gotten rid of her like the runt of the litter?

"Yes, they kept the other two girls."

The crowd gasped and murmured in dismay.

Casey clutched Matt's hand. She had to face the possibility of losing her mom, but she'd never had to face being abandoned by her mom. This story might be good for her after all. Help her count her blessings.

"But that's not the worst part."

It wasn't? How much worse could it get?

"The worst part was that they'd gone through in vitro fertilization with such positive results that there were six of us."

Matt frowned. Six? But Rosie said she was a triplet.

"They decided to do a selective abortion and only keep two babies."

Matt's whole body went numb.

"They thought they'd gotten rid of me, but they only chopped off my toes and some of my fingers."

Casey's hand slipped from his so she could cover her mouth. Matt checked on her but didn't make a move to comfort her. She was feeling something for someone else, and that was a good thing. As for Matt, what he really wanted to do was shake Rosie's disfigured hand again. Congratulate her on being such a fighter.

She struck a dramatic pose on stage, feet wide, one hand on hip, the other arm extended straight overhead. "Surprise!"

The audience tittered with nervous laughter.

Rosie's arm lowered slowly, her voice deepening with sadness. "But the surprise was on me. Because of all the scenarios I'd imagined could take place when meeting my parents, this had never been one of them. I'd never imagined that my deformity was a result of my parents trying to terminate me. They explained this through an email because they didn't want to meet me in person."

Matt shook his head. He'd always considered himself pro-life, but after hearing Rosie's story, he wanted to go rescue all of the unwanted babies. The fetuses who would never be able to tell their stories.

"As you might imagine, I sank into a pretty deep depression. Four years ago, today, I didn't think I could handle it anymore. I laid down in a bathtub and slit my wrists."

His chest constricted around his heart. Her arms weren't mutilated from her deformity. It had been a scar from attempted suicide.

"My sister Genevieve found me in that bathtub."

Matt's lips parted as his breath whooshed out.

Casey leaned toward his ear. "Did you know that?"

"No," he whispered. He'd had no idea. The sisters were so close and so happy. He'd never imagined.

There were probably a lot more things he didn't know about Gen. More things he would never know.

"Gen saved me, both physically and emotionally. She called an ambulance, and after my release from a mental hospital, she invited me to live with her near the Redwood Forest."

Matt's throat clogged. Gen was a hero, and he'd never realized it. Because she'd never shown it. It was like she didn't even know.

"I'm going to come back to my healing in the Redwoods after I tell you about where I'm at now."

Oh boy. Was this where she told everyone how she was hurting because Gen had been hurt? By him?

"Last year Gen was supposed to read through the entire Bible with me. She's never admitted it, but I could tell when she stopped. It was at the part about how families are cursed for up to four generations."

Matt frowned. He'd never really thought about that part before. Could that be because his parents were great people?

"She thinks I was cursed to repeat the sins of my father by trying to kill myself."

Matt blinked. That was harsh.

"But it's not only because of me. She thinks all six of us are being punished for the sins of our fathers."

Matt leaned forward, resting his elbows on his knees. He hadn't known any of this. Gen made her family sound idyllic. If she'd told him this, would he have broken up with Casey earlier to be there for her? He might have.

"My youngest brother is mentally handicapped like his mother." She ticked her siblings off on her hands. Since she had five siblings, it took both her hands. "I've got another brother staying with us right now after a stint in drug rehab—his mom was in jail for dealing drugs when she gave birth to him. My older sister Trina was adopted from China, and exactly like her birth parents separated themselves from her because their country didn't allow more children, she's separated herself from us because we don't have the same beliefs as her birth parents. She moved away after graduation and hasn't spoken with us since."

Wow. Gen may have a big family like his, but their history was completely different. Yet she seemed to love her siblings the same way he loved his. How would he feel about his brothers if one took off and didn't speak to him again or one lied to him about drugs? He'd be pretty angry about it, honestly.

Rosie sighed into the microphone. "Then there's my oldest brother who is in prison for rape."

Damon? The doctor? Matt had seen his photo, though Gen had never told him the guy was in prison. And for rape? That was horrible. How could she still display pictures of him?

"Damon was one of my favorite people in the world. Then he made an awful decision."

No kidding.

"It's the same decision his dad once made. If his dad hadn't raped his mother, he never would have been born. But in Haiti, where he's from, his dad didn't have the same consequences. Apparently Damon justified this in his mind."

Oh, man.

"Damon's had to learn the hard way, and I believe he really has learned from it. In fact, he was eligible for early parole this month."

Matt could barely handle all this new information. Besides Gen having to deal with losing Matt, she's been taking care of her druggie brother and likely preparing to take in a released felon as well. How would her life have been different if he could have been there for her?

Rosie shook her head. "I'm hurting because Damon won't be released after all. He got into a fight with another inmate who was making fun of my hands. He is staying in prison because of a fight over me."

Matt's mind whirled. Why wasn't someone taking care of these women? Where were Gen's parents in all of this? She shouldn't have to face this alone.

"It hurts." Rosie's voice pulled him back to the present. To her spilling her guts on stage. "But I get it. Of all people, I get why Damon started that fight. Neither of us thought we could rise above our condition. We might not have called it a curse the way my sister does, but we both felt it. We both thought our failures defined us."

Whoa. That was deep. How did this apply to Matt? Did it have to do with the way he strived for perfection? The way he tried to protect everyone else?

"So back to my own recovery. To my move to the Redwoods." Rosie took a moment to gather her thoughts. Or perhaps her emotions.

Casey wiped at her eyes next to him. He wrapped an arm around her.

"I learned a lot about the oldest trees on earth, on what helps them survive. Of all the places in the world for them to live, they live on the California coast. That means they've faced earthquakes and typhoons and mudslides. They've continued to grow even when their world is shaken. And do you know how?" She waited. Silence. "They deform."

Matt frowned. That didn't make any sense.

"When not on solid ground, they have the ability to grow faster on the lower side than the higher side. They buttress themselves up." Rosie leaned forward. "Their deformity is not a curse. It's a blessing."

She shook her head in wonder. "God created us all in His image. He created us perfect. Then the pain of life in this fallen world comes against us. If not for God, it would have the power to destroy us."

She lifted her hands again, and Matt saw them in a whole new light. "If not for my deformity, I would not be standing in front of you right now. Though I may sometimes have seen this as a curse, God can use it as a blessing. Same with Damon's existence. God didn't create the sin that brought Damon into the world, but He used it for good. And once Damon sees himself the way God sees him, he will be able to stop hurting people. He will stop hurting himself. He will realize he's been blessed."

Casey sobbed silently next to Matt as the event came to a close. Rosie's message had been powerful, but was it always true? He hugged Casey tight, wondering how her mother's cancer could possibly be a blessing. Wondering how Gen's destructive family could possibly be a blessing. Wondering how his feelings for the wrong woman could ever bless anyone.

Casey wiped her chin and swallowed. "I want to meet her." Her voice squeaked on the last word.

Rosie was talking to people up front and autographing her new book, but how would she feel about seeing Matt with his arm around Casey? She'd forgiven a rapist, so maybe she could forgive him too. He grimaced.

"Let's go." He led Casey to the line and listened to the encouragement Rosie offered others as well as to the encouragement they gave her.

The people in front of them finally moved, allowing Rosie's gaze to land on him. She gave a caring smile. "You came."

He nodded because if he spoke, he couldn't be as authentic as she'd been, and he didn't want to dim the light in the room by masking his pain or faking enthusiasm. She already knew more about him than anyone else there.

Casey stepped forward and clutched Rosie's beautiful hands, fresh tears pooling in her eyes. "Thank you so much for giving Matt the tickets for tonight. Your words touched me because I'm going through a painful time too. Halloween night I found out my mom has cancer."

Rosie leaned back, stretching their arms between them as the weight of understanding hit her. "I'm so sorry." Her eyes flicked his way, a deep sadness changing her expression. She'd been the one to stop him from explaining his situation to Gen earlier. Now she knew what she'd interrupted.

Casey bit her lip. "My grandma died of breast cancer, so it could be considered a curse too I guess."

Matt stilled. He'd known Casey's grandma had passed away before she was born, but he'd never realized cancer ran in her family. Would her mom pass away before Casey had kids? Was Casey getting regular exams to check for lumps? He'd have to make sure. At least their family had the money needed to get the best treatment possible.

As for Gen, would she consider Casey's situation a curse? It sure felt like one.

Rosie reached for his hand so the three of them were linked. "I will be praying for you both."

Earlier he'd wanted to rescue Rosie, and here she was, lifting him up. Despite the way he'd hurt her sister.

Casey sent him a grateful glance before focusing on Rosie once again. "I have one more question, if you don't mind my asking. But what is Gen's curse? She seems so healthy."

Matt stiffened. It wasn't that he didn't care to know, it was that he cared too much.

Rosie twisted her lips in thought. This time when her eyes peeked his way, it was with a measuring look. Like maybe she didn't know if she wanted him to hear the answer. Or maybe he was the answer.

He swallowed hard.

Finally Rosie faced Casey again. "Gen is afraid to track down her birth parents because she's afraid of finding out her curse."

Matt's world spun. This wasn't what Gen had told him. She'd claimed to be content with her adopted family. Though after Rosie's talk, he knew that couldn't be true.

Casey's light eyes reflected concern. "Does she think not knowing about a curse will stop it?"

Rosie's cheeks softened. "As I said before, I believe what Gen sees as a curse, God wants to use as a blessing. Since she's afraid to go through any more pain, she's going to deny herself both."

Pain. Matt had caused her pain. He hadn't meant to, but he had. And on top of all the other stuff she had to deal with. No wonder she was afraid.

Here he was, trying to protect Casey who was mourning the idea of losing her mother when Gen had never known hers to begin with. Maybe he could be there for Gen too. He could secretly pick up the birth certificate in Portland and track down her mother. If her parents really didn't want Gen in their life, Gen would never have to know. But if they wanted to reunite, he could make sure that happened. It was the least he could do.

CHAPTER TWENTY-ONE

GEN WOKE UP TO THE SOUND of a shriek. She jolted upright in bed.

Craig? No, the tone had been too high-pitched.

Rosie? She wasn't supposed to fly in until after noon. What would she be shrieking about anyway? They'd had the exterminator out last month, so there shouldn't be any more mice.

Gen kicked the sheets off her legs and scrambled out the bedroom door.

Craig still lay on the couch, having only pushed up to an elbow with one arm and rubbing the sleep from his eyes with the other. "What's going on?" he mumbled.

"I heard Rosie scream."

He swung his feet to the floor and reached for his phone. "What time is it? I didn't think Rosie was getting back until later."

"Either someone else is screaming in her apartment or she took an earlier flight." Gen scanned their surroundings, looking for a weapon. The spatula was still outside, and though she used to carry pepper spray, it got confiscated at TSA. At that time the security guard had suggested she carry a small flashlight that could be used to both blind or hit an assailant. He said it was safer too because then she didn't run the risk of getting pepper spray in her own eyes and lungs.

With shaky hands and a quivering heart, Gen tipped her purse over on the desk to find the weapon. Would she actually have to use it?

Craig watched her then sprang past into the kitchen. "I'll grab a knife."

A knife? Stabbing someone would be a lot bloodier than shining a light in their eyes. Gen's stomach revolted at the image. "Bring your phone to call the police." That would be the better option. Hers was still in her room, charging.

Craig continued to search through drawers. Should she wait for him or check on Rosie? Ideally he would lead the charge, but if their sister's commotion was over nothing more than a mouse, they would look pretty silly busting through her front door, brandishing weapons.

Gen tiptoed toward her door and peeked out, half expecting to see masked men carrying Rosie away. The deep blue horizon revealed nothing but the prelude to a rising sun. Rosie's door wasn't even open.

Gen glanced over her shoulder to see if Craig was ready to take the lead, but with as slowly as he was moving, he still had to be half asleep. Maybe he hadn't heard the scream because it hadn't happened. Maybe it had all been a dream and Rosie was still at SFO.

The apartment next door remained silent. Gen rolled her eyes at herself. She was going to be totally embarrassed if Rosie wasn't even there. She'd check quickly. But quietly, just in case.

After easing the deadbolt from its locked position, she cracked her door open and slipped out into the misty morning. Then she plastered herself against the pink siding and eased across the deck toward Rosie's window. With fingers clenched tightly around her flashlight, she tilted her head to peek inside.

Light shown from the bathroom in the hallway, so Rosie was home. But was she alone?

The woman in question stomped out of the bathroom. She headed toward her front door and ripped it open before Gen could move.

Rosie's amber eyes glowed in anger.

"What?" What had made her angry enough to scream and stomp around at six in the morning?

"Someone was in my house. They rifled through my medicine cabinet."

Gen frowned. She hadn't noticed anyone strange on their property. And how would they have gotten in anyway? "I'm the only one with a key…" Oh.

"Where's Craig?"

Gen closed her eyes. Their brother had stolen from them again. And all this time she'd been treating him like an honored guest.

Rosie pounded past her on the wooden planks. "Craig."

Gen sighed and turned to follow. "He said he was clean."

"Of course he said that." Rosie shoved Gen's door wide and disappeared into the apartment. "Craig."

No response. Probably because he couldn't lie his way out of this one. Gen trudged past the blankets on her couch toward the kitchen to confront him, but the kitchen was empty. Her stomach sank.

Rosie's footsteps pounded down the hallway.

Gen trailed behind to find Rosie in her bathroom, combing through her medicine cabinet. "Do you have any prescription drugs in your house, Gen?"

No, she'd hardly even used any of the pills the doctor had prescribed to help her through the Zika Virus. Oh crud. She'd never gotten rid of them.

She circled around Rosie from the mirror over the sink to open the cabinet over her toilet. She held her breath as she retrieved the orange bottle with the white cap. She shook it without hearing a sound. "Empty."

She slammed it into the garbage can. Craig had been happy to hang out in her apartment because she'd unknowingly kept him medicated. Once he'd run out of pills in her bathroom, he must have gone in search of Rosie's.

Rosie didn't say, *I told you so.* She hadn't wanted to be right. Instead she continued the hunt for Craig through Gen's bedroom onto the back porch. He wasn't there.

Rosie threaded her fingers into her hair. "He didn't even close the gate. The goats are loose."

Gen stopped and stared. "He let the goats loose?" Like dealing with the realization she'd been used by her brother again wasn't enough? He had to send her on a roundup through their neighborhood in her zebra striped pajamas? Not to mention everything else on her plate? Did he not care for her at all?

Ugh. He made her so mad. She wanted to...she wanted to...shine her flashlight in his eyes.

"Come on." Rosie scuffed down the stairs.

As much as Gen wanted to crawl back under her covers and pretend this was all a nightmare, she couldn't let Rosie chase down the farm animals by herself. At least Gen's minivan came in handy here. She drove behind her sister, and every time they found a goat, she stuffed him in the back. Finally they rounded up Alfred, freeing Rosie to climb into the passenger seat beside Gen.

What must they have looked like to all their neighbors? Gen moaned. "I don't know whether to laugh or cry."

"You've been doing enough crying lately. Let's laugh."

"Easy for you to say." Gen motioned to Rosie's jeans then her own silk pajama set. "At least you were dressed for the chase."

They laughed then. Hard enough that Gen was crying too. Those kinds of tears, she didn't mind. She wiped her eyes as she pulled up to the curb by their back gate. "First time Matt saw my van, he asked if I had four kids he didn't know about. I should have told him that no, I have five."

Then she was crying real tears too, but still laughing. Because she was that big of a mess.

Rosie cried along with her. Gen had lost Matt, but they'd both lost Craig. Would they ever get him back? She wouldn't give up.

"We have to find Craig. Where do you think he went?"

Rosie wiped her eyes. "Why do we have to find him?"

Gen shrugged. It should be obvious. "To help him."

Rosie leaned against the seat and sighed. "If he wanted help, he'd still be here."

"Of course he doesn't want help, but he *needs* help." How could Rosie let him go so easily? She'd been right about him not being clean, but that didn't mean he couldn't ever be clean.

"Gen." Rosie stroked the silky fabric covering her arm. "We can't fix him if he doesn't want to be fixed. He gets that choice. If we do for him what he can do for himself, we ultimately harm him."

Gen didn't want to believe it. She didn't want to admit she didn't have the power to keep him from leaving her. Though she should know better by now. "He's cursed," she said.

Rosie let go to wipe at another tear dripping off her chin. "If he's cursed, it's with good looks. He's never going to have to change because there will always be some girl he can charm with his rugged smile and piercing blue eyes, and she'll take him in like a homeless kitten."

Gen had been "some girl" this time. "Thank you for not leaving me, Rosie."

Rosie gave a sad smile. "I tried."

"I know. But you're here now." Where would she be without Rosie? She didn't even want to think about it. "You're the only one here."

Rosie reached for her hand, fingers damp. "Gen, I'm here right now because I flew home early. I wanted to be able to talk to you before you went to work."

Gen rummaged through the pocket in the van door for an old napkin she could use to wipe her nose. If Rosie hadn't come back early, she'd just be getting up. She'd be showering while Craig continued to sleep on her couch. She'd probably even offer to run to the store to get more milk for him to put on his cereal. The heartless jerk.

A goat bleated from the back seat. She'd worry about Alfred later.

"What did you want to talk about?" She found a semi clean napkin from Los Bagels and pinched at her nostrils. Whatever Rosie had to say, it couldn't be as bad as what their brother put them through.

"Matt came to hear me speak last night."

Gen lowered the napkin, her heart dropping as well. She knew Rosie had given him tickets. It had been the distraction she'd needed at the airport. But she'd never imagined he would actually show. He'd chosen Casey over her, and he should have been separating himself from her family. "Did you talk to him?"

Rosie met her gaze, her eyes full of compassion. "Both him and Casey."

Gen's heart rose then. Straight into her throat. But why wouldn't Casey have been with him? He wouldn't go alone. It was probably their date night, and he'd needed somewhere to take her.

"Casey's mom has cancer."

Gen clutched her chest. The space where her heart should have been throbbed with emptiness. Not only for herself, but for the loneliness Casey would have to face if she lost her mother. "I had no idea."

Rosie's lips curved down as if she was trying to keep them from quivering, but her chin puckered anyway. "I think maybe that's what Matt was trying to explain to you the other day."

Gen's hands rose to her mouth. Could it be? Could Matt have possibly been headed to break up with Casey like Sam had said, then she'd dropped this bomb on him. He never would have left Casey alone. He would commit to never leave her, even if he'd had feelings for Gen at one time.

This was all speculation on her part, but were it true, did it help or hurt even more? Did it matter? Nothing had changed. Matt was with Casey as he always had been. And she was still rejected.

Matt took a direct flight from San Francisco to Portland to pick up Gen's original birth certificate from Oregon Vital Records. She'd once wanted the information enough to put in the order. He'd be the middle man to make sure she'd still want it.

The building was all cement blocks and glass with a large alcove as an outdoor entryway held up by two pillars. Each block over the alcove contained one letter and together they spelled out OREGON — Gen's birthplace. Would he find out any more than that? He took a deep breath before dashing from the Uber through the rain and into the building.

Was he crazy for doing this? Probably. But he had the unique ability to travel to another state for the day, so how could he not? Nobody even had to know.

Say he looked up Gen's parents and tracked them down through Facebook to find out they'd been one of those couples who'd had a baby in secret before their wedding to avoid judgment, and now they were happily married and living in the West Hills? Say they were never able to conceive again and dreaming of their long lost daughter? He'd tell Gen then.

Matt checked the directory and entered an elevator, shaking his head at himself. The chances of a beautiful reunion were slim. Had Gen's parents wanted to get to know her, they could have found her ages ago. For all the texts he'd sent and the stories he'd made up, Gen's parents could just as easily be dead. Would he tell her then? Would she want to know? And was this all nothing more than a way to ease his own guilt?

The elevator chimed and the doors slid open. Matt was going to do this. Not for himself. But for her. Because it was the only thing he *could* do for her.

He found the right office and took a number. It would have been better if he was doing this with Gen. It would have been better if she was sitting right there with him in the hard plastic chairs, and he was holding her hand to ease her anxiety. It would have been better if they'd been a couple and he'd given her the courage to do this together, but there would be no together. He was together with someone else.

"Forty-two."

His number. He stood. Made his way to the correct desk, heart pounding in his ears.

"How can I help you?" A young woman peered at him over her cat eye glasses.

Was this even legal? Would she release the document? "I'm here to pick up an original birth certificate for a friend."

"Name?"

"Genevieve Wilson."

The woman typed the information into her computer then quirked an eyebrow over her glasses. It looked like the eyebrow was drawn on as did the mole above the woman's red lips. "She requested this years ago."

"Yes." He pressed his mouth shut. This might be the end of the road. How could he convince her otherwise? "Gen was scared of what it might say, so…uh…I'm going to pick it up for her."

The woman studied him then sank deeper into her seat with a sigh. "That's so romantic. Even if she doesn't ever find her birth parents, she has you."

Shame pricked his conscience. Gen didn't have him, and she might not want him doing this. "I'm here for her," he repeated his mantra.

"I'll need your ID."

Oh, man. He hadn't thought this through. What if he never told

Gen about the birth certificate because he found out her parents were in jail or raising a million other kids in the welfare system? Then later she came to pick up the certificate for herself and discovered he'd already been there? She'd track him down. And possibly find him married with children. Would she be hurt all over again? Would his feelings for her have died by then? It wasn't too late to back out.

Except she might never come—and her parents might be longing for her but were afraid the way she was afraid. Maybe they were waiting for her to track them down, and he was the only one who could unite them. She needed him.

He pulled out his wallet and flipped it open.

"Thank you." The woman took his license and typed his information into her computer. "I'll be right back." She rose and disappeared behind rows of shelves and file cabinets.

Gen may not have been there, but he was nervous enough for both of them. The information he received could affect her life forever. He didn't blame her for being afraid. Not after the story Rosie told. But finding out how her parents failed didn't have to change who she was. Though it had hurt Rosie at first, she'd become stronger from it.

This was Gen's chance to find out no curse had any power over her. As for the blessings Rosie spoke of? Didn't the Bible say those went on to the thousandth generation? He hoped she would be blessed through his discovery today.

The woman in glasses stepped out from between two shelves, walking his way efficiently yet absentmindedly, not realizing how big a role she was playing in the drama of his life. She was like the jury coming back with a verdict. Would Gen be set free or remain locked up in the prison of fear?

"Here you go." She smiled as she passed him an envelope. "I hope your friend finds her parents."

"Me too." Matt studied her as he took the papers. Had she looked at the birth certificate? Did she use the plural form of parent because there were two names written down? That would be good if the mother knew who the father was and if he stuck around for Gen's birth.

The woman's expression remained neutral as she turned from him to check the next number in line. "Forty-three," she called.

Matt stepped back to make room. But now where did he go? Did he rip the envelope open right there? Did he head to a coffee shop first so he could use their Wi-Fi when researching the names he found?

Who was he kidding? He couldn't wait. He dropped into the same chair in the waiting area that he'd vacated and turned the envelope over. His hands shook like he was playing Let's Make a Deal with Gen's life.

He pried up the metal tabs and ran his finger under the flap, ripping the paper more than peeling it apart. The tearing sounded like a bad omen.

Finally, he reached inside and pinched the stiff paper. He slid it out slowly, the blue scrollwork showing first. Then the script appeared with spaces where names had been printed. Genevieve's name appeared. Genevieve Sine Harper.

His throat constricted with a visual of a redheaded baby being held in her mother's arms. Her birth mother had named her Genevieve. Did she plan to call her Gen, or had that only happened because of the family who'd raised her. There was a time when Matt had mistaken Gen for Jen. He hadn't even known her name. Now he knew more about her name than she knew. Genevieve Sine Harper. How did you even pronounce Sine? What nationality was that?

His eyes scanned the writing to find her father. Blaine Harper. So she bore her father's name. The next question was if the mother shared their same name. Had Gen's mother been married to the father at the time of her birth?

His gaze dropped one more row. Olivia Harper. Yes. She'd been married to Gen's father.

The name rang through his head once again. Olivia Harper. Why did it sound familiar? He squinted his eyes. Did he know an Olivia? Only the one who flew from Portland to Eureka every month or so...to visit her family.

Matt sprang from his chair, energy coursing through his limbs. Could it be? Could Gen's mom have found her and been flying to Eureka to see her?

His mind whirled with implications. Olivia was the right age. But if she knew she was Gen's mother, why hadn't she said anything? And where was her husband? Could he have left her when she lost the function in her legs? Could that be why she'd given Gen up for adoption?

His free hand rose to his head as if he needed to screw it on straight. Because if Olivia was really Gen's mom, then she loved Gen. And Gen needed to know. That information really could change her world.

Oh, man. He needed to talk to Olivia. He'd start by making sure the Olivia who flew on his planes had the last name of Harper. He clamped the birth certificate under his arm so he could use his phone to log into the airline computer system. He entered the name Olivia Harper. Three names appeared in a list. Was one of them really Gen's mom? He checked birthdates. The only one in the right age range lived in Oregon.

Matt took a deep breath and tapped the screen. An information page opened up. He scrolled directly to her special requests. WC. Wheelchair. She was his passenger.

Olivia Harper was the tiny woman Gen lifted from her seat every time she arrived. She was the woman Gen loved pushing to and from the gate. She was the woman who told Matt Gen's name and took a copy of the newspaper with Gen's photograph home with her. She had to be Gen's mom. And Gen had no idea.

Now what? He had her phone number and address in front of him. He could call or he could simply show up at her house. If she was home…

He tapped on the list of itineraries. The date popped up. Today's date. She was flying to Eureka today.

And Matt was going to fly with her.

CHAPTER TWENTY-TWO

MATT RAN DOWN THE FUNKY TURQUOISE carpet originally designed to look like intersecting runways at the Portland airport. As a pilot, he was allowed to go through the pre-check line, so he should have had plenty of time to make his flight, but some impatient lady in front of him got frustrated with the TSA agents wanting to open up her bag and yelled out, "Yeah, like I'm a terrorist." Not something anyone should ever yell at an airport. Especially if they didn't want to make everyone behind them late for their flights.

Matt didn't even pause to check his watch. Instead, he prayed he'd make it in time.

"Final call for flight 348 to Eureka, California." A voice announced over the PA. "Doors will be closing in approximately five seconds."

Great. They had a gate agent like Bianca.

He rounded the corner and caught site of a big lady in a navy blue skirt, pulling the large door away from the wall.

"Wait." He waved a hand overhead.

She caught sight of him and paused with the door only halfway shut. "You're the pilot who wants the jump seat?"

Matt slowed and wiped sweat from his brow. "Yes, though if there are any seats left in the cabin—"

"There aren't."

Now he wouldn't have a chance to talk to Olivia before they landed. He'd have to confront her between the time Gen removed her from the plane and when she pushed her to baggage claim. Though that could cause even more issues since he'd have to face Gen, and she'd have no clue he was coming.

He did his best to stay out of the way of the pilots, though Stella from Australia was particularly chatty. At least her stories behind Australia's recent law requiring co-pilots to eat different meals before flying in case of food poisoning made the time fly too. But as they neared the airport in Eureka, the queasiness of his stomach made Matt wonder if he'd gotten food poisoning himself.

He steeled himself when the plane taxied to the gate. He couldn't see into the jet bridge from his spot behind the pilots. "Who's working today?" he asked.

Stella waved out the window. "The bluey is here today. I like her."

Did Matt hear her correctly? It was sometimes hard to tell with her accent. "The…bluey?"

Stella's co-pilot flashed him a smile. "Bluey means redhead in Australian slang. They're sarcastic like that."

"Oh…" Gen. The bluey. He hoped he didn't make her any more blue. That wasn't why he'd come. In fact, if he'd been able to talk to Olivia during the flight, he wouldn't even get off here.

Stella set the brake and twisted toward him. "You're continuing on to SFO, right?"

Matt rubbed his face. He could still stay in the cockpit. Except then he'd be aborting his entire mission. "I am, but I'm going to get off here for a few minutes. Stretch my legs."

"I could use a little smoko myself." She rose and squeezed out the cockpit door to merge with passengers.

"That means smoke or coffee break." The co-pilot stood and headed toward the lavatory.

Matt nodded. "Right."

He was too jittery to go for his normal coffee. Instead, he rubbed his hands down his pant legs, waiting for the passengers to clear completely off. Because that's when Gen would come for Olivia.

It took forever.

Finally the plane stopped bouncing with footsteps. He pushed to stand and made his way into the galley.

"Matt." Olivia waved from her seat a few rows back. She probably wouldn't be smiling like that when she found out why he was there.

The aisle chair bumped onto the plane. It stilled as Gen froze, staring at him. She wet her lips with the tip of her tongue. "Why are you here?"

His heart picked up speed like the chugging of a train engine in his chest. "I'm on my way home to San Francisco. Thought I'd see i could help out with Olivia."

Gen's eyes flicked toward Olivia for a second before giving him one more measuring gaze. "Olivia and I have a system."

"I know." He held his palms up. "I'll stay out of the way. I just thought you might have your hands full."

Her chin lifted—almost in defiance. Was she trying to prove to the world that she could take care of herself? That she didn't need help? Was she annoyed he'd listened to Rosie speak and knew her part of the story?

She pushed the aisle chair forward, bringing her closer. She looked down as she passed. "I heard you have your hands full too."

Casey. She was talking about Casey. Giving him an out. Trying to diffuse this strain between them.

"Yes," he said. Though Gen had no idea how tangled up he was in her life at the moment.

She rolled the chair past him to line it up with Olivia's seat then removed the armrest between the two. "Ready, Olivia?"

"I'm ready."

Matt made eye contact at the older woman over Gen's shoulder as she scooped Olivia up. She had Gen's same brown eyes. How had he never noticed? Was it because he'd expected Gen's mom to have bright red hair while Olivia's hair was a silvery blonde?

What did Olivia feel being held in her daughter's arms the way she'd probably once held Gen? When had she first realized their connection? Had she flown down here after hiring a private investigator, or had she flown down here for vacation and somehow recognized her child? And why had she kept her identity a secret all this time?

"How long have you been coming to visit your daughter here?" he asked.

Olivia settled into her seat. "It's been a little over two years now," answered cautiously, avoiding eye contact.

With Olivia buckled in, Gen had to let the flight attendant behind ‍e chair push Olivia. She turned slowly to face him, her gaze ff his then dropping to the floor. She held onto each headrest as if she needed help with stability. She didn't. She only needed an anchor should the storm inside him attempt to blow her off course. Which it was threatening to do. If he tugged her hand and pulled her a couple of extra steps, they could be alone in the cockpit.

Gen made it to the front row of seats and skirted around him into the jet bridge. He let the flight attendant and Olivia exit before he followed. No matter how much he wanted to watch Gen or listen to Gen or tease Gen until her laughter spilled over him, he was there to speak to Olivia.

The electric wheelchair had already been carried up the stairs from the ramp by the baggage crew. Matt waited for Gen to transfer Olivia onto her other wheels.

Olivia frowned at him over Gen's shoulder this time. "I feel like I've missed a lot since the last time I was here. What's new?"

Even she could tell there was something between them? Of course she could. Ethan had. Rosie had. Sam had. They'd probably all known before he had.

Gen adjusted Olivia's legs, a good excuse not to look at him. "Matt got me a job photographing the Giants players."

Oliva stared up at him in wonder, and he could see Gen in her more than ever. The shape of her face. The tilt of her nose. "Really?"

The flight attendant pushed the aisle chair away, and Gen moved into place behind Olivia, careful not to accidentally brush Matt in the confined space. Though that didn't keep him from sensing her presence. Her warmth. Her soft scent.

"Really." He responded to Olivia, his mind rewinding to their last conversation where Olivia was showing off Gen's photo in the newspaper. Would he ever have gotten Casey to hire Gen if Olivia hadn't bragged up Gen's work in the first place? "And actually, your excitement over her photo in the newspaper played a part in that."

Her cheeks ripened into a blush very similar to Gen's. Is this what Gen would look like when she was older? If so, she was going to get even more beautiful with age.

Gen gripped the wheelchair handles. "I need to push Olivia out of the jet bridge so I can load for the next flight." She gave a little sigh and lifted her eyes to meet his. "So, goodbye?"

Matt had never hated that word so much. He'd thought he'd said it to her before, but he was back, and he had more to say. Except it was to Olivia. "I'll walk with you." He motioned in front of him to let her pass.

Her eyes narrowed in a warning, but she preceded him down the jet bridge anyway. Was she wishing Rosie was here to protect her again?

Olivia twisted in her seat to look at him, her eyes shining in delight at the entourage. "If you're not the pilot, Matt, what were you doing in Portland?"

His stomach warmed. He was here to answer that question, but not in front of Gen. "I was…uh…doing a little research."

Her smile slipped. For only a second. "What were you researching?"

"The correct question would be, 'who were you researching'?" He glanced at Gen to see if she was following the conversation or perhaps jumping ahead.

But she emerged into the terminal, eyes scanning her employees like she was looking for an escape.

Olivia checked on Gen too. "Who were you researching?"

Gen parked Olivia out of the way by a column. Matt stood in front of her and crossed his arms. "A mutual acquaintance."

Olivia twisted her earring in a way that reminded him of Gen. Her eyes widened.

"I'll be back, Olivia." Gen set the wheelchair brakes as if she hadn't heard a word they'd said. "I'll see if Bianca wants to finish up here for me. Then you won't have to wait so long for me to push you down to baggage claim."

It would also give her the chance to escape Matt sooner. Bianca would surely be willing to help with that. He watched Gen toss her long hair and stride away. If he had it to do all over again—

"Who is our mutual acquaintance?" Olivia spoke primly, drawing his attention down to her. Did she still have any hope that he didn't know? And why was it so important for her to keep the secret?

Matt met her gaze directly so there would be no misunderstandings. "Your daughter."

A frail hand slid from her ear to her chest. She gripped it like she might be having a heart attack. But her pain wasn't physical. It was emotional.

He tilted his head and blinked to soften his stare. "When are you going to tell Gen you love her?"

Olivia sat up straighter, her brown eyes burning in defiance. She may not be a redhead, but she had the Irish disposition. "When are *you* going to tell Gen you love her?"

He opened his mouth to argue, but no sound came out. Other people had seen his attraction, but this was Gen's mom. She had a mother's intuition. She knew he loved Gen because he did love Gen.

Matt was in love with Gen.

Gen hated to leave her team early, but she had to get away from Matt. What was he doing here anyway? Why was he following her around? It was his day off. He should be spending it with his girlfriend.

She lifted one finger to hold Bianca's attention for final instructions, but she couldn't think of anything to say. She could only think of Matt coming here. He was probably watching her right this minute.

Did he assume Rosie had told her about Casey's mom's condition? Did he think they could be friends now? She'd been fooling herself to think they could be friends before.

"What?" Bianca prompted.

Bianca already knew everything. Except... "No boarding music."

Bianca stuck a hand on her hip. "If you're not here to be bothered by the music, why does it even matter?"

"Fine." They could all have a party without her. "I'll see you tomorrow." Though if Matt was going to be flying in again, she'd let Bianca and Tyler work the gate without her.

Matt. He still stood by Olivia though he was staring at Gen. It was the kind of stare appreciated most over a candlelight dinner. The kind where you were seeing that person in a new light, and you liked what you saw. But what could he possibly see in her that Casey didn't have?

She busied herself unlocking the wheelchair brakes, but when she stood to push Olivia, Matt remained in their way. With the magnetism of his gaze, it was a really good thing there was a wheelchair between them.

She looked down to the top of Olivia's greying bob. She would have thought her sassy passenger would have said something by now. Was nobody else as perturbed by Matt's presence?

Gen had to speak up for herself. "You're in the way, Matt."

He ran a hand over his face like one of those comedians when changing expressions. Then he took a deep breath and stepped to the side. "I'm sorry."

"It's okay." She pushed Olivia past him. "Just a little weird."

Matt chuckled from behind, leaving her feeling a different kind of warm. Despite the way seeing him brought with it the painful reminder of how he'd chosen someone else over her, a giggle still slipped out. More than she wanted to cry over him, she wanted to laugh with him.

Olivia kept quiet until they were out of hearing range. Then she kept quiet some more. Matt must have weirded her out too.

"I've decided not to have a crush on him anymore," Gen announced, as if that might explain some of the weirdness. "I met his girlfriend on the photo shoot, and she's perfect."

"Genevieve..."

Gen didn't need another pep talk. She needed to let him go. Again. "Not every girl can marry a Gilbert Blythe and live happily ever after."

"I know." Olivia sounded as if she were depressed by Gen's rejection as well. "There's something I have to tell you."

Gen glanced over her shoulder to check on Matt. He stood staring after her in that same way he'd been staring before. Did he realize he was staring? Was she doing the same thing and not even realizing it?

She faced forward. "What's that?" she asked Olivia. Hopefully the woman's words would distract her from the shaky feeling inside.

"I'm...I'm..." Olivia paused as they passed a TSA agent.

Gen nodded at the man in uniform. Had Matt watched her do that too? In a moment she could round the corner and be out of his sight. Then she could breathe.

Had Olivia finished her sentence? "You're what?" Gen prompted.

"I'm not able to hold it in any longer." Olivia's voice trembled. "Matt's in love with you."

Gen's ears rang as if she'd forgotten to wear earplugs outside onto the gate ramp, and her world spun like she'd gotten sucked into one of the airbus turbines.

"Why…why do you think that?" She slowed to a stop in front of the glass doors that would release Olivia to roll out to the curb and be picked up by her family. Gen couldn't let Olivia go without having her questions answered. Not without finding out why Olivia knew Matt loved her. If it were true, which was highly unlikely.

Matt loved Casey. He may have been attracted to Gen, but it didn't matter. Even if his girlfriend's mom hadn't been sick and he'd broken up with her, he probably would have eventually realized what he was missing and returned. That's what she'd been afraid of from the beginning because that's what people in her life did. People like Craig. They didn't make sacrifices for her.

Olivia looked straight ahead and wrung her fingers in her lap. The older woman didn't know what had happened in her absence. She didn't know Matt had flown Gen home alone from San Francisco, and she'd hugged him goodbye. She didn't know Matt's brother said he was leaving Casey for her, but then he didn't. She didn't know Casey's mom had cancer.

The woman peeked up, her eyes watery and wary. Like she wanted to help Gen, but she was afraid her words might have the opposite effect. "He…he was talking about you, and I asked when he was going to tell you he loves you, but he didn't respond."

Olivia was right to be wary because that hurt. Matt wouldn't deny that he loved her, but he wouldn't admit it either.

What if he did love her? That didn't make her any less dispensable, did it?

She wasn't only replaceable in his life. She was upgradable.

No wonder everyone rejected her. She was like vanilla creamer in Matt's coffee. She could add to the flavor of his life, and while he liked her, he could do without her.

CHAPTER TWENTY-THREE

CASEY MET MATT ON THE CATHEDRAL steps after church on Sunday. He'd excused himself to use the bathroom after the service, but really he was checking his phone to see if he had any messages.

How could Gen find out Olivia was her mom and not thank him? Unless it hadn't gone well. But he couldn't imagine that. Olivia loved Gen. Their reunion would have been an Oprah moment. He'd really been hoping to see it, but they'd apparently turned the corner at the airport before Olivia muscled up the courage to reveal her true identity. He couldn't imagine that she didn't. It wasn't something you'd want your child to learn from a stranger.

It didn't help that Matt had to face his own feelings. He didn't only care about Gen, he'd fallen in love with her. As a result, he felt all the more guilty for it. As much as he'd been itching to talk to her for days now, he'd made himself remove her from his contacts list on his phone. That should make him feel less guilty, except for the fact that he was hoping she'd contact him.

He told himself he only wanted to clear the air. He wanted her life to be better off because of him, not worse. The truth was that he couldn't help thinking his life would be better with her.

But if love was an action, a choice, then he'd chosen Casey. She needed him. She was the one who could lose her mother while Gen now had two.

Casey looked at him, uncertainty dimming her light eyes. "Stephanie asked if we want to go to lunch with them."

Stephanie? Ethan was supposed to have dropped his bomb already. Had he not told his wife he was leaving yet? Was Matt going to have to keep pretending he didn't know things?

Casey leaned forward and lowered her voice. "She said Ethan cheated on her with a flight attendant. Did you know about this?"

Oh. Man. "I knew Ethan was attracted to Michelle, but I tried to talk him out of doing anything—"

"It's Michelle? The new girl I met when your company came to a game at the ballpark?"

His stomach twisted into a knot. "Yes, but don't say anything." Had Ethan not told his wife who he'd cheated with, and Matt was going to make things worse? Well, Stephanie would find out eventually, if not from Casey at lunch. But why in the world would Ethan want to go out as a group? He scrunched his face. "Is Ethan here?"

Casey nodded, her forehead reflecting his concern with a wrinkle of her own. "They're going to try to make their marriage work, so they want to find a few couples to help keep them accountable. Stephanie's parents are watching the kids for the weekend. It's only the two of them."

Matt huffed. Ethan was going to stay with Stephanie? This was news. Good news. He could get on board with accountability, and maybe Ethan would even be more understanding of Matt's commitment to Casey now. "Yeah. Okay. If you're up to it. How are you doing?" That question was really the extent of their conversations of late.

Casey fiddled with her purse strap. "I think it will be good to get my mind off my own problems. We can always visit Mom after lunch, right?"

"Right." Valerie would be starting chemo that week. They had one last visit before her energy was sapped away and her hair started to fall out. It was sure to be emotional.

Ethan picked Waterfront Restaurant at Pier 7, and Matt was really curious to see if he was giving his wife the royal treatment to make up for his mistakes or if he was simply putting on a show. The man didn't say much through the meal, but neither did Matt. It was mostly Casey encouraging Stephanie then opening up about her own pain. Somehow both women seemed comforted to know they weren't the only ones hurting.

Matt studied Ethan, wondering if his change was truly genuine, or if he and Casey would be sitting with an abandoned Stephanie next week. His co-pilot met his gaze without the usual prideful sneer.

"Want to walk down the pier?" Matt asked. If he was going to keep Ethan accountable, it would have to be done privately.

Casey twisted her head his way. "That's a good idea. Give us a bit of time for girl talk."

Ethan placed a hand on his wife's back. "Do you need girl talk?"

Matt had never seen Ethan so sensitive. Even with Michelle.

Stephanie met his eyes, hers as guarded as they were sad. But she was still with him. "Yes, thank you."

Matt pushed his chair back and placed a supportive hand on Casey's shoulder as he walked past. She was a good woman to be here for Stephanie.

Ethan followed him toward the door that led to the outside eating area with an iron railing separating them from the water below and giving a beautiful view of the bay bridge when it wasn't foggy. Today it was foggy.

The chill bit at Matt's skin, and he stuck his hands in his jacket pockets. Where did he begin? "Is it over with Michelle?" he asked. That was the most important question if he was going to keep Ethan accountable.

Ethan placed his hands on the railing and looked into the water. "Yes. I've requested to fly a different route."

Matt nodded. That couldn't have been an easy choice. "What changed your mind?" he asked.

Ethan hunched into himself. "When I told Stephanie I wanted a divorce, she was devastated. I didn't even think she would care. I told her I'd still support her and the kids, and I'd still go to all the baseball games and dance recitals and parent teacher conferences, but that didn't help." His voice cracked. "She loves me."

Matt's own throat constricted. His friend really had felt alone in his marriage. If only he'd spoken up about his loneliness rather than try to fill the void with someone else.

"You're speechless, huh?" Ethan's tone lowered with sarcasm as if he had to lighten the mood with humor. "So am I. I did something that should make her want to leave me, but instead, for the first time in a long time, I realize she actually wants to be with me."

Matt *was* speechless. Not only by the fact that Stephanie was going to forgive Ethan but that he was so humbled by her forgiveness. "I'm really glad, man."

Ethan took a deep breath. "Me too."

Matt scratched the back of his head. This wasn't the same guy he'd shut out on their last flight to Eureka. Had he given up on Ethan too soon? "Was there anything else I could have said or done?"

"Nope." Ethan lifted a hand in a shrug. "I'm sorry you had to be in the middle."

Matt had definitely felt in the middle when he'd made the decision to time out. He cringed. "Did you spend the night with Michelle in Eureka?"

"Yes. Only time."

Matt closed his eyes. That had been his fault. He could have prevented the physical affair if he hadn't been battling his own attraction…

"That's not your fault." Ethan let him off the hook. "I made it hard on you."

Yeah, he had. "So you understand why I'm staying with Casey now?" Matt motioned with his head back toward the restaurant. "With her mom battling cancer and all?"

Ethan shot him a sideways glance, eyebrow lifting. "Nope."

Matt jolted with the impact. He'd thought Ethan was in a better place. Clearly he'd been wrong. "I can't leave her to handle that on her own. She needs me."

Ethan pressed his lips together as if trying to keep his mouth shut, but then he turned to face Matt squarely, eyes confident with wisdom—the kind of wisdom that came from learning things the hard way. "Casey has a savior. And it's not you."

The words stabbed Matt like an arrow to the heart.

But…but…

He wasn't trying to be a savior. He was trying to save her. That was a good thing.

Like he should have saved Tracen from almost killing himself in a Class-VI rapid as a teen. Like he should have prevented Sam from joining the military. He took it upon himself to keep others from getting hurt. Kind of like he was doing with Ethan's affair.

"Who do you want to be with?" Ethan challenged.

Matt shook his head. He would not admit to loving Gen. "That's not the question here. You want to be with Michelle, but you're choosing Stephanie because it's the right thing to do."

Ethan narrowed his eyes. "Did you not hear anything I said? The only reason I was miserable in my marriage was because I didn't think Stephanie wanted to be with me. Don't put Casey in a situation like that."

Matt's heart constricted. If he did what Ethan was suggesting, he'd have to break up with Casey right when she was dealing with her mom's illness. He'd be kicking her when she was down. "I don't want to hurt her."

Ethan rubbed his jaw and looked towards the windows of the restaurant. "Sometimes the most loving thing you can do *will* hurt someone."

Matt wanted to argue, but then he thought of chemotherapy. That was going to hurt a lot. At the same time, it was the only thing that could save Valerie's life.

Was he staying with Casey for her own benefit? Or was it for his? So he could be a hero? Because he wanted it to be his identity.

He'd enjoyed rescuing Casey from the very beginning. It made him feel like he was a better person than all those other men out there. All the men who didn't really want to be with her for her. They just wanted to show her off and spend her money. Was he any better?

He told himself he was staying with her to protect her. Yet wouldn't she be better off if he protected her from himself?

Matt clenched and unclenched his fingers around the steering wheel on the way to the Holloways' penthouse on Nob Hill. If he broke up with Casey now, would she want him to go in to visit her parents? Would she ever talk to him again?

How did he even lead up to such a conversation?

Casey rested her elbow on the windowsill and her head on her hand. She stared out up into the gray sky. "I used to want to meet with Ethan and Stephanie as part of premarital counseling, but now I hope we never end up like them."

There's the opening he was dreading. His stomach clenched as tight as his fists. "I hope we never end up like them either."

Ugh. He'd effectively shut that door by agreeing with her. Now what?

She dropped her head onto the headrest. "How do we prevent it?" she asked.

"Well..." He definitely wasn't her savior. He was a failure. "My dad always said you don't commit to not having an affair, but you commit to never having coffee alone with someone of the opposite sex. So I guess commitment is the key."

She nodded. "Is there such a thing as committing to the wrong person?"

He stilled. Did she know about Gen? Had Ethan said something to Stephanie, and Stephanie brought it up during girl talk?

"I...uh...think you can most definitely commit to the wrong person." As he spoke, the truth of his words resonated in his soul. He'd been congratulating himself on being so self-sacrificial, when self-sacrifice had been a mask for selfishness. He hadn't wanted to fail at a relationship or be the bad guy, so he'd made himself a martyr. "You met my oldest brother and his fiancée. She pretty much ran away from the altar on her wedding day."

"That's right." Casey bit her lip. "How are you supposed to know if you're with the right person?"

Was she breaking up with him? If so, she was much better at this than he was. "I think you both have to question your motives."

She turned her head to look at him, her eyes more steel than blue as if reflecting the weather. He avoided her gaze, wishing for an emotional umbrella.

"Why are you with me, Matt?"

This was it. His chance to be honest. Because honesty was as important as commitment. Even when it hurt like hail. "I'm with you because I want to be your hero." Matt paused at a stoplight on the steep hill and gave her the respect of his full attention. "But I can't help thinking you deserve more than that."

She didn't argue, just studied him. Her chest rose and fell. "Is there someone else you'd rather be with?"

Numbness washed over him until the car behind them honked. Why did they have to have this conversation when he was driving? Though it could be worse. He could be driving down the famous curves of Lombard Street. He flipped on his blinker and circled around the block, looking for a parking garage or open space. A spot in front of them opened up, and he pulled into it, barely noticing the view of the Transamerica Pyramid that spired into the air from far below. The weight of dread pulled all his senses from the outside in.

He shifted into park and turned toward Casey. From the lack of expression on her pixie face, she looked to be dazed as well.

"Case, you're everything I thought I wanted."

A corner of her mouth twitched at the word thought, which made him feel thought*less*. But there was no heroic way to say what he had to say.

He reached for her hand in hopes of softening the blow. "There is someone else. Nothing has happened, and once I realized my attraction, I kept my distance, but…" He worked with Gen. Even when he wasn't with her, he was thinking of her. He wanted to be there for her. "But I think there's the possibility she and I could become more than friends."

He held his breath, inflating his lungs like airbags against the impact of his heart.

Casey's fingers gripped his tighter as if her whole body had tensed. Her eyes turned to ice. "Is it Gen?"

She knew? Stephanie must have said something, which was unfair to Casey. He should have been the one to tell her.

"I'm sorry."

Casey looked down so all he saw were the tops of her lashes. "I could tell she liked you, but I didn't think it would ever become mutual. I assumed you were trying to help her with the photography job the way you help everyone."

So she hadn't heard it from Stephanie? She'd seen it with her own eyes. "I *was* just trying to help her." Hey, if Casey had been suspicious, why had she sent that text about wanting to kiss Gen? He narrowed his eyes to study her closer. "You made everything more awkward with that text you sent, you know."

"I know." Her gaze lifted, and she pulled her hands into her lap, away from his touch. "It was a test. I thought if it was something you could laugh at, you'd tell me. I expected you to tell me."

Oh, man, had he failed. He leaned back and ran his fingers through his hair.

"I brushed it off at the time because I was so busy with the team. I figured once the World Series was over we could reconnect. Until Gen showed up to the party in her puffy sleeves, and you looked at her in a way you've never looked at me." She gave a helpless shrug. "I was going to say something, but then Mom went to the hospital, and I...I didn't want to visit her alone."

"Oh, Case, I didn't want to leave you alone."

"Thank you for that."

She was stronger than he'd realized. Not to mention honest and intelligent and kind. "You're a hard person to break up with, you know? You've got it all. So much so that anyone who leaves you has to be an idiot."

"Or a fool for love?" She gave a small half-smile. She was going to be okay.

"Yes." He was a fool. For all he knew, Gen's reunion with her mother had gone terribly wrong, and she blamed him. He could have hurt both the women he'd tried so hard to protect, and he'd be all alone. He'd worry about that later. For, perhaps the first time, he was going to be there for Casey without any ulterior motives. "What now?"

She faced forward, taking in the view of her city. Her home. "Now I might have to invite a certain actor—and Giants fan—to cheer from the owner's suite."

Matt arched an eyebrow. Casey Holloway deserved more than a boring pilot from Idaho. She was designed for the limelight. "Jack Jamison is a lucky guy."

Casey faced him again, not quite herself, but definitely more relaxed than he'd seen her in a while. "What about you? What are you going to do?"

Well, he couldn't call Gen as he'd deleted her phone number, but he'd want to talk in person anyway. "Tomorrow I fly to Eureka, and I guess I'll see where life takes me from there."

CHAPTER TWENTY-FOUR

GEN HIT SEND ON THE EMAIL with her resignation letter. With all the photography jobs pouring in, she didn't need to work for the airline anymore, and she definitely didn't need to see Matt Lake fifteen times a month. This would be easier for him too—if he was really in love with her. Why put themselves through that? What did she think this was, Casablanca?

Bianca stared from the office doorway. "Did you just do what I think you did?"

Gen spun her desk chair to face her friend. She'd been planning to tell the team when they were all together. Now she wouldn't be telling them at all because Bianca would beat her to it. "I'm quitting," she confirmed. "Going to work my photography business full time."

Bianca stuck a hand on her hip. "Does this have something to do with Matt the pilot?"

Matt the pilot. It wasn't that long ago that a pilot was all he'd been in her life. Now he was nothing. "Yes, because he got me the deal with the Giants."

Bianca cocked her head. "And?"

Gen's heart burned in an attempt to destroy the evidence, but it was too late. They'd all had a front row seat to her feelings for the man. As well as the way he'd trampled them. "And..." Maybe she could redirect Bianca's energy. "I think it would be best if I close the ticket counter and let you go to the gate as part of training for taking over my position."

Bianca clasped her hands at her chest. "I'm being promoted?"

Mission accomplished. Gen's success stung a bit in the way she was being so quickly forgotten. But that was life. "The job is yours."

Bianca shot her hands in the air. "I'm being promoted." She pointed a finger at Gen and lowered her voice. "I know you're trying to distract me, but we'll talk later in partner yoga." Then she did a little raise-the-roof move and ran down the hallway. "I'm being promoted."

Gen spun to face her computer again, but the email blurred before her eyes. It was too late to keep her job. She'd have to step out of the plane and hope her parachute worked.

She reached for her earlobes and rubbed. If ever there was a moment when she needed inner peace, it was now. Because as much as she loved photography, she didn't want to leave the airport. She didn't want to leave Matt.

How was he going to feel about her decision? Probably relieved. If he'd wanted to talk to her, he could have. But he didn't call. He'd created as much distance as possible. So she'd finish the job. Literally. They'd never speak again.

"Flight 348 calling Eureka station." Matt's voice on the radio interrupted her thoughts.

Her heart crashed into her ribs like a landing gone wrong. Had she been so busy daydreaming that she hadn't realized it was time for the inbound call? She'd been planning to have Bianca answer.

She checked her watch. Matt was early. The station notes showed he'd left on time, so he must have had a tailwind.

Gen leaped from her seat and rushed into the hallway to grab Bianca. Tyler leaned through the doorway. He'd do.

Grasping Tyler's arm, she drug him into the office. "Do you know how to answer an in-bound call?"

Tyler blinked. "I tried one time, and Matt laughed at me."

Matt's voice echoed around her once again. This time a little louder than before. "Flight 348 calling Eureka Station."

She grabbed the receiver and placed it in Tyler's hands. "Tell him he's reached the Eureka station."

Tyler's eyes bugged, but he pushed the button down. "Thank you for calling the Eureka station. This is Tyler at your service."

Crud. Matt was going to know something was up. Tyler never spoke like that.

"Uh...hi, Tyler."

Gen covered her mouth to smother a nervous giggle. If Matt were nothing more than a friend, they would have laughed about this together. But no. He was Matt the pilot, and she was Gen the nut job.

"We're twenty minutes out, and there are no wheelchairs on board."

Thank goodness. Now she wouldn't have to help out at the gate by pushing a wheelchair and run the risk of having Matt watch her with those hypnotic eyes of his.

"Now what?" Tyler whispered, not that Matt could hear him.

"Repeat what he said, and tell him we're at gate 3B."

Tyler nodded then concentrated really hard on pressing the button. "You're landing in twenty minutes, and you have no wheelchairs on board."

Gen nudged him. "3B."

He clicked the button again and practically shouted, "3B."

"Three-bravo," she corrected.

"Three-bravo," Tyler yelled.

Matt's chuckle washed over her, warm like the waves in Costa Rica. "We'll see you at gate three-bravo, Tyler."

His laugh. She wanted to bathe in it. But Tyler pulled the plug by replacing the receiver in its cradle.

"Good job," she said.

"L-O-L." Tyler rubbed his palms down his pants. "If you're trying to avoid Matt the pilot, I have some bad news for you."

"What?" Were there engine troubles she hadn't heard about yet? Was the flight grounded and he was stuck at her airport? He could go to a hotel like he had the time before. That didn't necessarily mean she had to speak to him.

"Olivia rescheduled her flight for today. She's waiting for you to push her to the gate."

Gen moaned as her body wilted. "Olivia?" Of all the things she'd do to avoid Matt, ignoring Olivia wasn't one of them. She needed to tell her favorite passenger that she was quitting anyway. With a deep breath, she stood straight. "Okay."

Tyler held out an arm in an offer to help. "I can push her if you want me to."

Gen pressed his arm back to his body. "I've got this. Go ahead and shut down the ticket counter, and I'll assist Bianca at the gate."

"Okay." Tyler punched a fist into his palm but didn't move. "B-T-

W, we are going to miss you when you're gone."

She was going to miss him too. She didn't only love Matt; she loved all these guys. She swooped in like a mother hen to wrap her arms around the kid. "You'll still see me when I fly to The City for photo shoots." Preferably on days Matt didn't fly.

Tyler stood stiff. Emotional overload perhaps?

She stepped back and racked her brain to speak his language. "T-T-Y-L?"

"Talk to you later."

One of the best parts about working at the airport had been knowing she wasn't the only weirdo. She headed out to the ticket counter to say goodbye to another one of the best parts. "Olivia."

The woman sat shriveled in her wheelchair. Was she sick? Was that why she was headed home early?

"You okay?"

Olivia gave what might be considered a smile. "I think so."

Whatever that meant. Gen stepped behind the wheelchair and gripped the handles. "You weren't in town very long. Your family okay?"

"As far as I know." Olivia gripped the armrests as Gen pushed her forward. "How are you doing, dear? Any new developments with Matt?"

"No." Gen sighed. "I never meant for my crush to go this far. I pretended Matt was in love with me, but I didn't expect it to really happen." She rolled Olivia to the TSA agent at the security checkpoint. "So I'm quitting."

Olivia's ticket slipped from her fingers. Gen let the security guard bend to retrieve it while she badged in at the box on the wall. She'd known the older woman would disagree with her choice, but she'd already made up her mind, and she didn't have the energy to argue.

Gen felt Olivia's gaze as she walked through the metal detector and waited for TSA to run their wand around Olivia. Her passenger may be upset to lose Gen, but Gen was the one losing. Besides Matt and her daily interaction with the staff here, she'd lost two brothers in one week. Life was going to hurt for a while.

The guard rolled Olivia forward. Gen moved to circle behind her, but Olivia grabbed her hand. "You're not a quitter."

Gen squeezed. It was nice to have someone believe in her. "You're right. I'm not the one quitting. Matt quit on me." Exactly like everyone else in her life. She gently tugged her hand away and resumed her role as wheelchair pusher. "But because of him and the boost he gave my career, I don't need this job anymore. So I will always be grateful."

Olivia wiped at an eye. "I'm so proud of you, dear. Matt doesn't deserve you."

Gen gave a wry smile. Olivia was right. Matt didn't deserve her. He deserved Casey. Beautiful, rich, stunning Casey. No sane man would give that up. "Thanks."

"Will you be coming to Portland for any photo shoots?" Olivia's voice quivered.

Gen should have expected an invitation. The woman had become a good friend. "Maybe. If you give me your phone number, I'll let you know. I'd love to see you again."

Olivia pulled her purse open and rummaged through it. Probably for her phone.

Gen slowed as she neared the gate. The plane had landed and the door stood open, ready for passengers to disembark.

If she didn't have to transfer Olivia to her seat, she could take off now. The next time Olivia travelled, someone else would have to do it, but Gen would consider it an honor to make the transfer one last time. Even if it meant facing Matt.

Her stomach churned, wondering if he'd get off the plane for coffee.

Bianca appeared in the doorway, leading the parade.

Gen parked Olivia behind a column to wait out of sight.

"I'm ready. What's your phone number?" Olivia had her fingers poised over the screen of her phone.

Gen rattled the number off then pulled out her own phone from her pocket to do the same. Her mind whirled back to the time she'd given Matt her number, when Tyler had taken a picture of her for his contact list. Her chest ached with longing. Matt wouldn't text her anymore, but Olivia could. She pulled out her camera app and bent down next to the woman. "Can I get a selfie with you?" she asked.

Olivia lowered her phone into her lap. "I'd love a picture with you. Could you send it to me too?"

"Sure." Gen smiled at their image on the screen. They looked good together with their big brown eyes, heart-shaped faces, and contrasting hair.

"Hey." Matt's voice.

Gen stood to face him, and her breath shimmied in her lungs. He looked more relaxed than he had last time. Friendlier. Open. Her pulse sent out warning signals like a cop car with sirens blaring.

"You two look like you are doing well," Matt said.

She did? Because she felt the opposite of well. She felt like she might have to lean over and heave into the trash receptacle at any moment. She shoved her phone inside her pocket to be prepared.

He tilted his head toward Gen and rubbed a hand over his mouth. "Can I talk to you alone for a second?"

Alone? As in stepping away from her wheelchair shield? She scooted behind it and gripped the handles. She knew he was in love with her. And she'd told him explanations would only make things worse. What more did he have to say? "I have to put Olivia on the plane."

His gaze caressed her face, resting on her lips. "Afterward?"

Her cheeks burned. Her whole body warmed. Because if he was going to look at her like that, then they wouldn't be doing much talking.

What was wrong with him? So what if he thought he was in love with her? Those feelings would die. He couldn't destroy what he had with Casey.

"I…I can't today. I have other plans." She shoved Olivia forward with no warning and scurried to keep up with the rolling wheels.

"Next time then," Matt called after her.

Olivia leaned to one side, looking behind them. "There will be no next time. Gen quit."

Gen wouldn't look back. She wouldn't torture herself with Matt's reaction.

"You quit?" His voice rose from right behind her. He was following.

She picked up her pace, but he was chasing her onto a plane. It wasn't like she could lock herself in the lavatory until they landed at PDX.

Olivia squealed as they entered the jet bridge, and its slope pulled the wheelchair faster. "Slow down, dear."

Gen glanced behind them. Matt had stopped at the door inside the terminal. His coffee must have been more important than talking to her.

The PA system rang an intro to announcements. "Genevieve Wilson," Matt's voice blared through the speaker. "I'm in love with you."

Gen stopped. The wheelchair attempted to tug her forward, but she resisted. She had to quiet her footsteps, quiet her breathing, quiet her heartbeat so she could hear. Because he couldn't have really said what she thought he'd said. That would mean…

"It's okay if you don't love me back, but I want you to know I'm single. And if you ever want to go on a date, I would be thrilled to fly you anywhere you want to go. Europe, Asia, Costa Rica."

He was asking her out. Over the intercom. And it was even more amazing than she'd once imagined.

"Even Idaho so you could meet the rest of my family."

Her lips parted. Her chest heaved. His family? What would his family think of her? They knew he'd been dating Casey Holloway. How would they feel about him trading the heiress in for her?

Besides Sam, they'd be shocked. Horrified even. Because surely, they would want Matt to marry into affluence. His parents wouldn't want redheaded grandchildren. Even if they didn't care about that, there was still the fact that if a relationship continued, Matt would be marrying into a family of jailbirds. Addicts. The disabled.

She reached for her earlobe, and the wheelchair rolled slightly on an axis.

"Oh my," Olivia breathed. "Roll me back there so he can ask you out in person."

No. She couldn't. Matt didn't know what he was getting himself into. She didn't even know. Because she'd never been brave enough to discover her generational curse.

It could come out to haunt them. What would he do then? Stick around so it would be passed on to his own children?

Was that silly to consider? Her head told her yes, but her heart screamed even louder. Her heart refused to let her hurt him. Or was it trying to protect itself?

She didn't know, but she knew she had to get out of there. She had to leave him before he could leave her. Again.

Gen shifted the wheelchair forward.

"Gen?" Olivia's voice rose hesitantly.

She had to steel herself against it. Against the questions the woman was sure to ask. She pushed harder.

"Genevieve? Are you turning around?"

Gen rushed them both down the jet bridge, creating a breeze that lifted her hair. She would leave soon and put all this behind her. "No. This is a mistake. People don't give up other things for me. They give me up for other things."

She'd never put it that way before, but it fit. And it hurt as bad every time. Maybe worse.

"Genevieve Sine Wilson." Olivia used her full name, which was strange, but not as strange as her next words. "I am your mother, and I'm telling you to stop."

CHAPTER TWENTY-FIVE

GEN ROLLED THE WHEELCHAIR TO A stop at the door to the plane then hung on for dear life. The man behind her had professed to love her and the woman in front claimed to be her mother. Where did she go? What did she do? And how could she go anywhere or do anything when the ground was dropping out from under her like a plane flying through turbulence?

"Gen?" Olivia said.

That voice. Was that her mother speaking? Had this woman named her Gen when she'd been born? Had she even picked Sine for her middle name, pronounced Shin-ay—Irish for *God is merciful*? How else would Olivia have known? Though if God was so merciful, why had Gen not been raised by her? And where was her father? Blaine. Blaine Harper. Gen had assumed he'd abandoned his wife, but had he really abandoned them both?

Her throat clogged.

Footsteps pounded down the jet bridge. She turned to find Matt standing there, arms hanging by his sides, aqua eyes filled with hope.

She'd been running from him, but now she didn't have the energy to either run or to face him. He'd asked her out, so she had to do something.

She shook her head. Shrugged her shoulders weakly. No words would come.

"Matt, you probably want to give her a few minutes." Olivia spoke for her the way mothers often did for their children. "I just told her who I am."

Wait. Matt knew? He faded in front of her like an old-fashioned television screen losing its signal. None of this made sense. "You knew?" the hoarse whisper ripped from her chest.

He took a step forward then stopped, his eyebrow dipping in concern, but with the way he lowered his chin contritely, it could have been concern for himself. "I picked up your birth certificate the day I went to Portland. I wanted to find your real family for you."

The words should have stunned her, but her mind was like an Etch A Sketch that had already been shaken clean. There were no dots to connect or images to evaluate. Nothing made sense.

"He only discovered my identity this week," Olivia amended. "He wanted me to tell you, but I was scared."

Gen turned toward Olivia to find her wringing her hands in her lap. Why was she scared? She knew Gen. Did Olivia not want a relationship with her? "I don't understand."

The jet bridge bounced. Bianca bounded around the corner. "I'm ready to load." She glanced from person to person. "You're not planning on hijacking this plane to take Gen to Costa Rica right now, are you, Matt?"

"I wish," Matt said, and Gen pictured TSA agents busting through the door and swinging through the windows on ropes to stop him. She was clearly not in her right mind, and neither was he if he was saying things like that.

"Gen," Olivia spoke up. "I'd like to stay in Eureka another day with you if that's all right."

Were Olivia truly her mother, then they had a lot to talk about. All this time, they'd been talking, but like acquaintances. Olivia had been giving her guidance with Matt, showing off her photography, telling her stories about her own family without Gen knowing who she was. Oh my… "You come down to visit your daughter in Eureka? Does that mean I have a sister?"

How could that be possible? Was her sister someone she passed on the street every day? Was it someone she'd taken a photo of? Did they both have red hair?

Bianca tromped closer. Gen ignored her coworker as she held her breath and waited for an answer.

"No, Gen." Olivia twisted an earring. "I came here to visit you. You're my only child."

All this time. But where had Olivia been before that? Why was Gen only finding out now?

Bianca planted her hands on her hips. "This is your mama? Well haven't you hit the jackpot today?"

The jackpot meant luck. Now that Gen had met her mother, was she going to find out her curse? Could it be multiple sclerosis? Was she going to lose control of her limbs? Because she was suddenly starting to feel that way.

"Tell you what. I'm gonna roll your mama back into the terminal and let you say goodbye to Matt right here. We gotta, you know, load the plane in a second."

Gen didn't move, which resulted in being alone with Matt all too soon. How could he love her when he didn't know her? She didn't even know herself. What was Olivia's last name again? Harper. Gen had been born Genevieve Sine Harper.

"Want me to pinch you?" Matt asked.

Would that lead to another hug? Could it lead to more than that? Did she want it to? She didn't know if she could handle anything more. "Probably not a good idea right now."

"Gen, I know you're overwhelmed..."

Overwhelmed didn't begin to describe the whirlwind of numbness and hope and fear inside. She'd always wanted to find her mother. She always wanted to fall in love with a man who loved her in return. But she'd never imagined it would leave her feeling so helpless. He'd pretty much taken control without her permission. "This doesn't feel like love," she said, eyes rising to accuse him. "This feels like an ambush."

He held up his hands as if under arrest. "I understand, but that wasn't my intent."

"Your intent?" She sucked at the air. "This isn't what I intended either." As he reached for her, she pointed to hold him back. "I picked you to have a crush on because you're out of my league."

He held his arms wide to give her space, but his forehead wrinkled in confusion. "No, I'm not. Not even close."

"Ha." The laugh escaped, kind of wild and completely self-deprecating. But once let loose, it couldn't be reeled back in. "I know it. You know it. Everybody in the airport knows it, and I'm sure they are all thinking about it after your crazy announcement."

His hands stilled. His eyes darkened. "Nobody thinks that but you."

That's exactly what she thought of herself. The realization hit with the force of A-Plus hitting a homerun. The player had broken bats before. He'd ripped the stitching from the baseball. That was how her heart felt. The stitching that held her together had unraveled to reveal her core.

In her heart, she believed he was too good for her. There was evidence everywhere. Including the fact that her own mother didn't want to confess their relationship. And the fact that Matt didn't ask her out until he tracked down her birth mom. Coincidence?

"Isn't that why you picked up my birth certificate? Because I wasn't enough on my own?" She'd never spoken such words aloud before, and the emptiness of them left her even emptier. "Now I'm like Anastasia when she discovers her link to Russian royalty. All of a sudden, I'm somebody."

He shook his head, his mouth hanging open a moment before he could form words. "You've always been somebody to me."

She wanted to call him a liar. She wanted to shove him away and scream. Just as much as she wanted to believe him. But it couldn't be true. "Then answer my question. Why did you track down my birth mom?"

His restless hand ran through his hair. "To help you, Gen. I wanted the best for you. I wanted to do something for you even if I couldn't be there for you." His arm dropped to his side. "I know I hurt you. I know I tried to be a hero, and I failed. I'm so sorry."

Why did he have to sound so kind? So caring? He probably sincerely believed his words. They sounded good. He was apologizing. But he still thought she needed a hero. He thought she couldn't save herself. Kind of like the way she felt about Craig.

Rosie's words came roaring back. They burned in her chest. Exploded like fireworks. "When you do something for someone else that they could do for themselves, you ultimately harm them."

"I never..." Matt's chest heaved. "I never meant to harm you."

Her chest constricted. If he could hurt her like this—even unintentionally—when they had no relationship, then going out with him would give him the power to destroy her. "I can't."

His face angled away as if flinching for a blow. "You can't what?"

The words echoed through her mind. I can't... I can't... "I can't go out with you. I've already lost a lot of people in my life, and now I have a new relationship with a mother I don't want to lose. I have to focus on that."

"Gen..." He reached for her.

The door to the jet bridge stairs swung open. Kevin stuck his bald head inside. He glanced back and forth before settling on Gen. "Uh...sorry to interrupt, but Shane is sick. He's vomiting in the bathroom right now. He thinks it's food poisoning."

She knew the feeling, but she was still in charge here. She had to find someone to replace him as wing walker.

"You guys didn't all eat the same thing before coming to work today, did you?" Matt asked.

Kevin frowned. "I doubt it. My wife made French toast for breakfast."

"Okay, good." Matt crossed his arms before focusing back on Gen. He was even trying to rescue her here, wasn't he?

The saddest thing was that she'd love to be rescued. But then she might start depending on him. And she couldn't let herself do that.

Kevin cleared his throat. "Can you send someone else out to wing walk, Gen?"

"Yes." She looked into Matt's eyes one last time. He didn't look like someone who would leave her. But he'd chosen Casey over her before. And she didn't blame him.

The door swung shut.

Matt stepped forward, lowering his head to keep their gazes locked.

Oh, no. They were alone again. Her chest throbbed as if her heart was trying to pull her toward him. She wouldn't let it.

She jerked toward the door and shoved it open. "I have to fill in for Shane."

Matt nodded slowly, his gaze never leaving hers. "And I have to fly out. But I'll be back. This isn't over for me."

She took a deep breath of gasoline and tar, its scent the only normal part of her day. She had to get back to normal. Back to safety.

"It is for me."

She stepped onto the grated stairs to tear herself away, letting the door swing shut to separate them. It hurt to be away from him, but it was the best thing for both of them.

Only she hadn't gotten away. She'd put herself directly in his path. If she'd thought this through more carefully, she never would have volunteered to be a wing walker.

Her pulse throbbed in her throat as she stood to the side of the plane and raised the orange marshalling wands in a right angle. Lance stood in a similar position on the other side, while Kevin attached the push back cart and climbed behind the wheel. Once they reached the tarmac, Lance would join Kevin to unhook the cart while she'd move to the front of the plane and signal with the wands for when Matt could release the brake. He'd be talking to Kevin through the headsets, but he'd be looking at her.

The closer she got to the tarmac, the more her breath wheezed from her lungs.

She could do this. She would focus on scanning the ground for loose debris that could get sucked into the engines. That was her job.

It didn't matter if her biological mother was watching through the windows.

It didn't matter if this was going to be the last time she ever saw Matt.

It didn't matter if he loved her and could be hers for the moment.

The plane angled sideways as Kevin lined it up. Time for her to change positions.

Her pulse pounding louder than her footsteps, she walked professionally to the nose of the plane.

She faced the cockpit. Lifted the wands overhead in the X formation.

Matt stared down at her. The same way he had in the jet bridge, only now they were separated by a lot more than a few inches. She couldn't read his facial expressions the way she could before. But she could feel them. She could feel the heat of his gaze and the ache in his gut. And she wasn't allowed to look away.

An itch clawed at her chest from the inside. An itch that would never be scratched.

The pushback cart stopped. Released its connection. Rolled away.

Her turn. She'd go through the motions the way she always had. It was her job. For one last day, it was her job.

She lowered her wands to her side. Matt flashed his lights to let her know everything was all right. But it wasn't.

This time, as she raised the wands to her forehead in a salute, she knew she'd never see him again.

Because he was no dented minivan. He was a jet. She wouldn't be able to keep up, and she'd get left behind. The same way he was leaving her now.

Gen ignored the stabbing pain in her chest as she helped Olivia into the front seat of her minivan then stored the wheelchair in the back, careful to avoid muddy goat prints. She liked minivans because they were so functional. A relationship with Matt would not be. He didn't even live in the same town.

She climbed behind the wheel, her thoughts in a tailspin. Matt was gone. She had to focus on her mom. On the explanation she'd just given. She repeated it the way she repeated flight information back to a captain over the radio. "Every time you fly into Eureka, you take a taxi to a hotel where you stay in your room for a week and do nothing?"

The idea was getting closer and closer to arriving on the tarmac of her mind. At least she knew Olivia. And the woman wasn't a serial killer or a hooker or anything. Gen had it better than any of her adopted siblings.

"I don't do 'nothing.' I don't even stay in the room the whole time. I do my therapy exercises in the pool and lift weights in the workout room. I also teach online." Olivia adjusted her glasses. "I knew of your family because I taught Damon in second grade. I saw how they handled his struggles and how they'd adopted so many other kids, and I knew you'd be in good hands."

Reality had been about to land when Olivia's words made it lift off again—and reality was no innocent airbus. Gen was dealing with a bomber. The bomb being that her birth mom knew her family—had chosen her family.

Gen emotionally defended her base as she exited the parking lot. "Why?" That was the real question. The only one that mattered. The only one she could get out.

"It's my fault." Olivia's face crumpled. "I insisted Blaine drive us to Portland to spend Christmas with my parents even though they were having an ice storm. He lost control on the Terwilliger Curves, and the next thing I knew I was in a hospital. He was dead, my baby was born, and my spine was broken."

Gen's exhale trembled. Olivia was talking about her. Gen's birthday. The day her father died and her mother became a paraplegic. Not a day to be celebrated. "My dad died before I was born?"

"Yes, but he loved you more than any father has ever loved a child." Olivia wiped her eyes. "He would sing to you in my womb, but that was only one of the Irish superstitions he followed. He wouldn't let me visit my grandpa's grave on Memorial Day because he thought if I entered a graveyard it would cause you to starve and be weak. He also made me wear a medal of St. Elizabeth to protect you. And he tried to feed me lots of honey so you would have a sweet disposition." She gave a faltering smile. "I'd say that worked."

Gen wiped at her own eyes. She could never be with either of the men who loved her. "You...you didn't think you could take care of me without him?"

Olivia sniffed. "I couldn't even take care of myself. I stayed at my parents' home in Portland, and I felt I had nothing to offer you. I believed you would have a better life with two parents and siblings."

The tears flowed freely and Gen considered pulling over, but Eureka was small. They'd be home in a minute, and then they'd cry together on her ugly couch. "Why didn't you do an open adoption? Then I'd have been raised by them but still known you."

"It...hurt too much." Olivia waved her hands looking for the right words. "But, oh...I regretted it every single Mother's Day. And every one of your birthdays. And every Christmas when I only had my dog's stocking to stuff." She covered her lips with her fingertips until she could speak again. "As soon as Oregon passed the law about birth certificates, I hoped you would track me down. I hoped you wanted to know me as much as I wanted to know you. But you never did. And I couldn't wait anymore. So I found you."

If only Gen had known. If only she'd picked up that birth certificate as soon as it had been ready. They would have been able to spend so many more years together. "I ordered my birth certificate, but I was afraid to pick it up. My brothers and sisters don't have as sweet of stories."

Olivia nodded. "Matt told me."

"I wish I hadn't been afraid." Story of her life.

Olivia reached across the seat to brush Gen's hair out of her eyes. "It's okay. I understand your fear. What matters is that you're here now."

The words were meant to comfort, but something in them snagged at Gen's soul. The part about how Olivia understood her fear. Could fear be her curse?

"You live in a pink house?" Olivia sat up straight as if she found the revelation to be a gift. "I love it."

Gen smiled and shifted into park. She'd never have a relationship with Matt, but she could make the most of a relationship with her mother. One step at a time. "That's not even the half of it. You've got a lot of catching up to do."

CHAPTER TWENTY-SIX

MATT WAITED FOR THE PASSENGERS TO debark before heading up the jet bridge to the terminal. Olivia had rescheduled to fly home Sunday, and he knew Gen would be there with her birth mom. He had to see her again. He had to change her mind. She'd only rejected him because she'd been so overwhelmed at the time.

His revelation hadn't played out the way he'd hoped it would. Of course, he hadn't realized Olivia was going to trump his Jack of Hearts with a Queen of Hearts. He also hadn't realized revealing their hands would make Gen want to fold hers.

He'd saluted her goodbye with the rock of hopelessness in his stomach, but after spilling his guts to Sam over the phone and dissecting their relationship repeatedly all night from beginning to end, he'd started to believe she might change her mind. Once she got over the shock of it all.

Because they were good together. They could travel the world together, him flying her to take pictures. They'd laugh and joke the whole time. She was his best friend.

Who could give that up?

"Hey, lover boy." Bianca greeted him at the gate with a wry smile. Not his favorite way of being greeted, but he'd take it as a good sign.

"Hi, boss lady." She was his new boss according to Gen's theory of airport hierarchy. Had Gen overheard his response? Would it make her smile? He scanned the waiting area for Olivia's wheelchair.

There. Where she usually waited by a column. But she was all alone.

He trotted across the tile, looking up and down the walkway. Maybe Gen had run to the bathroom or to pick up a water bottle. She couldn't avoid him if he was with her mom. And he had a feeling Olivia was on his side too.

"Matt," Olivia said, her features missing the extra creases that had been carved into her face earlier that week.

"Hi, Olivia." He stopped, the palms of his hands itching in anticipation. "How did the rest of your visit to Eureka go?"

She leaned back, her cheeks blossoming in a way that made her look ten years younger. "I learned more about my daughter in one day than in the rest of my lifetime combined. I can't thank you enough for bringing us together."

Speaking of together... He rubbed the back of his neck, crossed his arms, stuffed his hands in his pockets. "Where is she now?"

The sparkle in Olivia's eyes faded. "Her adopted parents flew in today. She left with them."

Energy drained out his fingertips and toes. "You mean they were on my plane?" How had he not known? Did they know who he was? If so, they hadn't stuck around to meet him. "Are they gone now?"

He should have run down the jet bridge ahead of the passengers, but he hadn't wanted to seem desperate. He didn't want to scare Gen any more than he probably already had.

"I'm afraid so." Olivia pressed her lips together.

"Oh, man." Matt rolled his head back. He'd lost her.

Olivia's fragile fingers grasped his hand. "It's going to be okay, Matt."

He lifted his head. Did she know something he didn't? Had Gen said something to her about him?

Olivia studied him thoughtfully. "If Gen is anything like me, she thinks she's giving you up for your own good."

Matt grimaced. How did that help? That only made things worse. Like even if Gen did love him, she couldn't be with him because of it. What good did her love do from a distance?

Olivia shook her head sadly. "The truth is she's scared."

Matt lifted his arms. In his stupidity, he'd given Gen a reason to be scared. He'd chosen another woman over her. This was his fault. "I wish I could fix it for her, but that's what got me into trouble in the first place."

Olivia patted his hand. "If she wants to be saved, she's going to have to put her trust in God."

As much as he knew Olivia's words to be true, Matt hated leaving it in God's hands. Because with all his failures, he didn't deserve to have God rescue him.

Gen answered questions about her birth mom as Rosie drove her, their parents, and their youngest brother Kyle to Crescent City. Mom and Dad were thrilled for her, but the beauty of her reunion was marred by the fact that they weren't picking up Damon to take him home the way they'd planned. Also by the memories of saying goodbye to Matt, though she didn't tell anyone besides Rosie about that.

The guard at the gate let them through without any problem this time, and Gen wondered if Rosie was going to tell their parents about Craig's visit. One of them probably should before Rosie told the story during one of her speaking engagements and their parents learned about it through the grapevine.

She sank into one of the hard metal chairs in the visitor's room, watching her family interact. Mom and Dad loved on Damon the same way they'd loved on her and Rosie when they arrived. They were pretty wonderful that way.

It was weird to think what life might have been like if Olivia had raised her or if her father had never died. Would she have gotten a job with an airline and been able to travel? Would she have moved to California? Would she have even taken up photography?

She loved Olivia, and she loved that finding her had finally filled part of the emptiness inside from not knowing her identity, but would she have wanted to give any of this up? What if she hadn't been there to find Rosie after she slit her wrists? Or if she hadn't been able to visit Damon? Or she wasn't there to hug Kyle when he described the same movie over and over for her like he was still nine instead of twenty-nine? She was blessed the way Rosie always claimed she was.

She'd been afraid to find out who her mom was because she hadn't wanted to know her curse, but she'd been living out the curse of fear by not tracking down her mom. Now that Olivia had found her, had her curse been broken? Maybe she hadn't had anything to fear in the first place.

Her birth parents were good people. They'd simply been in a car accident. And despite that, she had all this to be thankful for.

Though, even with all this love, she still felt alone. Her thoughts returned to Matt.

"Oh, Damon." Rosie's voice drew attention as usual. "Did Gen tell you she went out with a guy you knew in college? He plays for the Giants now. What's his name again?"

Damon looked Gen's way. "You went out with A-Plus?"

Gen blinked. "Uh, yeah." All eyes focused on her. She had to change the subject before it circled around to Matt. "He liked the promo photos I took of him and wanted me to take more pictures at the end of season party. I think he only called it a date so I'd feel special."

Dad leaned forward, his bushy eyebrows lifting toward his clean-cut hairstyle. "Your photos were fantastic, Gen, but don't sell yourself short. Any man would be lucky to go out with you."

Dad's sweet words might have been a soothing balm were Rosie not there to potentially slather them all around and make a big mess. Gen shot her a warning look.

Rosie's eyes grew wide with fake innocence. "Matt Lake certainly thinks so."

Mom's eyebrows rose in interest this time, though they weren't as bushy as Dad's. The corners of her mouth lifted in curiosity. "Who's Matt Lake?"

Gen shook her head as if the subject was of little importance, though her belly fluttered at even the mention of Matt's name. "He's a pilot."

"Really?" Damon crossed his arms and studied her. It was like a repeat of Craig's surprise over the interest in her.

"I met a pilot," Kyle interjected. "He gave me wings." He pointed at the airplane wings pinned to his Sponge Bob shirt.

Gen's chest squeezed tight. Matt had been there for her brother without even knowing.

Rosie nodded. "That was Matt."

Dad scrunched up his face, bushy eyebrows dipping low this time. "No, the lady next to me said the pilot was dating the daughter of the

Giants' owner."

Rosie shrugged, a twinkle in her eye. "Who do you think got Gen the photography job in the first place?"

Gen glared and shook her head. Why was Rosie doing this now? They were supposed to be here for Damon.

Mom sighed dreamily. "The pilot broke up with an heiress for you? That's so romantic. Why didn't you say anything?"

There were a lot of reasons Gen hadn't said anything. She rubbed an ear and willed her heartrate to slow down. "Matt broke up with Casey, but it's a mistake. He'll regret it, and I don't want to be with him when he does." Her hands slid to her mouth to catch the words, but it was too late.

Her family stared at her in horror. Yes, her admission sounded weak, but it wasn't something anyone should be horrified about. Out of all the things her siblings had done, her parents were horrified by this?

She threw her arms wide. "Don't look at me like that. I'm the good kid."

Rosie gasped. Her gaze hardened.

Gen closed her eyes and shook her head. Rosie's response was bad enough. She didn't want to see how her parents took it. "I didn't mean it like that."

Keeping her eyes shut couldn't keep out the stiffness in Rosie's voice. "I think you did."

"Genevieve." Damon's deep tone took over. "Look at me."

Gen pried her eyes open. She'd do anything for these people. She tried so hard. That's what she'd meant to say. Not that she was good, but that she did good things.

The peace on Damon's face told her he knew. Maybe he knew too much. "You are the good kid the same way I was the good inmate. I followed the rules and encouraged others to do the same. That's what I have to do to earn my way out of here."

Her heart pitter-pattered at the analogy. She loved her brother, but she'd never compared herself to him.

"I could have been released today." Grief washed over his face. "But I got scared. I got scared I might mess up again. Scared I would hurt someone else if I didn't have guards watching me all the time. So I started a fight."

Gen's chest constricted at the admission. At the pain he'd caused. At the pain he was now causing them. She glanced at Rosie to see how Rosie was taking it. Her sister had felt pretty guilty when they first heard about the fight. Now her eyes filled with unshed tears.

Damon cleared his throat, likely uncomfortable with Rosie's emotion. "You're doing the same thing, Gen. You've been set free, but you're afraid to trust yourself enough to spread your wings."

That's not what she was doing. She wanted solid ground under her feet because creating stability was part of making wise choices.

Damon spoke like a professor. Like his statements were facts. "I know you're afraid to fall, but what if you soar?"

Those words. Matt's words when he'd given her control of the Cessna. She'd been afraid of crashing even though he was right there beside her and would never let that happen.

Damon studied her from behind his glasses. "All this time you and I both worked to prove how good we were, when really we never believed it about ourselves."

Shame crept under her armor. He was right. She didn't think she had what it took. She was afraid. In that way, she wasn't only like him. She was like her birth mom.

Gen entered the yoga room, but stayed close to the door. Mom, Dad, and Kyle had already gone to their hotel, and she felt like she needed to apologize to Rosie again. Though it was kind of hard to be serious when her sister was hanging upside down in a Spiderman pose from her yoga hammock.

"Hi." Gen bit her lip to keep from grinning.

Rosie laughed. She wasn't one to hold a grudge. She'd given Gen a piece of her mind at the prison, and now she was over it. "Do I look funny?"

Gen released her smile, glad to be rid of the tension she'd been processing for hours. "Your face is a little red, but you're not nearly the mess that I am."

Rosie flipped to the ground like an acrobat. "I'm glad you're finally admitting it. Now you can do something about it."

Rosie made it sound so easy. She wouldn't admit the discovery of her curse to her sister and complicate everything. "Should we go do some laughter yoga? Laughter is supposed to be the best medicine, right?"

Rosie crossed her arms and tapped the stub of one foot. "You need more than laughter yoga."

"Oh." She was going to have to do something even more painful.

"Gen, I do yoga because the chiropractor suggested it when I was little to help me keep balanced. But it also helps me balance spiritually. During the meditation time at the end, I meditate on God's word."

Gen looked away. She didn't like what God's word said.

Rosie swiped a Bible from her stereo cabinet and handed it to her. "You're off balance, Gen."

Gen fingered the gold foil letters in the bottom corner of the leather cover. Rosie's adopted name. But she didn't see her adoption as a curse anymore. Could Gen ever get there?

If admitting her issues was the first step to fixing them, she might as well be honest. "I didn't finish reading the Bible in a year the way you did. I stopped when I got to the Ten Commandments. I didn't like the part where God said he would punish children for the mistakes their parents made, but obviously He does, and here I am."

"Oh, Gen." Rosie's eyes warmed. "You missed out on the best parts."

Really? Gen shrugged. "I know all the Bible stories."

"But have you meditated on them?" Rosie grabbed a yoga mat from the corner and unrolled it on the floor. "Here."

Gen was supposed to meditate right here? Right now? Well why not? It wasn't like she had to go to work in the morning. She lowered to the mat and crossed her legs. "What do I meditate on?"

Rosie clasped her hands to her chest. "You'll have to listen to your heart for that. Maybe check the concordance and see if there are any words that jump out at you. Look up all those verses."

Gen didn't want to listen to her heart. It hurt too much. She flipped to the back of the Bible, specifically avoiding the word love. She was not going to go there.

Rosie backed out of the room, but not before she pressed the button on her remote control and surrounded Gen with the gentle melody of familiar worship songs. How long would Gen have to sit here to satisfy her sister? She glanced down at her watch and realized she'd put it on her right arm automatically even though she didn't have to hide her tattoo anymore. She squeezed the clasp and removed it, revealing the tree on her right wrist.

Her family tree with all its crazy branches. Gen brushed a thumb over it then looked up to the wall where Rosie had also painted a tree in a soft sage color. It gave a peaceful and relaxing vibe, but it was also a part of Rosie. A part of how the Redwoods had helped bring her healing.

Gen looked down at her Bible and slid the crinkly pages sideways to see if there were verses about trees in the Bible. That seemed relatively safe, right?

The verses started in Genesis. Oh crud. She'd forgotten about the Tree of Life. Adam and Eve lost the right to eat from it in the very beginning of the Bible. God had cursed them right there. Cursed to die. The whole earth had been cursed because of them. How had Gen missed that the first time through? If punishing children for four generations was extreme, this was even more extreme. She wasn't the only one cursed. Everyone was cursed—and no one had access to the Tree of Life anymore.

She stared at the tree on the wall again. At her wrist. Rosie had told her she needed to keep reading. Was there something in the Bible that gave Rosie the confidence to declare her curse a blessing?

Gen continued on to the next verse. Then the next. There were lots of pretty verses about trees too. Verses about being planted by streams and flourishing like a palm. She remembered the one about the mustard seed turning into a huge tree. She found another verse about a curse. Only the one in Galatians 3:10-13 wasn't as bad.

"Christ redeemed us from the curse of the law by becoming a curse for us. For it is written: 'Cursed is everyone who hangs on a tree.'…By faith we might receive the promise of the spirit."

Jesus took her curse on Himself.

Gen stared at the tree on the wall again. She'd known Jesus died for her sins. She'd been grateful for that. But he'd died for her parents' sins too. The ones that she believed her family was being punished for.

It said by faith she could receive the promise of the spirit. What was that? She had to know. She kept going. All the way to the end of the Bible. Where, in the very last chapter of the very last book, the Tree of Life was given back to humanity.

"No longer will there be any curse" Revelations 22:3.

The words echoed through her mind. She'd been set free. She'd been saved.

All of humanity had lost the Tree of Life in the beginning, but they'd get it back in the end because one Man took it on himself by being hung on a tree in the middle of two others. All she had to do was have faith in Him.

That was all.

Her birth dad never had to feed her mom honey or refuse to let her go to a graveyard to protect Gen. All he'd had to do was have faith.

Yeah, her life was affected by the choices of her parents. For all she knew, she'd even inherited her father's superstitious nature. But that nature had no more control over her.

Craig could kick his addictions. Trina could come home. Kyle could live the rest of his life with childlike jubilation. They could all learn to overcome the way Damon and Rosie were learning to do. It was up to them. They got to choose whether to have faith or not.

Gen got to choose whether to take the risk her heart yearned for. She didn't have to have faith that Matt would never leave her and return to Casey. She only had to have faith that no matter what happened, Jesus had already paid the price to save her.

Yes, death was in the world because of a curse. But like the dead leaves on a Redwood fell onto other branches creating an environment for the growth of moss and ferns, new life could always be found.

She wanted new life.

CHAPTER TWENTY-SEVEN

MATT NODDED TO BIANCA THROUGH THE window in the jet bridge. Would he ever stop hoping Gen would be standing there?

"I was sad to see the bluey go too," his new co-pilot said. "I'll buy you a cuppa to cheer you up."

Was he that obvious? Matt smiled his thanks. Coffee did sound good, but he didn't want to go inside and have to face the memories of Gen. Or even the employees who had heard him profess his devotion to her. Plus, since he was still committed to her in his heart, he really shouldn't have coffee with any other woman. Even if that woman had ten years and ten pounds on him. He'd learned the hard way. "I'm going to pass."

"Your loss, mate."

Yes. His loss. He hoped Gen was doing well wherever she was. Knowing her, she was probably in Ecuador or Morocco or Rome. Rome would be cool. Maybe he'd make plans and travel there anyway. Sam would go with him. One last hurrah before he joined the military.

Matt pulled out his phone to text the kid while he waited for the next flight to board, but he accidentally hit his camera app and got distracted by the old photos he'd taken for Gen. His favorite was the Scottish guy in the kilt. He hadn't been able to talk to Gen about her real father, but Olivia had opened up after they'd landed at PDX. Apparently Gen's father had been a little Irish man, and he'd loved Gen until his dying day. Exactly like Matt would do.

"I brought you coffee."

Stella's voice lost its dialect, and it actually sounded like Gen's, but he was seeing and hearing Gen everywhere he went lately. He'd accept then pay Stella back.

"You didn't have to…"

A redhead stood in the doorway to the cockpit. Gen? She didn't work there anymore. Did she buy a ticket? Was she flying to SFO? Did she have another date with Alan?

She extended the steaming cup, her eyes glistening. "Isn't this how you apologize when you make a mistake?"

He jumped to his feet. He didn't know what mistake she was talking about. He was just thrilled to see her.

He wrapped his hands around the cup, but only as an excuse to brush his fingers over hers. She didn't move hers away, and they stayed there, connected. "If anybody should be buying coffee, I should be buying it for you."

"No. You've already done so much for me." Her gaze sharpened, direct and powerful. "You flew a plane up for the emergency drill, you got me a dream photography job, you brought my mom back into my life. I need to tell you how grateful I am."

Okay, that coffee had to go, even if she was only here to say thank you before taking her seat in the plane. He set the cup on a tray table then reached for her hands. She didn't back up. She didn't pull away.

"Gen, there's so much more I want to do for you." He continued stepping closer, turning her hands around until their fingers were interlaced.

She stayed open. No more running outside to wave orange marshalling wands at him. Her rust-colored eyelashes lifted to look up at him. "Are you still interested in taking me on a date?"

Did she even need to ask?

He stepped closer, wrapping her arms behind her so he was holding her as well as her hands. Her breath tickled his collar bone. How had he known they were going to fit together this well? "Name the time and place."

Her lips curved, and he had to drag his eyes away to meet hers. "Since I already bought a plane ticket, I was hoping you'd take me to the Fisherman's Wharf or Chinatown in, say, an hour?"

How did this happen? He hadn't done anything to deserve her. In fact, he'd done the opposite. "Why are you giving me a second chance?" He didn't want to push her away; he just needed to make sure they were on the same page. He needed to be real and communicate and partner with her rather than try to save her.

Her hands slipped from his and brushed all the way up his arms on the way to hook behind his neck. This wasn't like the one goodbye hug she'd given him before. This wasn't even the friendly way she'd checked out his pirate sleeves at the Giants' party. This was the embrace of a woman.

She looked into his eyes with transparency, all walls and jokes and even desire aside. "I've been thinking about family trees a lot lately, and though I haven't had any say in my past, I get to choose what direction to grow in the future."

He'd known she cared about family. He'd known she wouldn't get involved unless she was serious. But he'd never expected this. She might as well be proposing. He had to be sure. "Are you choosing me?"

"I'm choosing you."

He smiled from the inside out. Despite his mistakes and his selfishness and the way he'd hurt her, she still chose him. He was no hero, yet he was loved like one. Or was he? She hadn't said it yet. "You love me as much as your dented minivan?" he challenged.

Her lips pursed with a sultry air. "More."

"Oh, man." He teased right back. "That's pretty hard to believe."

"Yeah?" She let go of his neck with one arm at the same time she leaned forward. Was she going for a kiss? Nope. She leaned away, intercom in hand. She held it to her lips. It dinged on through the cabin before her tinny voice played overhead. "Ladies and gentlemen, this is your captain's girlfriend speaking. On behalf of the entire station here in Eureka, I'd like to announce that we love him. And when I say we, I mean me. I am in love with Matt the pilot."

Cheers rose from the cabin.

Matt shook his head in mock shock, and removed the receiver from her hand to give himself better access to her lips. "Is that how it's gonna be?"

Her arm found its way behind him again. "Oh, that's just the beginning."

"Are you kidding me?" Bianca busted in. "I wasn't even allowed to play boarding music, while you can hijack the intercom?"

Gen didn't look away. "You're in charge now, Bianca. Do what you want."

"I. Will." With that the new station manager whipped out her phone, tapped on the John Denver song, and held it to the microphone.

Matt could have kicked her out, but then he couldn't have pulled Gen even closer and swayed to the music. The passengers joined in the song, their voices rising in harmony.

"Leaving you was the hardest thing I've ever had to do," he whispered.

Her fingers sent goosebumps down his spine as she wove her fingers into his hair. She repeated the lyrics to the song. "So kiss me."

Usually a first kiss was done at the end of the date. And usually not in front of a hundred and fifty people, unless, of course, those people were witnesses at a ceremony. But they'd done everything backwards already anyway, so why not?

He lowered his mouth until it was a breath away from hers, enjoying the electricity zapping back and forth between them. "You know this has to be our wedding song now, right?"

She nuzzled her nose against his. "As long as we can use my minivan as the getaway car."

He couldn't think of a better idea. Except maybe getting to work on filling her van up with kids. For now he'd settle for that kiss.

And now . . . for the REST of the story . . .a few things you might enjoy

DISCUSSION QUESTIONS

1) Gen is triggered by the idea of generational curses in the Bible. What are some Biblical ideas that have triggered you, have you worked through them, and how?

2) If you had a "curse," what would it be, and what have you learned from it?

3) Gen started out at the beginning of the story ashamed about her family and later realized she was blessed to have them. What is something you wish had been different about your family and what would you have missed out on if your life had been more ideal?

4) Matt had guilt from the time his little brother almost died whitewater rafting, and he tried to make up for it by playing the hero and rescuing others. This made him a good person but a good person who thought he could do good things on his own without God. How are you tempted to do good without God?

5) Matt judged Ethan for adultery, and Ethan accused him of doing the same thing in his heart. Have you had an experience where you judged someone else then later realized you were no better? Have you ever done what Ethan did and used blame to justify your own sin? What opened your eyes?

6) Both Matt and Gen received life-changing advice and encouragement from people who had really messed up in their own lives. What is the most unexpected way you've received life-changing advice? How was that experience different than if the wisdom had come from a respected mentor?

7) Gen's adopted family was filled with people who could be considered "hard to love." Have you ever been considered hard to love, and what was it that finally reached you? How do you love the unlovable? How can you love them better?

AUTHOR NOTE

My Resort to Love Series was originally contracted for three books, but I loved hanging out with the Lake family so much that I wanted to go back and write love stories for the oldest two brothers. I ended up including Dave's story in a novella anthology *Finding Love at the Oregon Coast*. After that released, I had other options, but I couldn't leave Matt hanging. I had to write his story, and I'm so thankful Mountain Brook Ink extended my contract to let me do so.

For this book, I wanted the heroine to come from a family that was as dysfunctional as Matt's family was extraordinary in order to show two things. First, even if we come from rough backgrounds, there is the same amount of hope for us, and we still have something to offer. Second, if we come from great backgrounds, that isn't going to make us perfect or give us the ability to rescue others. We are all in this together, and we all have the same Savior.

I consider *Finding Love in Eureka, California* to be my least "Christian" novel with the strongest message for Christ. Writing it made me think deep and feel even deeper, and I'm honored to be able to share the story with you. If you haven't met the rest of the Lake brothers yet, I invite you to check out my other books, and if you'd like to get to know me, you can find me at www.angelaruthstrong.com, where you can also sign up for my newsletter. I know there's something I can learn from you too.

https://www.facebook.com/groups/1557213161269220/
https://twitter.com/AngelaRStrong

ANGELA RUTH STRONG'S BOOKS

Resort to Love Series

Finding Love in Sun Valley, Idaho
Finding Love in Big Sky, Montana
Finding Love in Park City, Utah
Finding Love in Eureka, California

The CafFUNated Mysteries

A Caffeine Conundrum
A Cuppa Trouble
A Latte Difficulty

Suspense

Presumed Dead
Love on the Run (False Security)
The Princess and the P.I.

Fun4Hire Series for Ages 8-12

The Pillow Fight Professional
The Food Fight Professional
The Snowball Fight Professional
The Water Fight Professional

Body and Soul Series

Lighten Up